Praise for the Shadow Falls Series

"The Shadow Falls series belongs to my favorite YA series. It has everything I wish for in a YA paranormal series. A thrilling tale that moves with a great pace, where layers of secrets are revealed in a way that we are never bored. It continues a gripping story about self-discoveries, finding a place in the world, friendship, and love. So if you didn't start this series yet, I can only encourage you to do so." —*Bewitched Bookworms*

"The relationship Kylie has with both Lucas and Derek is addicting! How could anyone choose between the two? It's not often that I love a series as much as I have with Shadow Falls. I find myself thinking of nothing else! This has been one of my favorite series of all time!"

—*Open Book Society*

"Ms. Hunter handles this series with such deftness, crafting a wonderful tale that speaks to the adolescent in me. I highly recommend this series filled with darkness and light, hope and danger, friendship and romance."

—*Night Owl Reviews* (Top Pick)

"*Taken at Dusk* has even more drama and answers for Kylie. Jam-packed with action and romance from the very beginning, Hunter's lifelike characters and paranormal creatures populate a plot that will keep you guessing till the very end. A perfect mesh of mystery, thriller, and romance. Vampires, weres, and fae, oh my!" —*RT Book Reviews*

"Fans of the Twilight series will love this series. I cannot wait to see how this all plays out in book three." —*Fallen Angel Reviews*

"*Born at Midnight* is addicting. Kylie's journey of self-discovery and friendship is so full of honesty, it's impossible not to fall in love with her and Shadow Falls . . . and with two sexy males vying for her attention, the romance is scorching. *Born at Midnight* has me begging for more, and I love, love, love it!" —*Verb Vixen*

"The evolving, not-always-easy relationships among Kylie and her cabin mates Della and Miranda are rendered as engagingly as Kylie's angst over dangerous Lucas and appealing Derek. Just enough plot threads are tied up to make a satisfying stand-alone tale while whetting appetites for sequels to come."

—*Publishers Weekly*

"With intricate plotting and characters so vivid you'd swear they are real, *Born at Midnight* is an addictive treat. Funny, poignant, romantic, and downright scary in places, it hits all the right notes. Highly recommended."

—*Houston Lifestyles and Homes Magazine*

"I laughed and cried so much while reading this. . . . I LOVED this book. I read it every chance I could get because I didn't want to put it down. The characters were well developed and I felt like I knew them from the beginning. The story line and mystery that went along with it kept me glued to my couch not wanting to do anything else but find out what the heck was going on."

—*Urban Fantasy Investigations Blog*

"This has everything a YA reader would want. . . . I read it more than a week ago and I am still thinking about it. I can't get it out of my head. I can't wait to read more. This series is going to be a hit!"

—*Awesome Sauce Book Club*

"The newest in the super-popular teen paranormal genre, this book is one of the best. Kylie is funny and vulnerable, struggling to deal with her real-world life and her life in a fantastical world she's not sure she wants to be a part of. Peppered throughout with humor and teen angst, *Born at Midnight* is a laugh-out-loud page-turner. This one is going on the keeper shelf next to my Armstrong and Meyer collections!"

—*Fresh Fiction*

Chosen at Nightfall

ALSO BY C. C. HUNTER

Born at Midnight

Awake at Dawn

Taken at Dusk

Whispers at Moonrise

Chosen at Nightfall

• a shadow falls novel •

c. c. hunter

ST. MARTIN'S GRIFFIN NEW YORK

This is a work of fiction. All of the characters, organizations, and events portrayed in this novel are either products of the author's imagination or are used fictitiously.

 Printed in the United States of America. For information, address St. Martin's Press, 175 Fifth Avenue, New York, N.Y. 10010.

www.stmartins.com

ISBN 978-1-250-01289-0 (trade paperback)
ISBN 978-1-250-01290-6 (e-book)

10 9 8 7

To Val Sturman.

The first time I met you, my life became a little brighter. You danced your way through life with a smile, an infatuation for storytelling, and with a kind word for anyone who paused long enough to listen. I'm honored and blessed to have been called your friend. You will be missed.

Acknowledgments

To Rose Hilliard, my editor, who yanked me into the young adult genre and helped me achieve this unbelievable and fantastic publishing dream. You rock! To my agent, Kim Lionetti, who helped me navigate my career of ups and downs and crazy U-turns. It's been a hell of a ride and I can't wait to see where we go next. To my hubby, Steve Craig, who started it all when he said, "If you want to be a writer, then just do it." And thanks for keeping me going by cooking dinners and doing laundry. By the way, hon, the bras do not go in the dryer. To Kathleen Adey and Shawnna Perigo for their assistance in all things writing related. You two make me look good, thanks. To my fans: those e-mails you send, the Facebook comments you post, and the things you tweet all add joy to this writer's soul. You keep me inspired. A huge nod to all the parents who pay for my books so their teens can get lost in my fictional world, and especially to the moms and dads who drive them to book signings and take the time to tell me how much their children enjoy my books. To all the adults who confess, "I'm not a young adult, but I love your series." And last, but not least, to those writers out there with an unending determination to find their own place in the publishing world: with thousands of rejections to my name, believe me when I say, Never, ever give up the dream.

Chosen at Nightfall

Chapter One

Kylie Galen looked up from the slice of pepperoni pizza on the fine china plate and tried to ignore the ghost swinging the bloody sword right behind her grandfather and great-aunt. Her newfound family members were . . . good people, but a tad on the proper side. And proper people probably wouldn't appreciate an uninvited ghost getting their dining room walls bloody.

The spirit, a female, dark flowing hair, in her early thirties, stopped in mid-swing and stared directly at Kylie. *You kill or be killed. It's really rather simple.* The words reverberated in Kylie's head. They were communicating telepathically, and considering the topic being discussed, that was probably for the best.

That's not simple, Kylie shot back. *And I'm trying to eat, so would you mind leaving?*

That's rude, the ghost said. *You're supposed to help spirits. You need to abide by your guidelines.*

Kylie twisted the cloth napkin she'd placed in her lap. Okay, was there something written in the rule books about a ghost whisperer having to be polite to obnoxious spirits?

Oh, wait, she didn't have a freaking rule book, or guidelines. She was winging it. Winging everything, in fact: ghost whispering, being a supernatural, being someone's girlfriend.

Being someone's ex-girlfriend!

Lately it felt like she was winging her whole damned life, and making a fine mess of things, too. Like her decision to leave Shadow Falls, the camp/recently turned boarding school for paranormal teens. It had felt like the right thing to do at the time.

Had.

She'd been here at the chameleons' compound less than two weeks, and she wasn't so sure anymore.

True, she'd had a good reason to come—to discover more about her paranormal heritage. To get to know Malcolm Summers, her grandfather, and her great-aunt Francyne.

Months after learning she wasn't all human, she'd finally discovered she was a chameleon, a rare species that had gone into hiding after an organized unit of the paranormal government, the Fallen Research Unit, the FRU, had used them as lab rats to try to explain their abilities. Kylie's own grandmother had died as a result. And now the same branch of the FRU wanted to take Kylie in for testing. That was so not happening!

However, Kylie's main motivation for leaving Shadow Falls didn't have anything to do with the FRU, or with finding out about her heritage. Nope. It had everything to do with running away.

Running away from Lucas, the werewolf she'd fallen in love with. The werewolf who had promised his soul to another werewolf and expected Kylie to believe it meant nothing. How could he have done that? How could he have kissed Kylie with all that passion for the last month, yet every time he went to his dad's house, he was seeing that girl? How could Kylie stay at Shadow Falls and continue to face him?

The problem was, she might have run away from Lucas, but she'd brought the heartbreak with her. And now, she wasn't just hurting over a certain werewolf; she was hurting because . . . every cell in her body missed Shadow Falls. Okay, so maybe not really Shadow Falls, but she missed the people. Friends who had become as close as family: Holiday, the fae camp leader, who was like a big sister. Burnett, the stern vampire, the other camp leader who was a friend and sort of a father figure wrapped into one. Her two roommates, Della and Miranda, who'd felt abandoned by Kylie when she left. And Derek, who'd vowed his love to her, even when he knew she loved Lucas.

Oh God, she missed everyone so much. Amazingly, she was only a few miles away from Shadow Falls, tucked away in a secluded spot in what Texans referred to as the hill country, and yet it might as well have been across the world.

Sure, she'd spoken to Holiday every day. At first, her grandfather had refused her this right, but her aunt had insisted he see reason. He'd relented, but only if she used a certain phone and kept the conversations very short, so the calls couldn't be traced. And by no means could Kylie tell anyone where she was.

Because of the camp's affiliation with the FRU, her grandfather didn't trust anyone at Shadow Falls. And his distrust only added to Kylie's feelings of isolation from everyone she loved. Even her mom, who called to inform her that she was about to fly to England with John, her mom's new boyfriend, whom Kylie wasn't so sweet on. Sure, her granddad allowed her to call her mom back every time she called. So they had spoken twice. But only twice.

Kylie's throat knotted with tears, but she refused to cry. She had to be strong. Pull up her big-girl panties and be an adult.

"Is the pizza to your liking?" Francyne, her great-aunt, asked.

"Yes, it's great." Kylie watched the two older people slice into their piece of pepperoni pizza as if it were steak. She knew they served it just for her—because after barely touching her meals these last few days, they'd asked about her favorite foods. Feeling obligated, both to eat and to comply with their show of manners, she forced herself to cut a bite of pizza from her slice and slip it into her mouth.

She wasn't vampire right now, so she should be able to enjoy food. But nope.

Nothing tasted right.

Nothing felt right.

Not eating pizza with a fork off a fine china plate that looked old and rare enough to be in a museum. Not sitting at this fancy dining table with a formal place setting. And especially not feeling right was the spirit who now moved in closer to her grandfather and held the sword over his head.

Kylie stared at the spirit. *Either tell me exactly what you need, that doesn't involve murder, or go away.*

A drop of blood splattered onto her grandfather's forehead. Not that he could feel it or see it. But Kylie could. The spirit performed this show just to get Kylie's attention.

And it was working.

Stop it! Leave. Kylie shot a warning glance at the spirit.

You are in a nasty mood, huh? the ghost said.

Yeah, she was, Kylie admitted to herself. A broken heart would do that to you. It pretty much sucked the joy out of life. Or maybe what sucked the most was missing everyone.

Not that Kylie's time here had been in vain. She'd discovered a lot about herself, about chameleons, these thirteen days. Chameleons had only come into being in the last hundred years. While they considered themselves a species, they were really a blend of all paranormals—individuals who retained the DNA and powers of all the species.

Problem was, learning to control that power was a real bitch. Most chameleons didn't even master the feat until their mid-twenties. Not that there were a lot of young chameleons trying to master things. Chameleons were rare. Her grandfather said about a hundred compounds existed across the world, but in total there were less than ten thousand of her kind. And only one in ten chameleon couples had been able to produce a child. Hence the low population.

Kylie couldn't help but wonder if she'd ever be able to have a child. But damn, she was sixteen, too young to start worrying about being infertile.

"How did classes go today?" her grandfather asked.

Kylie focused on the man. In his seventies, his hair held tight to its strawberry blond color, with only a few signs of graying. His eyes, a vivid light blue, matched hers and her father's.

Another drop of blood landed on his cheek. Kylie scowled at the smirking spirit who sliced the sword though the air only an inch above his head.

I said, stop it! Kylie tightened her eyes.

"So it didn't go well?" her grandfather asked, obviously reading Kylie's expression.

"No, it went fine. I'm . . . I was able to switch my pattern from a werewolf to a fae." Supernaturals all had patterns that could be seen by other supernaturals. Chameleons had their own pattern, one they hid. And unlike any other supernatural they could change into any other species, and attain this species' powers with the transformation.

Problem was, like their other powers, it wasn't easy to control. Classes here didn't involve so much English, math, and science, but training on how to control one's powers and to hide their true pattern from the world.

"That's amazing. Then why the long face?" her grandfather asked.

"It's just . . ." *I'm miserable here. I want to go back to Shadow Falls.* The words sat on the tip of her tongue, but she couldn't say them. Not until she knew for sure that she'd given this a shot. And until she knew how she would survive facing Lucas.

"I wasn't frowning at you. It's—"

"Kylie has company," Francyne said. Her aunt wasn't a full-fledged ghost whisperer. She claimed she couldn't see them or hear them, but she could pick up on a spirit's presence easily.

The ghost held the sword up, pointing it at the ceiling as if making some big declaration. *You're about to have more company.*

Kylie didn't know what that was supposed to mean, but she focused on her confused-looking grandfather now and not the spirit.

"Company?" Her grandfather looked at his sister-in-law. "Oh." He tensed. Then his eyes widened. "Is it my wife, or my son, Daniel?"

"No." Kylie wished Daniel, her father, who'd died before she was born, would come for a visit. She could use some TLC, and her father was really good at offering it. However, he'd used all his allotted time on earth.

"It's not them. It's . . . someone else," Kylie answered.

Someone who had yet to explain what she wanted or needed. Well, except to tell Kylie she needed her to kill someone. What did the spirit think Kylie was? A killer for hire?

The spirit leaned down close to her grandfather's ear. *It's a shame you can't see me. You're kind of cute.* She proceeded to lick the blood from his cheek. Slowly. And she looked at Kylie when she did it.

Kylie dropped her fork. "Stop licking my grandfather, right now!"

The spirit brought her tongue back into her mouth and stared at Kylie. *Stop fighting your fate. Accept what you must do. Let me teach you how you must kill him.*

"Kill who?" Kylie blurted out, and then flinched when she realized she'd been speaking aloud.

"Lick? Kill? What?" her grandfather asked.

"Nothing," Kylie insisted. "I was talking—"

"She was talking to the spirit, I think," her aunt said, her brows pinched in worry.

"About killing someone?" her grandfather asked, and shot Kylie a direct look.

When Kylie didn't answer, Malcolm glanced around the room as if nervous. His expression of fear reminded her so much of the other supernaturals at Shadow Falls.

That's when a thought hit. She'd come here thinking she'd fit in, and yet, even living on a compound of about fifty acres in Texas hill country, with about twenty-five other chameleons, she still didn't fit in. And it wasn't just the ghost whispering, but the fact that she was so much further advanced than the four other teens here. And they weren't overly thrilled to be shown up by the newbie, either.

The elders of the group—which included her grandfather and

great-aunt and about four others—guessed that Kylie's early development was because she was also a protector, a supernatural with amazing strength. While that sounded pretty cool, she would argue with that definition for so many reasons.

Topping those reasons was that she could only use those powers to protect others, and never herself. Which to Kylie didn't make a lick of sense. If she was in charge of protecting others, wasn't it important that she kind of stay alive? Who the heck had made that rule?

Kylie sighed, a sigh that felt as sorrowful on the inside as it sounded leaving her lips. Was it simply her destiny to always be a misfit?

Her grandfather leaned forward and set his silver fork and knife beside the expensive piece of china. "Kylie, I hate to intrude with your . . . spirit matters, but why would a spirit be conversing with you about killing someone?"

Kylie bit down on her lip and tried to find a way to explain without completely freaking them out. Especially when it freaked her out. She opened her mouth to say something, but was saved by a bell. A very loud bell, more like a siren. The lights in the chandelier over the table started flickering.

Her grandfather, his frown deepening, pulled out a cell phone from his perfectly pressed white dress shirt, punched one button, and held it to his ear. "What is it?" He paused. "Who?" he snapped, and cut his eyes to Kylie. "I'll be right there!"

He turned the phone off and shot up from his chair, and then faced his sister-in-law. "You and Kylie disappear. Hide out in the barn. I'll be there shortly."

By disappear, Kylie surmised he meant vanish, another thing a chameleon could do. Vanish. Like into thin air.

"What's going on?" Kylie asked, remembering the ghost saying she was about to get company.

"We have intruders." His deep, matter-of-fact tone sounded deeper, more serious.

"Intruders?" Kylie asked.

His eyes tightened. "It's the FRU! Now vanish."

Her aunt came around the table and reached for Kylie's hand. Then the woman vanished, and in a fraction of a second, Kylie looked down and her own legs had disappeared.

Chapter Two

Three minutes later, Kylie was led into the barn by her aunt. Or at least she assumed it was her. Because everyone was invisible.

Breathing in the earthy smell of stored hay, Kylie added another thing she'd learned about her powers. A chameleon had the ability to make other people vanish. Or it would appear that way, because she hadn't been wishing to vanish and it seemed her aunt's touch had done all the work.

"Are we all here?" Her aunt's voice broke into the odd, tense silence. Kylie cut her eyes around the empty barn. Not a soul was here that she could see. Of course, she couldn't see herself, either.

Listening, she heard the slight sound of feet shuffling.

"Let's do the count," her aunt's voice echoed again. "One," her aunt said.

"Two," another voice added.

The count went up to twenty-four, but there had been several pauses, and several numbers missed, before someone moved on to the next number. Kylie recognized most of the voices. Especially the four other teen chameleons, plus Suzie, the six-year-old, and her parents, who were the teachers of the groups. The numbers missing were obviously her grandfather and the other four elders.

"And I have Kylie," her aunt said. "Kylie, your number is twenty-five. Remember it and whenever we have the need to vanish, you must say it so we will know you are here."

She nodded, then remembering they couldn't see her, she said, "Okay." Her mind raced thinking about everything that was happening, from being number twenty-five to being invisible and especially to what the FRU wanted. Were they here for her? Then her racing thoughts stopped on one subject.

Her grandfather. She was worried about his safety and the possibility of what the FRU could do to him and the other elders. Was he okay? Did she need to find him in case he needed . . . protecting?

"Maybe we should go find the others," she said, her blood starting the fizzling sensation she got when she feared someone was in danger.

"No," her aunt said in a voice that left little doubt that she was the one in charge. "We wait here. That was the plan and we never stray from a plan."

Kylie heard something in her aunt's voice. Edginess, concern. Kylie's blood grew hotter in her veins.

"Have the FRU come here before? Do they know we can vanish?" Kylie asked.

"Only if you told them," Brandon snapped.

Brandon, the teen who didn't like her. Oh, he had liked her plenty in the beginning, but when Kylie pretty much told the seventeen-year-old that he was wasting his time coming on to her, he'd obviously been offended. He'd snubbed her ever since. And anytime Kylie accomplished something that the teachers taught, shifting their patterns and such, he seemed personally insulted at her success. This wasn't a competition. She just wanted to learn all she could and then . . . then go back to Shadow Falls.

Go back home. The thought hung up somewhere inside her, a place very close to her heart.

"I never told them," Kylie said.

"This is no time for bickering," her aunt stated.

"She brought this on us," Brandon spit out. "We've never had the FRU break in before. And God only knows what they will do to us if they find us."

"Be quiet," Aunt Francyne ordered.

But in the silence that followed, Kylie heard what wasn't being said by the others. They agreed with Brandon. Because of her, the FRU had discovered their compound.

Guilt crowded Kylie's chest. She had never considered that her coming here could have put anyone in danger. Yet it had, hadn't it?

Her blood fizzed faster; thoughts of her grandfather being hurt—of it being her fault—made her heart race.

Kylie tried to pull her hand free. "No," her aunt said. "You let go, you'll become visible."

"I need to make sure they're okay. And . . . I can become invisible myself."

"That's impossible," Brandon snapped. "You can't do that until you're in your twenties. Everyone knows that."

Kylie rolled her eyes. She was tired of his petty jealousy.

Footsteps sounded. Numbers were called out. She recognized her grandfather's voice as well as the other elders.

"They'll search in here," her grandfather said. "Adults, make sure you hold tight to your child's hands. Go to the south end of the property." The sounds of people making their way out echoed through what, even to Kylie, looked like an empty barn.

Kylie felt her aunt's hold on her wrist, directing her to walk, but then her grandfather spoke again. "Everyone but Francyne and Kylie. You two go down by the edge of the woods in the back."

Kylie couldn't help but wonder why she and Aunt Francyne were being singled out.

"Why?" Kylie asked after she heard the last footsteps leave, still finding it so strange to speak when no one could see her.

"When we are in a state of emergency, one never asks questions." Her aunt's voice rang in the emptiness of the barn. Then, still holding Kylie's hand, the woman started moving, and in careful steps, she guided Kylie out of the barn.

She moved with her aunt, but she couldn't remain silent. "What's going on? Why should I be taken to a different place than the others?" Kylie asked as she moved through the barn door. The afternoon light had her pupils adjusting.

"Obviously, it is you they search for," her grandfather answered, his voice sounding close, but his form still invisible.

"But I'm a protector," Kylie insisted. "If someone needs help, I should stay close."

"I can feel you, damn it! Where are you?" a voice, a familiar voice that wasn't her aunt's or grandfather's, called out behind Kylie.

Her breath caught and she looked over her shoulder. About fifty feet away, standing in the tall grass, was someone she cared about.

"Derek," she called out. Then she remembered that no one, other than another unseen chameleon, could hear her when she was invisible.

"We should go." Her aunt gave Kylie's hand a tug, but she didn't budge. Stiffening, Kylie soaked up Derek's image, hungry for anything that was linked to her life at Shadow Falls.

His light brown hair resting on his brow stirred in the wind, giving him a carefree look, but his green eyes, with flecks of gold, held concern. What was he doing here?

"Where are you, Kylie?" he asked, and the breeze whisked his words away.

She remembered what her grandfather had said about who was here. This wasn't the FRU.

"Go to the creek!" her grandfather demanded. "You should not have told them where you were."

His accusation and his tone put Kylie on the defensive. While she couldn't see her grandfather, she could imagine his expression—stern and uncompromising.

She turned to where she heard his voice. "I didn't tell them, and no, I will not leave. You lied. It's not the FRU." The feeling of betrayal hit.

"When I told you it was the FRU, I was repeating what I was told by those guarding the gate. But even still, it is not a lie. They both work for the FRU."

They? Who else was here? She heard footsteps coming from the house. Her first thought was it could be Lucas. Her heart gripped at the possibility of seeing him. The pain of his disloyalty weighed heavy on her heart and still tasted bitter. Yet as those footsteps grew closer, she could not turn away any more than she could stop breathing.

Looking back she saw Burnett James, one of the camp leaders. Not Lucas. Disappointment swelled in her chest, but she refused to believe it was due to Lucas not being there. She didn't want him to come. Didn't want to see him, not now and maybe not ever. Even as the thought whisked through her mind, she felt her heart race with the lie.

But she knew that at least some of the disappointment she felt was about Burnett. She hadn't said good-bye because she knew he would have tried to stop her from leaving. Now she wanted to go to him and embrace him. Apologize for neglecting the courtesy of a simple good-bye.

"Kylie." Her aunt spoke again, and gave her hand a slight tug. "Your grandfather knows what is best. Listen to him. We must go."

Kylie inhaled and tried to not let her emotions control her. But it seemed almost too late. Her head spun as too many feelings swirled inside her. Loneliness, regret, and anger at being lied to. "He knows what is best for him, but maybe not so much for me."

"You must trust him," her aunt said, her grip on Kylie's wrist tightening. "Come, please. We only want to protect you."

"I don't need protecting from Burnett or Derek." She spoke calmly. "And it appears my grandfather needs to trust me, as well. I didn't tell anyone where I was. I gave you my word and I didn't break it." She heard the hurt resonate in her voice.

"That's not important," her grandfather said, but Kylie disagreed. Before she could voice her feeling, he continued, "What is important is that they will try to force you to go back. If we leave now, we will avoid a confrontation."

"She's around here somewhere," Derek called back to Burnett. "I can feel her. Seriously, she's here somewhere."

Kylie focused where she thought her grandfather stood. "No one will force me to do anything that I do not want to do. Not them . . . or you," she added. "My plan all along was to go back to Shadow Falls. I told you that from the beginning."

"A plan that I also told *you* I do not agree with." Her grandfather's voice rose slightly.

Kylie, lured by the sound of footsteps, looked over her shoulder again. She watched as Burnett drew closer. Proud, strong, a bit too headstrong. In so many ways, he reminded her of her grandfather. Inhaling, she glanced back to where she'd heard her grandfather's voice earlier. "I came here of my own free will and when I choose to leave, I will."

"You are too stubborn for your own good." Her grandfather's voice boomed from nothing.

"And I fear I might have inherited it from my grandfather," Kylie snapped. Then she glanced back at Derek and Burnett.

"Come with me, Kylie," her aunt pled, and she held tight to Kylie's hand.

"No," Kylie repeated, and watched as Burnett drew closer. He stopped beside Derek, only fifteen feet away from Kylie. She longed to run to him and throw herself in his arms.

"The pizza in the main house was still warm," Burnett said. "Are you sure she's here?"

"I'm certain," Derek answered. "And she's upset about something, too."

Not seen or heard, but still felt, Kylie thought. How odd was that?

Her aunt started patting Kylie's hand as if the gentle touch would convince her. But Kylie was beyond convincing. "Please let me go," she told her aunt. But her aunt held on.

"Is she in danger?" Burnett growled.

Derek closed his eyes as if internally trying to touch her emotions. When he opened his eyes, he looked at Burnett. "I don't think so," Derek answered. "She's frustrated and I sense . . . loneliness. And . . . she's feeling . . . something . . . something like being torn between two loyalties."

Tears welled up in Kylie's eyes. Leave it to Derek to always get her emotions right. She knew her grandfather and aunt cared about her, knew they only wanted what was best for her, but how could she not make herself visible to Burnett and Derek? Why did she feel as if doing so would be seen as disloyal to her grandfather?

She'd tried to play by their rules, she had. But enough was enough.

Burnett looked around and Kylie would swear he looked right at her. "Are there others here?"

"I'm not sure," Derek said. "I can only sense Kylie because . . ." He didn't finish, but she knew the answer. He could sense her so well because he loved her.

Burnett stood a little straighter. "Mr. Summers, I need to speak with you. Now!"

"How do you know he's here?" Derek asked.

"If Kylie's here, he's around." Burnett shifted his vision back and forth. "Show yourself."

Kylie heard her grandfather move in beside her.

"You belong with us, child. Just let them leave," her grandfather said.

His invisible shoulder brushed against hers. Even though she was angry at him, his touch and the tenor of his voice reminded her of her father's. The ties binding them to each other could not be denied. "I can't," Kylie said.

"Let them leave and we will talk about this in a rational manner later," her grandfather offered, and she could hear in his voice that he tried to temper his mood.

"I am being rational," she said. Her aunt's hold on her hand tightened and Kylie had to fight not to jerk away.

"No, you are not," he said.

Suddenly, Kylie's own mood was beyond tempering. Maybe he hadn't actually lied to her when he'd claimed it had been the FRU, but no doubt he had planned to get her away so she wouldn't know who had arrived. Since when did he feel he could decide who she could and couldn't see?

The answer came no sooner than the question whispered across her mind. *Since I came here.* She hadn't missed how limited her connection to the outside world had been since she'd arrived. No phone. No computer. And it wasn't just her. The chameleon lifestyle encouraged isolation.

"No." She touched her aunt's hand. "Release me." She spoke slowly but in a tone she hoped they understood was serious.

"Do as she asks," her grandfather said, and he sounded defeated. Kylie had only blinked when his image started appearing before her eyes. It wasn't like a ghost materializing. It was somehow different. As if the air parted and he was pulled back into the world.

Her aunt released Kylie's wrist and she felt a slight tingling in her feet and she looked down and watched as her feet and legs became visible.

"Wow," Derek said. Lifting her face, she saw him stare at her, and she fought the urge to throw herself into his arms.

Glancing at Burnett, she saw surprise appear in his eyes as well. His gaze met hers briefly, then he focused his attention on her grandfather, who stood protectively at her side.

"Why have you come here?" her grandfather asked, his tone dark and menacing. Immediately, she knew his stance was out of protection for her.

"Kylie's life is in danger, and if I can find you, so can the rogue who's after her."

"It is not the rogue who I fear the most," her grandfather said, leaving little doubt he considered the FRU, as well as Burnett, the biggest threat.

"You are letting the past blind you from seeing the truth," Burnett said. "Yes, the FRU would like to test Kylie, and some of us have decided not to let that happen, but it is Mario and his team who have already killed trying to get to her."

"I will protect my own," her grandfather said, his wide shoulders drawing tighter.

"How? By turning invisible? Do you not know that Kylie has already been taken hostage by this man, and she's discovered that Mario is a chameleon just like you and that means he knows about your trick. And if he knows about it, that makes you all that more vulnerable to him."

"I know this," her grandfather said, sounding defensive.

"Then you should know enough to be scared. Mario has not spent the last fifty years hiding as you and your friends have been moving from one place to another. He's been killing the innocent. He has taken the powers you have and mastered them to slaughter others. Even his own grandson died at his hands in front of Kylie because the boy defended her. If Mario will sacrifice his own blood, he will think nothing of killing his own kind."

"Wait," Kylie said, trying to keep up. "How do you know Mario is back?"

Burnett glanced briefly at Kylie. "He has been spotted."

"Spotted by whom?" her grandfather asked, disrespect coloring his tone. "The FRU? Like we would believe them?"

"I see that you have reservations," Burnett said, his words slipping from thinned lips pursed in what appeared to be anger. "But you must understand—"

"You dare to ask for my understanding?" Her grandfather's face grew red with fury. "What I understand is that you and your kind killed my wife. Because of you, I never knew my son. What I understand"—he pounded his chest with his fist—"is now you wish to do the same to my granddaughter!"

Kylie saw Burnett try to hold himself in check, but he couldn't hide the bright anger filling his eyes. She had to intervene, but how? Unfortunately, Kylie had no time to come up with a plan. Her grandfather took a step toward Burnett.

"Stop." Kylie attempted to move between the two men. But too late.

No one stopped.

Her grandfather swung his fist and Burnett took the blow square on the jaw.

While not nearly as young as Burnett, her grandfather didn't lack strength, and Burnett hit the ground. The sound of pure fury leaked from someone, and Kylie assumed it was Burnett. Before a second passed, her grandfather dove on top of Burnett and the scuffle continued.

Derek barreled forward, but two male chameleons appeared out of thin air and grabbed him by each arm.

How had things gone so wrong, so fast?

Chapter Three

"Stop this!" Kylie felt her protective mode start to kick in, the familiar fizzy-like feeling moving through her body, but for the life of her, she didn't know where to apply the strength. *Torn between two loyalties.* Derek's words rang in her head. Chameleons were her own kind. Her grandfather was blood. Yet Burnett and Derek were . . . they were family, too.

Out of nowhere, another figure appeared, this one snatching her grandfather off Burnett in an extremely rough manner. Her grandfather managed to stay on his feet but swung at the newcomer.

Feeling forced into action, even before considering what she was doing, she moved in, grabbed the newest member of the fight by his T-shirt, and tossed him away from her grandfather. The helpless figure was about ten feet in the air and making his way down to the ground—fast—when his blue eyes found hers and Kylie realized who she'd tossed.

Lucas.

So he *had* come.

The memory of him kissing his fiancée flashed in her head and echoed painfully in her heart. And for a flicker of a second, she wished she'd tossed him twice as hard.

She turned away, barely managing to catch her breath, when her gaze found Derek, still struggling against the two chameleons who held him. "Let him go," she seethed to the men. She recognized them as part of her grandfather's group, but it didn't matter. She wouldn't let them hurt Derek.

Her words hadn't completely left her lips, when suddenly the guys who held Derek dropped to the ground like dead flies. Derek scowled down at their bodies and stood straighter, almost with a sense of pride that he'd accomplished something.

Seeing the lifeless bodies on the ground brought on a wave of panic. What had Derek done? She'd wanted them to release Derek, but she hadn't wanted them . . . She remembered Derek's ability to mentally knock people out, but leave them basically unharmed. Or at least she hoped they were left unharmed.

Swinging back to her right, she refused to look at Lucas, but she heard him getting to his feet, and she felt him staring. Felt his gaze begging for just a glance. He could beg all he wanted; he wasn't getting it.

Yet less than two weeks ago, she would have given him her heart. Who was she kidding, she *had* given him her heart. That's why this was so hard.

Blinking, she refocused on her grandfather, who looked prepared to charge Burnett again.

Burnett, blood oozing from his lip, stood up. His expression and body language held ferocity; he was a man about to even the odds, but the one hand he held out suggested an attempt at peace. Thank God someone had sense, because with her broken heart replaying a painful song over and over in her head, she didn't think she was completely in control.

When her grandfather took another step forward, Burnett spoke up. "You and I have no fight between us. Stop this before someone gets hurt."

Kylie, realizing she needed to react, rushed to her grandfather's side. "He's right," she said. "Stop, please!" She wrapped her hand around his arm. Heat filled her chest. The warmth traveled down her arm and into her fingers. Then she felt it flow from her touch into her grandfather. She instinctively knew that she had passed the emotion of calm to her grandfather. And it was obviously working, because he dropped his head down and breathed in as if to collect himself. Chin still lowered, he must have spotted the men Derek had caused to pass out, because he hurried to them.

"They're fine," Derek said, and stepped away from her grandfather as if he half feared the man might come at him. But the signs of aggression her grandfather had worn minutes earlier were gone.

Kylie recalled the calming touch she'd passed him. Had she instinctively transformed into fae? She had to have, hadn't she?

Lucas took a step closer, not that she gazed at him directly, but from her peripheral vision she noted his movements. She attempted to tap into some of the serene emotions that she'd just passed to her grandfather. But it didn't work. The pain of Lucas's betrayal rose in her heart, crowded her better judgment, and knotted in her throat.

Her grandfather spoke up. "Everyone leave but Kylie and Mr. James."

"So you can attack him again?" Lucas asked, his tone hard, angry. And yet she could swear she heard remorse in his tone, too. She imagined his expression, his eyes filled with shadows of regret, but she still didn't look at him.

"Do as he says," Burnett ordered. Kylie could tell that, like her, Burnett recognized that her grandfather had seen reason.

People started walking away. Kylie again sensed Lucas moving, but his footsteps faltered as he moved in behind her. His scent filled the air she breathed, and his whispered question reached her ears. "Do you hate me so much that you can't even look at me?"

If only she could hate him, Kylie thought.

Then he continued in a voice meant only for her. "I never cared about her. Only you." The sound of his footsteps moving away sounded like the last beats of a sad song.

Physically he had left, but his words hung on. They filled Kylie with wave after wave of emotion. She knew Lucas spoke the truth—knew because, still being fae, she felt his sentiments—felt them seep into her skin, slip into her heart, and swell to the point of pain. But knowing he spoke the truth didn't change anything.

Whether he'd intentionally set out to hurt her or not didn't alter the fact that he had. How could he not have known how devastated she would be to learn he'd promised himself to someone else? Could he not see how hurt she'd be, knowing that for the months they'd been together, he had been seeing this girl, and at least pretending to care about her?

Right then, someone else's footsteps moved behind her. She felt the light touch of fingertips brushing across her shoulder blades. A slow, soft touch, not meant to seduce, not meant to draw attention. Meant only to soothe.

The warm calm of the touch left little doubt of the person's identity. Derek.

The pain in her chest lessened and she blinked the beginnings of tears from her eyes.

Trying to gain control of her wayward emotions, she stood there, eyes closed, concentrating on the feel of sun on her skin and the breeze against her cheeks.

"Kylie?" Burnett's voice had her jerking open her eyes.

Her grandfather and Burnett stood in front of her. Concern darkened both of their eyes.

"You okay?" her grandfather asked.

"Great." She produced a smile, one that probably came with as little believability as had her one word.

"Then come," her grandfather said. "We need to talk. At the house and over tea."

As she moved in step beside them, she saw Burnett give her a quick glance and she knew he'd picked up on her untruth. She wasn't great. She wasn't even marginally okay. Then she saw something else in his gaze. Or had she read it in his emotions? Fear. Fear of disclosure, as if he worried she wasn't going to like what he had to say.

Little did he know, she didn't like much of anything being said lately. Then instantly, she realized she'd been thinking only of herself. Selfishly, she'd focused on only her own pain. There was a reason Burnett was here and it might not be just about her.

Coming to a sudden halt, she grabbed the vampire by the elbow. "Is everyone okay? What . . . what happened?"

Five minutes later, Kylie sat at the dining room table and waited for her aunt to serve them iced tea before the conversation started. She just prayed it wouldn't lead to more of what had happened out by the barn. The tension between Burnett and her grandfather was slowly building again. Kylie's, however, had already hit its peak. Someone had better start talking or she was going to lose it. And by someone, she meant Burnett.

He'd postponed answering her question until they got somewhere to . . . talk. Which basically put Kylie on high alert that she'd been right. Something more than just Mario had happened. Someone wasn't okay.

On the walk to the house she'd gone crazy imagining the worst. Now sitting here, cold pizza centering the table, she fought back a sense of nausea as different versions of the worst threw darts at her heart. She knew Derek and Lucas were okay. And yeah, she shouldn't care about Lucas, but she still did.

Holiday had to be fine or Burnett wouldn't have been able to function. He loved her too much not to have been a physical mess if something had happened to her. That left . . .

Her thoughts immediately went to her two closest friends—friends her grandfather had insisted she not speak with for a while. But because he'd relented on her conversations with Holiday, she had tried to accept it. Now . . . if something had happened to them . . . Oh, God! Without knowing the answer, tears stung Kylie's eyes.

Kylie's mind turned first to Della. The stubborn vamp was on a mission for the FRU. Had something gone bad? Was Della okay?

Kylie recalled telling Della she didn't like her working for the FRU, but when Della came right out and asked her if she wanted her to decline helping them, Kylie hadn't told her no. She had known how much Della had wanted to work for the agency.

But now . . . if something had happened to Della, Kylie would forever regret her answer.

Worry chewed Kylie's patience down to a fine thread.

"Is it Della?" she finally bit out, as the glass of tea was set in front of her and her aunt left the room. "Did something happen to her?"

Burnett looked at her. "No, Della is fine . . . as far as I know. She is still on the mission."

"Then who . . . what happened?"

Burnett cupped the cold glass in his palm, but didn't sip from it. If it wasn't blood, he seldom drank anything except the strong coffee she'd seen him consume on some mornings. "After Mario was reported having been seen in Fallen, there was an incident. We aren't sure it's connected."

"Was anyone hurt?" The words stung as they left her lips, but somehow she knew with certainty someone hadn't walked away unscathed.

He turned the glass in his hands twice before answering. "Helen was attacked."

Kylie's breath caught. Helen, a half fae, was the shyest, most docile person at Shadow Falls. Who in the hell would hurt her? The answer bounced back like an unwanted echo. Mario.

"Is she . . . okay?" The word *alive* lingered on her lips, but she feared saying it because, damn it, it would have hurt too much.

"Yes," he answered. "She's going to be fine. And we don't even know if any of this is connected."

"So it wasn't this Mario, seeking Kylie," her grandfather said.

She looked at her grandfather and then said the obvious. "Burnett wouldn't be here if he didn't suspect that."

Burnett begrudgingly nodded. "We suspect it." He glanced at Kylie. "But there is really no proof to substantiate it. She was attacked from behind. She can't remember what happened."

"How bad is she?" Kylie asked, praying Helen wouldn't have scars—emotional or physical.

"She's stronger than any of us thought." He hesitated. "Her injuries were serious, but not life threatening. As you can imagine, Jonathon isn't leaving her side. Her parents are there at the hospital and there have been some awkward moments. Apparently, Helen hasn't told them of her newfound love."

Kylie envisioned the tall, lanky, and pierced vampire holding Helen's hand while her parents looked on. "I can also imagine that he's beyond pissed and wants revenge."

"I see you know Jonathon very well." The slightest hint of a smile passed Burnett's lips. But the smile didn't linger. "We have guards at the hospital, just in case the attacker returns."

"Should I go there?" Kylie asked.

"No," Burnett and her grandfather said at the same time.

Burnett continued. "If it was Mario, this could have been his ploy to get you to go to the hospital."

The thought that she and she alone was the reason Helen had been attacked sent an achy feeling crowding into her chest. Then anger crawled in and found its own spot in the tight space. She was so damned tired of people suffering at Mario's hand because of her. But how could she stop it? That was the million-dollar question and one Kylie decided needed to be answered. And sooner rather than later.

Burnett sat up straighter and refocused on her grandfather. "It was after Helen's attack that I got worried about Kylie's safety. I figured if I could find you then I'm sure he can. I think Kylie would be safer back at the camp."

"And I don't agree," her grandfather said.

"You don't agree?" Burnett seethed out the question. "Mario has made it clear, he wants Kylie to either join his group of rogue chameleons or he plans to kill her. He's threatened by her power as a protector."

"Again, I know this," her grandfather insisted. "You are not the only one who Kylie confides in. But if this attack on the other girl was to draw Kylie out, then it means he doesn't know where she is."

"But for how long?" Burnett asked. "Mario isn't one to let up."

"Perhaps, but if he's already found his way into the camp to get to this girl, why would you have me believe that he couldn't do it again to get to Kylie?"

"But—" Kylie spoke up, yet Burnett's direct glance at her seemed to ask for her to let him deal with this. She clamped her mouth shut, although it irked her to do it.

"I see your concerns," Burnett said. "However, the attack didn't take place on camp grounds." He gave the glass of tea another twirl in his hands and looked down at the amber-colored liquid as if debating whether to drink it. Then he raised his gaze. "Another factor to consider is that we have more bodies to help fight this rogue and his followers. And while I know the idea probably enrages you, I also have the FRU's assistance. With the office in Fallen, near the camp, I can have a hundred trained people there in a matter of minutes."

Her grandfather frowned. "You are right, it enrages me." He paused and Kylie saw him grinding his teeth before he spoke again. "I must tell you that the only reason I sit at the table with you is because my granddaughter holds you in such high regard. In the absence of her real father and the situation of her home life, you have in many ways stepped into the role of a father figure for her."

Burnett ran his finger over the condensation of his tea, almost as if uncomfortable at hearing how highly Kylie thought of him.

"I pray you deserve her respect." Her grandfather breathed in again. "That said, your logic here confuses me. You claim to be keeping my granddaughter from the FRU and yet you would call them to assist in protecting her. How is this feasible?"

"I'm assisting in preventing them from testing her simply because I'm not sure the tests are one hundred percent without risks. I believe their eagerness to find answers might prevent them from completely considering Kylie's best interest. But please don't take this to mean that I think they are capable of doing what they did to others in the past. The FRU isn't perfect, Mr. Summers, no organization is, or ever will be, but it's not the same organization that it was back then."

Silence filled the room. The tension hung thick in the air.

"Let me take Kylie back to Shadow Falls where I believe she is the safest," Burnett continued. "I will have guards waiting and watching for Mario to make his move. When he does, we will be ready. We will catch him and put a stop to this once and for all."

"And we can do the same," her grandfather added, his tone tight again.

Burnett's grimace deepened. "Look me in the eyes and tell me honestly that you believe you and your people are capable of handling this."

Her grandfather laced his fingers together—tight—and set his gripped hands on the table. Then he stared at his hands as if weighing Burnett's words.

When he raised his gaze, he met Kylie's eyes, and then returned his frown to Burnett. "I do not agree with your plan, nor your assessment of my or my people's ability to protect one of our own. Albeit I may be holding on to my prejudices of the past. Prejudices I am certain will be a part of me until I take my last breath."

He cleared his throat and let go of a sigh. "However, if my granddaughter has told me anything since she's been here, it's that she is her own person. So while I hope she will listen to my counsel on this, I'm aware that the decision will be hers. I have lost too much family in this life and I care too much about her to push her away by trying to hold on too tight."

Tears stung Kylie's eyes again. She reached over and touched her grandfather's hands. He turned his palm over and held her hand. His gaze found hers. "Stay here, Kylie. Stay and continue to learn who you are and where you belong." His touch, so much like that of her father's, sent warmth through her.

And a part of her wanted to give in. But at what cost?

Chapter Four

Before Kylie spoke, she saw in her grandfather's expression that he already knew her decision. And she saw the pain she was causing him. She felt it, too. His pain.

"You won't lose me. Where I live won't change anything. I'll always be your granddaughter. But I think Burnett has made some good points. I need to go back." It was, she thought, the only choice she could make.

Shadow Falls was her home, but that was only half the reason for her decision. Deep down she knew that Burnett was right. As gifted as her grandfather and his compound of chameleons were, they had spent the majority of their lives avoiding confrontation, not preparing for it. They were no match for Mario and his murdering kind.

Problem was, Kylie wasn't sure Shadow Falls could take on Mario, either. And if they did, how many more like Helen would be hurt, or worse, killed? It wasn't as if it hadn't happened before.

As she matched Burnett's steps to the front gate, they remained quiet. Night was encroaching on them. Part of the western sky, with shades of pink, hinted at the sun's departure. When they arrived at the gate, he looked at her. "I'll call your grandfather to set up a time to pick you up tomorrow."

Kylie nodded; she had insisted she have time to say good-bye to her grandfather. But now her heart didn't want to see Burnett leave. They hadn't really gotten to talk. That last fifteen minutes had been her grandfather asking how Burnett had found them. Burnett explained that it had been through the real estate office. When her grandfather had sold his house, Burnett was able to find out who had handled the sale, and through sales records he'd discovered another property her grandfather had owned.

Now with good-bye on her lips, she wasn't ready. "Promise me that Helen's really okay."

"It is as I told you. She will heal."

"And things with Della's mission are going okay? She's not in any danger?"

"My last communication with her confirmed everything is well."

Kylie nodded. "And Holiday's okay?"

"She's worried. But she's always worried about you guys. It's her natural state of being."

"But things between you two are . . . good?"

He smiled. "Yes. Very good."

Burnett's smiles were few, so she could guess how good it was.

"And Miranda?" Kylie asked.

"Lonely," he said. "With both her roommates gone, she's feeling rather out of sorts. She, as well as many others, will be happy to hear you are returning."

"Right. With no one there with evolving patterns to check out, I guess it's pretty boring."

Burnett shrugged. "I think you would be amazed how many people have inquired about you. You aren't nearly as unaccepted as you perceive, Kylie."

"I miss everyone, too," she admitted. "Can I hug you good-bye?"

He arched a brow in disapproval, and Kylie immediately knew why. Burnett wasn't one to completely let someone off the hook.

"I didn't think I warranted a good-bye hug," he said, reminding Kylie that she hadn't said good-bye to him when leaving the camp.

"I was wrong," she said, accepting she deserved this comeuppance. "I just knew that you would argue with me. It would have made leaving even harder."

"I would have argued. I would have insisted it was wrong," he said. "And I would have been right."

"Maybe not all right. I have learned some things. Plus, he's my grandfather and she's my great-aunt. My time here hasn't been a complete mistake."

"I understand your need to learn about yourself and I agree, there is a time to reunite with family, but not when your life is in danger."

Kylie looked at him. "So one's welfare is more important than . . . family. Like Holiday's your family?" She knew she had him.

He didn't even try to bullshit his way through that one. "I concede."

"Wow, this is a rarity." She smiled.

"Well, enjoy it," Burnett said. "Then again, you knew my one weakness and used it against me."

"Loving someone isn't a weakness," Kylie said. And then concern chased the levity of the moment away. "How certain are you that Mario did this to Helen?"

"Enough that I'm here," he said. "And enough that I will have guards monitoring this place tonight. Mario has seen your power, Kylie. You threaten his existence."

And yet, she felt powerless against him. She looked past the front gate and saw two figures. Two figures she recognized as Lucas and Derek. They stood a good fifty feet apart as if they weren't even together. Or as if . . . they were stationed to . . . Were they going to serve as guards? The idea that Lucas might be the one watching out for her, when he'd been the one to hurt her so deeply, sent another wave of pain to her chest.

"Not Lucas," she muttered.

"Not Lucas what?" Burnett asked.

Kylie felt a little childish for feeling the way she did, and even more for voicing it, but she didn't want to have to think about him being this close tonight. She'd have to deal with him being close tomorrow when she returned to Shadow Falls, but not tonight. "I don't want Lucas guarding me."

Burnett opened his mouth to say something, then shut it as if he thought better of it. Then, with a frown, he nodded.

Kylie ignored the look of disapproval and went in to collect her hug.

Burnett's embrace, even cold because of his vampire core body temperature, sent a warm feeling right to her chest. Knowing that tomorrow she would go home made letting go easier, but knowing that she would be forced to be in Lucas's presence made thoughts of her homecoming bittersweet.

Kylie started back to the house, but as she drew closer she grew leery of the conversation that would no doubt take place inside. Needing a few minutes to come up with a way to help her grandfather and aunt understand, she passed the house and started toward the gazebo. The sky glowed a hot pink and the setting sun bathed the scene before her in a golden hue. As she moved between the live oak trees, her gaze caught on the Spanish moss swaying ever so gently in the breeze.

She wondered if her grandfather would feel compelled to move now that Burnett had explained how easy it had been to find him. She hoped not. As discontent as she'd felt here this week, the beauty of the property hadn't gone unnoticed. The echoes of nature seemed to announce the coming of nightfall—a bird, a few crickets.

Then the pre-night seemed to hold its breath and the peacefulness of the moment shattered at the sound of a snapping twig. Kylie's heart skipped a beat as her gaze shifted toward the line of trees. Why the slight noise felt intrusive, she didn't know. It could have been just an innocent creature making its way back home before dark.

Yet it didn't sound innocent.

Suddenly a shadow appeared and then disappeared between the trees. Kylie couldn't explain it, but instead of running from the figure, she felt compelled to go to it.

Starting for the trees, she saw the figure again, a feminine silhouette, darting in and out of the shadows. For a flash of a second, Kylie thought she recognized *her*.

Kylie came to an abrupt stop.

How could that be? How could she be here? What was she doing here?

She'd followed him. She had to have followed Lucas. Why else would his fiancée be here?

Unsure if she wanted to confront this girl, she turned to leave. She got only a few steps before she heard someone's feet hitting the soft earth even with Kylie's own steps.

"What do you want?" Kylie bit out, without looking at the person who now moved beside her.

"To talk," the person answered, but the voice wasn't right. It wasn't the light flowery tone she'd heard promise her soul to the person Kylie loved. It wasn't Monique.

Kylie stopped and looked at Jenny, the seventeen-year-old chameleon from the compound. She had dark hair, and was the right height. Had Kylie mistaken her for . . . ?

"Was that you?"

"Was what me?" Jenny asked.

Kylie looked again at Jenny's features, a straight nose, square chin, and light grayish green eyes, and remembered the vague feeling that she looked familiar. Not like she knew her, but just that she looked like someone she knew. "You . . . were in the woods?"

"I . . . guess. I was coming from our house."

Kylie envisioned a quick glimpse of the person she thought was Monique. It hadn't been Jenny—or had it? "Did you see anyone else?"

"No. Why? Was there someone else out there?"

Kylie looked back at the woods. "Probably not," she said, but she wasn't completely convinced. Being werewolf, Monique could be very quiet if she willed it. Or very fast getting away. Kylie returned to walking, her mind racing faster than her pace.

"So . . . do you mind?" Jenny asked.

Lost in her thoughts, Kylie glanced up. "Mind what?"

"If we talk," Jenny said, and she gripped her hands together as if worried about something.

"I . . ." Kylie looked back up at the house. "I need to speak with my grandfather and aunt now, but why don't you stop by in a bit." Kylie noted again Jenny's worried expression and she found it odd that she was even asking to speak with her. Jenny hadn't been rude to Kylie during her time here, but she hadn't been friendly, either. "Is something wrong?"

"The rumor is that you're leaving. Are you?"

Kylie nodded. "Yes. Why?"

Jenny nipped at her bottom lip as if nervous. "When?"

"Tomorrow," Kylie answered.

Voices came from her grandfather's house. Kylie looked toward the door.

"I . . . gotta go." Jenny darted off in a hurry. Kylie turned back to the house and noticed that on her grandfather's porch stood the four other elders, as if they'd just stepped out to leave.

Kylie looked back and tried again to convince herself it was Jenny and not Monique she'd seen. But she wasn't completely buying it.

As she headed to the house, the elders passed her. All nodded a quick hello and kept walking, but just in passing Kylie felt the tension radiating from them. Somehow Kylie sensed that they had been at her grandfather's discussing her. While she'd been relieved that her grandfather had made at least some level of peace with Burnett, it didn't mean the other elders had. And that, Kylie realized, could mean trouble. If not for her, for her grandfather.

Kylie hesitated as she stepped into the house. Having been here thirteen days, she still felt as if she should knock. Not that her aunt or grandfather made her feel unwelcome, but she just didn't have the sense of belonging. Maybe because, deep down, she knew she didn't fit in here. She belonged at Shadow Falls. She recalled Burnett saying that her coming here was a mistake. And even though it didn't feel right, she wasn't prepared to call it that.

Voices drifted from the dining room and she moved that way. As she entered the hallway, the voices stopped. Stopped too quickly, as if they knew she was there and didn't want her to hear them. She paused at the threshold. Her aunt and grandfather sat at the table looking at her. She wished she knew the right thing to say. Yet a part of her knew that no matter what she said, it was going to hurt them. Maybe Burnett was right. Coming here had been a mistake. If for no other reason than the pain she'd brought on her grandfather and aunt.

"I'm sorry if I've caused problems. I'm sorry that—"

"No worries, child. Sit down," her aunt said. "Do you want me to heat your pizza?"

"No, I'm not hungry." Kylie sat down and gazed at her grandfather. "Are the elders upset at what happened? Are they upset at me, or you?"

Her grandfather sighed. "Upset, yes, but not at a particular person. They do not like change, and lately there has been a lot of change."

And mostly because of me. Kylie bit down on her lip. "I know someone who told me that it's when things don't change that a person should start to worry."

"I'm betting this person wasn't a chameleon," her grandfather said.

"No," Kylie answered.

He nodded. "Right or wrong, we have a tendency to like our comfort zones."

"Is there anything I can do to help?" she asked.

The wrinkles between his eyes tightened. "Stay with us and continue to learn what your heritage means," he said. "You've only scratched the surface of what there is to learn."

"Malcolm," her aunt said. "Do not put the girl in a bad situation."

"I worry that the bad situation is the one she will go back to," he said.

"I'll do most anything to make this right, but I can't stay," Kylie said, feeling her throat tighten.

"I'm sorry." He held up his hand. "Your aunt is right, I'm putting pressure on you and I shouldn't. I have already said my piece. But I will say that I'm going to miss you."

"And I'll miss you," Kylie said. "Will you remain living here?"

He shrugged. "If the other elders get their way, we will leave."

"Because they don't trust Burnett?" Kylie asked.

"I'm sure that's part of it," he said.

"How will I get in touch with you?"

"Hayden Yates is still working at your school."

Hayden was the chameleon whom her grandfather had hired to keep an eye on Kylie. For some reason, when she left, she had just assumed he would leave, too. "He stayed on as a teacher?"

Her grandfather nodded. "He convinced them that you tricked him into taking you off the grounds. They still don't know what he is, and it needs to remain that way."

Kylie nodded, but she couldn't help but be suspicious. Burnett wasn't that easily tricked.

"Actually, Hayden speaks highly of how things are run at the school."

"See," Kylie said. "It's really not a bad place."

• • •

That night, not knowing what time Burnett would come for her, Kylie packed her bags. Then she stretched out in the bed with the softest sheets and down comforter she'd ever felt, flipping through the pictures of her dad. You would think being with her grandfather would make Kylie miss her real father less, but no; it seemed to work just the opposite. Seeing this man who looked like an older version of her dad made her miss him more.

Finally, after spending too much time wishing things could have been different, she lay there and stared at the ceiling. She worried about how leaving her grandfather might hurt him. She worried about Della, and even a bit about Miranda feeling abandoned by both of them. She worried about her mom off in England, probably doing the dirty with a man who gave Kylie the creeps.

Oh, goodness, she had to push that image out of her head really fast, or she was going lose what little pizza she'd eaten.

She worried about how she was going to cope with Lucas.

But you aren't worried about me?

The cold hit so fast Kylie's breath caught when the frigid oxygen hit her lungs. She grabbed the comforter and pulled it all the way up to her chin.

"Should I worry about you?" Kylie asked, and looked over to where the ghost stood. Her hair hung loose and dangled almost to her waist. She wore the same white gown covered in blood.

And she looked . . . dead. Deader than before.

Kylie didn't understand. If a ghost had an option to look dead, or not so dead, why didn't they choose not so dead every time?

No, don't worry about me. I'm already dead. See? She pulled her skirt tight and showed a dozen or so bloody slits in the white dress. It looked as if someone had taken a knife to her and hadn't known when to stop.

"That's terrible." Kylie looked away for a second and then back. "Who did that to you?"

The ghost didn't answer; she just kept looking at the holes in her dress. *Actually, it's not so terrible. And to be honest, the person you should worry about is you. Because if you don't start listening to me, you're going to end up dead. Just like me.*

"Listen to what? Listen to you go on about my killing someone, you mean?" Kylie asked, frowning.

Yeah. She continued to stare at the holes in her dress. *And don't make it sound like a terrible thing. Taking a life is not the worst thing in the world.*

"Okay, I'm curious, how many people have you killed?"

The spirit looked up as if considering the question. And it seemed to take her too damn long. As if she actually had to count. "You really did it, didn't you? You killed more than just one?"

I'm up to twenty-something, but I know I've missed a few. Some didn't seem to count very much.

"What were you? A hit man . . . a hit woman?"

No, well, sort of, I guess. I didn't profit from my work. I just took care of someone else's problems. And a few of my own. Blood suddenly appeared on her hands. She held them up and stared at them. Blood dripped from her fingertips. Some of it fell onto her already bloody dress and some dripped to the beige carpet. The smell, the coppery scent, filled the room and almost made Kylie gag. She supposed she should be happy that it didn't smell good to her right now.

"Are you trying to take me to hell with you? Is that what this is about? I've heard about some evil hell-bound spirits doing that. But I'm not going there, and I refuse to help you kill someone, so just give it up. You got that?" Kylie closed her eyes and tried to think positive thoughts the way Holiday had said could prevent a ghost from getting control of you—from taking you places you didn't want to go.

She felt the cold ebb away, but the spirit's words whispered in her head. *I don't want you to go to hell. I want you to send someone else there.*

"Go away! Go away! Go away!" Kylie muttered both aloud and in her head. "I'm not killing anyone for you. Nope. Nope. Not me."

The cold was gone, and Kylie took in a deep breath. But the cracking sound at her window had the breath seeping out in a squeal and made her jump at least three inches off the bed.

Kylie's gaze shot to the window but she didn't see anything.

Once the initial panic slaked off, her mind envisioned the blue jay—the one she'd pulled from death. Had the thing followed her here?

Getting out of bed, she moved to the window, and with thoughts of hell-bound ghosts still too close to her mind, she cautiously pulled back the white lacy drapes. Out of nowhere, a distorted face appeared pressed to the glass pane.

Kylie screamed.

Chapter Five

"Kylie? Are you okay?" Her grandfather's voice sounded at the bedroom door at the same time she was able to make out the face at the window. *Jenny.* The young chameleon who had spoken with Kylie earlier and acted so nervous. The one Kylie thought might have been Monique. What was she doing at the window? What could she want this late?

Jenny's gaze shot to the bedroom door and she shook her head. Panic filled her face, making her eyes widen, and her expression pleaded for Kylie not to tell her grandfather that she was there.

"Yeah, I'm fine. I must have been dreaming," she lied, and then hoped her grandfather wasn't in vampire mode and could read her heartbeat. Glancing back at the window, she saw relief flash in the girl's green eyes.

"Sleep well, then," her grandfather said from behind the door.

"I will," Kylie said. She waited until she heard the footsteps moving down the hall and then inched to the window and opened it.

Jenny pressed a finger to her lips and motioned for Kylie to come outside.

Before she did as Jenny requested, Kylie poked her head out and glanced around. She wasn't sure what she was looking for, but she just didn't want any surprises. Jenny's presence already surprised Kylie enough.

Just as she started to crawl out, Jenny stopped her and leaned in. "Is that your packed bag?"

Kylie looked back at her suitcase sitting on a side chair. "Yes."

"Get it," Jenny whispered back.

Kylie's breath caught. "Why?"

"I have to get you out of here."

Say what? "No." Kylie shook her head. "I'm leaving tomorrow."

"No you're not. Or at least you're not going where you think you're going."

"What are you saying?" Kylie asked, and part of her wanted to slam the window shut, because instinctively she knew whatever news Jenny had to share, it wasn't going to be good.

Ten minutes later, traipsing through the very back of her grandfather's property, her old brown suitcase in hand, Kylie still couldn't come to grips with what Jenny had told her.

"I can't believe my grandfather would do this."

"I told you, it's probably not really him doing it. It's the other elders. To be honest, your grandfather is the most tolerant of all of them."

Kylie stopped. "But he wouldn't go along with it. He would not let them just kidnap me and keep me against my will."

"Look, to be honest, I don't even know if he knows. They could be doing this behind his back. But you and I both saw the other elders there talking to him."

Anger and doubt rose inside Kylie so strong that tears stung her eyes. "But leaving like this is . . . It feels so wrong. I should go back and talk to him."

"No! If you go back, there's a good chance they'll find us. I know the schedule of the guards, and if we don't hurry they'll catch you leaving."

Kylie inhaled. The smell of the forest filled her lungs and she tried to rationalize. The night seemed to crawl between the trees and the air felt thick. "Why? Why would they do this?"

"Isn't it obvious? You're a protector and you belong to the chameleons."

"I don't belong to anyone!"

"I didn't mean . . . I know you don't really belong to anyone. But that's the way they feel." Jenny stepped closer. "They're wrong, they're all wrong about so many things. Why do you think I'm doing this?"

She looked at Jenny and the girl's question vibrated in Kylie's head. "Why *are* you doing this? And don't say it's just because you think they are wrong, or because you like me or something, because you haven't said more than a few words to me. My gut tells me it's more and my gut is usually right."

She glanced away but not before Kylie saw the guilt in her eyes.

"Is this some kind of a trap?" Kylie started looking around.

"No, it's not a trap," Jenny said.

Kylie heard conviction in Jenny's tone, but she wasn't vampire and couldn't be sure if the girl lied or not. She peered harder at Jenny. "Either you explain yourself right now, or I'm turning around and going back."

"Explain what?" Jenny asked, sounding frustrated.

"Explain why you would help me when you don't even like me."

She huffed. "Look, I didn't like you because Brandon did. I'm supposed to be matched with him, and while it makes me furious that they think they can tell me who I should fall in love with, it still pissed me off when he started falling all over you."

"Matched with him? You mean the elders try to arrange marriages?"

"They try to do everything. They are all crazy. Well, not your grandfather, completely, but . . ." Jenny rubbed her hand on her jeans as if nervous at telling her true feelings. "They keep us sheltered away from everything. They say it's because they don't want people to see us until we have the ability to hide our patterns. But look at you. You lived in the regular world; you weren't killed or thrown into slavery."

"Slavery?" Kylie asked.

"Yeah, they use fear to keep us compliant. To convince us to stay here and not go out into the world."

Kylie shook her head. "I haven't heard anything about this." But she suddenly realized how isolated she'd been since she'd come. She'd been so overwhelmed, she hadn't realized.

"They've been careful what they say in front of you. But you have to believe me. They want to keep us here. To protect us, they say, but . . . sometimes I think what we should fear the most is being suffocated by this way of life. And if they find out you don't agree with them, there's hell to pay."

"Which brings me back to my original question," Kylie said. "If you're so afraid, why are you doing this?"

She averted her eyes away again.

"What are you not telling me?" Kylie insisted.

Jenny exhaled. "It's Hayden."

"Hayden Yates?" Kylie asked.

"We talk sometimes. My parents don't know. The elders don't know. And you can't tell anyone."

Kylie did the math in her head, comparing Hayden's possible age and then Jenny's. "He's too old for you."

Jenny's green eyes widened. She shook her head. "He's not my boyfriend. He's my older brother."

Kylie tried to compute this new information. "Then why would your parents not want you to talk to him?"

"Because he left. When a chameleon leaves they're supposed to cut all ties to the family so they won't expose us."

"But my grandfather contacted Hayden," Kylie said.

"Like I said, your grandfather is the lesser of the evils here. Your grandfather actually lets me talk to him sometimes." Jenny frowned. "But we don't have time to stand around and talk. I'm serious, if we don't go now, the guards will catch us." The sound of footfalls coming, coming fast, punctuated Jenny's warning.

"Damn," she said. "Run. Just keep going south and you should come to the edge of the property. You should make it before the guards do if you hurry."

"But—"

"Go! I promised my brother I'd get you out of here!"

The urgency in Jenny's tone had Kylie bolting, but she only got a hundred yards when her chest constricted with a bad feeling. A bad feeling about leaving Jenny. Kylie felt the subtle change in her body at even the slightest thought that someone might be in danger. She wasn't leaving the girl, not until she made sure whoever hurdled toward her wasn't a threat. Swinging around, she started back.

"Damn it!" a gravelly sounding voice exploded in the dark of the forest. A voice that sounded familiar. "Get off of me."

"Leave her alone," Jenny screamed. "She's going back where she belongs."

Kylie's feet pounded harder against the ground as she hurried to the edge of the trees. She hadn't come to a complete stop when she recognized the voice. She saw Derek with a very angry Jenny clinging to his back, her hands over his eyes and her legs wrapped around his waist.

Derek yanked her hands from his eyes, but Jenny just shifted her hold around his throat.

"Where is Kylie?" he growled, and whirled around, as if half attempting to find her and half trying to throw off his assailant.

Kylie almost smiled at the sight of Jenny clinging to Derek's back. The smile faded when she saw him become still and close his eyes as if concentrating. She knew he was about to do that thing in his mind that would leave Jenny unconscious. "Stop. I'm here," Kylie belted out.

"You know him?" Jenny asked, her legs still clinging to Derek's back.

"Yes. I know him. Get off of him," Kylic suggested, not completely sure Derek understood Jenny wasn't a threat.

Jenny slipped down and then quickly stepped back, as if now the moment of panic was over, she felt a sense of fear. Derek turned, no doubt scowling at the girl, if Jenny's expression was any indication. After only a second, his angry posture weakened. The two of them clashed gazes, neither of them looking happy, but assessing each other.

"Then . . . then go, both of you." Jenny waved her arms and quickly diverted her gaze away from Derek. "Go before the guards find you."

"What's going on?" Derek asked, and finally looked away from Jenny to Kylie. She saw his gaze cut to the suitcase in her hand.

"She says the elders are going to try to stop me from leaving." Kylie felt the pinch of betrayal as she said it. Was her grandfather in on this or not?

"But Burnett said—"

"You do not have time to talk about this!" Jenny snapped.

Derek looked at Kylie as if waiting for her to make the call.

"We should go," she said, and sadness fluttered inside her about leaving this way. About not knowing if her grandfather had betrayed her or not.

She cast Jenny one more look. "Thank you," she said.

Jenny offered Kylie a shy smile and nodded right before she and Derek took off.

She kept her pace even with Derek's, knowing he couldn't keep up. The suitcase in her hand felt light in her firm grip, but the bouncing back and forth felt cumbersome.

"I could've knocked her off. You know I just didn't want to hurt that girl."

"I know." Kylie bit back a grin. What was it with guys and their egos?

Their footfalls seemed to bounce off the trees and fill the darkness. But the mood suddenly felt different. While she couldn't explain it, her skin felt ultra sensitive and her blood seemed to pulse a bit fast. Fear. Danger. It built inside her, like a slow fire, and the scent of it seemed to fill the air, stinging her flesh.

And from the quick glance Derek shot her, Kylie knew she wasn't the only one feeling it. Their pace suddenly increased.

• • •

They got within a hundred yards of the gate in less than five minutes. Kylie could have made it in half that time, but Derek couldn't. As they drew closer, Kylie spotted the gate. They could easily jump over. Kylie was about to tell Derek the plan, when suddenly she remembered. Just because she couldn't see the guards didn't mean they weren't there.

She grabbed Derek's arm and pulled him behind a tree. "Wait," she whispered under her breath.

"It's clear," he said, and looked back around the oak's trunk.

"We don't know for sure," she said. "They're chameleons."

His gaze shot back to the fence, his brow wrinkled with puzzlement. She saw the exact second he realized what she meant.

"How could we know if . . . they're invisible?" he asked.

Kylie suddenly recalled that while she couldn't see anyone when she was invisible, she could hear them. "Let me check on something." She closed her eyes and concentrated on disappearing. For a second she feared it wouldn't work, but then the odd kind of tingling started with her feet and went to her knees.

Derek's eyes grew round as she faded. The second she couldn't see herself, she concentrated on listening. Her gaze moved between the trees, trying to see anything in the dark. Beside her, she could hear Derek breathing. She glanced at him, saw him still staring as if finding her disappearing act a bit too much. Then she heard it. Footfalls.

Shit.

Someone was coming upon them. It had to be the guards.

Panicked, she searched for the right thing to do. They could hear her whether she was invisible or not. But at least she couldn't be seen. But what about Derek?

Remembering something she had learned, she yearned to be visible again, and when she appeared, Derek just eyed her in a bit of amazement. She leaned in and whispered in his ear. "They're close by." She took his hand and laced her fingers through his. Normally, Kylie wouldn't worry so much about facing the guards. Chameleons weren't known as fighters, but the feeling of fear that still pricked her skin said she shouldn't take chances. Not now, not when they were so close to escaping.

She leaned closer to his ear. "I'm going to make you invisible with me. You have to be very quiet, because while they can't see us, they will be able to hear us. You understand?"

"Wait? You're going to make me—"

She cut off his words by pressing a finger to his lips. Then, not really knowing if she could do it, she closed her eyes tight and thought of nothing but disappearing—and taking Derek with her.

Slowly, her legs started to fade, and then she saw Derek's hand start to shimmer. She heard his light gasp when he saw it, too. It didn't occur to her until right then that the whole invisible thing might not work the same for non-chameleons. What if this hurt him? She almost let go of his hand, but instead she listened to her gut and her gut said it was okay.

Dear God, she hoped her gut didn't let her down now.

As the vanishing slowly climbed up her body, she saw his arm completely disappear. She held tight to his wrist and felt him brush his thumb on the back of her arm. When she looked up into his eyes, she saw his gaze was directed at her mouth. He leaned in just a bit. Oh, crap! Thankfully, before his lips pressed against her, he was visually gone. And so was she. As she felt his breath on her lips, she shifted back just a bit.

"Can you hear me?" She breathed the words, her mind still on the kiss that almost happened. Why did it feel so wrong? She didn't need to be loyal to Lucas now. But she did need to be loyal to what felt right, and that almost kiss hadn't felt right. Maybe not all wrong, but not right, either.

"Are you okay?" she asked.

She heard his quiet reply. "Yeah. This is so cool."

Odd, how different people interpreted situations. The first time this happened to her, she'd freaked. Of course, she hadn't had anyone with her, or even known it was possible.

"Don't pull away from me or you'll become visible," she whispered. At least that's how she thought it worked. Oh, great. What if it wasn't that simple?

"Holding on to you is easy," he whispered, and he brushed his thumb over her wrist again. "I never wanted to let go of you."

"Now's not the time . . ."

"I know." A bit of guilt sounded in his tone.

Kylie tried to calm her racing mind that darted between the almost kiss to the fear that turning him invisible could have done some damage. Thankfully, he appeared to be fine. Now she just prayed undoing this was as easy as making him vanish. God, she hoped this hadn't been a mistake.

"Now what?" he asked in a voice barely audible, and she felt his breath against her cheek. She shifted back.

"If I understand what Jenny meant, the guards walk the property. I can hear footsteps, and I'm assuming it's them now. They aren't too close, but it sounds like there are two of them. I'm hoping they will walk on by."

"Sounds like a plan."

It sounded like a shot in the dark, Kylie thought.

They stood completely silent and invisible. The footsteps drew nearer. Close.

Then closer. But they remained invisible. The sound of their breathing echoed too loud in the night air. Kylie tried to listen to see if their own breaths sounded.

Derek must have shifted because the sound of a twig snapping filled the air.

Kylie stiffened and prayed it didn't give them away.

"Did you hear that?" one voice asked.

Kylie recognized it as one of the chameleons' voices. She didn't know him well enough to call him by name. Not that knowing his name would help right now. If he discovered them, they would probably call the elders. And just what the elders would do was beyond her.

"Who's here?" a different voice called out, and the footsteps drew closer. So there were definitely two of them.

"Speak now if you are one of us!" the second voice said, and moved so close to Kylie she could swear she could feel the warmth of his invisible body.

And that warmth left Kylie cold with fear.

Especially when the body materialized and stood within an inch of her. Derek's grip on her fingers tightened, telling her he was sensing her fear.

The redheaded chameleon guard glanced around and called out. "Hello? Is someone here?"

Chapter Six

Another set of footsteps filled the darkness, but this one came from behind them.

"It's just me," a feminine voice called out several feet behind where Kylie and Derek stood, invisible and silent.

Kylie recognized Jenny's tenor just before she appeared from the shadows. The girl had obviously followed them—to make sure they had made it. Kylie felt slightly guilty for doubting the girl in the beginning.

"Jenny Beth? What are you doing traipsing out in the woods at this time of night?"

Derek squeezed her hand and Kylie could only assume it was out of concern for Jenny. But her gut said that Jenny should be able to handle this. She almost said that to Derek, but remembered the other guard would hear her.

Jenny moved in a few more inches. "I couldn't sleep. I stepped outside for a quick walk and then . . . I saw someone."

"Saw who?"

"I don't know, he didn't look familiar. Sandy brown hair, almost six feet. Medium build. Young. And when the moonlight hit him, he looked like he had light eyes."

Kylie bit down on her lip. Why was Jenny describing Derek?

Derek squeezed Kylie's hand a little tighter, silently asking the same question.

The other chameleon materialized beside his partner. "Sounds like one of the guards that dirty FRU put on us. The one that knocked our asses out. I'd love to get another stab at him."

Tension traveled through Derek's grip and up Kylie's arm. The need to protect him stirred in her chest.

The new guard cut his gaze toward Jenny. "Why did you stay out here with a stranger running loose?" the man asked.

"I didn't. I mean, that's why I came this way. He was between me and my house when I spotted him. He walked toward the north part of the property. I was going to Mr. Summers' home to report it."

"I knew this wouldn't end well," the guard snapped. He pulled a cell phone from his pocket and dialed. The other moved closer to Jenny. "I'll walk you home."

"I think I can make it."

"Not with strangers running amok."

Kylie saw Jenny cut her eyes toward her and Derek, almost as if she knew where they stood. And in the gaze, she seemed to send a silent message that said once she got the guys away from here, they needed to run.

It was a message Kylie didn't need to receive twice.

The one on his cell started talking to someone about finding Jenny. "She says he was headed north." He paused. "We will." He hung up and looked at the other guard. "Get her back home and join me in the north end to find this guy. Our orders are if we don't find him quickly, we'll have to sound the alarm."

"Twice in twenty-four hours, I think that's a record," the other stated with disgust.

Silence reigned in the dark. "Yeah, that's what happens when we start bringing in strangers. Protector or not, I knew that girl's coming here would stir up shit. And to think they want to keep her."

Kylie's heart pulled at hearing this. It wasn't that she hadn't believed Jenny, but hearing it somehow made it feel more real. And it hurt deeper.

Derek's touch grew warmer and Kylie knew he was attempting to console her.

One of the guys shifted closer to where she knew Derek stood. Derek shifted, obviously freaked out about someone taking up his space, even when he was invisible.

The guard glanced around as if he almost suspected he wasn't alone.

"Should one of us go check and see if she's still in her residence?"

"Yeah, we probably should," bit out the other guard.

And as soon as they discovered her missing, it would make it more difficult to escape, Kylie realized.

The guards and Jenny walked away. Kylie waited until they were out of hearing range to speak. She had words on the tip of her tongue when she heard another pair of footsteps echoing around them. Had one of the guards gone invisible and turned around? Or was this someone new?

Kylie squeezed Derek's hand, hoping to make him aware of the newcomer.

Derek's grip tightened as if he understood.

The footsteps stopped only a few feet from her. She tried to control her breaths in and out, praying the slip of air into her lungs, or Derek's breathing, wouldn't give them away.

Several very long minutes passed. Finally, whoever hung around let go of a deep, emotion-filled breath and began walking away. The crunch of twigs popping filled the air as he left. The temptation to call out her grandfather's name was strong. For the cadence of those footsteps, as well as that long sigh had sounded familiar. But she couldn't be sure, could she? Maybe it was just wishful thinking.

Wishful thinking that he'd discovered her missing and was worried and came looking for her.

Wishful thinking that he didn't know what the other chameleons were up to.

But wishful thinking could land her and Derek up to their eyebrows in trouble. So she stood frozen in one spot and waited. As soon as the footsteps faded between the shadows of the trees, Kylie said to Derek, "We have to go and go fast."

"I'm not arguing," he said.

"I'm going to let go of you and I think you should just go visible again."

"You *think*?" Derek asked, and yes, there was a tad of fear in his tone. "Oh, shit. You haven't done this before?"

"Not really," Kylie confessed.

"Okay, let's hope it works." He released her hand. Kylie closed her eyes and willed herself visible. A second or two passed and she opened her eyes. When she didn't see Derek, her heart pounded and fear swirled in her chest.

"Derek?" she whispered. Tears filled her eyes. Oh shit, had she done something terrible?

"I'm behind you," he said.

Kylie swirled around and her breath eased out of her at the sight of him.

"You ready?" he asked, and smiled as if he'd read and liked that she'd been freaked out at the thought of losing him. Because face it, that meant she cared, right?

Not that it was a surprise. She'd never stopped caring. She just didn't know if her caring was in the same way he felt about her.

"Ready," she said. "We have to hurry." And they did.

They ran, side by side. She never pushed it to a level he couldn't make, though.

When they reached the five-foot fence, Kylie took his hand, ready to help him if needed. He didn't seem offended. If anything, he smiled and pressed his palm against hers. The smile, and the contentment that filled his gaze, reminded her that he'd tried to kiss her and only added to her anxiety.

Was it just too soon after her heartbreak with Lucas?

Or was it just too late for her and Derek?

Realizing this wasn't the time for contemplation, she started running faster. Holding Derek's hand tight, they leapt over the fence.

They came down with a good thud. Derek caught her around the waist. His breathing, heavy enough that his chest moved in and out under the dark T-shirt, matched her own. Their gazes met for one second, a second that felt as if it came out of some romantic movie. The kind where soft music played in the background. The kind that ended in some hot kiss. She pulled away. "We have to go."

Disappointment flashed in his eyes, but in a blink it disappeared. She knew he'd read her emotions. Probably felt her confusion. And being Derek, he wouldn't push, or at least not too hard. Then again, trying to steal a kiss earlier had been pretty bold for him.

Maybe this was a new Derek?

Maybe she'd have to be a bit more careful?

Derek snatched the suitcase from her hand and they started running again. Running away from her new problems, but right back to her old ones.

They got a good mile away before Kylie gave in and stopped. She glanced around. They stood beside a road, and while she'd lost her bearings, she felt certain they were less than five miles from Shadow Falls.

In the distance, a bird called out to its mate. Soft insect sounds vibrated in the night air. The verdant smells of plant life swirled around them. The pending danger should be over. They were far enough away—the guards wouldn't come this far. But some tiny sensation in the pit of her stomach said not to be so sure.

"I should call Burnett," Derek said.

"I guess." The hint of danger stirring in her gut faded at the thought of how she would explain all this to the stern vampire. Frustration swelled inside her. Burnett would be furious and assume her grandfather had been lying all along. And yes, Kylie would admit it almost appeared that way, but she couldn't believe it. She wouldn't stop believing in him until she spoke with him—until he looked her square in the eye and wouldn't deny it. Maybe she hadn't known him very long, but for some reason, she felt she knew him. Knew him well enough to believe that if he'd done this, he wouldn't deny it. He'd own up to it, maybe claim he had reasons, but he wouldn't lie.

Again, she wondered if it had been him hanging around earlier, before they'd made a run for it. The ache in her chest, the one she recognized already as missing him, tugged at her heart.

"Hey . . . you okay?" Derek asked, and ran his hand down her forearm.

"I will be," Kylie said, and she had to believe that.

"So . . . you don't want me to call Burnett?" Derek dropped the suitcase and pulled his phone out of his pocket, but he hesitated to dial, waiting for her permission.

"No, call him," she said, accepting it was the right thing to do. She'd just have to deal with Burnett's disapproval of her grandfather.

He punched in a button and frowned. "My phone's dead." He punched in a couple more numbers. "I know I charged it. Shit." He jumped and tossed the cell to the ground. "What the hell? That thing shocked the fire out of me," he blurted out.

Kylie watched as sparks started shooting from the phone, then a buzzing sound came from the device, followed by smoke.

"I didn't know that could happen," Derek said.

"It doesn't."

"It's a new phone, too," he complained. "My mom's going to have a fit."

Remembering some ghosts could do things with phones, Kylie

put her feelers out for ghosts. No cold brushed up against her flesh. She looked around, searching for . . . She didn't know what she expected to see, but something told her the phone's demise wasn't an accident. As her gaze shifted from side to side, the night gave nothing up. Darkness swallowed up the terrain. The paved street looked abandoned. The street lights stood dark, not a flicker of illumination flowed from their bulbs.

Something was out there, but what? It didn't feel like a ghost.

"We'd better run."

He reached for her arm. "What is it?"

"I don't know, but I don't like it."

"That makes two of us," Derek said.

"Three," a voice said beside Kylie.

Kylie turned and the spirit of the murderous woman stood beside her. "You did this, didn't you?"

"Why would I blow up my own phone?" Derek asked.

"Not you," Kylie said, but didn't look away from the spirit.

No! I stopped blowing up phones years ago. I found much better ways to make my presence known.

Kylie turned to Derek. "Let's get out of here." He picked up the suitcase and they started to run.

No! This way. The spirit started in a separate direction.

Stopping, Kylie reached out and snagged Derek's arm, bringing him to a jerky halt.

The spirit turned and looked at Kylie. *This way. Go to the graveyard. You'll have help. For some crazy reason all the dead people there like you.*

"Why should I trust you?" Kylie asked, and in the corner of her vision, she spotted Derek frowning. No doubt, seeing her hold a conversation with a ghost would be unsettling. He ought to try having one and see how unsettling that could be.

Because you want to stay alive.

Kylie's breath caught and she looked at Derek. "Let's go this way," she told him, praying her gut was right and she could trust this spirit.

Praying this wasn't some ploy to get her at the cemetery and then take her to hell.

They ran. Ran hard. But Kylie felt something following them as they ran. Felt it from the inside out. And felt it was ready to pounce.

She saw the front gates of the cemetery. Her heart pounded against her breastbone and if she was running out of steam, Derek surely couldn't go much farther.

"Wait!" Derek stopped and reached for her.

"Why . . . are we . . . going to the cemetery?" His breath came out in gulps.

"I have friends there," she said.

"Dead friends," he said, not happy.

"Let's not be choosy right now."

He shot a glance at the rusty gates. "We should head to Shadow Falls. We're close."

"We won't make it," Kylie said, and something inside her said she was right. Something inside her said the thing that followed them wasn't playing around. Something inside her said it was Mario. Dear God, she hoped she was wrong.

She grabbed Derek by the arm and started running again. Unfortunately, they didn't make the gate before the man made himself visible. Mario—the super-powerful rogue who wanted Kylie dead—stood only a few feet from them. The same rogue who'd hurt Helen, killed Ellie, murdered his own grandson, and didn't mind taking the life of any innocent being who got in his way.

The man's dark eyes shined with nothing but evil. His skin looked aged and leathery, and he wore a dark robe as if he considered himself some sort of royalty.

Memories of this man sending bolts of lightning through his grandson had Kylie's fury and protective nature raging full strength in a fraction of a second. Grabbing Derek by the arm, she pushed him behind her.

Chapter Seven

"We meet again," Mario said, a hot, dark breeze stirring the bottom of his robe. The sky seemed to grow darker. Even the moon and stars seemed to cringe in his presence.

"Very unfortunate," Kylie said, and breathed in. The night air tasted of his wickedness. She felt her blood fizzing in her veins and the sense of danger nearly sucked the oxygen right out of the air.

Derek shifted behind her and Kylie reached back and caught him, holding him in one spot.

Protect him. Protect him. The words repeated in her soul like a litany.

Mario chuckled as if he could read her mind. "Do not worry, child. I want nothing to do with your boy toy. He is in no danger from me."

The old man smiled. His teeth—thin and slightly yellowed with age—appeared below his lip. The creepiness of the moment sent a shiver crawling down her backbone.

"You can calm that protective side of yours down," Mario said, as if he sensed her defensive side surging to life. "It will do you no good. For you see, the only one I'm after here is you. I mean the weakling no harm."

Derek yanked free and went barreling into the freakish old rogue.

Kylie took a protective step forward to intervene. Mario turned invisible and Derek crashed to the ground.

Mario reappeared a few feet away. "How cute," he mocked. "The little man wants to protect you."

Derek didn't hesitate to go at him again. But, like before, Mario disappeared into thin air and reappeared again a few feet from Derek.

"Stop it," Kylie said to Derek.

He ignored her and stared daggers at Mario. "I'm not the one who's disappearing, you bastard. Fight me like a man."

Mario laughed, and the evilness of his tone raked over Kylie's nerves like broken glass. "You want me to fight so your girlfriend can protect you. I am no fool, child."

As much as she resented it, Mario was right; if he didn't harm Derek, she couldn't draw upon her powers to fight him. Fear settled in her gut.

"Leave," Kylie insisted, and right then, she saw the spirits gathering at the gates, their mutterings filled with concern for her.

"Not without you," Mario demanded, but his confidence seemed slightly lessened when he cut his eyes toward the graveyard gate. Could he sense the spirits, too? He took a step closer to her—or was it just a step away from the graveyard gate?

She took a step back. In the corner of her eye, she saw Derek reach for a large stone at his feet. She knew his plan was to anger Mario enough to pose a threat to him so she could protect them both, but Kylie wasn't sure she could do it. Indecision filled her chest whether to stop him or not. Because like the plan or not, it might be their only one.

Mario, focused on her, didn't see the rock coming. It hit him in the temple with a thud. But she knew it would come with ramifications. And she had damn well better be ready to face them.

Tension thickened the air around them as the rogue's eyes brightened to a lime green color and red blood spurted from his brow. A low growl snaked out of the man's lips as he glared at Derek.

Kylie felt the strength start to build in her muscles, but it was nothing like what she should feel to draw upon her true power.

"Come get me, you coward!" Derek taunted.

Mario wiped the blood from his forehead and the fury in his eyes faded. "You do not interest me."

"What about me, you bastard vamp?" Lucas, appearing out of nowhere, shot out from behind the trees and took the old man down.

Kylie had no time to consider her emotional havoc. Derek, obviously seeing the opportunity, barreled forward. Kylie moved in, her strength now full force. But her strength and speed were nothing compared to Mario's. She hadn't reached the pile of swinging fists when the rogue tossed first Lucas and then Derek off him. Their bodies were flung into the air like rag dolls. Breath caught at the sight, she bolted up into the air and snagged both of them. After only a fraction of a second, she dropped both of them to the ground and then lunged at the rogue.

Proving his abilities again, before she got to him he'd bounced to his feet and shot out of her path. She came to a startling jolt and looked around. He stood several feet away watching her as if she was nothing more than a form of entertainment.

He was toying with her. And she didn't know how to turn the tables on him.

Gripping her fist so tight her hand hurt, she forced herself to accept he was out of her league. He may be old, but his power obviously kept him agile and quick.

He stared at her and smirked, then with eyes thirsty to see more, he held out his hand toward Lucas.

"How far will you go to save them?" Kylie saw a fireball extend from his fingertips. She darted between the fireball and Lucas. She snatched the circle of flames and threw it back at Mario. He managed to dodge it, but then he tossed two more. She caught one of them and the other shot past her. She glanced over her shoulder and saw the other fireball knock Lucas down. The taste of fury, bitter and salty, spilled onto Kylie's tongue. In spite of her emotional befuddlement over Lucas, her heart begged her to go to him, to assure herself his injuries were not bad. But the need to stop Mario had her facing him again.

"Will you die to save him?" A grin filled his aged gray eyes. "Which one will you save first?" Mario studied her as if amused, definitely not afraid, and apparently so occupied with tormenting her that he didn't see Derek coming at him again. And neither did Kylie, or she would have stopped him. Stopped him before someone died.

The moment Derek crashed into Mario, the man reached for Derek and tightened his gnarled fingers around his neck. Kylie surged forward, her fury, her need for revenge strong. Wrapping one hand around Mario's throat, she used her other hand to peel the old man's hands from Derek's neck. The second she felt Derek slip free, she used both her hands on the rogue's throat.

"Let go!" the voice echoed in her ear at the same time the ghostly cold shimmied down her spine. *"Stop!"*

Kylie ignored the spirit. This was so not the time.

She heard Derek gasp for air. Now it was Mario who could not breathe. She felt his tendons roll beneath her tight grasp. Her goal was simple. Stop him. Stop him now and forever. All she had to do was squeeze a bit tighter.

She would crush his windpipe with just a little more force.

She would send him to hell where he belonged.

Her mind went to Ellie, who Mario had taken too young from this world. She thought of this man's grandson, who had died knowing his own blood had brought him to his death.

Mario deserved this death.

A thought raked through her mind. Killing wasn't easy. Not even when it was the right thing.

"Let him go!" the spirit yelled. *"You are blind. Nothing is as you see it!"*

She could see just fine, thank you! She tightened her hold on the old man's neck, trying to convince herself to finish what needed to be done. The raspy sound of Derek bringing air into his lungs echoed behind her. Mario's arm swung at his sides, trying to find something to hang on to. Trying to find life.

She heard Derek blurt out her name, his voice hoarse, but she ignored him. Ignored everything but the fact that she was about to take a life.

Suddenly, a sick feeling filled her stomach—as if something was terribly wrong. And that's when she saw Mario. Standing several feet back and smiling. Her breath caught and her gaze cut to the face of the person she was in the process of killing.

Lucas.

Mario's laugh echoed around her.

Panic shot through Kylie like raw pain. She released her hold around Lucas's neck. He fell into a heap on the ground, but Kylie didn't remove her gaze from Mario.

Lucas shifted at her feet. Tears filled her eyes at the realization of how close she'd come to taking the life of someone she loved.

"I should kill you now," Mario said, "but it's so much fun to see you suffer."

Kylie's next intake of air shuddered in her lungs.

"Oh, he lives, but for how long?" Mario asked, his tone expressing the excitement he felt at the pain he'd caused her.

The wickedness in the man seemed to flavor the air. She had no idea how Mario had traded places with Lucas, but what mattered was stopping him from doing more. And if she couldn't think of something quick, he would take her down. And she wouldn't go down alone.

Her blood raged faster, the air she breathed tasted carbonated with emotions raging though her like viruses. Then fear, like a liquid trying to drown her, rose in her chest.

Her pulse raged with horror that this was a battle she could not win. For one second, she accepted defeat and mourned. Mourned not for her life, but for Derek's and Lucas's. They had come here to save her, and now would die for their efforts. And then others would follow. Mario wouldn't stop.

A voice seemed to come with the wind. *You are not alone. Ask and you will receive.*

Were the death angels here? She focused on Mario, but prayed for assistance. Prayers without faith, her heart seemed to whisper. Doubt filled her and echoed in her soul. If the death angels were going to help her, would they have not already been there? Why would she feel so alone, so unprotected? Would they not have offered her help before she almost killed one of her own?

Like a flash of lightning, she remembered the dead at the gate, and something Holiday once said floated through her mind like a thought she needed to grasp on to. *Sometimes I think all the dead are my death angels.*

Kylie drew in a breath of hope. *Help me.* The plea echoed in her mind. *Be my death angels.*

A loud, bone-chilling creak echoed in the dark. The gate started to open. The squeal of the rusty metal being forced to move rang in her ears. Then the dead came barreling out by the hundreds. Male, female, young, old, they all came running, their hands outstretched. Their eyes haunted. But their expressions didn't beg for help, they offered it.

The icy feel of their presence burned her skin. The air in her lungs seemed too cold to breathe. But even in her pain, she saw she wasn't alone. And that offered her hope. Hope she clung to.

Mario's face, old and wrinkled, grimaced in anguish. Pain, perhaps the same cold ache filling her body, reflected in his gray eyes. He slung his head back and roared. Steam rose from his mouth and danced above his lips. He caught his breath and bolted backward a good ten feet.

As if the distance offered him a reprieve, his gaze turned to her. Kylie tightened her eyes and saw his pattern. He was for sure a chameleon. Oddly enough, with her vision slightly unfocused there was something about him that felt different. Familiar in a different way. The thought seemed important, but like a storm cloud that promised to return, it blew past.

"You might have won this time, but my moment draws near," he spat out. "You will come to me, Kylie Galen, come to me willing to die, to suffer at my hands for my pleasure, because the price will be too great! Your weakness will take you down."

Her weakness? What was her weakness? Kylie wondered, but with her mind churning with pain and hope at the same time, the question remained unasked, and unanswered.

Instead, she focused on the hope. Hope that she had spared Lucas and Derek. And somewhere in the depth of her soul, she wanted to be spared, too.

The spirits still crowding around rushed at Mario again. Purposefully. Their intent—to protect her—showed in their concerned and ash-colored faces. Holiday had been right. All spirits were in some way death angels—death angels being spirits of supernaturals. Spirits who while known to protect the innocent, were mostly feared for their stern judgment of those misusing their powers. A quick glance at the graveyard gate and Kylie saw even more phantoms stumbling out. Some moved slow and uncertain, as if they had just been awoken from a deep sleep.

"Thank you," Kylie managed to say, even though her teeth chattered and the cold of the presence of too many dead made being alive difficult.

As the spirits re-gathered around the rogue, Mario roared again and the sound of his disappointment and agony was the last thing she heard before the icy throbbing in her body became too much. Her vision blurred, ice coated her lips, and she felt herself being pulled into a dark spiral of nothingness.

Chapter Eight

"We wait on Burnett."

"We get the hell out of here now!"

Kylie slowly became aware of the voices. Who? Wait on Burnett for what? Questions rolled around her confused mind. Where was she? Who was holding her so . . . ?

She heard the sound of a rhythmic thump. A heartbeat? But not her own. The warmth, the heat of someone pressed close felt like heaven. She'd been so cold. Why? If she focused she could figure it out. But part of her didn't want to focus; part of her wanted to stay just like this. Unaware, warm, and feeling safe in the arms of someone holding her close.

Holding her tenderly.

Holding her as if she were treasured.

"We can't leave," one of the voices said. The voice in the distance. Not the one holding her.

"He could come back. We should leave while the leaving's good." She heard the words vibrate deep in the speaker's chest.

"I don't think so. You said Burnett was on his way. We don't leave."

"Just because you're afraid—"

"I'm not afraid, damn it. I'm being rational. Kylie came here for a reason. The spirits, I'm betting they're the ones who sent that bastard packing."

Kylie recognized Derek's voice.

Everything came rushing back. Her grandfather's betrayal, Jenny's assistance, Derek finding her, Mario showing up, the fight, and Lucas . . . The familiar feel of the arms wrapped around her told her who held her, whose warmth she now absorbed. Stiffening, she pushed herself off Lucas's chest. "Put me down."

His dark blue eyes, now glowing light orange, no doubt still sensing danger, shot to her face. "Can you stand on your own?"

"I can," she said, and when she saw the bruising around his neck, her heart clutched. Dear God, she'd almost killed him. She'd had her hands around his neck, squeezing the life out of him, and had almost finished the job.

Tears stung her sinuses, but she blinked them back. Now wasn't the time to fall apart. Later, she'd let that happen. Later, she'd have a good, long pity party. She deserved one. Just not now. Not now, she repeated in her head, trying to fight the emotional overload.

"Are you hurt anywhere?" Lucas asked.

"She asked you to put her down," Derek insisted, his tone tight, no doubt reading her battling emotions.

"I heard her," Lucas growled, and Kylie glanced up from his bruised neck to his face. His dislike for Derek made his eyes a brighter orange. "I'm making sure she's okay."

"I'm fine," she lied, her emotions ping-ponging all over the place.

Betrayal.

Fear.

Her gaze shifted to his bruised neck.

Guilt.

"Please put me down," she insisted.

He did as she requested. Her knees felt weak, but she focused on not letting them turn to Jell-O, and was able to remain standing.

Lucas kept his hand out as if to catch her if her legs wouldn't hold her up. She didn't want to need him to catch her. Why was he even here? Hadn't she told Burnett not to put him on guard duty? Then she remembered thinking she'd seen Monique. Had it been her?

Her emotions did an about-face and she realized how unimportant that was at this time. Right now, she had to make sure they got back to Shadow Falls safely. Like the pity party she'd mentally scheduled, she could spend time mourning over Lucas and her issues later.

"Are you up to heading back?" Lucas asked her.

"We're not leaving here until Burnett shows up," Derek snapped again.

Kylie looked at Derek and then back to the gates, which were now closed. The spirits stood guard, their faces peering out between the rusty metal bars. "Derek's right. We stay here until Burnett shows up."

A flash passed by Kylie and then another.

Burnett, along with about three other FRU people, as well as several of the campers, Perry included, suddenly surrounded them.

"I'm here," Burnett said. His bright eyes seemed to say he was prepared to fight. He glanced around as if checking for danger, before focusing back on them. "And someone better tell me what the hell's going on."

When no one spoke up fast enough for his impatience, his gaze zeroed in on Kylie. "I was supposed to come get you in the morning." His gaze shot to Derek. "You were supposed to be guarding her at her grandfather's place." He glanced at Lucas. "And you told me you were going to your father's."

"Well, I lied," Lucas bit back, never one to take a reprimand easily. "I wanted to make sure Kylie didn't need me. And she did."

"What happened?" Burnett asked again, his tone implying he was losing patience.

"Mario," Kylie answered.

Burnett's eyes brightened and he glanced around again. "Are you sure it was him?" he asked.

"Positive." Kylie shivered, remembering the wickedness she'd felt from him. She recalled the sensation that he'd enjoyed toying with her—like a cat with a mouse. But the mouse had won this time. Thanks to the dead, no one had died at Mario's hand, but what about next time? She heard Mario's threat ring in her head. *You will come to me, Kylie Galen, come to me willing to die, to suffer at my hands for my pleasure, because the price will be too great!*

He spoke with certainty as if he already had a plan in place. Fear tiptoed up her spine.

Burnett continued to glance around. After a few more seconds of putting out his feelers, he looked back at Derek.

"He's gone now," Derek said.

"I can see that."

But was he really gone? Being a chameleon, he could turn invisible. He could still be here. Kylie almost said something to that effect, but remembered the other FRU members. And her lack of trust in them kept her mouth closed. The less they knew about her and the chameleons as a whole, the better.

"What were you even doing out here?" Burnett asked, seemingly getting more frustrated the longer he considered things. "The orders were to wait for me until tomorrow. Why do I give orders around here if no one listens to them?"

"We couldn't. They weren't going to let her leave," Derek said, and looked at Kylie as if knowing how hard the truth was for her to hear. And he was right. The ache in her chest tightened.

"They?" Burnett asked. "Who was not going to let her leave?" His gaze shot between Derek and Kylie.

"The chameleons," Derek answered.

Burnett's focus landed back on Kylie, and her chest constricted, knowing Burnett was laying the fault on her grandfather.

"My grandfather wasn't aware of it," Kylie said, but for the life of her she couldn't say it with certainty. And she knew Burnett read her white lie for what it was.

His expression softened for a fraction of a second, as if he could relate to her pain. "You should have called me." Burnett glanced back at Derek.

"He tried," Kylie spoke up again, unwilling to let Derek take the blame for this. "We had to hurry to try to beat the guards and then . . . then when he tried to get you, Mario . . . he fried Derek's phone."

All of a sudden, the night's blackness was sliced by the beam of headlights. A car came to a screeching halt. Holiday's car.

She barreled out of the Honda, her red hair hanging loose as if she'd just risen from bed. And when her teary-eyed gaze lit on Kylie, she muttered, "Thank God," and put her hand over her lips.

Seeing the emotion in Holiday weakened Kylie's resolve to wait until later to fall apart. She ran up to Holiday and fell into her arms.

As Kylie buried her head on the camp leader's shoulder, she heard Burnett scold, "I thought I told you to wait at the camp."

Kylie felt Holiday tense at the reprimand, and then she raised her head. "And I thought you knew I don't follow anyone's orders."

"Does anyone listen to me around here?" Burnett asked, his frustration making his tone sound almost comical.

"Obviously not," one of the FRU agents said, and chuckled.

Burnett groaned, but Kylie heard his sheer relief. She knew he saw the protection of everyone at Shadow Falls as his personal responsibility. And she loved him for it, too.

"What happened?" Holiday asked, tightening her comforting embrace around Kylie's shoulders.

"Let's discuss it later," Burnett said. "We need to get back to Shadow Falls now."

Kylie knew that discussion would include accusations toward her grandfather. Even as she hurt thinking of that conversation, right now with Holiday's warm, comforting embrace around her, and even hearing Burnett and Holiday bicker, made this moment feel right. It felt like she was almost home.

And that felt really good.

• • •

Walking back through the Shadow Falls gate sent a warmth right though Kylie. This was where she belonged. Even the next hour of facing Burnett's questions didn't completely chase away the sensation of being home.

"I'm sorry I have to do this now," Burnett said several times. He'd already gone over everything with Lucas and Derek, while Kylie sat in the office with Holiday. They hadn't talked about what happened tonight because she knew Burnett would want to be present, so they talked about what she'd learned while with her grandfather.

When Burnett came in, the mood grew more serious. "I know you haven't slept at all tonight, but statistics say the longer the wait the more likely you'll forget something."

Kylie, sitting on the sofa beside Holiday, nodded. "I know." She bit into her lip and tried to focus and fill him in on everything that happened. She covered Mario and his parting threat. Then she started at the beginning again and told him about Jenny coming to the window.

The thing she didn't tell him was about Jenny being Hayden Yates's sister. She wasn't even sure if Burnett had figured out Hayden was a chameleon. Then she explained one more time about Derek showing up in the woods. She purposely told him again about the invisible person she sensed there before they took off. And she reminded Burnett that she believed this person to be her grandfather and he'd been there not to stop her from leaving, but to check on her.

"But you didn't speak to him?" Burnett asked. "So you don't know for sure it was him, or even if his being there meant he wasn't behind all this."

Kylie frowned. "I know my grandfather. I don't think he'd do this. Even Jenny said he was different from the other elders. And I don't want you to start thinking of him as the enemy."

Burnett's jaw tightened. "He cares about you, Kylie. I sensed this when we spoke. But he never hid the fact that he didn't trust me or Shadow Falls. He very well could justify his actions because he felt your life was in danger. He may think he has your best intentions at heart, but he's wrong. And while I know it's difficult for you to accept this, we can't trust him anymore."

Burnett's remark had her throat tightening with emotion. She understood his point of view, but she couldn't let go of what her heart told her. And her heart told her that her grandfather hadn't been behind the attempts to keep her against her will.

"*You* can't trust him," Kylie said. "I've yet to make up my mind. And why are you spending so much time worrying about him when the real villain is Mario?"

"I'm aware of who the real villain is," Burnett answered. "But it's because of your . . . thanks to someone's actions with your grandfather's people, Mario almost got to you."

"They had nothing to do with Mario's showing up."

"I agree, but they had everything to do with you finding yourself in a vulnerable situation."

"I made the choice to run away." She wrung her hands in her lap.

"Don't you think we should call it a night?" Holiday intervened. "Let's stop now and pick this up in the morning."

Burnett frowned at Holiday, then moved in and knelt down in front of Kylie. He placed his palm on her gripped hands. His touch was cold, but caring and tender. The knot in Kylie's throat doubled. When he looked at her, she saw the struggle in his eyes to keep his cool and not let his temper rule. He wanted to make demands, to call the shots. Yet Kylie also sensed he struggled to do what Holiday had tried to instill in him, to compromise and not dictate.

Staring at his hand over her locked fingers, she knew Burnett cared—knew his intent wasn't to hurt her, but to help her. Yet wasn't that exactly what her grandfather felt?

"Kylie, I know this is hard for you," Burnett said. "I do. But I need your promise that you won't be sneaking off to see your grandfather."

He squeezed her wrist. "Please. I won't get a moment of peace unless you give me that."

"I won't." She couldn't deny him this, not when his expression practically begged for her compliance. Yet deep down she wondered if her heart said it was an untruth, and if it did, had Burnett heard it. God help her, because if her grandfather did ask her to meet him, how could she tell him no any easier than she could Burnett? Her loyalty was truly torn. She only prayed it didn't come to that.

The eastern part of the sky was a bit lighter than the rest when Burnett and Holiday walked Kylie to her cabin. The stars sparkled in the sky as if they knew they were about to be shut down by the sun and wanted to give out a bit more light.

She should be exhausted, and part of her was, but she doubted she'd fall in bed and go right to sleep. Her mind chewed on so many things that turning it off seemed impossible. Plus, she had an appointment to attend her very own pity party. The knot that she'd felt in her throat earlier was now caught in her heart area. In the past, Kylie had learned that nothing but a good cry could ease that kind of ache.

Obviously, the soothing effects of Holiday's touch were wearing off. Or maybe this was too much to completely be eased by a fae's magic. Some things just needed to be worked through. Things like leaving her grandfather's house without saying good-bye. Things like the fact that she'd almost killed Lucas. Things like wondering if it was really Monique, Lucas's fiancée, she'd seen tonight. Things like missing her mom, and she was halfway across the world sleeping with some creep.

Things like having a psychotic murderer wanting to take her down.

His threat rang in her head like a bad line in a song that you couldn't forget. *You will come to me, Kylie Galen, come to me willing to die, to suffer at my hands for my pleasure, because the price will be too great! Your weakness will take you down.*

And working through things like that might include shedding a few tears. Who could begrudge her that? Of course, she should probably spend some time trying to figure out what he meant by her weakness.

"How about we take a trip to the falls tomorrow?" Holiday piped up, and then as if reading Kylie's emotional status, she reached over and gave Kylie's arm a squeeze.

Kylie nodded.

"I'll figure out when's a good time first thing in the morning," Burnett added, making it clear he would be going with them.

Silence fell on them like a soft rain. The sky had turned slightly purple as if morning would be in the next hour. Burnett cleared his throat. "You do know we will have to go back to you being shadowed?"

"I figured that," Kylie said.

"Before I work out the shadowing schedule, is . . . is there anyone you don't want to be shadowing you?"

"Only one," Kylie said. "And I think you know who that is."

Burnett just nodded.

Their footsteps fell on the graveled path and sent out crunching sounds in the darkness. "How is Helen?" Kylie asked.

"She's much better," Holiday said.

"Has she remembered anything yet? Do we know if it was Mario or not?"

"No," Holiday answered.

"We're still investigating it," Burnett said, and a bit of frustration sounded in his tone. "But we know that Mario was spotted in Fallen that same morning. And with his appearance tonight, everything points to Mario being behind this."

They got almost to the turn in the path. In the distance Kylie could make out the cabin. Not a light flickered inside. Kylie glanced to Burnett. "Is Della back yet?"

"No, not yet," he said, and something about the way he said those three words set off alarms.

She caught him by the arm. "What happened?"

Burnett held up his hand. "She's fine. She ran into some trouble late yesterday, but everything's fine now. She should be back either later today or tomorrow."

"What kind of trouble?" Kylie asked, her concern over Della giving her a reprieve from her own problems.

Burnett hesitated to answer and that made Kylie even more suspicious.

"What happened?" Kylie insisted.

"She got into an altercation with some gang members. But—"

"Are you sure it wasn't Mario?"

"I'm positive," Burnett said.

"Was she hurt?" Kylie's chest ached. "I knew her working for the FRU was a bad idea."

"She was just bumped and bruised a bit," Burnett said.

"How bumped and bruised?" Kylie asked.

"Not so bad that I can't say that I think her ego received the most damage," Burnett replied.

"She's really fine. I promise," Holiday added. "I spoke with her myself."

Kylie inhaled, knowing she was probably overreacting, but her emotional dam was almost ready to spew over. She started walking again, hurrying to the cabin, wanting to be alone before that dam broke.

Holiday picked up her speed and slipped her hand into Kylie's, bringing her to a stop right before taking the steps to the porch. "Do you want me to come in and we can talk for a while?"

"No," Kylie said, feeling like an idiot. "I just need some rebound time." She hugged Holiday, absorbing a little more of her soothing touch. When Kylie pulled back, she started to turn for the door when Burnett cleared his throat. She looked up.

The man held out his hands. "I don't get one, too?"

Kylie saw the surprise shine in Holiday's eyes, then she couldn't help it, she grinned. "Be careful, people might think you've gone soft on us."

"I doubt that," he said, and gave her a quick embrace. With his chin pressed against her hair, he whispered, "I'm going to get the bastard. I promise you."

She didn't have to ask which bastard. She knew he meant Mario.

"Thank you," she said, and pulled back. And before she really broke down and cried, she moved inside.

The smell of the cabin filled her senses. She wasn't even sure exactly what contributed to the scent, but whatever it was, it offered some calming effects. And then she realized it smelled like the people she loved. Miranda, Della. And there was the woodsy scent that she registered. A smell that belonged to . . . No!

It just smelled like home, she told herself.

Della's bedroom door stood open—like a flashing neon sign that she wasn't here. The vamp, a very private person, always kept her door closed.

Kylie's gaze shifted to Miranda's door.

"Rebound time," she whispered to herself. If she was going to fall apart, she wanted to do it alone. She started to her bedroom, had barely opened the door when she heard the slight creaking of the wood floor. She wasn't alone. Her gaze shot up to the corner of the room and she saw the figure standing there.

Saw and recognized the figure.

Maybe she wasn't going to get that rebound time after all.

Chapter Nine

Kylie twirled around on her Reeboks, probably leaving skid marks on the wood floor, and started out of her room.

"Don't go," Lucas said. "Please! You're going to have to talk to me sooner or later."

Later would be really nice. Then anger made her clutch her hands. It wasn't right. She stared at the wall, still not wanting to face him. "Why? Why do I have to talk to you? I don't owe you anything. Not an explanation, not an apology. I'm not the one who . . ." Her throat tightened and she just shut up. She heard him shift behind her.

"I know . . . I screwed up. I admit that. I . . . should have told you. No, that's wrong, I should have never let it go that far. I should have told my father to go screw himself in the beginning. I'm at fault here, but I didn't do anything . . . else. I didn't sleep with her. I kissed her twice. You saw one of those times. And both times I was put on the spot. I only did it to try to convince my dad that I would go through with the marriage. But I never, not for one damn minute, planned on marrying her."

That knot in her throat tightened. Her eyes stung right along with her heart. She shook her head, and managed one word. "No." She wasn't even sure what she was saying no to. Then she turned and faced him.

It didn't matter what she said, because he wasn't listening to her. He stood there staring at her in his own world of hurt and pain.

"You love me," he said. "I know that."

Now was when she should be saying no, but she couldn't get the word out. Oh, it sat on the tip of her tongue, but it felt super-glued in place. Sure it would have been a lie, but wasn't it okay to lie at times like this? When the truth was just too painful. When the truth felt like it could tear you apart.

"I also know you're punishing me. And it's working, because I'm hurting like hell. Not that I don't deserve it." He reached up and ran his hand over the back of his neck.

Kylie blinked away a wash of tears. Even in the darkness she could see the bruises around his neck. Bruises she'd put on him. She gripped her hands at the memory of just how close she'd come to crushing his windpipe.

"I didn't mean to choke you," she spit out. "It was a trick on . . . Mario's part. I don't know how he did it but—"

"I know that. I don't mean . . . punishing me with this." He ran his hand over the bruises. "This isn't anything compared to what I feel inside. I'm talking about you not wanting to talk to me, not wanting me close to you. You have no idea how much it hurts to stand right here, this close . . . Can you even imagine how hard it is to stand here and know you don't want me to touch you?" He moved in a step as if testing her.

While it was only a few inches, his scent came with him. She remembered inhaling his particular smell when she walked in. She should have known. Should have known that part of the scent of home that had welcomed her, was his essence. He was home to her. Or he had been.

Now she felt homeless.

He must have gathered a bit more courage because he took another step closer.

She inched back. And that little inch said so much.

"See," he said, and his intake of air sounded painful. "But I know you still care because . . . because you saved my life. You could have stepped out of the way and just let Mario kill me. You didn't. You caught the fireballs that were meant for me."

His emotion echoed in the room, and she'd give anything if she didn't have to feel this. How much more emotion could she take in? Wasn't there a limit? Surely she'd reached hers.

"Yeah, I saved your life, but don't make me regret it." She waved toward the door. "Leave. I don't want you here." And it was the truth. She didn't want Lucas, the guy who'd betrayed her, here. She wanted the guy she'd trusted, the guy she'd thought would go to the end of the world to protect her. And yet they were one and the same.

He took one more step. She saw his Adam's apple go up and down. It looked painful to swallow.

"I hurt you," he said. "I know that, and I'm willing to take whatever it is you want to dish out at me. I deserve it. That's what I came here to say. That I accept what I did was wrong. But I didn't do other things that you might think I did. And when you're over being mad, I'll still be here. I don't care how long it takes."

She glanced away, remembering him standing up in front of his family and friends. He'd worn a fancy tux and looked so handsome, so much like a man and not a boy. The image of him reaching for Monique's hands played across her mind and she heard the promises he made. The kind of promises you didn't break.

A wave a fresh pain washed over her. She looked at him again. "You gave her your soul."

He shook his head. "No, you're wrong. I didn't give her my soul. I lied. I couldn't have given her my soul. Because my soul was already given away. You took it when I was seven years old." His voice shook. "And if I had any of it left, you took the rest of it when you walked into Shadow Falls that first day. In the were culture, it's believed that there is only one soul mate. And you are mine, Kylie Galen. I knew that then, and it hasn't changed."

Her vision blurred with tears. She inhaled, hoping to get her watery weakness under control. But she felt a tear slip from her lashes onto her cheek.

She swiped it away. Her breath shuddered as she drew needed oxygen into her lungs. Why did it hurt to breathe?

You are mine, Kylie Galen. His words echoed in her heart. She couldn't deny that part of her wanted to go to him, to make him say that over and over again until the pain bubbling in her chest went away. Until she could look at him without remembering how it had felt to see him making promises to someone else. But she couldn't go to him, because she knew the pain wasn't going to go away.

Not now.

Maybe not ever.

She couldn't be sure.

He paused and she saw the same pain she felt in her chest reflected in his eyes. Her own pain doubled knowing she hurt him. But wasn't that his fault? Why should she feel guilty that he was hurting now?

"I'm sorry that I caused you this hurt," he said. "And as mad as you are at me right now, you need to realize that I'm madder at myself. I did this to you. To us. I hurt the most important person in my life. If someone else had hurt you this badly I'd rip their heart out."

He stood there and just stared. The silence in the room seemed too loud. Or was it the pain echoing in the room that pierced her ears?

"I'll go now," he said, and she couldn't remember ever hearing him sound so defeated. So lost. "I've said what I wanted to, and just know I'll give you all the time you need to forgive me. But not forgiving me, that isn't an option. Because I love you."

She moved out of his way and he walked out the door. She went to the bed. Sat down. Kicked her shoes off. "Kitty, kitty?" she said, wanting something to hold on to. But Socks didn't come out. He really didn't like weres. Right now, a part of her agreed with him.

She brought her legs up, hugged her knees to her chest so tight it hurt.

Then she waited.

Waited for the tears to flow full force.

Waited for some of the pressure building in her heart to fade. But the tears didn't flow. The pressure remained.

Closing her eyes, she bit down on her lip. Why couldn't she cry? Was she just too emotionally exhausted?

And confused?

Yes, she was so damn confused.

How could Lucas suddenly see how wrong he was now, and not have seen it earlier? How could he have stood up there and vowed his soul, promised to marry someone else if he loved Kylie?

But why would he lie? Why would he come here and tell her all these things if they weren't true?

She sat there in the dark room for several long minutes. She felt alone. Lonely.

A crazy and somewhat childish thought ran though her head: *I want my mama*. But her mama wasn't here. Not at Shadow Falls. Not even in the country. Her mom was in England banging some guy that Kylie hated.

But she could still call her. Heck, maybe she'd even cause a little hiccup in John's plans to seduce her mother. That made calling even more tempting. She wanted John to know that her mom wasn't alone in the world.

She reached for her pocket and then groaned. She'd left her phone at her grandfather's.

"Damn it," Kylie muttered. As the frustrations of her lost phone bounced around her brain, her thoughts went to Jenny, to her conversation about talking to Hayden, and to some of the accusations she'd made about the elders. Were the young chameleons really being forced to live in a world of isolation? That seemed so wrong.

Just like that she felt compelled to find Hayden Yates. He would have answers. Maybe he could even assure her that her grandfather wasn't behind this. Popping up, she started out, then immediately slowed down when she got to the door. Oh, just friggin' great! She was supposed to be shadowed.

Burnett would flip if he thought Kylie was out wandering alone at night. But damn it, she needed answers. And sometimes you just had to break the rules. She went outside, quietly shutting the door so not to wake Miranda. Moving down the porch steps, she started toward the path that would lead to Hayden's cabin. He'd probably still be asleep, but she didn't care.

She only got a few feet when she saw someone move out from the trees. Her breath caught in her throat when she saw who it was.

The thought that came to mind was a phrase her Nana had often said when she'd found herself in a bad situation. She was up shit creek without a paddle.

"I . . . I'm sorry," Kylie mumbled.

"Don't you even try to talk your way out of me being pissed!" Burnett growled. "Not a word!"

"I just . . ."

"That's two words and I said not one!" he snapped, and he swiped his hand through the air for emphasis.

Kylie bit down on her lip, and wouldn't you know that's when the tears started flowing. Big, fat, and fast tears. She sniffled and wiped her cheeks with the back of hand. Her breath caught in her chest. But damn it. Why couldn't this have happened when she was alone?

"Those tears do not affect me, young lady!" He pointed a finger at her. While she couldn't hear his heart beat to the rhythm of a lie, she heard it in his voice. They did affect him. Not enough to stop him from him being mad, but enough that his voice tightened with emotion.

And knowing she'd disappointed him added another layer of pain to her chest. Just what she needed . . . more pain.

She hugged herself and tried to stop crying. But the tears kept coming. He didn't say anything. Just paced, back and forth in front of her.

Back and forth.

Back and forth.

Staring at her with complete discontent and disappointment the whole time. She started to move back to her cabin, and he growled. Just a growl. No words, but enough inflection to know he didn't want her moving. Obviously, her punishment was to stand here and accept the fact that she'd let him down.

In the back of her mind she wondered if this was how Lucas had felt.

She swallowed another trembling breath. "I just . . ."

"Did I say you could talk?" he asked. He did three more pacing laps, as if working off steam, before he looked at her again. "Where were you going?"

When she just looked at him, he bit out, "Answer me."

"You said I couldn't talk." She wiped at her cheeks again.

"Where were you going, Kylie?"

Dear God, she didn't know what to say. She couldn't tell him the truth. She'd made a promise to her grandfather never to give up Hayden Yates.

Yup, she was really up shit creek and not a paddle in sight.

"Were you going to see Lucas?" Burnett asked.

She started to nod, but felt her heart race at just the thought of a lie.

"So it wasn't Lucas," he seethed, obviously hearing her heart and knowing her temptation to spout out untruths.

He stepped closer and his dark eyes studied her. Studied her too closely. Up close, she saw again the disappointment in his eyes, and the knot in her throat rose again.

She tried to think of what to say, something to help this, something that wouldn't give anything away. Something that wouldn't be a lie. "I just—"

"Don't talk to me if you're going to lie."

Okay, so her heart wasn't going to even let her white-lie her way out of this one.

"I want the truth," he said. "Were you going to meet your grandfather?"

"No," Kylie said with honesty, and with it came an enormous amount of relief.

He studied her closer. His eyes tightened. "Okay, I'm going to ask you a direct question and I want a yes or no answer. Don't you try to talk around the truth, because I'll know." He paused for effect, or maybe just to collect his thoughts. "Were you going to see Hayden Yates?"

Kylie's mind raced. What did Burnett know? When her grandfather had told her that Burnett believed Hayden's lie that Kylie had simply tricked the teacher into thinking she had permission to leave, she hadn't believed that Hayden had fooled Burnett.

He knew something. But just how much, and what he knew, remained unknown.

"Okay, your silence pretty much answers it for me. Come on." He motioned for her to start walking.

"Where to?" she asked, afraid of what he was going to say.

"You wanted to see Hayden, so let's go see him. And then you two are going to tell me what the hell is going on, or somebody's ass is grass! And I'll be smoking it!"

Chapter Ten

Kylie had heard the term "walking the green mile" when convicts walked to their execution, and the trek to Hayden's cabin sort of felt like her green mile. Burnett didn't speak. She barely heard him breathe. And yet his rock-hard posture moving beside her told her of his impatience. Her loyalty to her grandfather and Burnett had her heart torn in a game of tug-of-war.

"Can we go talk to Holiday first?" Kylie asked, knowing that maybe Holiday could calm Burnett down and make him understand.

"No." Burnett's one word came out coarse. "I'm going to get the truth."

But at what price, Kylie thought. Would Hayden realize that Kylie hadn't just turned him over? She hoped so. But would her grandfather understand her breaking her promise to him?

She didn't think so.

Like the man moving so brusquely beside her, her grandfather was not so forgiving.

As they came to the bend near Hayden's cabin, Kylie desperately searched for a way out. "Do we have to wake him up? Can't we just—"

"He's already awake," Burnett said with sternness. "He's tossing and turning in bed worrying about something. Was he expecting you this morning? Are you already late?"

"No," she muttered.

They kept moving and got all the way up the cabin's porch steps and suddenly Kylie realized something. Anger stirred her gut, and she grabbed Burnett by the elbow. "That's right, you can hear everything!"

"And your point?" he asked, obviously noting her new disposition. And yes, being angry gave her guilt over being caught hiding secrets a slight reprieve.

"Earlier, when you dropped me off at my cabin, you knew Lucas was there, didn't you? You knew he was waiting to talk to me!"

Guilt whispered across Burnett's brow. "He pleaded with me to give him ten minutes."

"And you gave it to him. You thought that was your choice to make," Kylie accused.

Burnett frowned, but the guilt didn't completely fade from his eyes. "If I remember correctly, you put your two cents in Holiday's and my romantic affairs."

"Neither one of you ran off and got engaged to someone else!"

He didn't flinch, but in his expression she saw her argument hit his conscience. "Everyone deserves their chance to explain themselves," he offered, but his tone lacked complete conviction.

"There's no explanation for what he did," she bit back.

Burnett inhaled and pinched the bridge of his nose. "Okay, I concede I might have been wrong allowing him that privilege. And I will forego any such actions in the future. And now maybe you and Hayden can make amends by explaining what you two are keeping from me!" He arched a brow at Kylie, raised his fist, and banged on Hayden's door so hard it shook the hinges.

Once he'd taken his mood out on the door, Burnett cut his eyes to her again. She saw his mind churning, searching for answers. It was the first time she got the feeling that Burnett didn't know as much as she feared he might.

"Be forewarned," the vamp said, "if I learn that there's anything romantic happening here, I'm sending him packing . . . less a few body parts."

Kylie's mouth dropped open. "Romantic? Oh, please, he's old. He's as old as you."

Burnett's brow creased. "Which is my point." His frown deepened. "Not that I'm *that* old."

Hayden opened the door and his gaze zipped from Burnett to Kylie.

Burnett growled. Then the vamp stepped across the threshold as if he ran the joint. Which he did.

Hayden wasn't happy about Burnett's grand entrance, but he didn't attempt to stop him. He backed up, allowing Burnett to come all the way inside.

Kylie swallowed, not sure how this was going to play out. Burnett was going to be furious, and as soon as her grandfather learned Burnett was on to Hayden, he would be furious.

"Okay, let's get one thing straight," Burnett said, getting things started. "No one is leaving this room until I have answers. And I don't care if I have to use force to get them." He stared directly at Hayden. "And since I don't hit girls, I'd suggest you start explaining."

Hayden tilted his head up. "Explaining what?" he asked, not showing the least bit of intimidation.

Kylie had to admire Hayden for it, too. She loved Burnett and knew he wasn't unfair or unjust, but she still had a quiver in the pit of her stomach. The man had intimidation down to an art. And one he excelled at.

"What's the tie between you two?" Burnett asked.

"Tie?" Hayden asked.

"At first Kylie was certain that you were the one behind the dead girls, and then suddenly you are her ally. You lied when you told me she asked to be let out at the cemetery."

"I did let her off at the cemetery."

"Then you lied about her coming to you. I know Kylie, and she wouldn't have just gone to you for help without a reason, without a connection of some sort."

"I'm her teacher," Hayden answered. "I thought helping a student in difficult situations was a plus around here."

"And I thought you were smart enough to know when to come clean!" Burnett's eyes glittered with specks of angry green. "The only reason I haven't already kicked your ass out of here is that I want answers first. So start talking!"

Kylie, afraid this might get out of hand, moved between the two men. "Can Hayden and I have a moment of privacy?"

Burnett's expression hardened.

"Please," Kylie said. "I . . . I think it will help get to the bottom of this."

Burnett's jaw tightened to the point it looked about ready to crack.

"And when you come back, I'll have answers for you."

His frown tightened. "I'll be right outside the door."

"But you can still hear—"

"That's all I'm giving you!" he demanded.

She suddenly realized that was enough—for she and Hayden could go invisible and their chat wouldn't be overheard by intruding vampire ears. She nodded and watched the angry vamp step out. As soon as the door closed, she pressed a finger over her lips and then grabbed Hayden's hand and took him into the invisible realm with her.

"You can already do this?" Hayden's voice echoed but he remained unseen.

"Yes." Kylie held on to his hand, so she'd know where he was.

"That's amazing, Kylie. Do you realize how far advanced you are? When did you—"

"Sorry, but we don't have time to talk about that right now. What are we going to tell Burnett? I think we should come clean."

"He'll insist I leave," Hayden said. "And you'll lose my protection."

"First, I don't need protecting from anyone here. But I don't want you to go, I want to have someone I can go to if I have questions. Second, I'm not sure Burnett will make you leave. But if we don't tell him, he's for sure going to send you packing. Our best chance of you getting to stay is telling him the truth."

"I see your point," Hayden said. "But . . ."

"I didn't tell him, you know. He doesn't even know you're a chameleon. He just—"

"I know," Hayden said. "He's been suspicious of me since before you even left."

"That's my fault. I—"

"I know," Hayden said.

The sound of the front door slamming brought Hayden's words to a halt. Burnett stormed back into the room, his eyes glittering with fury.

"That man is impossible," Hayden said.

"God damn it!" Burnett's words rang out. "Kylie! Where are you!"

"I'm going to talk to him," Kylie said to Hayden. "You stay invisible." She released his hand and willed herself to be seen.

Burnett's scowl landed on her immediately. "Where is he?" he bit out.

"He's here. We're still talking. In private, like I asked."

"You can make others invisible?"

She nodded. *Not that I had to make Hayden invisible—him being chameleon—but Burnett doesn't know that.*

"This is foolish. I want answers!"

"And you'll have them if you allow me this time!" she demanded, not backing down. "I'm asking you to trust me as you have asked me to do so many times in the past."

He growled and turned his gaze to the ceiling as if pleading for patience. Kylie willed herself invisible again.

"I'm right here," Hayden's voice came beside her. "So exactly what all do you want to tell him?"

"Everything," Kylie said to an empty spot, but she trusted he was there. "That you were sent here by my grandfather and that you're a chameleon. And that you want to stay on here." She paused. "And it wouldn't hurt to add how impressed you are with this place. If we can get him to see you as our ally then maybe . . ."

"Maybe what?" Hayden asked.

"I don't know if it's possible, but I was thinking that a lot of the younger chameleons like Jenny could benefit from Shadow Falls."

"I've entertained that thought myself," Hayden said. "But the elders wouldn't—"

"Okay, time's up!" Burnett snapped, and started moving around the room. "Get your asses back here now."

"One more minute," Kylie insisted. "We're almost done."

"He can't hear you," Hayden said.

"Oh, yeah." She paused, questions for Hayden racing through her mind, but Burnett was about to flip. And a flipping Burnett wasn't easy to deal with.

"Are you ready?" Kylie asked. "I have so much more to talk to you about, but for now . . . I think we should deal with this. Wait!" Kylie snapped. When she didn't hear him, she called for him. "Hayden?"

"Yes?" he asked.

"Do you think my grandfather was in on the plan to kidnap me and keep me from Shadow Falls?"

"No. I don't think he was. He's been very worried about you—even called six times until you arrived."

Relief fluttered through her. "Will you tell him I'm sorry for . . . not saying good-bye?"

"I will."

"Kylie!" Burnett growled.

Taking a deep breath, she willed herself visible again. Hayden appeared at her side.

Burnett didn't look impressed. He came at Hayden and grabbed him by his shirtfront. "Disappear again and I'll see that you disappear permanently."

"Calm down." Kylie moved beside Burnett. "Hayden isn't the enemy. It's because of him that we were able to find Holiday when Warren had her. He's actually the reason I was able to escape tonight." Kylie saw Hayden look at her as if surprised she knew this piece of the puzzle.

Burnett released Hayden and then studied his forehead. "You are a chameleon?"

Hayden's body posture stiffened. "You say that as if it's an insult."

Burnett's shoulders grew tighter. "I say that as if you've been lying to me."

Hayden brushed off his wrinkled shirtfront. "I came here to make sure Kylie wasn't being sold out to the FRU by someone who has a problem throwing around his authority."

Burnett frowned. "I am the authority here. And I ran a background check on you. Everything states that you are half vampire, half fae. You are even registered as such."

"I am," Hayden said.

"But it's not true."

Hayden didn't blink. "It is how I choose to live my life."

Burnett shook his head, as if trying to understand. "But according to my research, Kylie's grandfather is listed as human by the FRU. And the few chameleons I saw outside the compound wore the human pattern. I thought that's what all of you let the world think. For that matter, why do you choose not to live in the compound with the others? Are you rogue?"

Hayden's posture tightened. "Are you rogue because you do not live within a community of vampires? One should live their life as they choose, is this not so? I simply prefer to live on my own and I chose to live it as a supernatural and not a human."

"So you just picked a species and fake that pattern?"

"I haven't done anything wrong to be judged by you," Hayden said.

Burnett still looked confused. "How many like you exist? Living as a different type of supernatural?"

"Not enough for us to feel comfortable with coming forward," Hayden said. "Not when history has proven what can happen."

Kylie saw Burnett try to absorb what he was hearing and file it away. "So when you saw I held no threat to Kylie, why didn't you come forward then?"

"So you could send me packing, or worse, have me arrested?"

Burnett might throw his weight around more than Hayden, and even outweigh him by quite a bit, but verbally Hayden held his own. And that fact wasn't appreciated by Burnett.

"You work for Kylie's grandfather?" Burnett asked.

"Work for him? No. Was I assisting him? Yes. As you know from the checks you ran on me more than once, I worked as a regular high school teacher for three years in Houston."

"Are you still assisting him?" Burnett's question hung in the air as if the answer would decide something.

"Depends on what you mean by assisting. Am I trying to go against you to cause Kylie any harm? No. But am I still keeping a watchful eye on her and answering the concerns of her worried grandfather? Yes."

"The same worried grandfather who had planned to kidnap her?"

"My grandfather wasn't behind that," Kylie said before Hayden could answer. "And I don't want you to send Hayden away, either. Please, Burnett, do this for me."

Burnett looked at Kylie. "I don't know if I can work with someone who doesn't know where his loyalty lies."

Kylie rolled her eyes. "You mean like you and the FRU?"

Burnett's eyes tightened. "My loyalty has always been to protect you."

"But you still work with them, too. Because as you say, you see the good the FRU does. Well, Hayden is the same. He wants to protect me, but he understands my grandfather has good intentions. Why can't you accept this?"

Burnett frowned, but Kylie could see her point had hit home. "I will take it under consideration and discuss it with Holiday."

Hayden nodded, his expression saying he wouldn't beg to stay on. Not that Kylie blamed him for not wanting to plead, but she didn't have so much pride that she wouldn't. Her life would just be easier with Hayden here, and it would help with her connection with her grandfather. She really, really needed Hayden.

"My rules, however, still stand," Burnett continued. "No matter what I decide with Mr. Yates's future at Shadow Falls," Burnett said, focusing on Kylie, "you are not to run off to see your grandfather. You will have shadows, and if I have to personally guard your cabin every night to prevent you from going against the rules, I will."

Kylie nodded, accepting she'd have to earn his trust back.

Burnett shifted his attention back to Hayden. "And if I choose to let you stay on at Shadow Falls, I will expect you to abide by my rules and help me keep Kylie in check. And assist me in learning how to cope with a rogue of your own kind."

"If you decide I can stay on, I'll consider your offer," Hayden said, the edge in his voice stating he obviously hadn't warmed up to Burnett's demeanor. Not that Kylie could blame him. It had taken her a while to warm up to the vamp. Until she learned how much he cared. "But I can tell you this, Mr. James, I refuse to be treated with disrespect."

"Disrespect?" Burnett growled.

And then everything went to hell.

Burnett and Hayden exchanged colorful verbal blows. According to Hayden, Burnett was a prick, and according to Burnett, Hayden was an overconfident jerk who had lied.

She didn't know if she felt confident the tension wouldn't elevate to physical blows, or if she was simply too tired to care anymore. If they broke each other's noses, so be it. She didn't think they would kill each other. Then again, she could be wrong.

But she was suddenly too tired to try to stop them.

Her knees wobbled and her eyes grew heavy. She had to sit down before she fell down. Ignoring the two arguing men, she walked across the room and plopped down on Hayden's sofa.

Feeling a chill wash over, she hugged herself. She was so tired it took a minute to realize the cold wasn't just a natural reaction from being exhausted. It also took a second to realize the men had stopped arguing and were staring at her.

Kylie ignored the men to deal with the spirit. "Not now," she muttered, and stared right at the coffee table in front of her, not wanting to have to face the ghost and her nonsense talk of murder. And not really wanting to face Burnett or Hayden, either.

"Not now, what?" Burnett asked.

"Nothing," Kylie said, and the ghost stepped in front of her. Her pale pink dress hung heavy, soaked in blood. Lots of blood. At least it looked like blood.

Kill or be killed. The spirit's words wiggled through Kylie's mind.

Kylie leaned back and looked the spirit in her cold dead eyes. *Right now, I'll have to go with "be killed." I'm just too tired.*

"Are you ready to go back to your cabin?" Burnett glanced around as if aware they had a visitor, but he couldn't see her. Not that he really should be able to see her ghost, but he had been able to see Hannah, Holiday's sister, so Kylie wasn't sure.

"Can you see her?" Kylie asked.

"See who?" Hayden asked.

"A ghost," Burnett answered Hayden.

"Shit!" Hayden mouthed, and took a step back.

"No, but I can feel her," Burnett said, and his concerned gaze stayed locked on Kylie. "You're not going to pass out, are you?"

"I don't think so," Kylie answered.

"Good. Are you ready to go back to your cabin?" Burnett asked again.

"Yeah," Kylie said. As she went to stand up, she saw Hayden's phone on the coffee table. Recalling she wanted to call her mom, she picked it up and shot Hayden a glance. "I'm gonna borrow this," she told him. "I left mine with my granddad."

Hayden frowned. "Just don't call my girlfriend like the last time you borrowed my phone."

She moved over to him, ignoring the spirit who she felt standing by the door, and hugged Hayden. Maybe she shouldn't have, because he stiffened. *What is it with men and hugs?* she wondered.

"Thank you," she said, pulling away.

"Yeah," he answered.

She glanced at Burnett. He looked upset, as if she'd just hugged the enemy. "You know, the problem with you two is that you are too much alike."

Both of them made some scratchy noise in their throat as if to deny it. Kylie just rolled her eyes and started out. And her ghost, carrying a bloody sword in one hand and . . . and somebody's head in the other, cut in front of Kylie. The head, apparently freshly severed and still pouring blood, dangled and bounced against her hip as she moved.

Kylie gasped and came to an abrupt stop. The spirit turned around, and smiled. Then, holding the body part up by a handful of dark hair as if it were a trophy, she gave it a good shake. *I told you, killing is a piece of cake.*

She shook the head. The eyes wobbled as if loose in their sockets, and blood squirted out of the neck. Kylie let out a frightened squeak.

Swinging around, Kylie slammed into Burnett and buried her face in his shoulder and hung on. "I'm too tired to handle body parts," she muttered. "Make her go away. Please, make her go away."

Chapter Eleven

Five minutes later, the ghost gone, Kylie walked up her porch steps and turned to say good-bye to Burnett behind her.

He studied her with compassion. He hadn't apologized for being so hard on her, and he probably wouldn't. No doubt, he thought she deserved it. And in a way, she guessed she did.

Burnett reached around her and opened the door. "Promise you'll go to bed and not try to wander off again?"

"I promise," Kylie said.

"And try to trust me," he said.

"I do."

"No, you don't," he said, sounding defeated. "If you trusted me I wouldn't just now be finding out about Hayden."

"Someone made me promise not to tell," she said. "If you had promised someone something, wouldn't you try to honor that?"

He sighed, probably offering her the best understanding he could. "But you need to be careful what you promise people." He glanced around, looking a little leery. "Is she still gone?"

Kylie knew who he meant by "she." She looked left and then right. "I don't see her anymore." But deep down she worried the spirit wouldn't stay away too long. Tomorrow she needed to confer with

Holiday about how to get rid of the ghost permanently. Holiday was right. Kylie had no reason to help someone so evil.

"Do you know what she wants? Or who the head belonged to?" Burnett asked.

"I don't know. It could have happened years ago for all I know. But as for what she wants, yeah, I sort of know."

"And that is?" he asked.

"She wants me to kill someone for her." Kylie was too tired to put the sarcasm in her voice.

Burnett scowled. "Who?"

"She hasn't made that clear yet," Kylie said.

"They don't ever ask too much, do they?" he said, but sarcasm rang in his voice. Obviously, he wasn't as exhausted as she was.

Kylie shrugged. She went to step back, but this time it was Burnett who surprised her, when he moved in for a hug. It was short, but sweet, and she realized she needed it.

"Do you want me stay a while?" he asked, looking awkward after the show of affection.

"No," Kylie said, letting him off the hook.

"Do you want me to get Holiday?" he asked. "I will."

"No, I'm fine. I just want to go to bed." Her gaze cut to the sky; it was almost morning. She really needed some sleep. And she was exhausted, physically, but the walk back had kick-started her brain again. Touching Hayden's phone in her pocket, she remembered she also wanted to call her mom. She moved up the porch, looking back once to see Burnett standing at the steps, gazing at her with parental concern.

She remembered her grandfather saying Burnett had stepped into the role of a father, and in a way she supposed he had.

"I'll be fine," she assured him. Not that she felt all that certain.

"Promise me you won't leave the cabin," he said again.

"I promise." She shot him a half-faked smile and shut the door.

Once she heard his footsteps leaving, Kylie leaned against the door and just stood there. Then something caught her eye at her bedroom door. Her heart sank when she saw the steam billowing up from the slit at the bottom, telling her she had company.

Oh, boy. Had she brought more show and tell? What body part had she dragged along this time?

But damn, Kylie didn't want any company.

Or at least not that kind of company. She needed a friend. She needed one of her best friends. She looked over her shoulder at Miranda's door. No steam was billowing out from the bottom.

Turning around, she opened her friend's door. It was early, but something told her Miranda wouldn't complain.

A much-needed smile bubbled up inside Kylie at the sight of the sleeping witch wearing her smiley pajamas and spooning a huge teddy bear like it was her lover. Kylie took in the witch's blond hair with streaks of pink, green, and black scattered over the pillow, and just like that she felt her heart lighten at the sight of her good friend.

As she took another step, the wood floor creaked as if announcing Kylie's presence.

Miranda's shoulders twitched, but she didn't roll over. "I thought we were going to wait to have sex," she muttered.

Kylie's smile widened. "I think that might be wise. I'm not sure our relationship could handle it right now."

Miranda swung around, bringing the teddy bear with her. Her sleepy eyes now popped wide open.

"Besides," Kylie added, "I think you and the teddy bear might have already done the deed."

Miranda squealed, threw the bear at Kylie, and bolted out of the bed. "I thought you were Perry." Giggling, the girl wrapped her arms around Kylie extra tight. "I can't believe you're home. I'm sooo glad you're back." She released Kylie, took a step back, and looked at her as if half afraid she wasn't real. "You *are* home, right? This isn't a dream?"

"It's not a dream," Kylie said, though part of her wished most of the night had been.

The witch's smiled faded and she stomped her foot. "Do you have any idea how miserable I've been? First you up and leave me and then Della runs off to play superhero! I should be furious at you and not happy to see you."

"No, don't be mad. Let's just be happy that I'm back." Kylie snagged the three-foot bear from the floor and tossed it back on the bed.

Miranda gave her an evil look. "Are you back to stay? No more running off on me?"

"No more running off," Kylie said.

"Pinky promise?" Miranda asked, and held out her pinky.

What was it with everyone wanting promises? Kylie looked at the girl's little finger, which was a witch's weapon. "I don't know if it's safe to pinky promise you when . . ."

"It's safe. It's a promise between witches. And since you are part witch, it's the most unbreakable promise you can make."

"Fine. I promise." Kylie held out her pinky to make the promise valid. And in spite of it being a silly gesture, the moment their little fingers locked, a surge of emotion filled her chest. Maybe pinky promises between witches were more than just a childish gesture. Or maybe she was just so damn happy to be home.

"I missed you so much!" Kylie reached out and squeezed the girl's forearms.

"Me too." Miranda bounced back on her bed. "Now, sit down and tell me everything that happened." She squinted her eyes and checked out Kylie's pattern. "You're back to being that strange pattern again."

"I think that strange pattern is a chameleon." If Kylie was the least bit paranoid, like ninety percent of the other chameleons, she should be trying to hide that pattern. But it was a little late for that, wasn't it? Too late to start pretending to be something she wasn't? Everyone here had seen her. And for that matter, could she pretend?

Sure, she'd been able to change the pattern a couple of times, but how did one maintain it? According to what she'd learned, most chameleons weren't able to do that until they were in their twenties.

And by God, she wasn't going to let anyone lock her away until her pattern quit misbehaving. Her heart went back to Jenny and the other teens at her grandfather's place. Suddenly, Kylie got a feeling that helping the young chameleons was part of what she was meant to do. But as Hayden had said, convincing the chameleon elders seemed impossible.

"But you can transform yourself into most anything, right?" Miranda's question drew Kylie out of her thoughts.

"Sort of," Kylie answered, and tried to keep her mind back on Miranda. "But it's still kind of tricky."

"What crazy stuff can you do now?" Miranda asked. Her green eyes glittered with excitement.

Kylie shrugged and dropped down on the bed beside Miranda. "Nothing new, just a little more control over what I can do. Oh, wait, there is one thing. I can make other people invisible."

"Seriously? Make me invisible now. Do it. Do it."

"Please, not now. I'm exhausted. Plus, I'm not sure . . . I mean, it's still kind of scary to do it." She remembered being scared shitless at the thought that she'd somehow lost Derek in the invisible world tonight.

Then, almost wanting a distraction from talking about herself, she reached for the bear and hugged it. "So you and this bear have a thing going, huh? It looked pretty serious when I came in here."

Miranda smiled. "Perry gave it to me to keep me company when he wasn't here. Though this guy's not nearly as good of a kisser as Perry."

Kylie smiled. This was what she had missed. Just having someone to talk to, to giggle with. "That's sweet," Kylie said.

"Yeah," Miranda said, and then asked, "Can you glow anytime now?" She pulled her knees up to her chest.

"No," Kylie said. "That only happens when I heal people." Or pull them from the dead, she thought. Realizing the crazy powers that seemed to come and go, it all scared her. She really hoped Hayden and Burnett could work out their differences. It would really be nice to have Hayden here to help her if things went wonky again.

"Too bad, the whole glowing thing was totally cool. I mean, I can make myself glow, but it's not as cool as when you did it. I don't know why, but it's different."

Kylie shook her head. "It wasn't that cool, believe me."

"Yeah, it was." Miranda made a funny face. "Everyone agreed that you looked like an angel. They were even wondering if maybe you didn't have a little angel in you."

"I'm no angel." *Just ask Burnett.*

"Everyone is still talking about it," Miranda said.

Great. But even at the thought of being everyone's topic of conversation, and getting all the awkward stares from some of the other students, she didn't dread it as much as she would have before. Face it, she was thrilled to be back, even if it did mean she was still considered a bit of a freak.

Pushing all that aside, she focused on Miranda again. "So what have I missed since I've been gone?"

"Everything. It's been crazy. Oh . . ." A frown appeared in her eyes. "Did you hear about Helen?"

"Yeah." Kylie nodded. "Holiday promised me she's fine."

Miranda made another face. "Did you hear who they think did it? That Mario creep was seen—"

Kylie nodded again. "I know."

Miranda frowned. "I think it was him, too. I had started feeling that weird presence again. Like someone was hanging around. Gave me the creeps. And I was all by myself, too."

"I know what you mean." An ugly shiver walked down Kylie's spine as she remembered her confrontation with Mario earlier. Then Kylie looked at Miranda. "And I'm sorry. It's my fault he's here."

"It's not your fault. He's evil."

"Yeah." And he was. Soon, Kylie knew she'd have to tell Miranda about what happened tonight, but she didn't have the energy to go into it now. "You don't feel him now, do you?"

Miranda tilted her head to the side as if putting out some kind of internal feelings. "No."

"Good." Kylie pushed back the feeling that he could come back anytime. She really wanted to believe that Shadow Falls was safe, but was she only fooling herself?

"You okay?" Miranda asked, studying her.

"Fine. How's school going?"

"We got a new history teacher. To replace that creep, Collin Warren. A cool guy. A were. He's young. Like only twenty. He was a whiz kid, but you wouldn't know it now. You should see Fredericka! She's all over him."

Kylie nodded but didn't want to get caught up in bad-mouthing Fredericka. They had kind of made peace. "And what other craziness has happened?"

Miranda arched her right brow. "Nikki happened, and if she doesn't stop happening I'm gonna give her a case of big fat pimples." She held up her hand, wiggled her pinky, and scowled.

It took a moment to remember Nikki was the new shape-shifter who had a thing for Perry. Kylie frowned, thinking about the Meet Your Campmate hour she'd spent with the girl. The girl for sure had it bad for Perry. "Yikes. How's that going?"

"It better not be going anywhere! I get so furious at Perry. I mean, he swears he wouldn't touch her, but I think he's eating up the fact that some girl has a thing for him. And I can tell that he likes it that I'm jealous. He mentions her in unimportant conversations. As if he likes to see me get all riled up."

Kylie bit down on her lip and wondered if Lucas hadn't been a bit thrilled that Monique had a thing for him. Or did Monique even have a thing for him? Was Lucas really telling the truth about them never doing more than just sharing a couple of kisses? Had it been Monique who Kylie had seen?

The questions came at her so fast, she wanted to mentally duck.

Miranda dropped back on the bed with a bit of drama, and Kylie realized her mind had taken her back to her problems when she should be focused on Miranda.

"Do you trust him?" Kylie asked. "If you do, then you have to stop fixating on it."

Miranda pursed her lips as if thinking. "Is that what you did with Lucas?"

"That's different," Kylie said.

Miranda propped herself up on one elbow. "Are you okay? God, I know that had to hurt."

"I will be okay," Kylie said. "Eventually." She stared up at the ceiling and tried to push her heartbreak back. It wasn't as if she didn't have a ton of other issues to worry about. Like the ghost carrying around severed heads who was probably waiting for her in her bedroom. A shiver ran down her spine from the memory.

Miranda shifted and rested back on the bed again. "You know after you left he came to talk to Della and me?"

Kylie turned and looked at Miranda. "He did?"

"Yeah. I think he hoped we would try to talk to you about him. Convince you to forgive him."

Kylie refocused on the ceiling and reached for the teddy bear and hugged it. "I'm sorry he bothered you."

"He didn't bother us," Miranda said. "I don't know if you want to hear this, but . . . he was really hurting. I'm not saying you should forgive him, but he swore to us that the only reason he was going through with the engagement was to get on that stupid were Council."

"I'm not sure the reason is important," Kylie said. "It's the fact that he did it. And behind my back. Not that I would have accepted it if he'd told me, but . . ." Her throat tightened. She hugged Miranda's teddy bear closer.

"I know." Miranda paused. "Della pretty much told him the same thing. And she gave him hell. The kind of hell only Della can dish out. Told him he was a piece of monkey shit and that he should go have himself castrated." Miranda let go of a deep sigh. "When Della first started unloading on him, I thought I was going to have a were/vamp fight on my hands. I mean, I thought he was going to come unglued. Weres don't often take lip off of a vampire, not that kind of lip. But he didn't even react. He stood there and took everything she said. Later, even Della said she couldn't help but admire him for taking his punishment like a man."

The knot in Kylie's throat doubled. "I don't want to talk about it."

"Okay." Silence filled the room. Miranda finally spoke up. "Then let's talk about something else. Something good. Did you know Holiday and Burnett are planning on having their wedding here at the camp?"

"No, I didn't know." That news did make Kylie feel better. "When is it planned?"

"They haven't set a date yet. I got the feeling she was waiting on you to come back. However, it will probably be soon. I went to see Holiday the other night, and Burnett's things were all over the place. I think he's staying there now. They're so hot for each other. I'll bet they have sex three times a night."

Kylie made a face. "Do people really do it that much?"

"I don't know," Miranda said, "but I hope so."

They both started giggling. A warmth filled Kylie's chest. "Burnett and Holiday deserve to be happy."

"Don't we all?" Miranda said, and then sighed again. "I'm gonna say this and then I'll shut up. I know you are really angry at Lucas and I don't blame you for it, but . . . maybe you shouldn't completely give up on him. You wouldn't let me give up on Perry."

Kylie shook her head and frowned. "Two weeks ago you were telling me that I should give him the boot and go back to Derek."

"That was before I saw how hurt Lucas was. I think he loves you."

Kylie shook her head. "I really don't want to talk about it. I don't want to think about it. I just want . . . I need to call my mom and then I want to go to sleep. Will you hate me if I leave now?"

"You aren't going to school today?" Miranda asked.

Kylie gave it a thought. "No, I think I'm going to play hooky. I haven't been to bed yet."

"Oh, then go to sleep." Miranda looked at her. "Why do I get the feeling you're not telling me everything that happened?"

Kylie frowned. "Because I'm not, but I'm just too tired to get into everything now. I'll tell you every horrible detail later."

Miranda nodded. "How horrible?"

"Really horrible."

"Okay." Miranda frowned. "But I may pop in and just look at you every now and then. I've really missed you."

Kylie smiled. "I missed you, too."

"You can borrow Teddy if you want." Miranda smiled.

"I think I will." Kylie reached over and squeezed Miranda's hand. "Thanks." She stood up and walked out, holding on to the oversized stuffed animal as if it could be her salvation.

If nothing else, she could use it to hide her face so she didn't have to look at severed body parts.

Chapter Twelve

Thankfully the ghost must have gotten tired of waiting, because Kylie found her room warm with Socks, her black-and-white tuxedo kitty, resting peacefully on her pillow.

When she joined Socks on the bed, the cat scooted over, giving her room, then with his front white-socked paw, he swatted at the teddy bear Kylie still held.

"Okay, I guess holding you is better." She set the bear on the floor. The cat climbed up on Kylie's chest and she gave the kitten some much needed attention. After several minutes, Kylie sat up, shifting the feline to rest at her side. "Sorry, buddy, gotta call Mom. But don't worry, I'll probably be short and sweet. She's much too busy with John to spend time talking with me."

The moment the words were out of Kylie mouth, she realized half her problem with John. She was jealous. She felt her relationship with her mom had just found solid ground when John had come along and snagged her mom's attention. Was it wrong for Kylie to want to be the most important thing in her mom's life for a while?

Probably, Kylie answered her own question. Especially when she was living away from home. Her mom had every right to need a life of her own.

But if Kylie's jealously was only half the problem, what was her other issue with the man? Plain and simple, she just didn't like him. She reminded herself that Burnett had done a background check on the guy and nothing suspicious came up.

Kylie remembered how shocked Burnett had been to discover that Hayden wasn't everything his background check had revealed. Maybe Kylie shouldn't put too much stock in Burnett's checks.

Then again, maybe Kylie should stop trying to paint John as a bad guy and start trying to accept him as a part of her mom's life. Especially when he seemed to be the only part of her mom's life that was making her happy. Her mom deserved to be happy, didn't she?

Kylie dialed her mom's number, determined to play nice.

It rang once. Then two more times. Normally her mom picked up quickly. Kylie worried she might be interrupting some romantic interludes. She frowned and looked at the time. It had to be almost lunch time in the UK, surely they really weren't . . . doing the deed, or as Della would have called it, having a nooner.

She pushed that thought from her mind as quickly as she could, and instead let her mind wander to Della. Burnett had said the little vamp had run into some type of altercation. Seeing Miranda had been super soothing, but having them both here would be just what the doctor ordered.

Another ring of the line brought her attention back to the phone. She expected it to switch to voice mail at any moment. Was her mom okay? Resentment stirred inside her for John again. If something happened to her mom on this trip . . .

"Hello?" Her mom sounded . . . distant. Somehow unwelcoming.

"Everything okay?" Kylie asked, her hand tightening on Hayden's phone.

"Kylie?" her mom said. "Whose phone are you using to call me?"

Realizing this to be the reason for her mom's delay and odd distant tone, Kylie sank back on the pillow. However, the aloofness in her mom's voice reminded her of when she'd been younger and tried so hard to win her mom's approval. A time when Kylie questioned her mom's affection for her. But that was the past. They had found a new place in their relationship. Or they had before now. Kylie prayed John's presence didn't change that.

"Where's your phone, young lady?"

"Oh . . . I . . ." She had think of a lie quickly and make it sound convincing. Her mom might not be able to hear her heart race with a lie, but she had some maternal lie detector that got Kylie in trouble more times than not. "I misplaced my phone last night, so I borrowed a friend's." For all intents and purposes, it wasn't really a lie.

"Well, that explains why you didn't return my call last night," her mom said in a scolding tone. "Oh, goodness, do you realize how much it's going to cost to replace your phone?"

"I . . . think I might be able to find it. And I'm sorry." Kylie stroked Socks when he moved to brush his face against her chin. "Is something wrong? Why were you calling me?"

"No, just . . . your dad was worried."

Stepdad, Kylie wanted to correct, but didn't.

"He said he called you three times late yesterday and you hadn't responded. And then he called me three times while John and I were . . . I mean, while I was in bed."

Ew! Kylie's capacity for being grossed out hit maximum overload, triggering her brain to block out all inappropriate mental images. "I'm sorry," Kylie offered, and then bit down on her lip. She'd told herself she had to give up hoping her mom and stepdad might get back together, but it was tough at times. Still, where it mattered most—a place where she cherished the memories of what her family used to be—a spark of hope existed.

"Three times is ridiculous," her mom said. "Especially when he knew what time it was here."

"I know," Kylie said, but thought, *Give it a break, Mom! He was worried about me!*

"Well, it's time your dad learned I'm not his phone buddy," she said.

"I'm sure he will in time," Kylie said. "I'll get in touch with him today and see what he wants."

"Do that," her mom said, and paused. "Wait. If you didn't know I called earlier, then what's up? Is everything okay?"

"Yeah, I just wanted to check in. I hate thinking you're so far away."

"I know . . . I sort of feel like that, too. I miss you. Not that I'm not having a great time. England is gorgeous, Kylie. Maybe when John and I come back next time you can come with us."

Next time? Were they already planning another trip? "Yeah," Kylie muttered, and reminded herself she was playing nice.

"Guess what, baby?" her mom asked.

Fear suddenly filled her chest. *God, please don't let her tell me they got married or something.* "What?" Kylie asked, her voice sounding like she'd swallowed a frog.

"John asked me if—"

"No," Kylie snapped.

"No what?" her mom asked.

"You don't know him well enough."

The line remained silent for a beat too long. "What do you think he asked me?"

Kylie cringed. "I don't know," Kylie said, and realized she probably was too tired to have called her mom. Too exhausted to hold a logical conversation—especially one where she had to pretend to like someone she didn't.

"He wants me to come work for his company," her mom said. "He's willing to pay me almost double what I'm making now."

Okay, so her mom working for the man wasn't as bad as her marrying him, but Kylie didn't like that, either.

"I thought you liked your job?" Kylie said.

"I do, but . . . twice as much money and free travel. I mean, that's hard to turn down."

"But . . . but you're"—*banging him*—"you're dating him. Isn't that like sexual harassment? I mean there's laws against that, aren't there?"

"Not if the relationship is consensual," her mom said. "John and I talked about how my working for him could be difficult. But he pointed out that I wouldn't be working directly under him. So, it wouldn't really be like we were working together."

Kylie could hear it in her mom's voice. Her mind was made up. She was going to take the job. "Yeah, but I just don't know if it's wise to work for someone you are . . . dating."

"I think John and I are mature enough to deal with this."

Yeah, like he behaved so mature the last time you brought him here when he socked Dad and started a whole free-for-all fight in the lunch room. Kylie bit her lip to keep from saying anything hurtful.

"I guess I just don't know him that well," Kylie said.

"Which I plan to remedy the next time you're home," her mom said. "I thought maybe we could all go somewhere for a weekend."

Please no! "I . . . don't think we need to do that. I . . . to be honest, I kind of like knowing those weekends are for just me and you."

"But you need to get to know him, Kylie. He's a great guy. I just know you'd love him if you really got to know him."

"Yeah, and that's fine. But let's not . . . not rush it, okay? All in good time."

Her mom got quiet again. "You okay, baby? I just realized what time it is there. What are you doing up at five thirty?"

"I had some homework I had to catch up on," Kylie lied again. "And I'd best get going and start working on it, too."

"Do you have boy problems again?" her mom asked.

Along with a ghost-carrying-a-severed-head problem. "Nothing I can't handle."

"What happened, sweetie?" her mom asked.

"I'm fine. Actually, I prefer not to talk about it. Maybe later."

Her mom's long sigh came through the phone. "I'm here when you're ready . . ."

"I know, and I love you, Mom."

"I love you, too, baby."

It was by replaying her mom's words over and over in her head that Kylie finally fell asleep.

"Where are we going?" Kylie asked Derek as she felt that haziness of being in a peaceful dream state. Correction, being in a dreamscape. And right then, the peacefulness of it floated off. It had been a while since she'd done this, but she instantly realized this wasn't her dream. She hadn't gone to Derek. He had come to her. And now he was leading her somewhere—walking ahead of her but with his hand held behind his back holding hers, and leading her down a path. A wooded path.

She tried to get her mind to work on a more alert level. What time was it? How long had she been asleep? She had to stop this.

But then Derek looked back over his shoulder and smiled at her. She lost her train of thought and got caught up in the world she was in. A safe world, her mind said. She looked up. The sun sent soft morning rays of light dancing through the trees.

"We're going to our rock. You like it there, don't you?" His hand gave hers a slight squeeze. His palm felt warm in hers. Comforting. Odd how just holding someone's hand could feel like a hug—like a warm embrace. Then again, she was talking about Derek. He had all those fae powers that made his touch . . . more.

Meaningful.

She vaguely remembered him trying to kiss her earlier on the escape from her grandfather's place and thinking he wasn't going to be as easy to keep at bay. Did she really want to keep him at bay?

The answer seemed to be somewhere between her heart and mind and she couldn't draw the conclusion. But this was just a dream, a part of her offered up as an excuse. Later she'd figure it out. She would, she promised herself.

"You always liked going to the rock before," Derek said.

"Yes, but . . ." She stopped and glanced down at herself. She was dressed in a pair of cut-offs and a T-shirt. But she was barefoot. It felt good. A soft bed of moist grass and earth beneath her feet. Definitely a dream. If real, she would be feeling the pebbles and thorns. This wasn't real. Not really. But she needed to be careful. She wiggled her toes and tried again to wake up enough to figure out what was right and what was wrong.

Derek turned, still holding her hand, and faced her again. "Just come with me, Kylie. Give me this, please." She could already hear the trickle of the stream flowing through the earth, splashing over stones that had been smoothed by time. The smell of the grass, the woods, and the tall trees scented the air she breathed.

A breeze stirred Derek's hair. "Give me some time to be with you."

She stared at him through her own hair dancing in front of her eyes. Saw the pleading in his gaze.

The word *no* rested on the tip of her tongue, but then she saw the bruises on his neck. Bruises that looked just as bad as those on Lucas. Not that she'd given those bruises to Derek. Mario had. But it had been because of her. He'd thrown himself at Mario to protect her.

Derek had been willing to die for her.

He loved her.

"Please," he said, and the sound of his voice echoed in her heart like a sad song.

Going with him didn't feel completely right, but telling him no didn't feel right either.

"Just to talk," she said, and arched a brow.

"Right." He grinned and the gold flecks in his eyes glittered. She remembered that look, too. A sexy devil-may-care look that hinted he was up to something.

He turned around and she continued following him. In a few minutes, they arrived by the stream. He waved toward the rock.

"Your chariot awaits you, my dear lady," he said in a formal voice, and gave her a bow as if in some school play.

He looked so cute, she couldn't help but grin. "You're being silly."

"Yeah, but if that's what it takes to make you smile, I'll be silly all day long. You had a rough night. You deserve a little fun."

"I do, don't I?" she said, and then hopped up on the rock. On her chariot.

He jumped up on the rock right after her. His shoulder brushed against hers. She couldn't help but remember the first time they'd come here. It had looked so magical, so much like a fairytale, something from a painting in a children's book. Of course, back then that had happened a lot when she was with Derek, and it didn't have to be just there.

Kylie looked around at the woods and sights. No fairytale feel dominated the place. Maybe the fairytale feel didn't happen in dreams.

Not that it wasn't pretty or soothing to be here. The sun sent a golden color between the trees and their stirring leaves. The air smelled morning fresh. It felt nice to be sitting next to Derek, to feel his shoulder gently pressed against hers. Couldn't she relax? She wasn't going to let anything happen. They were here to talk, she reminded herself.

She looked at him and felt the tickle of attraction making her stomach flutter. For the first time, she noticed the subtle changes in him over the last few months. The boy she had once come to the rock with was almost gone, and a man had taken his place. The hair resting against his brow looked a little darker. He had a masculine profile, a strong jaw line, and beautiful lips.

He looked down at her. "You know, it was really cool when you turned me invisible."

"Yeah, but it scared the crap out of me when I didn't see you right away when I brought you back."

"I know. I could feel your emotions." He hesitated. "But that was kind of cool, too," he said. "Actually, that was the coolest part."

"No it wasn't," she said. "Seriously, it scared me."

"I know, but that's what made it so cool. Because that's when I knew for sure. That's when I knew you still loved me."

His words echoed in her head and bounced around her heart. He leaned down. His finger brushed across her cheek. His breath whispered across her temple. Oh damn, Kylie thought. Here she was again, up shit creek without a paddle.

The touch moved across Kylie's chin.

Gentle.

Caring.

Loving.

She remembered dreamscaping with Derek, but couldn't remember how it ended. The touch came again. The feel of bedsheets pressed against her side. Oh crap, was she still with Derek? In bed? What the hell had she done?

She jerked her eyes open, scared that . . . that . . . Yellow eyes stared right at her. Yellow feline eyes. And a white paw now rested on the tip of her nose.

"Socks." She chuckled with relief, her heart pounding with distant memories of the dream playing peek-a-boo with her mind.

"Hey, baby," she muttered when the cat's paw swatted at her nose. "So you really missed me when I was gone, huh?"

"Everyone did," a voice came from the other side of the room. Before she could force her brain to identify the voice, or to even know if it was male or female, she'd bolted out of the bed and stood wide-eyed, staring at . . . Okay, she took a deep breath. No reason to panic. It was just Holiday.

"I didn't mean to scare you. I just slipped in to check on you. I was getting a little worried. You've been out for hours. I checked on you two or three times and you didn't even stir."

Kylie blinked and looked at the clock on her bedside table. Three o'clock. "I didn't mean to sleep that long."

"I think you were exhausted," Holiday said, then frowned. "Burnett told me about the whole Hayden episode." Socks jumped off the bed and started doing figure eights around Holiday's ankles.

The camp leader ignored the cat and continued to stare at Kylie.

"About that," Holiday said. Her expression told Kylie that she was about to get a reprimand. Holiday didn't reprimand very often, so when she did, it always seemed to hurt twice as much.

And sure, Kylie might deserve it, but still half asleep, she didn't know if she could take it standing up. She plopped back on the bed, reached for the teddy bear, and hugged it.

"You can't hide stuff from us, Kylie."

Yup, here came the scolding.

Chapter Thirteen

"I know I shouldn't have hidden it." Kylie's chest tightened. "And I know Burnett was really disappointed in me and you're probably mad at me, too. And I get why. I really, really do. But . . ." She took a deep breath as the scolding look in Holiday's eyes remained strong.

Hugging the teddy tighter, she continued, "Can't you understand that I promised my grandfather not to expose Hayden? I wouldn't have kept that promise if I thought he was bad or trying to cause any harm. He's not a bad person. If it wasn't for him, I wouldn't have found you that night Collin Warren kidnapped you. And if I hadn't found you when I did, I probably wouldn't have . . . been able to save you. He helped save your life."

Holiday frowned. "I'm not saying he's a bad person, Kylie. And it's not that I don't understand why you would feel compelled to keep your promise, but Burnett is right to protect you. We need to know what's going on."

"Well, now you know everything. I mean, if Burnett told you."

"He did," Holiday said.

Kylie bit down on her lip and then pushed the teddy bear aside. "Have Burnett and Hayden spoken again? Did he tell you that they were at each other's throats last night? Burnett said he was going to consider whether he was going to let him stay on. *Consider!* And then

Hayden said he would then *consider* if he *wanted* to stay on." She let go of a deep gulp of air. "Burnett acted like a jerk."

Holiday frowned. "When it comes to protecting people he cares about, Burnett always comes off a little strong."

"A little? Really?" Kylie rolled her eyes. "You can say that with a straight face?"

A slight smiled pulled at the camp leader's lips. "Okay, maybe a lot, but most of the time, he's right." She pulled her red hair around to one side and started twisting it.

"But he's not right about this. And here's the thing. I'd kind of like it if Burnett didn't run Hayden off. I know he lied to get hired, but it would mean so much to have . . . to have someone around who understands what it means to be a chameleon. I mean, you're great. You've been there for me from the beginning, and so has Burnett, but it's like you've told me many times, you don't know anything about chameleons."

Holiday nodded. "I know it would be good to have Hayden here, and I told that to Burnett, too. And I promise you, he's taking that into consideration."

"You're going to let him decide?" Kylie asked, not liking that. "What happened to you being the head honcho around here?"

"Now that we're really together, we've decided that Burnett gets the final say on anything that impacts the security of Shadow Falls."

"Oh, hell! You know he can be so damn unreasonable at times. You just admitted that yourself," Kylie said. Had loving Burnett messed with Holiday's head? Kylie had heard that love turned you stupid; now she knew it for sure.

"True, he can be unreasonable. Yet I can be too easy," Holiday admitted. "And on the security and safety of our students, I'd rather err on the side of caution. But don't worry. I really think Burnett feels that having Hayden around would be good. Not just for you, but to help us figure out precautions against . . . future attacks."

Kylie pulled her knees up and hugged them. She knew by "future attacks," Holiday meant Mario. While Helen still couldn't recall anything of her attack, Kylie knew in her heart it had been Mario. A wave of doom and gloom bit down on her gut and some of last night's events flashed in her head. She looked up.

"I don't think I can handle Mario hurting someone else." She gripped her hands. "First Helen, and then I nearly got Derek killed last night. And Mario almost had *me* doing the killing where Lucas was concerned."

"I know," Holiday interrupted, as if she knew just repeating it would be hard for Kylie. "That has to be hard to take. But it just emphasizes what Burnett says about you being careful. He's done tons of work to the security system since you've been gone and he really thinks it's infallible."

That should have made Kylie feel safe, and it did, but . . . "So I'm a prisoner here," she said, thinking if things didn't change it would get as bad as living on her grandfather's compound.

"No, not by a long shot," Holiday insisted. "I knew you would feel that way, and Burnett and I have already discussed it. You are not prohibited from leaving, but until things calm down, Burnett wants to be with you when you go anywhere. I don't know if he told you, but Mario was spotted in Fallen. So Burnett's adamant about being with you if you leave. Do you think you can handle that? He just wants to make sure you're safe, Kylie. You're special to him."

Kylie nodded. "I know, and I love him, too." She recalled her conversation with her mom. "But what about parents' weekend in a few weeks? My mom is already making plans. She wants John and me to . . . bond." Kylie's mind created an image of being forced to be polite to her mom's boyfriend for a whole freaking weekend. Good lord, the last time she saw the man, she'd completely lost it and was slinging insults at him left and right. It was like she couldn't stop herself. He brought out the bitch in her big time.

Holiday dropped on the edge of the bed. "We'll cross that bridge when we come to it." But Kylie saw the concern flicker in her eyes.

Kylie hugged her knees tighter. "To be honest, I wouldn't mind not being able to make that weekend. So if you can find a way to call that off, I won't fight you on it. You've got my word."

Holiday sighed with sympathy. "Now . . . what's this about a spirit carrying around a head?"

Kylie rolled her eyes. "You mean your ghosts don't do that?" she asked with sarcasm.

Holiday chuckled, even though Kylie hadn't really meant it to be funny. "I had one toting around his own arm and leg for a while. He'd lost it in an accident and wouldn't put it down. It was pretty gross."

"Lucky us," Kylie said, but then she thought about the spirits at the graveyard, and felt bad for being so cynical. Most of them were simply lost souls looking for a little help.

Holiday reached over and pressed a hand on her arm. "Lucky them to have us," she said as if she'd read Kylie's mind, or at least her emotions. "But not all of them deserve our help. I've told you this before, you can send them away. You have every right to say no to some of them."

"I know, and I tried, but I guess I didn't do it right. Or maybe I didn't try hard enough."

"From what Burnett told me, I think sending this spirit away is a wise thing. What's this about her wanting you to kill someone? Has she told you who it is?"

"No. She's short on facts like all ghosts. I'm not even sure if she knows the answers."

"Does she feel evil?"

Kylie thought about it a minute. "Yes and no. I mean, she's not an angel. She admitted she's killed a lot of people. Most of the times when I see her she has blood on her hands, but it almost seems like she feels guilt for it. Or at least sometimes she does," Kylie said, remembering how callously she'd carried around the severed head. "But I don't think she's out to hurt me. I even asked her if she was trying to take me to hell."

Holiday raised a brow. "And you think she'd admit it if she was?"

"No, but she didn't out and out deny it as if it was a lie. She matter-of-factly told me that she wanted me to send someone else to hell. And I think the whole head thing was because I started ignoring her. She just wanted to get my attention."

"And I bet it worked," Holiday said.

"Pretty much," Kylie said. "Kinda hard not to pay attention to that." She shivered, remembering the image of the head.

"I still think sending this one packing might be a good thing."

"I know, and last night I was even thinking it was a good thing to do, but there's one thing that makes me question doing that."

"What?" Holiday asked, and brought one of her legs up on the bed.

Kylie sighed. She hadn't really been too concerned about this earlier, but right now it seemed like something she should consider. "She says that if I don't do it, if I don't kill this person, that I'm the one who's going to die."

Holiday's brow tightened. "Okay, that does kind of put a new slant on things. Do you get the feeling she's trying to protect you, or just cause harm to someone else?"

Kylie considered the question. "I think she's doing both. I don't know why she would want to protect me. But then again, last night when Derek and I were leaving the compound, she's the one who told me to go to the graveyard. I think she was helping me."

Holiday frowned. "Okay, keep her around for now. But for God sakes, be careful. You've already got someone from this world trying to hurt you, you don't need someone from the afterlife trying to do you harm, too. You are too special for anyone to want to hurt you."

Holiday's words repeated in Kylie's head and she had a flash of someone else saying words so similar. Someone with green eyes and golden flecks, and warm . . . lips. Suddenly, she recalled part of the dreamscape, an important part of it. The part where Derek kissed her.

"Oh, crap!" she muttered, and dropped her head into her hands. "What have I done?"

"What?" Holiday asked.

Kylie looked up at her. "In the dreamscapes, the person who initiates the dream is in control, but the person who is brought into it, she can stop things from happening, right?"

"Right. As long as she feels strongly about it not happening."

"Shit," she muttered again, because she recalled feeling confused about what she did and didn't want. Confused about what was right and what was wrong. And if she was confused in the dream, then she might have let things happen that shouldn't have happened.

"Oh, damn," she said, and tried to remember the rest of the dream. Then she looked back up at Holiday. "Shouldn't I be able to remember everything?"

"Yes, except . . ." She made a face as if she didn't think Kylie would want to hear the rest. "Except when you're really exhausted."

"Which I was. Just freaking great," Kylie mumbled.

"Calm down. After you have something to eat and relax you'll probably recall everything."

"I don't know if I want to remember," she muttered. "Oh, hell, yes I do."

Holiday frowned. "Do you want me to talk to Derek about this?"

Kylie's brow wrinkled. "I didn't say it was Derek."

Holiday gave her a don't-be-silly look. "You two and I are the only ones who can initiate a dreamscape here. It had to be him."

Kylie bit down on her lip again. "Okay, it was him, but no, I don't want you to talk to him. I should handle this myself." She let go of a deep puff of air. "He thinks I'm still in love with him."

"And you're not?" Holiday asked.

"No," Kylie said. And she meant it. She did. Yes, she really did. So why did she sound like she was trying to convince herself of that? "I don't want to talk about Derek."

Holiday studied her. "Do you want to talk about Lucas?"

"No," Kylie said.

"Okay, but if you need to talk about him or anything, I'm here for you."

"I know." Then, just to make a liar out of herself, the words slipped from her lips. "I realized I loved him right before all that happened." Her heart felt like it folded over on itself. "I was going to tell him the next time I saw him. Then, the next time I saw him he was promising his soul to Monique."

Holiday pursed her lips as if hesitant to say what was on her mind. "I don't think he meant it."

"I don't care if he meant it; he shouldn't have done it."

"That's true. And I won't tell you what to do, but I do believe he's telling the truth about his intentions. And I'm just saying that if you still care about him, I don't think he's a bad guy."

Kylie drew in a deep breath. "I asked my mom once if she still loved my dad. She told me she didn't know. That maybe once she got over being mad at him, she'd have to see how she felt. Maybe that's what will happen with me and Lucas. But for right now, it's royally pissing me off that everyone is telling me what a good guy he is. It makes me feel like I'm the one who did something wrong." Tears tightened her throat, but she swallowed them and stiffened her spine.

"I'm sorry." Holiday held up one hand. "And you know you didn't do anything wrong. And I'll not say another word."

"Thank you."

Her gut suddenly let out a loud growl letting her know it was as unhappy as she was . . . and empty. She gazed back up at Holiday. "I need to eat something. I think my stomach is gnawing on my backbone right now."

"Here." Holiday reached over to the nightstand and handed her a paper bag. "I brought it to you earlier, thinking you'd need some food."

Kylie pulled out the plastic baggie and saw half a sandwich with a bite out of it.

"Sorry, I got hungry while I was waiting on you to wake up."

When Kylie unwrapped the sandwich and took a bite, Holiday reached back into the bag and pulled out a bag of opened chips. "I'm still hungry." She smiled apologetically and popped a chip into her mouth.

As Kylie ate the sandwich and watched Holiday eat the chips, the weight of the world sitting on her chest felt as if it lifted. Not all the way, but enough to give her a reprieve. She still had tons of issues to work through. But being back at Shadow Falls—this was right. And being here with Holiday helped make it so.

Kylie finished off the last bite of sandwich and reached into the chip bag Holiday held. Her fingers found the bottom of the bag.

Holiday made a funny face. "Sorry, I don't know what's up with me. My appetite has gone haywire."

"It's probably love," Kylie said. "You're just shining with it. Every time you say Burnett's name, your eyes start glowing."

"Actually, love does just the opposite on the appetite. You think you can live off love. No food needed."

Kylie arched a brow. "Then . . . maybe you're pregnant."

Holiday licked the potato chip grease and crumbs from her fingers. "Not possible."

"Oh, please. Miranda told me she was at your place and Burnett's things were scattered all over. You two are planning a wedding. Miranda told me that, too. The fact that you two are sleeping together is . . . is normal. And if you pretend otherwise, you're going to look stupid."

Holiday tilted her head to the side, offering Kylie a half-serious look. "I'm not pretending. And while I shouldn't have to explain this—" She paused. "I didn't say he wasn't staying at my place, or that we weren't . . . sleeping together. I said it wasn't possible. We're being careful. Using protection. Which is the best advice I can give any teenager out there." She pointed to the paper sack on the bed. "There's a few cookies in the bag. Sorry, I . . . ate some of those, too."

Kylie snagged the paper bag and pulled out another plastic bag in the bottom that had three Oreos. She grabbed one for herself, and out of politeness, offered one to Holiday—who took it with enthusiasm.

"I love Oreos," Holiday said, as if reading Kylie's surprise. Then the fae pushed the entire cookie into her mouth in one big bite.

"You know condoms aren't foolproof," Kylie said, opening her cookie and licking at the white icing between the chocolate wafers. "Some statistics state they are only eighty-five to ninety percent effective in preventing pregnancy. Some claim that as much as ten percent of that error is human error, or in your case, vampire error, and not condom error. Like a guy pulling out too quick"—she made a face—"causing leakage, or not putting the thing on right in the first place. And if a woman has long nails . . ." The look on Holiday's face gave Kylie a moment of pause. "Not that you have long nails or that Burnett wouldn't know how to put one on himself." Kylie felt her face heat.

Holiday blushed right along with Kylie. Then, still having a mouth full of cookie, the fae held up her hand as if to say she needed a minute before speaking.

Kylie, oddly over the embarrassment, felt proud of the knowledge she had, and kept talking between licks of icing. "And if a guy carries one around in his wallet too long, it can tear. Then there're product failures. For whatever reason the condom breaks, or has a tiny hole in it. And you would be surprised how little sperm it takes to get a girl preggo."

Having tasted away all the icing, Kylie took a bite of the chocolate cookie and spoke around the mouthful of Oreo. "To be on the safe side, you can buy the condoms with spermicide on them. That's supposed to help kill any of those little escaping sperms. But using spermicidal condoms all the time can cause vaginal problems. So it's not recommended for long-term use."

Holiday took a deep swallow. "You . . ."—she swallowed again, licking her teeth clean—"sure do know a lot about condoms."

"I told you, my mom left pamphlets on my bed about twice

a week. You wouldn't believe what information I have in my head. I could tell you about all the different kinds of STDs, but it isn't pretty. I don't want to think about those."

Holiday laughed. "I think when I have a kid I might ask your mom about where she gets the pamphlets."

"Oh, don't do that. It messes with a person's mind. I think that's why I'm still a virgin."

Holiday chuckled. "Which is exactly why I'll be getting my kid those pamphlets." Her smile faded. "Seriously, a teen should not take having sex lightly."

"True," Kylie said, and grabbed the last cookie and broke it half. "But too much information isn't a good thing, either." She offered one half to Holiday, who didn't hesitate to take it.

"Thanks."

"Are you sure you're not pregnant?" Kylie asked, watching Holiday pop half the cookie into her mouth as if she was starving. Or as if eating for two.

"Positive." Holiday talked around the Oreo. "Faes, or at least Brandon faes, always know when they're pregnant."

Kylie grinned. "Don't tell me, one of the signs is they get ravenous and eat their friend's food while they're waiting on them to wake up."

"No." She paused and her brow wrinkled. "Well, being hungry is a symptom, but the most common one is hiccups and burping. I had a cousin who was pregnant and she hiccuped nonstop for eight months. It was sad."

Holiday looked at the lunch sack as if wishing it weren't empty. "Why don't you get your shoes on and we'll go to the cafeteria and snag some more cookies. Then we'll find Burnett and go to the falls. Something tells me you could use some soothing ambience."

The thought of going to the falls sent a warm feeling through Kylie. "Yeah, that sounds really good." Maybe when she was there she could remember the rest of the dream. God, she really hoped she hadn't done anything stupid with Derek.

Not that she feared she'd . . . gone too far—as in all the way, too far. Face it, like she'd told Holiday, those pamphlets did a number on her. Too much information really could be a bad thing. Or in this particular case, a good thing.

Then she realized that if she hadn't been so cautious where sex was concerned, she might have already slept with Lucas. She was glad she hadn't. That achy pain tugged at her chest again, and she couldn't help but wonder how much truth there was to what she'd told Holiday. When she was over being mad at Lucas, could she forgive him?

Did he deserve a second chance?

Pushing Lucas from her mind, Derek stood in waiting and popped right into the forefront of her thoughts. She recalled the kiss in the dream. Had she stopped the kiss? Or had she let herself be pulled into it? Damn! Damn! Offering Derek hope was a bad thing.

And if she had offered him hope, she needed to nip it in the bud, before it led to some irreparable damage. The kind of damage where people got their feelings hurt. And the fact that she did care so much about hurting Derek's feelings might have given her pause, but she wasn't going to let her mind go there. Nope!

Kylie snagged her shoes, slipped them on, and walked out with Holiday. Remembering Hayden's phone, she stuck it in her pocket. Last night she'd considered calling her grandfather, but not knowing what to say, or how to say it, she hadn't. And if she called him, would Burnett see it as another betrayal?

She glanced up at Holiday. "Can we run by Hayden's cabin? I need to give him his phone back." When Holiday looked confused, Kylie explained. "I left mine at my grandfather's. And I wanted to call my mom."

"Sure," Holiday said.

They weren't out of Kylie's bedroom door when Holiday let out a light jumpy kind of noise. Then another escaped from her lips.

Kylie gazed at her. Holiday slapped her hand over her lips and panic filled her green eyes.

"Is that what I think it is?" Kylie asked. "Was that a hiccup?"

"Oh, shit!" Holiday said, and hiccuped again.

Kylie yelped with excitement. "I wonder if the baby will look like you or Burnett."

Chapter Fourteen

Hayden wasn't at his cabin, but Holiday, still a little panicked by her two hiccups, agreed to walk by his classroom to see if he was there.

"I'm sure this is nothing," Holiday said, tapping her chest. "It's psychosomatic. We mentioned hiccups and it just happened."

Kylie wasn't convinced, and apparently neither was Holiday, who repeated the same thing over and over again as if to persuade herself.

"Don't you want kids?" Kylie asked, remembering what she'd learned about chameleons having a hard time getting pregnant.

"Yes, but . . . Burnett's not completely on board with the idea. He says he didn't have a father, so he doesn't know how to be one."

"I think he'd make an excellent dad."

"I know he would. He'd probably be a tad overprotective, like most vampires, but still fabulous."

Thinking of another vamp who could be a tad overprotective, Kylie asked, "Is Della back yet?"

"Not until tonight," Holiday said. "But she's fine," she added, as if reading Kylie's concern. "Burnett spoke with Steve again this morning."

Kylie nodded. "And Helen's okay?"

"They let her out of the hospital late yesterday. Her parents wanted her to come with them for a while. Just to make sure she's okay. Of course Jonathon is having a fit."

"I'll bet he is," Kylie said, remembering how the two of them were practically superglued at the hip.

Holiday and Kylie came to Hayden's classroom. Kylie saw someone moving behind the curtain. "He's here."

Holiday agreed to wait outside, and Kylie walked in.

Hayden, alone in the room, sat at his desk with a phone in his hand.

"Hey," Kylie said.

Hayden glanced up and dropped the phone. "I was about to try and call you to see if you were okay. And check on my phone? Please tell me you haven't spoken with my girlfriend this time."

"No, I haven't spoken with anyone but my mom."

"And you're okay?"

"Yeah." Kylie pulled the phone out of her pocket. "I wanted to drop your phone off. Thanks for letting me borrow it."

He nodded. "You didn't call your grandfather?"

Kylie's mood went a notch down. She shook her head. "I don't know what to say to him. I'll call him in a day or so." Yes, she was procrastinating, but she decided to give herself a little break on this issue. "Have you told him that Burnett knows everything?"

A frown pulled at his eyes as he nodded. "I had to chance it and use the office phone, since I didn't have my phone," he said.

She shot him an apologetic look. "Is my grandfather . . . okay with it?"

"He's not happy." Hayden paused. "I still don't think he was in on any of the ploy to try to stop you from leaving. And he seemed eager to speak to you about it."

"I know. I believe you, it's just . . . I feel as if I hurt him by leaving, and now he's going to be upset that I told Burnett about you. The thought of him being angry with me is . . . just too much."

"I explained the reasons we had to tell Burnett." Hayden leaned back in the chair. It squeaked. "Your grandfather cares about you. I know he can be hardheaded, but he's lost so much in this life—his kid, his wife. Now, he's scared he's going to lose you, too."

"I know. And yet . . . even if I didn't belong here at Shadow Falls, I couldn't live like they want me to live. Isolated from the world."

"I know. It's not easy." The sudden stiffness in his shoulders told Kylie just how hard it had been on him.

"How old were you when you ran away?"

He picked up a pencil. "How did you know I ran away?"

"I was guessing," Kylie answered.

He hesitated. "Seventeen."

"Have you seen your parents since?"

He shook his head. "Your grandfather keeps me abreast of how they're doing and . . . he started letting me talk to Jenny when . . ."

"When what?" Kylie asked.

"When he started getting worried she was planning to run away."

"Is she?"

"I think I've calmed her down. She just has to stay there another year or so. She's almost mature."

"Mature?" Kylie asked.

"Yes. When you are able to change your pattern. The rule is that if you leave after maturity, then you're not excommunicated. You're frowned upon, but you can visit. But the elders are trying to push her into getting married. It's just another ploy by the elders to try to keep her living on the compound."

Kylie felt Hayden's pain and she felt for Jenny, too. "Don't they see that they're pushing the young people to leave? It's like one of those cults that forces kids to live like it's the eighteen hundreds."

"They think they're protecting them," Hayden said. "And perhaps in the elders' day it was the right thing to do. But things have changed and they can't seem to see that. I've managed to create a life for myself and I'm not living in danger."

Kylie nodded, but she couldn't help but wonder how good of a life it was if he had to hide his true identity. Nevertheless, she supposed it was the better option. "Are you going to stay here?" She held her breath with hope.

He leaned back in his chair. "Burnett hasn't gotten back to me."

"But if he says you can stay, will you?"

He picked up a pencil and rolled it in his hand. She jumped in. "Please. I'd kind of like it if you stayed. I still have questions and it would be really nice to have you around. And . . . I think I want to try to change things. You know, help the other chameleon teens. I haven't mentioned it yet to Holiday or Burnett, but I'm just waiting for the right time."

"I'll give it some thought," he said. "But let me just say that your friend Burnett makes leaving sound like the better deal."

"He's not all bad," Kylie said. "I know he can be . . . difficult. In a lot of ways, he sort of reminds me of my grandfather. And even you a bit."

"I'm not nearly as pigheaded," Hayden said. "He has no right to treat me like this."

Kylie could argue the point with Hayden that coming here and hiding his whole identity didn't instill trust in Burnett, but what good would it do? "Just promise you'll consider staying on. I really need you here."

"I'll consider it, but that's all I can promise."

With another sandwich, Oreos, and Burnett in tow, Kylie and Holiday made their way to the falls. Burnett moved with them, but the vamp kept tripping, mostly because his concerned focus stayed on Holiday, instead of watching where he stepped.

She hadn't hiccuped again, but neither had she stopped panicking. At least it appeared that way, because she hadn't lost that oh-shit look on her face. Obviously, Burnett picked up her oh-shit look, too.

"Everything okay?" he asked for the second time.

"I told you, it's just tummy issues," Holiday answered, and Kylie recognized her answer as a version of the truth, so her heartbeat wouldn't give away the fact that she lied.

"Do you need to see a doctor?" His brows tightened and the big bad vampire became a worried, normal-looking guy who cared a whole hell of a lot for Holiday.

A warmth filled her chest just looking at them. With it came a sense of accomplishment. A feeling that she'd not just played a part in getting these two together, but it had been part of her quest that she'd completed, and completed well.

"No, I don't need to see a doctor," Holiday said. "At least not yet," she added quickly to counter another lie.

"Probably wedding jitters," Kylie added, hoping to help the conversation move away from her tummy issues before Holiday couldn't find another half truth to throw out.

Looking away from the couple holding hands, Kylie could swear she heard the whispering sound of rushing water over the falls. She slowed her steps and tuned her ears to listen. Yup, it was the falls, and yet they were probably a half mile away. She inhaled deeply, longing for the peace she would find behind the magical wall of water—a place where all the wrongs in life didn't feel so wrong. Or at least they felt manageable.

"Wedding jitters?" Burnett asked as if he'd been considering Kylie's statement. "She has nothing to be nervous about." He almost sounded offended. "I will do everything in my power to be a good husband."

"Brides are always nervous," Holiday said.

"About what? It's not as if you don't already know all my bad habits. Or me yours."

Holiday shot him a funny face. "What bad habits do I have?"

"You're a cover hog." Burnett grinned and stared with devotion at her. Kylie had seen that look on his face before, but now he wore it with pride.

"But seriously," Burnett continued, "what would you have to be nervous about?"

Kylie noticed that when they talked, it was as if she wasn't even here. They were so tuned in to each other, everything and everyone else disappeared. And hadn't she felt the same about Lucas? She pushed that thought back.

"What if you get cold feet?" Holiday asked, and some of the teasing tone slipped from her voice.

Kylie remembered that Blake, Holiday's ex fiancé, had left her at the altar—after sleeping with her twin. No doubt, Holiday probably did have wedding jitters.

"My feet are always cold. I'm a vampire," he said in a teasing voice, almost as if he was trying to chase away Holiday's somberness. "And if I remember correctly, you complained about that last night." He slowed down and slipped his arm around Holiday. "Marrying you doesn't scare me a bit. It's the best thing that could ever happen to me. I'd never run out on you. I'll be the first one to the church."

Kylie's heart swelled at Burnett's words.

She heard Holiday let go of a sigh in the sentimental moment. "And it's when you say things like that I know why I put up with your cold feet." Holiday reached up on her tiptoes to kiss him. Burnett pulled her up so he could deepen the kiss.

"Hey," Kylie said, grinning. "You've got virgin eyes watching you right now."

"Then turn your head," Burnett said to Kylie, and he smiled. "I should be able to kiss my fiancée."

Kylie chuckled. "Yeah, but you'd better be careful, they are going to revoke your vampire license if you get any more romantic and mushy."

"Don't worry," Burnett said, his eyes pinched as if serious. "I can still be a jackass, and kick ass, when it's called for."

Yeah, like last night, Kylie thought. She still had a few bruises on her ego, and so did Hayden Yates, but she didn't say it. Down deep, she knew Burnett had justifications for coming off strong with her and Hayden.

Her thoughts went back to her conversation with Hayden, but already the calm of the falls had given her a sense of peacefulness, and she was able to push her worries aside. She glanced over at the two lovebirds holding hands and walking. Maybe it wasn't just the falls offering this sense of well-being, Kylie admitted. Being back at Shadow Falls and among her friends just felt so damn right.

Almost on cue, the sound of the falls grew louder, and a calm spread inside her chest. Kylie had to admit the falls were definitely contributing to the magical sense of ease. And after everything that happened this last twenty-four hours, she wanted to cling to that magic. Forget that seeing Holiday and Burnett reminded her that she loved someone, too. Forget that Lucas had betrayed her. Forget about running into Mario. Forget she'd probably hurt her grandfather by leaving without saying good-bye.

Oh yes, she wanted the calm that came with being in a place of grace, a place that fed one's spirit with peacefulness. That offered one a sense of wellness.

And courage.

A voice echoed in her mind. Kylie stopped walking. The voice somehow seemed to mean something, something more than just facing her usual tribulations. As if the voice knew something she didn't.

Why would I need courage?

If it wasn't for the peacefulness, Kylie might have started panicking at the little intrusion in her head. The words didn't come with the cold chill she got when a ghost visited. Not that Kylie hadn't heard the voice before; she had, several times. In the past, she'd attempted to chalk it up to being her subconscious. But this time, it seemed more.

The peaceful sound of the falls grew stronger and took the edge off her worry. She didn't want to fret about the voice, or even the reason she might need courage. She picked up her pace.

Five minutes later, they arrived at the entrance to the falls. The serene ambience embraced her. Even the leaves on the trees seemed to whisper their greetings. The water cascading down from the cliff above filled the air with sweet moisture. The light breeze, carrying tiny pinpoints of water, scented the air with some distant flower and natural herbs.

Burnett's normal stern expression dissolved into something more peaceful. He stopped at the line of trees and agreed to wait outside, allowing them to have their regular falls experience. Removing their shoes and rolling up their jeans' legs, Holiday and Kylie both walked through the wall of cascading water.

Once inside, it took a second for Kylie's eyes to adjust. It wasn't completely dark, but only filtered light snuck in from behind the falls. Iridescent shadows in rainbow colors played on the rock walls. Cool water dripped from her hair and ran down her back, but the coolness on her skin felt refreshing, like walking through a sprinkler on a hot day.

Both Kylie and Holiday found their spots on smooth rocks just at the mouth of the water's edge. Neither of them spoke for several minutes. The reverence filling the space seemed to mandate a moment of silence.

The calm of quietness completely chased away Kylie's worries and concerns.

After several minutes, Holiday asked, "Do you have a new quest in place?"

The moment the question found its way to Kylie, a need for direction swelled inside her. "Have I really completed my other quest?" The question wasn't just meant for Holiday, but for herself.

"You know what you are, and you understand most of your powers. Was this not your quest?"

"Yes, but I'm not completely in control of my powers yet." She paused. "And I don't know everything." The unexplainable need remained and a hunger to have a plan filled her chest. She had to know where to place her focus. She needed a new quest.

The flow of the falls seemed to grow a little louder. Kylie glanced up and then back at Holiday. "You're right. I have to figure this out.

How do I do that? How did I figure out what the first one should be?" She turned to Holiday, not so much panicked, but eager to get started.

"Well, you need to ask yourself what is important to you right now. Usually our quests end up being something that has weighed on your heart, pulled at your conscience, or has been on your mental to-do list that you've ignored."

Kylie inhaled another breath of calm and glanced back at the camp leader. "Okay, I know something, and I was going to talk to you about it, but I haven't had a chance to think it through yet."

"What is it?" Holiday asked.

"The chameleon teens, they . . . the elders are practically locking them away on compounds. They have very little contact with the outside world. They aren't allowed to have cell phones or computers. I don't mean to make it sound as if they are mistreated. It's just that the elders are stuck in this mindset of when they were being persecuted. They think the only way to stay safe is to remain in hiding. They have a strict policy that until you can control and hide your true pattern, you shouldn't be allowed out into the world." Suddenly Kylie realized something. "They are as bad as the werewolves. With all their backward beliefs."

"It sounds like that." Holiday paused and stared at the water. "That's a big undertaking." Her expression said her mind was reeling. "It's hard to change beliefs that are motivated by justified fear."

"I know," Kylie said. "But there has to be a way, doesn't there?"

"It's for sure worth contemplating. It's a good quest."

What else? The voice inside her said. The same voice from earlier. But like before, it didn't completely scare her. It was a question she was about to come to on her own.

Kylie pulled her knees up and wrapped her arms around her shins. "There's something else, too." And her heart searched for what it was, but it didn't come.

"What?" Holiday said, and inhaled as if absorbing the calm.

"I'm not sure." Her words hadn't completely left her lips when all the flickers of light in the cave started swirling and then shifted as if to dance on top of the water.

Kylie's breath caught as the shimmering of different colors formed a circle. Yet even with the movement of light, the water seemed deadly still, and the surface below became crystal clear. The circle of light appeared to frame an object below the water. Suddenly, whatever it was bobbed up to the surface with a small splash and started drifting toward the edge.

Freaked out, Kylie butt-scooted back a couple of feet. She felt a little less cowardly when Holiday did the same.

The object—floating atop the water's surface and moving as if with purpose—got about a foot from the rock's edge before Kylie could identify what it was. Oh, hell, what did this mean?

Chapter Fifteen

Kylie twisted around on her butt, searching for the ghost and trying to feel the cold. No cold found its way in the cave. No ghost, either. None that Kylie could sense, anyway.

But the sword now inching toward her had to be from the ghost, right? She'd been carrying one around for show and tell this last week and a half.

"Where the heck did that come from?" Holiday asked, her voice filled with concern.

Kylie couldn't take her eyes off the weapon as it slowly inched closer and closer. "From under the water."

"I know, I saw, but . . ."

"I think it has something to do with the ghost," Kylie said.

Holiday frowned. "You mean the one toting around severed heads?"

Kylie nodded. "That would be her."

"Why do you think that?" Holiday asked.

"I'm not completely sure, but I think it looks like her sword. Minus all the blood of course."

"Oh, hell," Holiday said. "What did you get pulled into?"

"I don't know. But it wasn't willingly." Kylie bit down on her lip. If not for the peaceful ambience of the falls, she'd be completely tripping out.

Holiday picked up the sword. She turned it over in her hands. "It looks real. And old. Do you really think it's the same sword?" She shook her head in puzzlement. "Ghosts can't deliver things like this."

"It looks like it. I mean, I'm not a sword expert." Kylie reached for the weapon, and as soon as she touched it, the dang thing started glowing. She flung it to the ground and did another scoot backward. "Why did it do that?"

"I wouldn't know," Holiday said, and stared back at the sword. "Did you learn anything about chameleons making weapons glow?"

"No."

"You sure?"

"I think I might have remembered that."

"Okay," she said, still thinking. She gave the sword another puzzled look and then glanced back at Kylie. "Are you ready to go?"

"Yup." Kylie got to her feet and saw Holiday reach down for the sword. "Wait. Can't we just leave it here?"

Holiday rose and looked at Kylie. "I don't think so. I think it was meant for you."

"You know, I was afraid you were going to say that. But how do you know it wasn't meant for you?"

"Because it didn't glow when I picked it up."

Kylie frowned. "I'm really tired of all this weird crap happening to me."

Holiday sighed. "If it makes you feel any better, I don't like it."

"Well, that makes two of us." Kylie nipped at her lip again in worry.

Holiday half smiled. "We'll get to the bottom of this. When we get back to the office I'll do some research and see if I can find anything about it. And we'll talk to Hayden, too." She carefully picked up the sword, keeping the sharp end pointing down. "We'll find the answer."

Yeah, Kylie thought, but she had the distinct feeling that if they did find the answer, she might not like it.

• • •

Kylie, Holiday, and Burnett, with sword in tow, found Hayden at his cabin. He had nothing to offer. Not even a good educated guess.

Burnett asked him to pick up the sword to see if it would glow for him. It didn't. Then, because Burnett hadn't seen the sword glow earlier, he asked Kylie to pick it up. Carefully.

Like she wouldn't be careful picking up something that looked like it had been used to decapitate hundreds of victims.

The moment she fit her fingers around the hand grip, the iron grew warm against her palm, and just as it had before, it began to glow. It reminded her of one of those glow sticks you bought at theme parks.

"Enough?" Kylie said, eager to put it down.

"Yeah," Burnett said, and looked baffled. It wasn't a look that she'd seen on the vamp's face very often. He reached for the sword and waited to see if it would start to glow, and even looked a bit disappointed when it didn't. Putting it back down on Hayden's kitchen table, he gazed at Kylie's forehead to check out her pattern.

On the walk over here, he'd surmised that Kylie had probably turned into a witch and had lost control of her powers as she had the day she'd sent the paperweight at him, bruising his boys. While Kylie almost wished it was that simple, she didn't buy it. She hadn't been thinking about a sword to have conjured one up.

"I'm not a witch, am I?" she asked Burnett.

"No," he said, and shrugged.

"I told you," Holiday said. "I checked her pattern as soon as the thing started glowing. As crazy as it sounds, I'm not sure it's Kylie doing it. But the sword."

"You think the sword's possessed?" Hayden asked.

"Say what?" Kylie asked. "Swords can be possessed? Okay . . . this is just too freaky for me." She started dusting off her hands to wipe off any possessed germs.

"No, I don't think it's possessed." Holiday touched Kylie to calm her. "I just think for some reason it reacts to Kylie. There's some connection between her and the sword."

"It's strange as hell," Hayden said. "I could ask Kylie's grandfather about this. He might know something that I don't."

Burnett frowned at the mention of her grandfather, but he nodded, and she saw him work to pull back his discontent. "I would appreciate that." He even sounded grateful. "Would you report back to me on that as soon as you get anything?"

Hayden nodded. "Of course."

As they went to leave, Burnett offered Hayden his hand. Hayden didn't hesitate to take it. Kylie got the feeling that the whole sword thing might have worked in her favor for convincing Burnett that Hayden needed to stay on. Even though Hayden didn't have the answers, she could see Burnett appreciated having a go-to person for something he didn't have a lot of knowledge on.

Maybe, Kylie thought, the sword wasn't a bad thing after all. But each time she looked at it held at Burnett's side, she recalled the spirit last night carrying a bloody sword and the severed head.

And she started to worry again that whatever this was all about might lead to more bloodshed.

They went to put away the sword in Holiday's office and then they all walked to dinner. As they stepped off the porch, Kylie was seen for the first time by her fellow Shadow Falls students and was greeted by several campers. Perry came running and swooped her up in his arms, swinging her around twice. When he dropped her back on her feet, Kylie was dizzy and content. He grabbed her arms to steady her. She hadn't even realized how much she'd missed the shape-shifter until he laughed and it sent a warm déjà vu feeling through her.

"Hey, are you groping my best friend?" Miranda's voice echoed from behind Perry.

Perry released her and shot Miranda a grin over his shoulder. "Just a little bit," he said, and glanced back at Kylie. "Damn, we missed you. Miranda was driving me crazy she was so lonely."

"I missed everyone, too," Kylie said, and meant it with all her heart.

Right then, a group of weres walked past. Kylie first recognized Clara, Lucas's half-sister. She met Kylie's gaze and her posture suddenly seemed to express an attitude. Okay, so not everyone was happy to have her back. She could accept that. But then behind Clara, another person moved into view, and Kylie's gaze slammed right into Fredericka.

She didn't smile, but she didn't scowl, and then she offered Kylie a slight nod. A welcome-back nod, maybe even a good-to-see-you nod. Kylie returned the gesture and even offered a slight smile.

For Fredericka, that little acknowledgment was probably more of a show of affection than Perry's. Especially when Clara shot Fredericka a disgruntled look for her action, and Fredericka gave her a get-over-it shrug.

Kylie drew in a deep breath. It felt good to know that while she might not have gained any friends at Shadow Falls, she'd managed to lose an enemy.

Miranda leaned in. "Did you just do what I think you did? Did you smile at that B with an itch?"

"I told you, her and I sort of came to terms," Kylie said.

"Which is a good thing," Holiday piped up. "And I think more people need to come to terms around here."

"And I think Della's right," Miranda muttered. "Kylie's just too nice." Ignoring Holiday's frown, the witch glanced at Burnett. "Speaking of which . . . is Della back yet?"

"She's due any time," Burnett answered as they moved to the dining hall.

When they walked in the door, the chatter filling the large room went silent as if someone had turned off the volume. Heads turned. The only sound bouncing around the large space was forks dropping onto platters. Then, simultaneously, at least fifty pairs of eyes squinted to check out her pattern. Kylie stopped moving a foot inside the door feeling—and not liking—the limelight.

Holiday brushed the back of her hand against Kylie's. "You want me to do something?" she whispered.

"No," Kylie muttered, determined to fight her own battles. Besides, she wanted to be here, this was home, and by God, she wasn't hiding her pattern. Sooner or later, they'd get used to her. Wouldn't they? Eventually they would stop staring and accept her as one of their own.

"Well, I'm gonna do something," growled Perry. He moved forward. "You wanna stare at something?" he yelled out. "Well, stare at this!" Perry swerved around, bent to the waist, dropped his pants, and mooned every pair of those fifty sets of eyes.

"Perry!" Holiday squealed, but there was laughter behind the tone. Burnett's chuckle bounced out of him, but then he slammed shut his mouth when he spotted Holiday's arched brow at his open show of humor.

"Don't be showing your ass, Perry!" Burnett said, his voice deep as if still trying not to laugh. "People are trying to eat."

Everyone in the entire room bolted out with laughter, even Kylie. Leave it to Perry to turn an awkward moment to one of complete humor. Kylie looked at Miranda, who was rolling her eyes, but pride sparkled behind them. And she should be proud. While pulling his pants down might have seemed extreme, it had been done with good intentions, to put a stop to an awkward moment—done to make Kylie feel better. And it had.

Pants back up, Perry turned around and winked at Kylie. As they started moving to the food counter, Kylie leaned in to Miranda and said, "Perry's a keeper."

Miranda rolled her eyes again in humor. "I know." She grinned. "And he has a cute ass, doesn't he?"

Kylie laughed again. "I didn't see his ass, it's his heart that did me in."

As Kylie stood in line to get served her hamburger and fries—which actually smelled a bit like heaven—several people came over to welcome her back: Mandy, one of Miranda's witch friends, Chris, the vampire, and Jonathon, who wore a long face, obviously missing Helen.

"How's Helen?" Kylie asked, and was suddenly washed with a bit of guilt knowing it was probably because of her that Helen was attacked. "I'm so sorry this happened."

"It's not your fault," he said, and bumped her with his shoulder. "But give me a chance to put my hands on that asshole who hurt her and he'll be sorry."

"Is she really okay?" Kylie asked.

"Yeah, she's fine. Her parents say she can come back here in a week."

"That's good," Kylie said.

"Good? That's like forever. A whole week. Seven days. I'm gonna go bat-shit crazy. She's like my drug. I'm not used to being without her." He took off, not a happy camper.

Kylie watched him slump off—his posture that of a hurt and defeated-looking boy. And she got a flashback to how she felt when Lucas would leave. Lonely, empty. Her touchstone in life missing.

Trying to push the thought away, she felt the hair on the back of her neck stand up and do a tickling tap dance. Trying to be inconspicuous, but fearing she knew exactly who was staring, she looked over her shoulder at the were table. Sure as hell, he sat there, studying her with wide, blue eyes. Eyes filled with a sad apology. Her heart dropped to the pit of her stomach.

Would she ever get over being mad enough to forgive him? The question painfully banged against her chest bone with each beat of her heart.

She looked away and shot forward at the same time and ran right into a wide chest—a familiar wide chest. One she remembered leaning against last night in a dreamscape. When she glanced up at Derek's face, it was as if her brain decided this moment was perfect to download everything that happened. All the missing pieces of the puzzle of last night in the dream came hurling back.

The kiss.

His arms around her.

The gentle way he'd held her.

Oh, shit!

Chapter Sixteen

Kylie had stopped the kiss, but not nearly soon enough. And then she'd rested her head on his chest and cried because she'd felt so confused. He'd held her so close and let her cry. It had been cathartic and soothing.

It had been wrong.

Wrong because of what she saw reflecting in his eyes. Hope. Optimism that when her heartbreak with Lucas was all said and done, they'd find their way to what they'd had before.

That thought brought on an epiphany—one of those startling realizations that usually caused havoc in one's life. And yes, she felt the havoc, but she also felt . . . a surge of questions and a need to understand.

Derek had cheated on her, actually slept with Ellie, unlike what Lucas had done—or what she'd thought he had done. And while she'd been hurt by Derek and felt betrayed, this thing with Lucas felt like so much more. Why?

Did it speak to how much she cared about Derek—that forgiving him had come easier? Or did it refer to the depth of her feelings for Lucas? That the feelings she held for Lucas were truer?

"You okay?" Derek asked, staring at her.

She nodded. "Just hungry," she lied, and moved in front of him in the line, so she wouldn't have to face him or the lie she'd just told.

He leaned down and whispered in her ear. "You're not mad at me, are you?"

She considered the question, and the answer came back. *I can't be mad at you, it's myself I'm mad at.*

She'd been weak. She should have called the end to the dreamscape before it got started. And she could have done that. So why hadn't she?

"No, I'm not mad," she whispered back. "I'm just . . ." Realizing they were surrounded by vampire ears that could hear all kinds of secrets, she said, "We'll talk later."

"That will work," he said. "I'm shadowing you tonight, so we should have plenty of time."

Kylie frowned. Maybe she needed to add Derek to Burnett's no-shadowing list. At least until she sorted out her feelings.

With a food tray in hand, Kylie moved to the table where Miranda and Perry sat. She sat down and glanced at Perry and again felt the wash of gratitude to the shape-shifter. "Thanks," she said.

"Anytime you need me to show my ass, I'm there for you," he said, grinning.

Kylie heard someone take the seat beside her and worried again about encouraging Derek. Picking up a fry, she looked straight ahead, trying to ignore the fae as long as possible. Her gaze shifted around the room, stopping on the were table and the four frowns being tossed her way from the weres sitting there. Frowns from everyone but . . . Lucas.

A certain woodsy scent of the person sitting next to her suddenly filled her senses. The fry slipped from her fingers. Slowly, she turned her head to confirm her mistake.

Mistake confirmed. Her breath hitched a little.

It wasn't Derek sitting next to her. But Lucas.

Reverting her gaze to the plate of food, she stared at the hamburger that suddenly didn't smell or look so appetizing. "Shouldn't you be with your pack?" she whispered without looking at him.

"Actually," he said, leaning in close. So close his shoulder brushed against hers. Pain, emotional pain from just that light touch, went right to her heart. "I'm exactly where I belong," Lucas whispered.

She scooted over a few inches at the same time a tray hit the table in front of her. It hit a little too loud. She suspected the owner of the tray might be one pissed-off fae. A glance up confirmed it. Derek dropped into the seat, eyeballing Lucas as if he was infringing on his space.

Just freaking great, Kylie thought. She considered the right thing to do, bolt out of here, knowing people were probably already watching to see what she'd do. Stay and hope no drama arose between the were and fae, and try to downplay all the gossip.

Feeling forced to pretend everything was fine, she picked up her hamburger and sank her teeth into the soft white bun. While she didn't think about how it tasted, her stomach must have approved, because it grumbled in appreciation the moment the first bite made its way down into the empty organ. She didn't give her stomach time to beg for a second bite before she went in for another. This time, the flavor of the slightly sweet bun, mixed with the cheesy beef patty and the tangy zest of ketchup, had her taste buds applauding. She really hadn't eaten right since leaving Shadow Falls.

Derek, probably reading her desire to avoid chaos, picked up his burger and started to eat. Lucas did the same. The tension let up, but not by a whole hell of a lot.

"Who's up for a game of basketball after dinner?" Perry asked.

A few voices broke in with a yes. Kylie thought both Derek and Lucas chimed in, but she didn't know for sure. She did most of her focusing on her food and avoided eye contact with anyone.

Then Derek added, "But it will have to be a short game. I'm shadowing Kylie tonight."

It was more how he said it, than what he said, that made it clear his goal had been to piss Lucas off. And it worked. Lucas gave his tray a quick shove and it flew across the table and slammed into Derek's, sending his French fries flying into his lap.

"Give it up," Lucas said. "We'll be back together in no time."

"Are you sure of that?" Derek asked.

"Stop," Kylie snapped.

"I'm sure," Lucas growled as if he hadn't heard her. "You see, I didn't sleep around on her like someone else did."

"Yeah, but I didn't get engaged behind her back," Derek tossed out.

"Neither did I," Lucas countered. "The engagement never went through because I didn't sign the papers after the ceremony."

Say what? Kylie looked at him, shocked. She had just assumed . . . "What about getting on the Council?" she asked.

"You're more important," he said. "I told you that already."

No, he hadn't told her that. Not really. And he hadn't told her he'd backed out of the engagement, either.

"I told you it was mistake. That . . ." He hesitated just a second. "That I love you."

She didn't miss how hard it was for him to speak his feelings publicly, and you can bet every ear in the room was straining to hear, but he'd done it. He told her he loved her in front of everyone.

And it annoyed the hell out of her. Perry's mooning had been much more appreciated.

"And why the hell couldn't you have figured that out earlier?" She dropped her hamburger, shoved her own tray back, and left the dining hall. As she did, she heard her own footfalls on the tile floor. Which meant everyone in the room, the whole freaking camp, had just been privy to her personal upheaval. Great. Just friggin' great.

• • •

Kylie got outside before she heard someone following her. Thinking it was Derek, and prepared to send him packing, she swung around and Miranda crashed right into her.

"Sorry," Miranda said.

Kylie blinked away what felt like the beginning of tears. "It's okay. You don't have to come. Stay with Perry and finish your dinner."

"I have to come," Miranda said.

"No, you don't."

"Yes, I do." Miranda nodded. "First, because you're one of my best friends and second, because . . . Burnett told me to. But I would have come anyway because of the first thing." She hugged Kylie. "You want me to tell Perry to moon them again?"

Kylie pulled back from the hug, chuckled, and swiped at her tears. "I don't think they could handle seeing it twice."

Miranda giggled. "Are you kidding? It's a gorgeous ass."

They walked back to the cabin and Miranda talked about Perry. A lot about Perry. Like, as in nonstop. Not that Kylie minded; she'd take Miranda going on about Perry over the silence she'd experienced at her grandfather's place anytime. So what if Miranda talked a bit too much? Kylie still loved her, loved hanging with her, too.

They got to the cabin, walked inside, and both of their gazes shot to Della's door. Della's closed door. And that could mean only one thing. Della was home.

Screaming, they both went hurtling inside the vamp's room.

Della stood, completely naked, in the middle of the room with her bra in her hands.

"Jeepers! Don't you guys know what a closed door means? Now, turn around while I get dressed."

"We don't care if you're naked. We're just so happy to see you," Miranda said.

"True," Kylie said.

"Yeah, but you shouldn't have to see all of me. You'll tease me about my little tits. Now turn around."

"They're not *that* small," Miranda said, and gave Della a good hard look.

"Turn around!" Della growled, and used one hand and arm to cover her breasts and the other to cover her pubic hair.

"No so fast," Miranda said, and pointed a finger at her. "First you got some explaining to do, girlie!"

"*Girlie?* I'm not anyone's girlie. And explain what?" she asked, but she was grinning, obviously as glad to see them as they were to see her.

"It's not your little tits you should be hiding. It's that hickey below your shoulder."

Della shifted her hand up from her boobs and hid the mark right below her neck.

"It's not a hickey." Swinging around, she reached for the robe on the bed and slipped her hands in.

"Really?" Miranda asked.

"It looked like a hickey." Kylie giggled, just so darn happy that the three of them were back together again. She didn't even care if they started bickering, or threatening to rip off each other's limbs. Just being here around these two . . . it was what home was supposed to feel like.

"When it looks like a hickey, and smells like a hickey, it's a hickey," Miranda demanded.

"Hickeys don't smell," Della snapped.

"You know what I mean. Besides, I know a hickey when I see a hickey." She pulled her shirt down to expose a rose-colored mark above her right breast.

Kylie laughed and then sighed. "I swear, you two are such bad examples for me. I'm not sure I can stay in the same cabin with you. You two might taint my reputation."

"Oh, please," Della said. "You've had more action than a wind-up doll on speed since you've been here."

"I have not," Kylie said.

"You've made out with three different guys since you've been at Shadow Falls."

"Three? I have not."

"You're forgetting Trey came here."

"Oh, hell, Trey doesn't count. Besides, I've never even had a hickey."

"Oh, you poor thing," Della said. "Did you know you can give yourself one with a vacuum cleaner? I gave myself my first hickey in sixth grade and told everyone an eighth grader gave it to me. It was a doozy, too."

Kylie rolled her eyes. "I can't believe you made out with a vacuum cleaner."

"Yeah, and it was better at it than my first boyfriend. He was totally hickey impaired."

Kylie and Miranda started laughing. Then Della got somber. "Gawd, it's so good to be back!" She jumped on her bed and bounced twice. Then Miranda and Kylie both dove onto the bed with her.

"So you aren't going to explain the hickey?" Miranda asked, and snatched one of Della's pillows and hugged it.

"Nope," Della said. "No hickey talk."

"At the very least tell us who gave you the hickey?" Miranda insisted.

"Okay. I'll tell you." She stopped smiling and cleared her throat. "I ran into my old vacuum cleaner. And we took a trip down memory lane. It was so romantic," Della said, and grinned.

That grin didn't fool Kylie. She saw something in Della's eyes. A glimmer of pain. Della really didn't want to talk about this.

"Was the vacuum cleaner named Steve?" Miranda asked.

Della frowned. "Forget the hickey."

"But that's not fair, we tell each other everything," Miranda said.

"It's okay," Kylie said, enjoying the easy banter and not wanting to lose it just yet. "How about let's talk about me seeing Perry's ass?"

"You said you didn't see his ass," Miranda said.

"Wait. What?" Della asked, and stared at Kylie. "You saw Perry's ass?"

"Just a quick glimpse," Kylie said. "But I think everyone else got a really good long look."

"Of Perry's ass?" Della asked.

Miranda nodded and then told the story about how heroic Perry had been coming to Kylie's aid by dropping his drawers.

Della smiled ear to ear. "I knew I liked that shape-shifter."

"He is sweet, isn't he?" Miranda sighed and got that droopy-eyed look.

"So what's up with you?" Della asked Kylie. "Have you kicked Lucas's ass and decided to forgive him yet? He looks like a puppy who lost his only chew toy."

Kylie frowned. "Let's not talk about that."

Miranda bounced up and down on her butt. "You should have been at dinner. Derek and Lucas both sat with her. I swear, I thought they were going to go to fist city. And then Lucas told Kylie he loved her, right in front of everyone. It was sooo romantic."

Kylie's chest grew heavy. "It wasn't romantic. It was . . . It was sad."

"Sad pretty much describes him when you left," said Miranda. "It was as if someone had reached in and yanked out his joy."

"I don't want to talk about this," Kylie said.

"So you're still mad at him?" Della asked. "I don't blame you."

Kylie cut Della a stern look. "Hey . . . I respected your wishes not to talk about the hickey. Now you should respect mine."

Miranda dropped down on her belly and grunted. "This isn't fair. I tell you guys everything. I don't hold anything back."

"Believe me, I know," Della said. "I know more about you and Perry's relationship than the law allows."

"Don't start on that." Miranda frowned.

"Why don't we go get a Diet Coke?" Kylie offered before the two of them started bickering in full force.

They all bounced off the bed and started for the kitchen. For the time being she wanted to forget all her issues. She just wanted to sit around the kitchen table and laugh some more. Laugh with friends, tell a few jokes, and remember that no matter what issues life dealt them, it would be okay as long as they had each other.

Della got to the kitchen first. "What the hell is that?" she mouthed out.

The moment Kylie saw what rested on the kitchen table she realized that forgetting her issues wasn't going to be that easy.

"Crap," Kylie muttered. "Can someone please call Burnett and Holiday and tell them to get here ASAP!"

Chapter Seventeen

"How did it get here?" Holiday asked, standing a few feet from the kitchen table and staring at the sword in disbelief.

"You tell me and we'll both know." Kylie gripped her hands together with concern. "How . . . how could this happen?"

"How?" Burnett bellowed. "It's obvious. Someone brought it here to play a practical joke on you, but I'm not laughing and neither will they when I'm done with them." Burnett's frown deepened into a scowl. "Removing something from Holiday's office to bring it here for a joke is going to get their ass in a sling." He stared at Kylie. "Who all did you tell about the sword?"

"No one," Kylie said. "I didn't tell anyone. Not a soul. I've been trying really hard not to think about it. So it can't be a prank."

"She's telling the truth," Della mouthed off. "She hasn't told us. And she tells us everything. Or she did." Della shot Kylie a frown.

"She doesn't tell us *everything,*" Miranda piped up. "Just like some people with hickeys don't tell us everything."

Della scowled at Miranda and then looked at Kylie. "Frankly, I'd kind of like to know why we're freaking out here. It's just a sword."

Burnett continued to stare at Kylie as if still contemplating. "Then how do you suppose the sword got here?"

Kylie shrugged. "I don't know, but maybe it got here the same way it got to the falls. Magic, voodoo, or by whoever left it there."

"You found this sword at the falls?" Miranda asked. "Who would leave it there? It looks like an antique and that usually means it's worth a shitload of money."

"I don't know that either," Kylie said to Miranda. "But what I do know is that I really don't like it. So just take the thing away. Nice and safe like. And maybe put it somewhere more secure this time. Like in a vault."

"Wow," said Miranda.

"Wow what?" Burnett asked at the same time Kylie blurted out the words.

Miranda pointed to the sword. "It has an aura."

"The sword has an aura?" Holiday moved beside Miranda, looking intrigued. Kylie took another step back because she wasn't at all intrigued.

"What kind of aura?" Holiday asked the witch.

"Maybe Hayden was right. It's possessed," Burnett said.

"Wait! Can inanimate objects really be possessed?" Kylie folded her arms, not from the cold, but from feeling freaked out.

"No," Della said.

Miranda rolled her eyes at the vamp. "Of course they can."

"Really?" Della asked. "Cool!"

"Not cool!" Kylie snapped.

Miranda stared back at the sword. "It takes a strong witch—or a demon—to possess an object. But I don't think that's what's going on."

"Why not?" asked Holiday.

"You said it had an aura?" Burnett piped up.

"Yeah," Miranda answered, looking proud to be the one with information. "But just because an object has an aura doesn't mean it's possessed. Some things, like weapons and such, will carry an aura because emotion sort of gets soaked up into the physical matter during an attack."

"So this thing has killed a lot of people?" Kylie asked, remembering the ghost's sword and the head she so proudly brought to show Kylie.

"Probably, but I don't think it's possessed. Normally when something is possessed, it's completely evil."

"Then what kind of aura is it?" Kylie asked.

"A little bit evil," Miranda said, contradicting herself.

"Love it." Della rubbed her hands together.

Kylie moaned and focused on Miranda. "But you just said—"

"I said something that is possessed is completely evil." Miranda looked back at the sword. "This is just . . . Okay, it isn't even really evil. But I can feel that it has taken lives. A lot of them. But most of its aura is about justice, and . . ." She tilted her head to the side and focused on the sword like she was trying to read the supernatural pattern. Her hair, streaked with pink, black, and lime-green, curtained the side of her face. "And it sounds crazy but it's also about . . . courage."

"Courage?" Kylie remembered the voice she'd heard on the way to the falls. "What does it mean by courage? Ask it what it means by that?"

Miranda snickered. "Auras don't answer questions. I'm just telling you what the aura seems to exude."

"How do you know what it exudes?" Della asked.

"The colors, the intensity of the colors, and how it moves and blends together. It's sort of like reading a mood ring."

"I wish I could see auras," Della said to Miranda. "Could you like zap me the gift to see auras?"

"No," Miranda said. "No more than you can give me your ability to fly."

Kylie continued to stare at the sword, remembering the sword the ghost carried. "I still think it's somehow tied to the ghost. She could have brought it here."

"Oh, damn! Do we have a ghost here now?" Della asked.

"Not now," Holiday replied to Della, then looked back at Kylie. "Ghosts can't transport objects of real matter."

"Not true. I had one knock my phone off my nightstand," Kylie said.

"Yes, they might be able to create enough energy to nudge something small, and they can play with electronics left and right, but they can't physically move an object from one place to another. That would take an enormous amount of energy. It's impossible."

"Well, that makes me feel somewhat better," Della said.

Holiday moved closer to the table. "This doesn't make sense."

"I know," Kylie said. "And that seems to be the theme song of my life right now. Not a damn thing makes sense."

Burnett carried the sword out. He refused to let Holiday touch it in case it came to life. Right as they went to leave, Kylie heard a light burpy sound from Holiday.

The fae bit down on her lip and her eyes shifted to Kylie. In spite of being weirded out by finding the aura-carrying sword on her table, she sent Holiday a sympathetic smile. She knew the fae was panicking about the possibility of being pregnant.

Not that Kylie saw it as a bad thing. It would be neat to see what a child that was half-Burnett and half-Holiday would look like.

When Holiday and Burnett were out of the cabin, Della and Miranda turned to Kylie. Della spoke first. "Okay . . . sit down and explain why you didn't tell us about the sword, and then tell us what else you've been hiding."

Kylie started to remind Della that she kept her own secrets, like just who had given her the hickey, but all of a sudden Kylie didn't mind telling them. As a matter of fact, it might help if she talked about it. It wasn't as if she'd kept any of it from them on purpose. It was like Kylie had said earlier, she hadn't wanted to think about it.

She moved to the kitchen, glancing around to make sure the

sword hadn't magically reappeared. Seeing the table clear, she dropped down in a chair with a defeated sigh.

Della went to the fridge and snagged three diet sodas and passed them out. The sound of the tops being popped echoed in the small kitchen. Then Kylie started talking. Between sips of fizzy soda slipping down her throat, she told them everything. About what happened at her grandfather's place, to how the teen chameleons were treated. She covered leaving in the middle of the night because someone had plans to abduct her. Then she blurted out the hardest part—Mario showing up and how she'd almost killed Lucas.

"Well, not for nothing," Della said. "Lucas did sort of have it coming. I'll bet it felt good."

"No it didn't," Kylie insisted.

"Wait," Miranda said. "Before we get off talking about the whole boy issue, you haven't gotten to the part about the sword." She took a big sip of Diet Coke and continued to eye Kylie over the rim.

Kylie went into her visit to the falls with Holiday.

"What about this ghost?" Della asked, and looked around. "Are you gonna wig out on us again with those vision things? I mean, the last time you had that whole episode during class and I had to break down the closet door in Miss Cane's room, it really freaked me out. I swear, now every time she sees me, she has to remind me . . . 'You know, I had a key to that door.' But damn, you were screaming bloody murder in there."

"I hope I don't wig out on you again." Kylie frowned. "And I apologize in advance if I do. But I have no control over that. Seriously, if either one of you were trapped in a grave with three dead girls, I'd bet you would go a little crazy, too."

"Oh, hell yeah, I would. I'd be kicking me some dead girls' asses." Della set down her soda a bit hard and the can crunched a little. "I don't know how you handle it. It must suck."

"Yeah," Kylie said, drawing circles in the condensation on her soda can. "Sometimes it sucks to be me."

"Speaking of sucking . . ." Miranda glared at Della. "Do you want to come clean about the hickey?"

Della rolled her eyes. "There's nothing to tell. It happened."

"How much happened?" Miranda asked. "Did you . . . you know?"

"No!" Della snapped. "I didn't 'you know.' We just made out. And afterward, I wished it hadn't happened. And it won't happen again."

"Who did it happen with?" Kylie asked, stepping right into the conversation and possibly pissing Della off. But if she was making out with Steve, then maybe, in spite of what the vamp said, just maybe it would lead to something.

Della frowned. "If I tell you, will you both swear on your lives that you won't say anything? Because if you say something, I'm gonna have to kill you and then I'll feel bad. At least for a little while."

"I swear I'll never tell a soul," Miranda said.

"Me, too." Kylie leaned forward, letting her own issues slide away to concentrate on Della's.

Della backed up in her chair. "It was Steve."

"Yes," Kylie said.

"I knew you liked him." Miranda rubbed her hands together. "Details, we want details."

Della placed both hands on the table and leaned down low, looking up at them with an angry glare and showing a bit of her canines. "I don't give details, remember?"

"Okay, no details," Kylie said. "But explain why it was a mistake. And why it won't happen again. Because I mean, it was obviously good."

"Because . . . I didn't say it was good."

"Oh, please," Miranda said. "You got a hickey, so you must have been into it for it to have gotten that far." Miranda glanced at Kylie for backup. "Right, Kylie?"

Kylie leaned her elbows on the table. "Not being a hickey expert, I wouldn't know for sure, but it would seem that way." She looked at Della. "So you weren't ever into it?"

Della let go of a low growl. "Okay, I might have been into it for a few seconds."

"It takes longer than a few seconds to get a hickey." Miranda wiggled in her chair, obviously loving that Della was finally talking.

"You are so dang pushy!" Della said.

"How long *does* it take to get a hickey?" Kylie asked.

Miranda picked up her diet soda. "A minute, give or take a few seconds, depending how hard the guy is sucking."

"Doesn't it hurt?" Kylie asked, trying to imagine someone sucking on her for that long.

"No," both Miranda and Della said at the same time.

"It kind of feels good." Miranda smiled at Della. "Doesn't it?"

"I guess." Della rolled her eyes as if hating to admit she enjoyed anything, but then the vamp grinned. "Do you want me to introduce you to my vacuum cleaner?"

"Oh, screw the vacuum cleaner," Miranda said. "Kylie should go after Steve. I mean, she's pissed at both Derek and Lucas, and Steve's available because you aren't into him anymore, and he obviously knows how to do hickeys."

Della scowled at Miranda. "I don't think so."

Miranda wiggled her butt in her chair again. "Because you still like him. Because you want him to give you another hickey. Admit it. Just admit it."

"You're obnoxious," Della said.

"Yeah, she is." Kylie arched a brow at Della. "But the witch has a point."

"Well, she can keep her points to herself!" Della picked up her can and crushed it in her hand. And then Della's eyes went wide. "Shit!"

"What?" Kylie asked.

"It's back," Della said in a singsong spooky voice.

"What's back?" Kylie asked, but she was afraid she knew. She turned around and sure as hell, the sword was on the sofa.

• • •

Kylie hadn't wanted to call Burnett and Holiday again, but Della refused to sleep with a possessed sword in the cabin. Miranda, who told Della again it wasn't possessed, wouldn't have minded either way.

Respecting Della's feelings, and completely understanding them, Kylie borrowed Della's phone and called Burnett and Holiday.

Before Holiday and Burnett left with the sword again, he issued an order. "This doesn't go any further. None of you tell a soul, you got that?"

"Why?" Kylie asked, confused why he saw this as some sort of a secret.

"I'm already explaining too much to the FRU. And this just makes them more eager to get you in for testing. This is best kept hushed until we figure it out."

If we figure it out, Kylie thought, but didn't say it.

As Burnett and Holiday started out, Kylie followed them out on the porch. Holiday leaned in and whispered, "We're taking it, but if it's done this twice, I'm not sure it won't just do it again."

"I know." Which was Kylie's reason for not really wanting to call them this time. Hopefully if the sword found its way back, it would follow Kylie into her bedroom and not disturb Della. Even with the chill climbing up her backbone at the thought of sleeping in the same room with an aura-carrying sword, it was better than having Della in a frenzy and making Burnett and Holiday come back again.

Kylie just hoped that Miranda was right and that the sword wasn't a weapon intent on evil.

Chapter Eighteen

"Okay, first on the agenda . . ." Chris, the lead vampire, said the next morning as he prepared to announce partners at Meet Your Campmate hour—which was an hour that students were paired with someone else from the camp just to encourage interspecies harmony. Chris held his top hat in front of him as if to add drama to the moment.

Kylie stood centered between Della and Miranda, and arm-locked to Miranda's side was Perry. Miranda had spotted Nikki, the shapeshifter who was crushing on Perry, waving at him earlier, and the witch hadn't let go of Perry since.

Kylie had also spotted Miranda's pinky twitching. If Nikki knew what was good for her, she'd give up on Perry. Kylie didn't believe Miranda would do something really terrible, other than pimples of course, but considering that Socks spent months as a skunk, any spell from Miranda could wind up accidentally terrible.

Kylie looked around, searching. Not for any one person—but for a certain sword. It hadn't shown up last night. Which was a relief. Maybe it was just a fluke. She didn't really believe in flukes, but she wanted to.

"Okay," Chris said. "Let's see who goes first." To paraphrase Chris, "let see who paid in blood to spend an hour with someone." At one time, Kylie considered the whole thing outlandish, but now she understood it was just a way to supply food, their main nutrition, to the vampires. They needed blood and this was just one way to get people to donate a pint.

It was still embarrassing to be the person someone paid blood to spend an hour with.

And damn if Chris's gaze didn't collide right into Kylie.

Not again.

Oh, just freaking great. Who was it this time? She glanced around to see if she could find Derek or Lucas. They both stood on opposite sides of the crowd, each staring at the other with accusation. Okay . . . so if it wasn't those two, who?

"I'd be careful, Kylie," Chris said. "I'm beginning to think Fredericka has a thing for you."

Kylie happened to be focused on Lucas when Chris made his announcement. Shock tightened the were's face, followed by a fierce look of protection. His eyes shot across the crowd apparently looking for Fredericka. When his gaze lit on her on the other side of the circle, his scowl deepened.

The girl frowned back and started walking toward Kylie. Walking with a sense of purpose.

Kylie heard Lucas's growl and watched him stomp over with an equal amount of purpose.

Great. Now she had two pissed-off weres coming at her.

"You want me to do something about this?" Della asked.

"No," Kylie said.

"You want me to moon everyone again?" Perry asked.

"No," Kylie said, and just to be safe, she moved several feet away from her friends so no one would be tempted to start a fight or pull down their pants.

The two weres arrived at the same time. One on Kylie's left, the other on her right.

"You don't have to do this," Lucas seethed, obviously talking to Kylie. "I'll pay for her blood. But you don't have to go with me, either."

Kylie looked from Lucas to Fredericka.

Hurt flashed in the female were's eyes. "If Kylie doesn't want to go, she doesn't have to. And I'll still pay for the blood. I don't need you covering for me."

"It's okay," Kylie mumbled, feeling the eager gazes of everyone standing around. A light tingling ran up her legs and pulsated in her knees. Her heart lurched when she recognized this as the beginning stages of vanishing. She focused really hard to stop it. The last thing she wanted to do was vanish right before all the other campers and become even more of a freak than she already was.

Lucas snarled at Fredericka, "If you lay a finger on her, I'll get your wolf ass tossed out of the pack. I'm done making excuses for you."

Kylie's emotions ping-ponged all over the place. She felt sorry for Fredericka having to face Lucas's wrath. Sorry that Fredericka had to face the knowledge that Lucas's loyalty lay with Kylie and not her—one of his own kind. Having to face that in public had to be hard on her werewolf soul. Harder still because she loved Lucas.

But empathy for Fredericka wasn't all Kylie felt. She felt . . . shocked. This was the first time that he'd chosen her over one of his own kind.

Oh, he'd told her a thousand times, but his actions had never proven it. Not until now. The realization was so damn bittersweet. She didn't want to feel cherished by him after he'd betrayed her. She didn't want to feel guilty that he was hurting.

But she did.

Guilt, that ugly emotion, swelled inside her and made her chest feel heavy. But why? Was it someone's fault when she couldn't forgive someone else for a wrong they'd committed?

He looked at her again, his pain visible in his dark blue eyes, and then he took off—leaving her in a cloud of hurt and the awareness that, once again, all the Shadow Falls students were privy to her private life.

Fredericka watched him shoot off and then faced her. Kylie saw the blinders go down on the girl's emotions as she tried to hide her own hurt. She swallowed as if trying to get a painful lump to go down, then she lowered her head and spoke. "I told him I'd made my peace with you but he didn't believe me."

Kylie nodded, and sensing Fredericka was as uncomfortable being the entertainment as she was, then started walking. Fredericka followed.

When they were out of earshot, Fredericka said, "Where do you want to go?"

"I don't care," Kylie said.

Kylie heard wings flapping above them and remembered Perry was shadowing her. "We're gonna have company," Kylie said. "My shadow." She pointed up.

"Yeah, I figured that," Fredericka said. "Do you think he can hear us from up there?"

"Beats me," Kylie said. "I don't know how good a prehistoric bird's hearing is."

"Then let's just pretend he can't hear," Fredericka said.

"Okay." And the burning question rose in her chest. "Does Lucas know you were the one to tell me?"

"Yeah, he knows." Fredericka hesitated. "He thinks I told you to break you two up."

Kylie remembered Fredericka denying it once before, but . . . "Did you?"

Hurt flashed in her eyes. "You don't believe me either?" She walked a few steps without speaking. "I'm not stupid. I knew if I stopped him from going through with Monique he'd turn to you for good."

"But you also admitted you love him, and you've tried to break us up before."

"It finally got through my head how pathetic I was. He doesn't love me. He loves you. Always has and always will. It was a bitter pill, but I swallowed it."

Kylie inhaled and realized she believed the girl. "Okay, so why did you pay blood to see me again?"

"For two reasons," the were said.

"And they are?" Kylie asked.

"I hear you're good at . . . giving people relationship advice."

Kylie's mouth dropped open. "You want advice on how to win Lucas back?"

Fredericka make a funny face. "No! I told you, I swallowed that pill already."

Kylie remembered what Miranda had told her. "Please tell me it's not the new teacher, Mr. Cannon."

Fredericka looked shocked. "How did you know about me and Cary?"

Cary? So they're on a first-name basis? "Rumor has it you're hot on him."

The were frowned. "I didn't think I was that . . . obvious."

"Well, you thought wrong. And let me tell you, it's not a good idea. He's your teacher."

"He's twenty. He's like some super-smart kid that finished college when he was nineteen. And I'll be eighteen next month. We're barely two years apart."

Kylie could hear Perry's wings flapping in the breeze. She cut her eyes up, and for Fredericka's sake, she hoped he wasn't listening. "Fine, it's not the age thing. It's the teacher thing."

"I don't see why that matters," Fredericka said.

Kylie let out a deep gulp of air. "It matters if he wants to keep his balls. Burnett already threatened to send Hayden Yates away minus his when—"

"You and Mr. Yates had a fling?" Fredericka's eyes widened. "I thought you loved—"

"No! Burnett thought we were."

"Why would he think that?" Fredericka made another face.

Kylie realized she shouldn't have mentioned this. "It's a long story. The point is that Burnett will be overly pissed if this new teacher gives you even a second glance."

"Why don't you let me worry about Burnett and Cary's boys and you just tell me how to . . . to make it happen for us the way you did for the others."

Kylie sighed. "Why does everyone keep saying that I'm good at offering relationship advice? Can't you see what a disaster my own relationships are? If I was good at that, do you think I'd be in the mess I'm in right now?"

Fredericka shrugged. "But everyone who went to you with problems says you fixed things. Perry and that little witch friend of yours. Helen and Jonathon. Burnett and Holiday."

"How do you know they wouldn't have worked things out on their own?"

Fredericka frowned. "They all sing your praises."

Kylie shook her head. "Look, I don't think you and the teacher is a good idea."

"So you won't help me?" Fredericka said. "Even after I set you straight on Lucas and saved him from having to spend his life with someone he doesn't love?"

Kylie exhaled. "Okay, here's my advice. Go talk to Holiday, tell her about your feelings and—"

"She'll say hell no. She doesn't even like me."

"Oh yes, she does. With all the trouble you've caused, she'd have kicked your ass out a long time ago if she didn't. And if you're worried about her completely disagreeing, why don't you start by telling her you have a thing for someone who's only two years older and see what she says before you tell her who it is. Get her to say it's not such a bad thing and then drop the bomb about him being a teacher."

"You really think she'll listen to me?"

"Listen, yes. Whether or not she'll tell you not to do it is another matter. But she's the fairest person I know."

"Okay." Fredericka seemed to be thinking. "Now what about Cary? How do I get him to . . . ?"

"Notice you?"

"Not notice. He's already noticed me. I know he's attracted to me, he's just putting up roadblocks, probably for the same reason you said. He's a teacher and I'm his student."

"Then why don't you go to him and tell him that you understand that this is hard, but you really like him, and would at least like to be friends until—"

"I don't want to be just friends."

"Fine, but you start by being friends, and when you get the green light from Holiday, then you two can . . . go run off in the woods and do the wild thing, or do whatever you want to do. You're not going to be in school but for nine more months. So the worst-case scenario, you two build a friendship, then take it to the next level when school's out."

She started nodding as if she agreed with Kylie. "Hell, I've waited for two years for Lucas, I could easily wait for nine months for Cary—if I had to." She smiled. "See, you *are* good at this. Thank you," Fredericka said with sincerity.

"Good, are we finished? I think Perry's getting impatient."

"No, there's the other thing."

"What thing?" Kylie asked.

"The thing about you needing to forgive Lucas."

"Look, you asked for my advice, I didn't ask for yours." She started moving faster down the path that led to her cabin. A nice, quick run.

Fredericka matched her pace, footfall for footfall. "He loves you. Don't you get why he walked away from getting engaged? He gave up so much for you. Maybe even his own pack."

Kylie came to an abrupt stop and faced the she-wolf. "Why did you tell me? Why didn't you just let him go through with it? Damn it! He shouldn't have done it!" And right then Kylie accepted that this was part of her angst over Lucas. She hadn't wanted to admit it. She hadn't even allowed herself to really let it soak in. But it was there, the truth right under all the betrayal she felt. Lucas had lost everything for her. His dreams. His quests. Even if she did forgive him, sooner or later, he was going to hate her for this.

"Why?" Fredericka threw the question back at her. "Because, you fool, if he'd gone through with it, he'd have lost you. And whether you believe it or not, you are more important to him than getting on the Council. It's you that matters most to him."

Kylie walked in a bit late to her first period class with Perry right behind her. She plopped down in the empty seat right in front of Della. Sitting her book on the desktop, she opened it and pretended to read.

She felt Lucas's eyes on her. She ignored him. Or tried to. Her heart started breaking all over again the second she felt his gaze fall on her.

She had a lot of thinking to do. But damn, she was still so confused.

Still so damn mad at him.

Still so much in love with him that she could hardly breathe.

"Miss Galen, it's so good to have you back with us," Miss Cane said.

Miss Galen? Kylie glanced up, but didn't speak. A nod of appreciation was all the lady was going to get. She hoped she'd be happy with it. Refocusing on the page in her English book, she didn't want to look anyone in the eye. Like Derek, who sat three seats away from her and was studying her with a shitload of worry because he could read her emotional state.

Then she felt Della lean in behind her.

"What's wrong?" the vampire whispered. "Do I need to bite some she-wolf's ass after class?"

"No."

"Your face is all splotchy. And that means you've been crying. What's up?"

"Allergies," Kylie muttered, and wished she'd skipped class. Was it too late? Too late to just get up and walk out?

"You'd think you'd know better than to try to lie to me," Della whispered.

Kylie clenched her jaw and whispered back, "And you'd think you'd stop asking questions that would put me in a position to have to lie!"

"Okay," Della said. "We'll just chalk this conversation up to Miss Galen being in a pissy mood."

Chapter Nineteen

Kylie's day hadn't gotten much better. But it hadn't gotten much worse either. She found herself finding things to be thankful for. Nana used to say whenever you start feeling like the world is taking a bite out of you, bite back by counting your blessings.

And number one on Kylie's blessing list was being back at Shadow Falls. Even with all the issues, she belonged here. Every hour or so, she'd recall how it had felt to be at her grandfather's place. And while she missed the man, and even her great-aunt, she didn't miss the cumbersome feeling that being there brought—the feeling of being in the wrong place.

Number two on that list was that the sword hadn't decided to magically appear again. Of course, it could be waiting for her back at her cabin right now, but she was thankful she didn't have to explain it to anyone for the moment. And last, but not least, on her list was that Mario seemed to have crept back under some dirty, slimy rock again.

At least Kylie didn't feel him, and Miranda agreed that she didn't sense any strangers lingering around. A part of Kylie wanted to believe he'd just stay there, but part of her still wanted to believe in Santa Claus, too.

Mario would be back. The question was, would she be ready? For the life of her, she didn't have a clue how one prepared to take on someone that powerful, that evil.

Waiting for the last bell to ring and school to be over so she could leave history, she looked up at Mr. Cary Cannon. He pointed to the written assignment on the board. His starched, white shirt stretched across his broad chest.

Giving Fredericka credit, the teacher wasn't hard on the eyes. If he would lose the tie and dress pants, and put on a T-shirt and pair of jeans, he could look like a student instead of a teacher. Tall, dark, with black eyes, he carried himself well. And taught even better. He obviously had a passion for history, because it came across in his lessons. For a werewolf, he was amazingly friendly. Probably something he'd learned in school.

Kylie had even seen the guy cut his eyes to Fredericka at least a dozen times. That told Kylie that the infatuation wasn't one-sided. She hoped so, for Fredericka's sake at least.

Three minutes later, school over, Kylie stepped out of class. Della, her official shadow, walked beside her. Kylie hadn't gotten a foot out the door when someone grabbed her around the forearm. She almost yelped, but the warmth of the touch told her it was Holiday before she looked back.

"Hey . . ." Holiday glanced at Della. "I need to borrow Kylie."

"Okay. Are you going to deliver her back to the cabin later? Or do I need to meet you somewhere?"

"I'll walk her back to the cabin."

Della looked a little concerned at having her shadowing duties yanked away.

And she wasn't the only one. "What's wrong?" Kylie asked as soon as Della was out of hearing range.

"Nothing's, *hiccup* . . . wrong. Except that—" She pointed to her mouth. "Actually, I have a few things to discuss with you, but first things first." She let go of a deep sigh, as if to impart bad news. "I kind of told a roundabout untruth to Burnett. And I kind of need you to back me up."

"You want me to lie to a vampire?" Kylie asked. "Wow, you don't ask very much, do you?"

"No, not lie." Holiday reached back for her hair and twisted it in a knot. "He's not going to ask you anything. I just need you to follow through with something."

"I don't understand."

"Okay, here's what happened. I told Burnett I needed to run to the drugstore and he told me he'd just pick up whatever I needed.

"So I went into this song and dance about how I'd told you that you weren't a prisoner here and I thought you might like to get out. I said you hadn't actually told me this, but I had a feeling you needed something from the drugstore, some tampons or something."

Kylie gasped. "You told Burnett I needed tampons?"

"No, I told him that you hadn't said it, but I had a feeling you might need them. And thankfully it wasn't a lie because Miranda told me while you were away that she had to borrow some of yours."

"Okay . . . ," Kylie said, still not understanding what was really going on. "So . . ."

"So I need you to come with Burnett and me, and when you go to buy the tampons, I need you to also . . . *hiccup* . . . buy me a pregnancy test."

"Oh, I get it. But what if he asks . . . Wait. He won't ask what I bought because he thinks I bought tampons, and guys can't stand any talk of tampons."

"See, I knew you'd get it," Holiday said.

"That's clever," Kylie said.

"You have to be smart to deal with a vampire."

They started walking. "But wait." Kylie stopped. "What kind of test do I buy?"

"I don't know, I've never bought one . . . *hiccup* . . . but buy two of them. Different kinds. Something that looks accurate. I'll have Burnett with me helping pick out something for my hiccups."

Kylie tried to think. "How does an accurate pregnancy test look any different from one that's not accurate?"

"Just buy two, but not the cheap ones." Holiday sighed as they made their way down the path back to the office.

"Here." Holiday handed her a couple of bills and Kylie stuffed them in her pocket with her small wallet. "Now that's taken care of, let me tell you the other stuff."

Oh, yeah, the other stuff. "What is it?" Kylie asked, suddenly concerned.

"Your dad called. You need to call him."

"Okay," Kylie said. "Can I use your phone?"

"Yeah." She reached in her pocket and handed Kylie her phone. "And the next thing—"

"There's more?" Kylie asked.

"Yeah. Tomorrow you're getting visitors. If you want them."

"Visitors? Who?" Kylie stuck the phone in her pocket.

"The Brightens. Your real dad's adoptive parents. They are back from Ireland and got all the messages. They're eager to meet you."

Chills ran down Kylie's arms. "I'd almost given up on meeting them."

"Well, they will be here tomorrow, at two, if you agree to it."

Kylie swallowed. "Yeah, of course I want to meet them." And just like that, Kylie started missing her dad again. More than that, she could swear she felt a touch of cold. Cold that reminded her of him. And oh boy, could she ever use a visit from him now.

When they arrived at the office, Hayden and Burnett were standing by the coffee machine—not talking. The awkward silence told Kylie that they'd recently halted the conversation when they heard them coming. Meaning they were keeping secrets.

Which frustrated the fire out of her, because after all, this was about her, wasn't it? She almost called them on it, too, but realized an argument might delay the trip into town. And Holiday needed her. So Kylie buried her frustration, vowing it would be unearthed, resuscitated, and dealt with full-force later on.

Holiday cut a glance to Kylie as if she'd read the emotional marathon happening inside her. After a few nods of uncomfortable greetings, Holiday glanced at Burnett. "You ready?"

On the ride to town, Holiday drove and hiccuped the whole way. Burnett fretted over her hiccups and kept a keen lookout as if he was worried Mario would drop in.

"We should call the doctor," Burnett said when Holiday let out another one.

"I'll just pick up some antacid or something," Holiday said.

When they entered the pharmacy, Kylie started to the feminine product aisle. Burnett started after her, but when he saw her walk up to the tampon rack, he turned around.

Kylie saw Holiday pull him with her to a different aisle.

Taking a deep sigh, Kylie went to look for the pregnancy tests. Feeling rushed, she scanned the different packages but was at a loss. There were numerous kinds, each offering a different promise. Realizing she didn't have time to read them all, she grabbed two and then just to be sure she got the right one, she grabbed another. Checking to make sure no one was looking, she bolted to the pharmacy counter to pay for them. It wasn't until she saw the older man standing there that Kylie realized how hard this was going to be.

The man, an elderly preacher-looking type, was going to think that the tests were for her. Oh, just great. She swallowed a big lump of embarrassment down her throat. Then, thinking of Holiday, she put the three boxes on the counter.

The man eyed her purchase, then looked up. Kylie could see the judgment in his old gray eyes as a frown marred his face. Lovely! She was getting judged for being pregnant and she was still a virgin.

"Do you know how to use these?" he asked in a very condescending voice.

Kylie felt her face flush red. "I . . . will read the instructions."

"Would you like my assistant Angela to speak with you about . . . anything?"

Like safe sex, Kylie bet he was thinking. "No," she blurted out. When the man just kept staring at her, she added, "Thank you."

He rang up the items slowly. Kylie's heart beat to a nice, steady rhythm of embarrassment. She opened her mouth to say: "These are for a friend." But what was the chance of him believing that?

"That will be forty-two and ninety-six."

Kylie went for the bills Holiday gave her. "Shit," Kylie mumbled when she saw she didn't have enough.

"Excuse me?" the little old man said, now not only offended that she was pregnant but because of her language.

And he should be offended—by the language. She knew better than to curse in public. But face it, the man's opinion of her was already in the pits, what was one little word going to matter? But still, she offered, "Sorry."

"Do you want to buy these or not?"

She nodded. "Yes, it's just . . . I don't think I need three. Just two."

Frowning, he looked down at the boxes. "Which one would you like to return?"

She took a deep breath, realizing somewhere along the line she'd stopped doing that.

Then, remembering her mom's credit card—to use only in case of emergencies—she pulled out Holiday's phone and then the little wallet. "Never mind, I'll take them all."

Tossing the card on the counter, she bit down on her lip. She wasn't sure this was the kind of emergency her mom was referring to, but getting away from this man's judging eyes seemed pretty important.

He studied the card carefully.

Friggin' great. Now he was suspecting her of credit card fraud.

"It's good!" Kylie said. "I swear."

He didn't look convinced. "Can I see an ID?"

She heard Burnett and Holiday somewhere a few aisles behind her. Biting her lip, she opened her wallet and let him see her driver's license. She had never seen anyone take so much time reading a license.

Fear that she was going to let Holiday down had her stomach clenching. "I'm kind of in a hurry," Kylie said.

Finally, he dropped her license and finished the transaction. She heard someone shift behind her, and her heart tightened. She glanced down to see shoes, praying they weren't going to be Burnett's tennis shoes.

It wasn't Burnett. A pair of dress shoes, the kind businesspeople wore, adorned the feet of the man standing behind her. Thank God.

The cashier pushed a receipt over to her. "Would you mind some informational pamphlets?" he asked.

"Fine." Kylie signed the receipt then watched him drop sex pamphlets in her bag with the pregnancy tests.

Little did he know, those pamphlets were outdated. She'd read those over a year ago.

When at last he handed her the bag, Kylie swung around to leave, but came to an abrupt stop when she saw the face of the man standing behind her.

"Oh, shit," Kylie said again.

Chapter Twenty

Holy hell! Of all the people in the world to have witnessed her buy three pregnancy tests, this was the absolute worst.

"They are for a friend," Kylie blurted out.

"What?" her grandfather asked, and his brow wrinkled with concern when he looked at her little white sack. Okay, so he obviously hadn't seen her purchases. But now he probably thought she was buying condoms or something. And with this size sack, she was stockpiling them, too.

All of a sudden, Kylie realized a concern bigger than her grandfather thinking she'd bought a bag of rubbers. If Burnett spotted her grandfather, there would be hell to pay.

"What are you doing here?" Kylie's nervous gaze zipped around praying she wouldn't spot Holiday or Burnett. She didn't.

"I wanted to bring you this." He pulled her the phone out of his shirt pocket. "And to make sure you believed that I wasn't behind the ploy to keep you from leaving. I gave my word to Burnett. I don't do that lightly. I will go now."

Kylie couldn't help it, she moved in for a hug and she clung to him a fraction of a second longer than she should.

For when she pulled back, she saw Burnett barreling down the aisle toward her.

Thankfully, her grandfather vanished.

"What the hell?" the cashier said behind her.

"This is why you wanted to come here!" Burnett bit out.

"Is there a problem?" the cashier asked, and then added, "Did you see . . ."

"It's fine," Kylie said, and waved at the cashier.

"I wouldn't say it's fine," Burnett said. "I'm tired of these lies!"

"Should I call the police?" the cashier asked.

"No," both Burnett and Kylie said at the same time.

Burnett took her by the arm and started leading her out.

"Are you okay, young lady?" the cashier called out.

"I'm fine." Kylie looked back. "He's my friend." Never mind he wasn't acting like it.

"What happened?" Holiday came running up.

"Let's get out of here first," he seethed, and glanced at Kylie, eyes bright with anger.

He led them to Holiday's car parked right out front.

"What happened?" Holiday looked at Kylie because obviously she knew Burnett was being unreasonable.

She clicked open the car locks a fraction of a second before Burnett yanked open the back door. The angry vamp motioned for Kylie to get inside.

Kylie hesitated, not sure what to say. She knew Burnett was furious about her grandfather showing up, but that wasn't her fault.

She held her shoulder back. "If you will let me explain . . ."

"Get in the car!" he demanded.

Now angry at him for being so damn unreasonable, she flung herself in the backseat. Burnett reached in and snatched the bag from her hands. And then slammed the car door shut.

Oh, hell! This was not going to go well.

Kylie peered out the window. Burnett shot around to the driver's side of the car and motioned for Holiday to get in the passenger side.

As soon as Holiday got in, she flipped around to look at Kylie with questions in her eyes.

"My grandfather was there," Kylie said.

"She lied to you!" Burnett snapped out. "She didn't need any damn tampons! This was a ploy to see her grandfather!" He shook the sack at her.

"It was not a ploy!" Kylie leaned up and gripped the back of the passenger's seat.

"She didn't lie!" Holiday pressed a hand to Burnett's arm. No doubt to calm the man.

All Kylie could think was she needed a touch, too. Because right now all the anger at the vampire for keeping secrets from her rose back up and was accompanied by her anger at being falsely accused. "I did not know he was going to be here!" she said, her voice an octave too high.

"She couldn't have known he was going to be here," Holiday said.

The fierceness in Burnett's expression lessened, but not enough to make Kylie happy.

He stared at Holiday. "She asked to come here and you expect me to believe it's a coincidence that he just shows up?"

"I didn't tell him I was coming here." Kylie bounced back on the seat and folded her hands over her chest and the whole incident reminded her of being in the car when she was a kid and angry with her parents.

"Wait," Holiday said. "Did you tell Hayden where we were going?"

The frown line between Burnett's eyes deepened. "You think he told—"

"You shouldn't even be upset!" Kylie snapped. "All my grandfather wanted to do was give me my phone and tell me he wasn't behind the ploy to kidnap me. And you get all vampire pissy on me!"

"I went pissy on you because you already lied to me several times!" Burnett shook the bag for emphasis. Shook it hard.

Kylie held her breath, fearing the worst. Then the worst happened.

It almost looked like slow motion. The bag ripped and three pregnancy tests along with a pamphlet on safe sex and one on gonorrhea landed on the front seat with Holiday and Burnett.

Burnett looked down, gasped, and then looked up at Kylie. "For God's sake!" he muttered.

"Wait!" Holiday spoke up, and then she burped. Really loud.

Burnett ignored Holiday and stared at Kylie. "If you are old enough to have sex, you are old enough to know about using protection!"

Kylie opened her mouth to speak, but she didn't have a clue what she was going to say. Then it just spilled out. "I know all about condoms."

He scowled tighter. "Then why the hell are you in this mess!"

"Wait, Burnett," Holiday said. "You don't understand. Kylie's not in the mess."

Burnett was too focused on giving Kylie hell to listen to Holiday's confession.

"Actually, condoms are only eighty-five percent effective at preventing pregnancy," Kylie said, still seething.

"If you use them right, they work! I spoke with Lucas about this very thing a couple of weeks ago. I damned well told him he'd better be careful."

"Burnett," Holiday scolded.

Oh, but Kylie wished she'd just shut up and let the vampire bury himself a little deeper. And right then she decided to hand him a shovel. "I didn't buy them for me," Kylie said. "I bought them for a friend."

"You're not . . . pregnant?"

"Not unless these pamphlets lie and you can get pregnant by sitting on a toilet. I told you, they are for a friend."

Burnett's eyes rounded. "Miranda? Shit! I had the same God damned talk with Perry."

"Sometimes this just happens," Kylie said, much calmer now that she had a sneak preview of his comeuppance.

"Just happens?" Burnett bellowed out. "Are you freaking kidding me! If you have sex, you use protection. It's that simple. This shit doesn't have to happen! This is nothing but carelessness. It's irresponsible. It's unforgivable."

"Burnett!" Holiday rolled her eyes at Kylie and frowned. The fae knew exactly what Kylie was up to now.

But Kylie wasn't finished yet. "Maybe we should put a rule in place. Any male who impregnates a girl should be neutered."

"Enough," Holiday snapped.

"Actually, that's not a bad plan!" he growled.

"Burnett!" Holiday said in a stern voice. "Shut up before you embarrass yourself more than you already have." When the vampire looked at Holiday, she continued, "Kylie didn't buy the pregnancy tests for Miranda. She bought them for me."

Kylie flopped back against the seat again, enjoying the look of disbelief on the vampire's face a little too much. "Would you like a name of a good doctor who will schedule your little snip-snip operation?" she bit out.

Chapter Twenty-one

The thing about sweet revenge was it was never as sweet in hindsight. Burnett was . . . stunned. He turned around and started the car. He drove back to Shadow Falls without saying one word. Holiday sat there hiccuping and looking as if she might cry. Obviously, Burnett's reaction wasn't exactly what Holiday had been hoping for.

Or maybe, Kylie realized, it was exactly what the fae had feared. She recalled Holiday telling her that Burnett wasn't sure he wanted to be a father. Kylie suddenly wanted to apologize for her part in announcing the fact so . . . hurtfully, but the moment didn't feel right.

After parking the car, Burnett saw Perry as they walked through the gate, and called him over and asked him to see Kylie to her cabin.

"What up?" Perry asked, studying Kylie and then looking back at Burnett walking away. "I've never seen him looking so . . . stunned. It's as if the lights are on but nobody's home."

"Nothing," Kylie said, and she wanted to cry, to smack herself for being so thoughtless.

As soon as Kylie got back to her cabin, she headed straight to her bedroom.

But Della shot across the room and blocked the door. "What's wrong?" Della asked. "First you come to class crying, then Holiday shows up acting all weird, and now you come in looking like a kicked puppy. And don't tell me it's none of my business, I'm your friend, that gives me all the rights in the world to butt into your personal life."

Kylie gave Della a hug. "I love you."

"Okay . . . I . . . I wasn't trying to get all mushy?" Della said, and pulled back.

"I know, but you were," Kylie said. "Unfortunately, I can't . . . talk about any of this right now. I need to make a few phone calls." She motioned for Della to step away from the door. She did, but be-grudgingly.

Kylie's first phone call was to warn Hayden that Burnett might possibly arrive and be on the warpath.

"Why? What the hell did I do this time?" Hayden asked.

"My grandfather showed up at the drugstore. I'm assuming you told him where I was."

"Oh, damn it! I did mention it, but . . . I never thought he'd go there. I guess I'll start packing my bags," he muttered.

"No," Kylie said. "Please. Just explain that you didn't know he was coming. Just . . . placate Burnett. Say anything. But . . . don't leave. I need you here. And . . . don't be too hard on him. He . . . he's having a hard day."

"What happened?" Hayden asked.

"He had to put up with me," Kylie said.

"Oh, that would be rough," Hayden said teasingly, but Kylie wasn't in a humorous mood.

Off the phone with him, Kylie called her stepdad. She talked to him a good five minutes, assuring him she was okay, and that she'd lost her phone, but now she found it and was sorry she missed his calls.

She could tell from his voice that he was upset to learn that her mom was in London. Or maybe it wasn't just his voice telling her this, but his words. "God damn, she should have told me she was leaving the country!"

"I'm sure she just forgot," Kylie lied, unsure of anything else she could say.

Hanging up with him, Kylie suddenly felt her left pocket vibrate. Oh, crap. She'd completely forgotten she still had Holiday's phone.

Pulling her phone out, she saw Burnett had sent Holiday a text. Her gut said that Holiday needed to read it. She ran out of the room and hollered at Della. "Let's go."

Knowing Della would catch up, Kylie lit out the door. In a matter of seconds, Della was moving beside her.

"Where are we going?"

"To the office. I need to see Holiday."

"And you're still not going to tell me what's going on."

"Sorry." Kylie picked up her pace.

She asked Della to wait outside. The vamp rolled her eyes, but did it. When Kylie walked into the office, Holiday's door was shut. She knocked.

"Who is it?" Holiday asked, and Kylie sensed the fae was hoping it was Burnett.

"It's me." Kylie opened the door.

Holiday stood behind her desk. She sighed. Her eyes were a watery mess. The fae didn't cry much prettier than Kylie. "I'm so sorry." Guilt caused a knot in Kylie's throat.

"It's not your fault."

"Yes, it is. He shouldn't have heard the news like that. I was just so . . ."

"Mad," Holiday finished for her. "And you had a right to be. He completely jumped to conclusions. He has a really bad habit of doing that." Her voice shook.

Kylie saw the pregnancy test boxes in the garbage. "Did you take them?"

She nodded.

"And?"

She nodded again. "All three say yes. What's the chance of them being wrong?"

"Does Burnett know?" Kylie asked.

She shook her head. "He didn't even come into the office. Didn't say one word to me. He got in his car and left."

"Wait. He did say something." Kylie pulled Holiday's phone out of her pocket. "You got a text from him. That's why I came here. I thought it might be important."

Holiday took the phone and hit a few buttons almost in a panic. Tears filled her eyes and she put a hand over her trembling lips.

"Is that a good or bad reaction?" Kylie asked.

Holiday looked up, tears in her eyes but with a smile. "He writes: 'I'm at the florist, trying to figure out which flower says I'm an idiot and please forgive me.'" She inhaled. "He is an idiot!" She hiccuped.

"But I'm *your* idiot!" Burnett said from the doorway.

Kylie looked back and saw Burnett walk in carrying the biggest, and the oddest-looking, bouquet of flowers she'd ever seen. Holiday dropped into her desk chair. A few tears rolled down her cheeks.

He moved past Kylie and set the flowers on Holiday's desk, pretty much taking up the entire desk, too. "You didn't get back to me with the kind of flower, so I got one of everything they had."

Burnett's eyes cut to the garbage, where he obviously spotted the pregnancy test packages. He looked up at Holiday. "Are we pregnant?"

She nodded and wiped her cheeks.

"Forgive me," he said with pure emotion in his voice. "I'm just scared. I didn't have a father and most of my foster parents weren't what you would call good examples. But then I realized that you are going to be such a great mom, that it won't matter if I suck at parenthood a little bit."

"You're not going to suck at it." Holiday hiccuped.

"But if I do, you'll straighten me out, right?"

She nodded. "You bet your cold feet I will."

Kylie grinned and started to back out. She almost got to the door when Burnett turned. "I owe you an apology, too."

Kylie nodded. "And I owe you one."

Burnett smiled. "Accepted."

"But no more secrets," Kylie said. "Even between you and Hayden. If it involves me, I want to know."

He sighed. "Deal. Now that we got most everything cleared up, can you leave so I can kiss the mother of my child and not worry about offending virgin eyes?"

"Make it a good one." Kylie smiled and started out.

"Kylie?" Holiday said.

Kylie turned back. "The Brightens called while we were away. They're still planning on coming tomorrow. I just wanted to remind you."

Kylie nodded and walked out, trying to figure out how she was going to approach the Brightens.

She hadn't gotten one step on the porch when Della ran up to her and squealed. "Holiday's pregnant?"

Kylie covered the vamp's mouth with her palm and frowned. "You weren't supposed to be listening in."

"I didn't mean to," Della huffed out behind Kylie's fingers. "Burnett's voice just carries."

"Right." Kylie cut her eyes at Della in disbelief.

Della squealed again. "This is so cool."

Kylie, pushing aside her worry about the Brightens, suddenly felt like squealing, too. "What's cool?" Miranda asked, walking up.

Della looked at Kylie. "We have to tell Miranda. Just Miranda."

"Yeah, you have to!" Miranda squealed. "I don't know what it is, but I want to know."

Kylie gasped. "Okay, but you can't tell anyone."

"Won't tell a soul," Miranda said. "What is it?" She rubbed her hands together, excited to know a secret.

Della moved them away from the office, and under a patch of trees beside the trail. "Guess who's pregnant?" Della whispered.

Miranda gawked at Kylie. "But you said you'd never done it."

"Not me!" Kylie said. "Holiday."

Miranda's mouth dropped open. "Oh my! We're gonna have a baby Burnett running around? That is cool." She grinned ear to ear.

"I know." Kylie suddenly couldn't stop smiling.

Or she couldn't until someone dropped a severed head from the tree above her and it landed on her foot. Kylie screamed and kicked the head, which rolled a good six feet away. She screamed again when she saw the eyes wobbling and looking up at her.

The next morning, Kylie got up and went and sat in front of the computer to check her e-mail before heading off to breakfast with Della and Miranda. She sat there and stared at the black computer screen in a daze. There hadn't been any dreams, no more severed heads falling from trees, and no visiting swords. She still hadn't slept worth a damn. What kept her up were all her other issues. Most of them matters of the heart.

She'd stayed awake a while thinking about meeting Daniel's adoptive parents today, wondering what she should say, or not say. She'd connected with her real grandfather, but he wasn't a parent who'd raised her father. He hadn't taught him to ride a bike, or play baseball. He didn't really know his own son, but these people did. What would they tell her about her father? Had they loved him, missed him since he'd been taken from this life too soon?

That made her start missing her dad. So she pulled out his pictures and spent a good hour just looking at them, talking to him. Yeah, she talked to him as if he were there listening to every word she said. She told him about her quests. How she wanted to find a way to help all the other chameleon teens. Now all she had to do was figure out how to do it. She told him about Mario, how she felt deep down that she was going to have to deal with him. Personally.

She confessed to her dad how much that truly scared her. Scared because of the evilness that emanated from the man, and how she didn't think she had what it would take to face him and win.

A couple of times during the conversation she could swear she felt her dad, a slight familiar type of chill—one that actually warmed her on the inside. One that whispered that she wouldn't be alone—not facing Mario, or the visit with his parents. Then she heard the words he'd told her not so long ago. *But soon. Soon we will discover this together.*

Was it fate that she face Mario and lose? Would she be joining her father on the other side?

She slipped the pictures back into their envelope, her heart beating a little faster, and again recalled Holiday telling her that she didn't think it was what he meant. Dear God, she hoped not. She wasn't ready to leave this world.

When she let go of worrying about Daniel's message—choosing to believe Holiday, or at least trying to believe her—and stopped fretting over the meeting of the grandparents, she started obsessing over what Fredericka had said. It was because of Kylie that Lucas probably wouldn't get on the werewolf Council. She knew it wasn't her fault—he got himself in this mess—but guilt still pricked her conscience. It was hard to feel so angry and guilty at the same time at the same person. How did one deal with that? She didn't know.

She also had to deal with Derek. Nip things in the bud before things got out of control, if they weren't already out of control. She remembered lunch yesterday, which was why Kylie had Miranda bring them each back a couple slices of pizza for dinner last night. Ahh, her ol' avoidance trick was still in good working order. She should be proud. Not.

But honestly, she knew she shouldn't and couldn't continue to avoid it.

Derek deserved to know the truth. Now if she could just figure out exactly what that was, she'd tell him. Wait! She did know the truth, didn't she? Or at least part of it. Hadn't she admitted she loved Lucas? Still loved him, in spite of what he'd done. Then why had she even allowed Derek to kiss her in the dreamscape?

Was it because down deep she still held a glimmer of romantic feelings for Derek? Was it because she feared losing Lucas and not having anyone? Was it because she was angry at Lucas, and somehow felt kissing Derek was his payback? Was it because she was over-the-top stupid?

Questions.

No answers.

"Are we going to breakfast?" Della asked.

"Yeah," Kylie mumbled, and looked at the black computer screen. "Just checking my e-mail."

Della let out a sarcastic chuckle. "I think you need to turn the computer on first. Or do your powers now allow you to read your e-mails with the computer off?"

Kylie clicked the computer on and glanced over her shoulder to frown at Della. "Don't you remember the rule? You can't be a smart-ass until after breakfast. I need energy to deal with that."

Miranda skipped into the living room from her bedroom. "I personally think she should wait and be a smartass after lunch. That gives us two meals of energy to put up with her crap."

"You two think you're so funny," Della bit out.

"We are funny," Miranda said.

"Just a couple of comedians." Kylie clicked open her e-mail to do a quick check. One from her stepdad.

To answer later.

One from . . . Sara.

Damn, she hadn't thought about her old best friend in almost two weeks. Funny how someone could be so important in your life and then . . . then you go a long period of time without them even entering your thoughts.

It wasn't anyone's fault. Life took people in different directions. She'd read in some teen magazine that it usually happened when you graduated from high school. She guessed her different-path part of life had just come a little earlier. It was still sad.

An empty spot seemed to open up in her chest. A spot Kylie knew used to be occupied by Sara.

She clicked open the e-mail from Sara, praying it wasn't bad news, as in: her cancer came back, or she thought she was pregnant again, or she'd decided to go into a convent and become a nun. With Sara, anything was possible.

> Hey . . . Got my hair cut. Thought you might want to see it. Don't laugh. I'm feeling spunky now that I survived cancer. I'll bet your friend Miranda will approve. Call me when you have a chance.

Knowing Della and Miranda were waiting, Kylie clicked open the picture for just a peek. When the image of Sara with short, spiked pink hair filled the screen, a smiled slipped across Kylie's lips.

She heard shuffling behind her. "I'm coming," she said, thinking any minute Della would complain. Kylie grabbed her phone and wallet, but right as she stood up, another e-mail came in. It was from her mom, who was supposed to have gotten back to the States on the red-eye flight. Obviously, she'd made it home.

"Really? I don't see you moving," Della said.

Okay, Mom's e-mail would have to wait, too.

Meeting the girls at the door, Kylie glanced at her two best friends and she felt a wave of sadness. Not for what was, but for what might be.

"Promise me something," Kylie said.

"What?" they asked in unison.

"When we graduate from here we won't lose track of each other. We should all go to the same college. And I'm completely serious. Holiday was talking about getting some college forms and we should send them out to the same colleges. And we could get an apartment together."

"We could become lesbians and have threesomes," Della said, and chuckled.

"Sorry," Miranda said, and snickered. "I've already seen you naked and it did nothing for me."

"It was the little bitty tits, wasn't it?" Della asked, grinning.

They laughed all the way to breakfast.

• • •

Derek and Lucas didn't show up for breakfast and that was just fine with Kylie. Less drama must be good for the appetite, because she actually ate her runny eggs and burnt bacon in record time. Her phone rang just when she was about to push her tray back. When she saw her stepdad's number, she decided to call him back a little later. She didn't think she could take his heartbreak over her mom this early.

Her phone chimed with an incoming text. Couldn't be her dad, the man didn't text. Kylie waited a second before checking to see who it was from. Three words popped up.

Miss you. Lucas.

Miss you, too, she thought, but didn't type it in. Emotion whispered across her chest.

The sound of another tray being placed on the table brought Kylie's gaze up.

Steve, the hot shape-shifter who'd left a hickey right below Della's left collarbone, sat down beside the little vamp.

Della sat completely still, frozen, and stared daggers at her uneaten breakfast. If looks could kill, that breakfast would be pushing up daisies.

"Hey," Steve said.

"You have to leave," Della said without looking at him.

"Why?" he asked.

Della hesitated. "Because I'm shadowing Kylie and don't need any distractions."

That was the lamest excuse Kylie had ever heard and Steve's expression said he knew it, too.

"So I'm distracting to you, huh?" he said, leaned against her, and half smiled.

"Leave!" She looked up, her eyes glowing a pissed-off green.

The half smile faded from his eyes, and he popped up, took his tray, and went and sat at the shape-shifter table.

"That wasn't nice," Kylie said.

"I know," Della said. "I don't know why he did it."

"I was talking about you." Kylie leaned forward and shot her a frown.

"Yeah, and it was a lie, too," Perry added, sitting two seats down. "I'm the one on shadowing duty right now."

Della made a face and stood up. "Are you finished eating?"

A few minutes later they walked outside for the announcement of Campmate hour—Della on one side and Miranda and Perry on the other. Kylie found herself looking around for Derek or Lucas. Still both no-shows. But then she felt the hair stand up on the back of her neck. Looking back, she saw Derek standing about eight feet behind her. His green gaze met hers and Kylie remembered the kiss from the dream again.

"Okay," Chris said, drawing Kylie's attention forward. "First up today we have . . ." He pulled a piece of paper from his top hat—which always looked silly to Kylie, but it was obviously his thing.

She couldn't help but wonder if Chris had wanted to be a magician when he was a kid. Reading the paper, the head vampire moved his eyes around the crowd. Kylie's heart thumped when his gaze came close to her and started slowing down. *Not again! Who was it this time?*

Then his eyes moved past Kylie, past Miranda, and stopped. For some crazy reason, Kylie got a bad feeling. The sneaky smile on Chris's lips told her she was right, too.

"Perry, my ol' friend," Chris said. "You get the pleasure of spending an hour with Nikki."

Chapter Twenty-two

The bad feeling wasn't just right on the mark, it was an understatement. This wasn't just bad, it was really awful.

Kylie's gaze shot away from Perry's shocked expression to Miranda. The little witch stood rock-hard stiff. The only thing that moved on her was her eyes as she scanned the crowd, obviously looking for Nikki.

And when Miranda's eyes stop moving—meaning she'd found the culprit—her gaze filled with jealousy. And just like that, there was another body part on the witch moving: her pinky.

"No," Kylie blurted out, but it was too late. Nikki the cute blonde disappeared, and standing in her exact spot was a very shocked, very angry-looking kangaroo.

Oh, but Miranda wasn't finished yet. Her pinky continued to wiggle.

Kylie gasped as pimples started popping out of the poor five-foot marsupial. Kylie could hear Miranda's favorite threat ring in her mind. *I'll give you the worst case of pimples you've ever seen.*

Miranda was right. Kylie had never seen pimples so bad. Of course, she'd never seen a kangaroo with pimples, period.

Everyone in the crowd started howling with laughter. Even though Nikki had brought this on herself, Kylie felt sorry for her. And frankly, if Miranda wasn't green with jealousy, she wouldn't think it was so funny either.

Kylie grabbed Miranda by the arm, leaned in, and whispered, "She was wrong to do this, but . . . change her back. Change her back right now before you forget how to break the curse!"

Miranda frowned, but Kylie saw the logic whittle its way into the girl's brain. She bit her lip, pointed her pinky, muttered a few things, and poof, Nikki magically appeared—no longer a kangaroo, but now a very embarrassed and angry shape-shifter.

The laughter from the crowd must have upped the embarrassment quotient. Instead of turning into something fierce and ripping the little witch apart, tears filled Nikki's eyes and she took off running.

Perry shot around and faced Miranda. "Why did you do that?"

Crap! Kylie thought, knowing Perry had said the wrong thing.

Miranda, already wearing an expression of remorse, frowned up at him. "You're taking her side? She's trying to steal you away from me and now you're taking her side!"

"No, I'm not . . . But that was stupid," he said.

Oh, shit! Kylie thought. Miranda didn't like the word *stupid.*

Miranda's face turned red and tears filled her eyes. "Stupid?" Miranda snapped. "Fine, if I'm so stupid, why don't you run after Nikki and console her. Because she can have you if that's how you feel!"

"What's going on?" Holiday came running out of the dining hall. While several people started to fill Holiday in, Miranda ran off.

Kylie turned to Perry, who stood there staring at a departing and very hurt Miranda.

"Hey," Kylie said. When he didn't respond, she gave his T-shirt sleeve a good yank. "Don't just stand there. Go after her and tell her you're sorry."

"What did I do?" he asked.

"First you called her stupid. Being dyslexic, she really hates that word. Second, like it or not, it sounded like you were taking Nikki's side."

"No, I said what she did was stupid. And it was." Perry looked over at Holiday. "She's gonna get hell from Holiday. Why the heck did Miranda have to do something like that?"

"Probably for the same reason a certain shape-shifter turned into a big bear and then a giant lion and tried to rip apart another shape-shifter for kissing someone. Because she's jealous. Don't you remember how it felt?"

Perry frowned. "Yeah, I do remember." Guilt shadowed his eyes. "Shit. I did screw up, didn't I?" He raked a hand through his blond hair. "But I wasn't taking up for Nikki. I just didn't want Miranda to get in trouble."

"Then go tell Miranda that. Explain what you meant. And then do yourself and Nikki a favor and go tell her to give it up."

"I . . . haven't encouraged her one bit."

"But have you come out and told her that you're with Miranda and it's just not happening between you two? Because obviously she still thinks you two have a shot. And it's not fair that Miranda has to put up with that crap, and it's not fair for Nikki to keep hoping when she shouldn't. Now go and fix this mess you're in before it's too late."

Right then Kylie's advice to Perry turned around and bit her in the ass. Because it was advice she needed to hear as well. Perry wasn't the only one who had some straightening out to do. She had to talk to Derek. She had to set him straight.

"I can't go," Perry said.

"Yes, you can, or you'll regret this."

"No, I can't. I'm shadowing you. Burnett will give me hell if I run out on you."

Kylie groaned. She turned around and Derek had made his way up to them. She grabbed him by the arm and yanked him in front of Perry. "You're not shadowing me anymore. Derek is."

"Great." Derek smiled and she knew he was reading something into this that wasn't there.

Perry shook his head. "But Burnett—"

"Burnett's not going to get mad. I'll explain it to him. Now go before it's too late and Miranda decides not to forgive you. Go!" She gave the little twerp a shove.

Perry transformed himself into his bird form and took off flying. Kylie knocked a few of the electric sparkles off her arm, and then confronted Derek.

"Come on," she said.

"Where?" The look he shot her came complete with a sexy smile.

"To talk," she said. "We have to talk."

"What about Campmate hour?" he asked.

She let go of a deep sigh. "Forget Campmate hour. You're coming with me!" She grabbed him by the arm and started dragging him.

And, of course, that was when Lucas walked up.

His blue eyes met hers. She saw the way he looked at her. She had the oddest desire to stop and explain, but when she tried to think of exactly what she'd say, or why she felt he deserved an explanation, it just seemed too hard.

So she just met his eyes with a look of apology and went back to dragging Derek behind her. Later, she would deal with Lucas. How she would deal with him, she didn't have a clue.

"Do you want to go to the rock?" Derek asked, now walking beside her.

"No." The hurt look in Lucas's eyes kept echoing in her heart. He'd hurt her, but hurting him, even unintentionally, sent regret tightening her chest.

"Why not?" Derek asked.

"Because we have to talk, and I think you know what it's about, too."

For a second she wished it wasn't so. It would be so easy if she could just pick Derek. He didn't have a pack trying to keep them apart. He hadn't given up his quest and wouldn't someday blame her.

But you couldn't make your heart take the easy way out, it felt what it felt, it wanted what it wanted.

Her heart obviously wanted Lucas. Whether or not she'd give it what it wanted was another matter. But she couldn't give Derek what he wanted either. It just wasn't right.

He exhaled a frustrated gulp of air. "Why do I have a feeling this isn't going to end well?"

She glanced at him. "It may not end the way you want it, but it's the right thing."

"I'm not so sure," he said.

She led him to her cabin and then remembering Miranda and Perry could be inside working out their own issues, she flopped down on the porch step and motioned him to do the same.

Giving the door a quick look, she hoped Perry had been able to calm Miranda down. Heck, maybe they were in there having a make-up make-out session.

Taking a deep breath, she faced Derek. "You know how I feel. Why are you trying to convince yourself that it's not true?"

"What's not true? Come on, Kylie. You love me, too," he said.

She pulled one leg up to her chest and hugged it. "Yes. I won't lie, but it's not the kind that I'm feeling for Lucas. And I know you know that, because you feel what I feel."

"But if you and I got back together, we could fix this."

She shook her head. "You don't deserve that."

"Don't deserve what?" he asked. "I want you back. You think I wouldn't be happy?"

"Not really," she said. "You shouldn't be. You deserve someone who's as crazy about you as you are about them. You don't deserve someone who . . . cares about someone else."

She bit her lip and realized another reason she felt so strongly about this. "This is what happened to my dad and my mom. She loved my real dad. She cared about my stepdad, but he always knew she loved my dad more. Even my mom says it's probably part of the reason he ended up cheating on her. She can't forgive him, but she knows it's partly her own fault."

He sat there frowning. "So you're going to take Lucas back. You are going to forgive him for running off and getting engaged to someone else."

She tightened her hold on her leg. "He didn't really get engaged. He stopped it before he got to that point."

Derek's frown increased. "Only because you showed up—because you discovered his dirty little secret."

"I know that. And I don't know what I'm going to do. I haven't forgiven him yet, but I haven't stopped loving him either."

"But if you gave us a chance, maybe you'd really fall back in love with me. I think you were really in love with me at one time. We could get back there where we feel that way again."

"We?" She sighed, realizing what he said. "See, you don't even feel the same way anymore, either."

"I didn't mean . . ." He shook his head.

"Yes, you did," she said. "Derek, I think we *were* in love with each other," she admitted. "And I don't want to hurt you, Derek. I really do care about you and I still love you, just not . . . that way. And I think it's the same with you."

He stared off at a line of trees and she knew he needed a few seconds to get his feelings in order. She saw him swallow and she felt his pain.

He inhaled. "But what we had was so great."

"I know and I'm so sorry." She felt her voice shake with emotion. Hurting him was so hard.

He looked back at her and she saw the honesty, the genuine concern in his gaze. And wasn't that just like Derek. He was such a great guy. And for that reason alone, he deserved someone who adored him, who loved him more than anyone else.

"You didn't do anything to apologize for," he said. "You really didn't. If anyone can be blamed for this it was me when I got scared and did what I did. Or maybe this is just fate. The way it was supposed to have turned out."

She nodded.

"I want one thing from you," he said. "One promise."

"What?" she asked, knowing she'd give it to him if at all possible.

"Don't stop being my friend. Don't avoid me because you think it's awkward. When you need something, don't hesitate to come to me. I can accept that we can't be boyfriend and girlfriend, but I don't want to lose you as a friend and I'm not saying that just to say it. I mean it."

She nodded. "I promise." Tears filled her eyes.

"And when you do go back to Lucas, make him understand that I'd like to still be a part of your life."

"I told you, I don't know if we will—"

He reached out and brushed an escaping tear from her cheek. "Yes, you will. Because when you love someone, you forgive them."

Her breath shook. "Like you are forgiving me right now?" And another tear escaped.

"I told you, you didn't do anything to be forgiven for. But if you did do something, yeah, I would have forgiven you."

She inhaled and stared down at her shoe. "Even if it was because of me that you couldn't complete the one thing you always wanted to do."

"I'm lost," Derek said.

"I'm sorry. I'm just thinking out loud."

"About Lucas?" Derek asked.

Kylie nodded and realized how insensitive she was being. "I'm sorry," she repeated.

"Don't be." He exhaled. "This is what I'm talking about you *not* doing. I want you to talk to me." He gripped his hands together. "Look, I don't like saying this, but Lucas does love you. I can feel it. And he's hurting like the devil right now. Whatever it is you think he can't forgive you for, well, you're wrong."

She ran her hand up and down her leg before talking. "Because of me he won't get on the were Council. He won't be able to change all the things he wanted to change with his own people. His own pack will probably disown him. Sooner or later . . ."

"But he chose you, Kylie. He made that choice. You didn't force him to."

Kylie nodded, but looked him in the eyes. "Maybe it was the wrong choice."

He leaned in, and his shoulder brushed hers with warmth. "I'll bet he wouldn't think so."

She shook her head. "Being a were means everything to him."

Kylie's phone in her pocket chimed with an incoming text; a second later Derek's did the same. She pulled it out and saw Burnett's name on the screen as the sender. She glanced at Derek, who looked at her at the same time.

"A text from Burnett," Derek said.

"Oh, crap," Kylie said, hitting the button to read her text.

Get to the office now! his text read.

Holy hell, Kylie thought. What could be happening now?

Burnett's message to Derek had read almost the same: *Get Kylie to the office now!* So Kylie and Derek ran to the office. She could have moved quicker if she'd left Derek in the dust, but she held back. What was a couple of seconds?

Nevertheless, by the time she got in front of the office, her heart was thumping in her chest. From exertion or fear of what awaited her, Kylie wasn't sure.

She hadn't made it up the office steps when she heard the voices. Shit, Kylie thought, what was her stepfather doing here?

"It's my stepdad," Kylie said to Derek. "I'd better handle this alone."

She hurried inside and found Burnett, Holiday, her stepfather, and Jonathon in the office. What the heck was Jonathon doing in here? Tom Galen stood in the middle of the room, facing Holiday's desk. Holiday sat relaxed like the essence of calm, but her stepfather's posture wasn't picking up on Holiday's mood. His shoulders were tight, his hands clenched.

And like her stepfather, Burnett appeared a little tight, but she could tell he was trying to contain himself. But Jonathon . . . the vampire just looked guilty. And Kylie got a bad feeling.

Holiday's gaze shifted briefly to Kylie, as did Burnett's, but her stepdad didn't realize she was standing there.

"What kind of school are you running?" Tom Galen bit out.

"The same kind of school that the state is running," Holiday answered, her voice tranquil. "We have a security gate for a reason. You went through it and set off alarms. You were mistaken to be a threat."

"I'm not a goddamn threat. I'm a student's father."

"Fathers don't usually try to break into a school," Burnett insisted.

"What happened?" Kylie asked.

Her father swung around and at least some of his tension subsided at seeing her. "I jumped the gate instead of pushing the button and you would think I'd just broken into Fort Knox. I was tackled by this wisecrack of a kid."

Holiday glanced up and Kylie could see from her expression she was trying to play nice. "Jonathon saw your father and made a bad judgment call. Instead of asking questions as he possibly should have, he detained—"

"Detained? He knocked my ass on the ground." Her stepdad rubbed his side. "And let me tell you, for a skinny kid, he has one hell of a tackle."

"We're sorry," Holiday said. "Aren't we, Jonathon?"

"Very much so, sir," Jonathon spoke up.

"Dad," Kylie said. "Jonathon's girlfriend was mugged last week. You could understand how he might now be a tad overprotective."

Jonathon nodded. Holiday glanced at Kylie as if to say, *good move.* Burnett seemed to agree.

Her father sighed. "I'm sorry to hear about your girlfriend. Is she going to be okay?" he asked Jonathon.

"Yeah," Jonathon said, then flinched as if remembering his manners. "Oh, I mean, yes, sir, and thank you."

With most of the tension lessening, Kylie looked at her dad. "What are you doing here, Dad?"

He frowned. "I came to see you. I e-mailed you late last night and called this morning. You would have known I was coming if you had taken my call or read my e-mail."

"I'm sorry," she said. "It's been a crazy morning."

"She is attending school," Burnett added.

Her stepfather looked apologetic. "My company sent me down here for a meeting with a sister company that's not happening until two this afternoon, and I thought maybe I could steal you away and we could grab brunch together."

Behind Tom Galen, Kylie spotted Burnett scowl. The vampire had made it clear she wasn't leaving the school without him until they knew Mario wasn't in the vicinity. Burnett looked directly at Kylie and shook his head with determination. He wasn't just saying no, he was saying *hell no!*

"Uh, I already had breakfast," Kylie said.

"Well, we'd just grab something to drink," her stepdad said.

Kylie shot Burnett another quick glance. The man was still shaking his head a firm hell no.

"I . . . I have classes," Kylie said.

Disappointment filled her stepdad's eyes. She hated hurting him. Today she'd already hurt Lucas, then Derek, now her stepdad. This wasn't a good day.

"Now, Kylie," he said. "I'm positive you can spare a few minutes of your time to visit with me."

She felt the tension building inside her and inside the room. Her stepdad wasn't going to back down, and from the looks of things, neither was Burnett.

This was not going to end well.

Chapter Twenty-three

Kylie concentrated on looking at her dad and tried not to focus on the scene happening behind him—the scene being a nonverbal argument between Holiday and Burnett. An argument that rivaled the old silent movies that included some very angry hand motions and some very unhappy and telling facial expressions.

"Uh," Kylie said, a complete stalling tactic because face it, she didn't have a clue what to say.

"Of course you should go spend some time with your dad," Holiday finally blurted out.

Burnett's jaw clamped down so tight, Kylie would bet his teeth had just shortened a quarter of an inch.

Holiday stood up. "However, Kylie has a test in her next class. How about you coming back in about an hour or an hour and a half and you two can go to lunch somewhere. I think Kylie was telling me the other day that there was a hamburger joint in downtown Fallen that she wanted to try. What was it, Burgers R Us?"

Kylie nodded, clueless about the restaurant Holiday had mentioned.

Burnett's expression lightened; either he was seeing reason, or he was on to Holiday's plan. Kylie just wished she was on to it, too, because she was clueless as to what was going on.

Her father turned to Kylie. "I guess I could go take a drive and come back around eleven. It is pretty country out here."

"That would be good," Kylie said.

"Okay," her stepdad said, and reached out and drew her in for one of his super heart-melting hugs. The warmth from his embrace seeped into her chest and it should have made her panic subside. And it probably would have if over her stepdad's shoulder she didn't see the sword falling point down from somewhere above. It hit with force and caused a sharp clank as it lodged itself, standing straight up in the middle of Holiday's desk.

Kylie's heart lurched and she felt her father flinch at the noise. One thought ran amok in her head. How was she going to explain this to her stepdad?

Burnett flew into action at vampire speed. He snatched the sword, knocked over Holiday's glass of tea, and then hid the weapon behind his back in one swift move.

Only a fraction of a second later, her father pulled loose and swung around to check out the clatter.

"What the fu . . . frack?" Jonathon muttered, and then blushed when he realized what he'd almost said.

Burnett scowled at Jonathon. Holiday smiled and should have won an Oscar for her acting. "Dang it, I swear this is the second glass of tea I've knocked over today."

Her dad just looked back at Kylie, who hadn't breathed since the sword's miraculous appearance.

"I guess I'll see you in an hour and a half."

She nodded and inhaled.

"You're up for this?" he asked.

She got another gulp of oxygen into her lungs and hopefully to her brain.

"Are you going to walk me out?" he asked.

Feeling a bit like a bobble head doll, she nodded again, then added a smile to it, hoping to appear more convincing.

Her stepdad took one step and stopped and looked at her. "Are you okay? You look like you saw a ghost."

A ghost she could have handled, she thought.

"I'm fine." The two words came out squeaky. Unfortunately, she simply wasn't an awarding-winning actress like Holiday.

"I think it's doable," Kylie told her dad, and glanced up from the brochure of a guided hiking tour through the Grand Canyon—a trip he wanted to plan for them this summer. "It looks great." It wasn't really a lie, but she'd bet Chris, the vampire sitting a table away from her and her dad at the restaurant, might have heard her heart say differently.

She felt Lucas, sitting across from Chris, glance at her and her heart gave a little tug. Burnett had picked two people—two he thought her father was less likely to recognize—to play secret bodyguards during her lunch. When he'd told her he would have two people stationed at the restaurant, she hadn't considered he would pick Lucas. Little did Burnett know, Kylie half feared her stepdad would recognize Lucas as the kid who'd lived next door to them. The kid Kylie had accused of killing her cat.

Thankfully, her stepdad hadn't given Lucas a second glance so far. Neither had he noticed the hawk following the car all the way into town. She'd bet her best bra that the hawk answered to the name of Perry.

Kylie had taken the time before her dad's return to find Miranda and make sure she was okay. The little witch was still shook up. She'd made up with Perry, but had an appointment to have a sit-down serious talk with Holiday. No doubt there would be some consequences for her actions. While Miranda didn't look forward to the consequences, she accepted her wrongdoing.

"I thought you would like it," her father said, drawing her attention back to the present. "It's sort of like the one we did in Taos, New Mexico. There'll be some kayaking, but nothing too dangerous."

Her dad's eyes lit up with excitement. Kylie felt bad not sharing his thrill. She'd pretty much spent the last forty-five minutes here, praying that sword wouldn't come and stab any of the restaurant's patrons. But now seeing her stepdad's eyes become worried, she tried harder to put on a good front.

"Remember the baby deer we saw on that trip," Kylie offered. "And that camp leader that got skunked."

"Oh, yeah." His grin widened. "We have had some great trips."

"I know." She put her hand on top of his and he turned his over and gave hers a squeeze. She felt his love seep into her palm.

"Do you know how much I miss you? I really wish you'd consider coming back and living with me."

She bit down on her lip, remembering how when he'd first left her mom, she'd thought that was all she wanted. Her life these three months had changed so much.

Giving her dad's hand another squeeze, she said, "I really like Shadow Falls. But we'll have this trip in the summer." God, she hoped Mario was dealt with by then and she wasn't lying.

He nodded. "I get it. My baby girl is growing up." Emotion filled his eyes and he looked around. And Kylie's heart clutched with fear he'd recognize Lucas.

"Did you like your hamburger?" she blurted out, drawing his attention to her.

"Loved it. You were right to suggest we come here. But you barely touched your food." He waved at Kylie's plate with her hamburger and fries growing cold.

"I had a big breakfast," Kylie lied. "But it was good." Kylie glanced at her watch. It was almost one. Burnett had had her stall her father so they wouldn't be in as big of a lunch crowd. Her chest clutched a little when she realized that in less than an hour, she would face the Brightens, her real dad's adoptive parents. Oh, hell, she still didn't have an approach plan.

She looked back at her stepdad. "You know, it's getting late."

"I know, you're gonna turn into a pumpkin if I don't get you back." He signed the credit card bill that Kylie had already asked the waitress to bring.

Suddenly the three Cokes she'd drank out of nervousness hit her bladder. "I'm going to run to the girls' room first before we head out."

"Go ahead, I need to make a call to work anyway."

When she started to the girls' room, Lucas frowned. Oh, please, Kylie thought, what was going to happen in the bathroom?

Okay, a lot could happen. Mario could happen. But she had to pee.

Chris and Lucas whispered across the table and then Chris got up and shot ahead of her toward the bathrooms. She hoped he knew he wasn't coming into the bathroom with her. With her shy bladder, she'd never get her job done.

She found him waiting beside the men's bathroom door. As if he planned to just stand guard and listen. And just knowing he could hear her pee would probably making peeing impossible.

"Do what you gotta do and get out," Chris said like some serious special agent.

"I will." Kylie pushed the door inside.

The moment the door whooshed shut, someone inside one of the stalls turned on some weird Cajun music. Each to her own, she thought, and went into the stall.

She hadn't been in there a minute, was finally warming up to the crazy rhythm of the tune, when she heard a noise above. She looked up and saw a pair of hands gripping the top of her stall. Then a foot appeared as someone came climbing over.

Crap.

There couldn't be anything worse than getting caught midstream and in an above-the-toilet-seat squat when confronted by an intruder.

She shot upright, prepared to face whatever was about to go down. Unfortunately, she hadn't managed to stop the flow completely.

Immediately she realized she'd been wrong. There could be something worse. Being caught midstream, in a squat, with pee running down your leg, when you faced the almost-fiancée of the guy you still loved.

"What are you doing here?" Kylie snapped, knowing that to show fear to a werewolf could be detrimental.

"Isn't it obvious? I was curious?"

"About my potty habits?" Kylie snapped.

She smirked. "About you."

Not thinking the girl was going for her throat—and hey, if she did, Kylie didn't want to die with pee running down her leg—she snagged her few squares and wiped the urine running down her thigh.

Panties up, jeans snapped, she faced Monique and decided to just get rid of her. "You should know any second now a vampire is gonna run in here. If I was you, I'd scoot."

Monique arched a brow. "So Lucas didn't teach you the secret trick of dealing with nosy vamps, huh? Just a little zydeco music and their super hearing goes to shit."

Kylie frowned. No, she didn't know that trick, and she was a bit miffed that Lucas hadn't enlightened her. But why would he? Keeping secrets from her was his specialty.

"What is it you really want, Monique?" Kylie asked.

Monique shrugged. "I told you. I'm curious. Do you know how many suitors have approached my father to marry me? And then . . . the lucky guy my father finally chooses to saddle me with for life doesn't even want me."

Kylie heard the resentment in Monique's voice. But oddly it sounded more about being forced into an arranged marriage than Lucas's unwillingness to go through with the engagement. Nor had Kylie missed the part about Lucas not wanting Monique. He'd told Kylie this, Fredericka had told her this, but something about hearing it from the other girl herself felt good. "So now you want to take it out on me, huh?"

"No." She tightened her brow and started checking out Kylie's pattern.

Kylie turned her head and tried to change her pattern, but obviously she wasn't quick enough.

"Wow, that is weird. What exactly are you?"

"Just a mystery," Kylie said, and grew leery of standing in a stall with Monique—leery because this was what all chameleons feared, being noticed, bringing attention to their race. "Do you mind backing out?" Kylie asked.

Monique shuffled back a few steps and unlatched the stall door by reaching back, never taking her eyes off Kylie. "Are you sure you don't have a brain tumor?"

"That's probably it." Kylie motioned for her to move back again.

The girl took one step and then stopped. "But they say you're a protector, too. And at the ceremony, I'm told you had a were pattern. How could you . . ."

Kylie squeezed past her to leave the stall and went to wash her hands. And as much as she didn't want to think about it, her mind re-created the kiss she'd seen Lucas give Monique.

"Are you still mad at him?" Monique asked. "I'll bet you're furious."

Kylie gave the soap container an extra-hard pump. When she glanced up in the mirror at the were's reflection, Kylie was hit again by how pretty Monique was. Her eyes were dark brown with long dark lashes that matched her black hair. Her lips were pouty and plump like some famous actresses. Yup, she had a pretty face, matched by her picture-perfect curvy body.

Scrubbing her hands together, Kylie said, "If you don't mind, I don't think this is something I want to discuss with you."

"If I were you, I'd be drilling me with questions." She tilted her head to the side and studied Kylie's reflection as if trying to figure her out. "Since you're not curious, that means you believe him when he told you that we didn't fool around. Or at least you want to believe him," Monique said. "Don't you want to ask me?"

A sharp, painful ache struck Kylie's heart. "You already said he didn't want you."

"Maybe I meant he didn't want to get married, but you know guys, they always want other stuff."

Kylie ran her hands under the faucet and rinsed. Then she looked up at Monique's reflection again.

"You were right the first time. I believe him." And the words slipped out of her mouth and didn't trip her heartbeat up a bit. Even she was a little surprised.

"Then why are you still mad at him? Clara says you hardly acknowledge him. That he's one sad puppy."

Kylie snatched some paper towels from the dispenser. "Let me repeat myself: I really don't care to discuss this with you."

Monique shook her head as if she was confused by Kylie's behavior. "It took guts to do what he did. To call off the engagement. To risk it all." She tilted her head to the side and studied Kylie. "You do know what all he risked, don't you?"

Kylie didn't answer. She closed her eyes for a second and wished she didn't have to hear this.

"His own pack is considering banishing him," Monique continued. "If he can't get on that Council, he has lost everything. His father has practically denounced him. I've heard the forefathers have called a meeting to discuss his actions. My father is still debating putting a hit on him."

Kylie twisted and stared at Monique. "And you are going to let him?"

"Let him? I've told him that I'm thrilled to be out of the union, but what I say holds no importance to my father. Like Lucas, I'm expected to follow the rules. Funny, it took him calling off our engagement before I kind of liked the guy."

Monique moved in a little closer. "Call me a romantic, but I think it's kind of sad that after he did that, you don't take him back. Not that you would have him for very long. A lone wolf's life expectancy is very short. You either belong to a pack, or you are considered free game for any hungry were on a hunt."

The bathroom door banged open. The lone wolf stormed into the bathroom looking prepared to kill. When his eyes lit on Monique, his killer instincts lessened, but his scowl tightened. "What the hell are you doing here?"

Monique shrugged. "When a girl's gotta pee, she's gotta pee!" She moved past him without a bit of shame and walked out the door. "Have a good life, Lucas."

Lucas didn't even watch her leave. He stared at Kylie, his gaze almost a caress. "I'm sorry. She had no right to—"

"She didn't do anything." Kylie twisted the paper towels extra tight, ripped them in two, ripped them one more time, and then tossed them in the garbage. She swallowed the knot of pain down her throat. "You should go to her. Agree to go through with the engagement."

"What?" He stared at Kylie if she'd lost her mind.

"You heard me!" she insisted.

He shook his head. "You don't mean that."

"Yes, I do!" she said. And she did with all her heart. How could she stand by and watch him lose everything? Watch his own pack push him out, knowing it was because of her?

"You're just angry with me."

"Yes! You're damn right I'm still angry at you." Tears filled her eyes as honesty echoed in her voice. "You betrayed me. It hurts like hell knowing you left me all those times and went to see her. But do you want to know who I'm angrier at? Myself. I knew for the longest time how this would end. I knew that me not being a were would end up destroying any chance we had."

"I don't care what you are!" he growled.

"You should. Because the price you'll have to pay is too much." She saw the hurt flash in his eyes. "Even if you hadn't betrayed me, I wouldn't let you pay it. It's over, Lucas, accept that and don't screw up your life because of me."

Head held high, she walked out. Unfortunately, her heart felt like the towels she'd just trashed—mangled and twisted.

• • •

Kylie watched Perry—still a hawk—follow her dad's car as they returned to Shadow Falls. While her stepdad drove, he talked about the possible hiking trip. When he slowed down to turn into the Shadow Falls parking lot, Kylie noticed the silver Cadillac in front of them with its blinker on, also pulling into the parking lot. The car's tinted windows prevented her from seeing who drove, but she couldn't help wonder if it might be the Brightens—her real dad's adoptive parents.

Kylie's stomach started to flutter. She still didn't know what to say, what not to say. Her heart kept echoing the pain she'd felt when talking to Lucas, but she needed to shift mental gears now. Unfortunately, she had too many issues to give herself over to just one.

She glanced at her watch. It was twenty till two. It could actually be them if they were the type to be early.

Glancing at her dad now talking about the camping gear they would need, she realized how awkward this would be if he had to meet the Brightens. It would probably lead to having to explain a whole hell of a lot of things that Kylie didn't know how to explain. And it would probably end up hurting her stepdad, something she didn't want to do.

The silver car pulled in and parked in a visiting parking spot. Her dad pulled in and parked two spots down. Releasing her seat belt, before her dad even had a chance to turn the car off, she leaned over and gave him a kiss on the cheek.

"Thanks for lunch. I'll see myself in."

"Not so fast, I have time to walk you in. I need to take advantage of every second with you."

Chapter Twenty-four

"Okay," Kylie said, in a bit of a panic. "Well, it's gonna be a quick walk because I . . . I have to go pee."

"You went to the bathroom at the restaurant," her dad said as if her peeing habits concerned him.

"Tiny bladder." She popped out of the car. She cut her eyes briefly at the other car and saw the passenger side door opening and then she saw . . .

"Oh, crap!" It was *not* the Brightens. And right now she really, really wished it were.

Her mom and . . . She watched in sheer horror as John's head appeared on the other side of the car.

"Kylie?" her mom called out in a stern voice.

She turned to her dad. "You should leave before . . . before things go crazy."

"It's okay." Her dad looked embarrassed. "Just because of what happened last time doesn't mean we can't be civil to each other."

Her mom's posture and expression as she came stomping over to the car didn't seem to agree with her dad's "civil" declaration. Oh, lord, Kylie was so not in the mood to deal with her parents' drama right now.

But as she got closer, Kylie noticed her mom, her hair mussed, her clothes wrinkled, and her eyes bloodshot, didn't have her frown zeroed in on her dad, but on Kylie.

Okay . . . whose drama was this? Her parents'? Or . . .

"Is it true?" her mom snapped.

Kylie instantly remembered her mom had just flown back from England, which explained her appearance, but it didn't explain what was wrong.

Kylie looked to her dad to see if his expression would tell her if he had a clue to what her mom was talking about. But he looked equally puzzled.

"Is what true?" Kylie asked, and noticed John walking up to stop beside her mom. He didn't appear wrinkled or jet-lagged. But just seeing the man sent a bad feeling wiggling its way inside her.

"You called your dad about this, but not me?" her mom asked.

Kylie saw Holiday and Burnett high stepping it out of the office, probably thinking another free-for-all fistfight was about to occur.

Glancing back to her mom, Kylie sent up a prayer that this—whatever this was—wouldn't escalate into chaos.

"I didn't call him about anything. What are you talking about?"

"Did you use the credit card I gave you?"

Kylie nodded, her mind running circles and then landing on a possible answer to what this was all about. But Kylie really *really* hoped she was wrong.

"Are you pregnant?" her mom blurted out.

Okay, so Kylie wasn't wrong. Her mouth opened but nothing came out.

"She's pregnant?" Her dad looked at Kylie with a stern parental glare. "We won't be able to go on that hiking trip now!"

"Unfreakingbelievable," her mom seethed. "You hear your daughter's pregnant and you're worried about a hiking trip."

"No, I was . . . I'm just in shock."

He wasn't the only one shocked. "Stop!" Kylie said.

"Just answer me, young lady," her mom demanded.

"No, I'm not . . . pregnant." Kylie shook her head back and forth, imitating Burnett's hell-no head shake. "I haven't even . . . I'm . . ." *I'm still a virgin!* The words sat on the tip of her tongue, but she couldn't spit them out.

"Then why would you buy three pregnancy tests?"

"You bought three pregnancy tests?" her father echoed.

Kylie suddenly noticed another car parked beside John's Cadillac. It didn't have tinted windows, but it didn't matter if it did, because the windows were rolled down and the elderly couple in the front seat both had their faces turned, listening to the fiasco that was going on.

It suddenly hit Kylie who these people were.

The Brightens.

It had to be, didn't it? With Kylie's luck, yup, it had to be them.

Lovely.

Just lovely.

Kylie's knees started to tingle, signaling her desire to vanish.

Not now. Not now!

Take a deep breath and just relax. The voice came with a certain familiar chill.

Kylie looked around and didn't see him, but could hear him. *Daddy?*

I'm here. It's gonna be okay. I promise.

Your parents are going to think I'm a slut.

Nah. They are going to love you. You'll see. You will impress them. And soon, soon we will be together.

Kylie gasped. *Am I going to die?*

Daddy? Daniel? He, and his familiar cold, were gone.

Kylie took a big gulp of air. Now on top of worrying about her possible upcoming death and convincing everyone that she wasn't pregnant, she had to worry about the Brightens liking her. Because if they didn't, it would no doubt hurt her dad.

Oh, hell! Maybe she *should* just vanish.

• • •

Daniel, her dad, was right, at least about everything being okay. Well, she still had to face the Brightens. But within two minutes, Holiday had the Brightens by the arms and was escorting them into the office. Much to Kylie's relief, her parents were clueless as to who they even were.

And within five minutes, she had her stepdad on his way to his meeting, and her mom had calmed down. Not completely chilled, but calmer.

Holiday had explained the whole confusion with the pregnancy tests in a much more rational way than it actually went down. Claiming the test had been for her and that she'd forgotten her purse and Kylie had been so kind to offer the credit card, and she'd already mailed a check to her mom. And so on and so on. Yeah, Holiday pretty much lied, but it sounded really good.

Her mom explained that after the flight she'd found the credit card company had called and thought the charges might be fraud because the card had never been used and charges were made in Fallen, not in Houston. Her mom wanted to make sure the card hadn't been stolen so she called the drugstore to check on the purchase. That's when she was informed it was for three pregnancy tests and the buyer had been a Kylie Galen.

Now that her mom had calmed down, Holiday walked back to the office. Kylie spent about five minutes visiting with her mom, pretending to be interested in her off-the-wall ramblings about England. Finally, her mom confessed she was too tired to think, much less talk. She kissed Kylie's forehead, told her she was so proud she wasn't pregnant, and asked John to take her home.

John had barely said two words the whole time he was here, but Kylie had caught him watching her in a way that made her antsy. However, when the man put his arm around her mom and gently kissed her brow and told her she could sleep while he drove, Kylie felt a flicker of guilt for not liking him.

Maybe Kylie needed an attitude adjustment where John was concerned. Because face it, if he made her mom happy, that made Kylie happy.

Liar, her heart seemed to say as it skipped some beats. She wasn't happy with John. But maybe Kylie should work on that. Work on trying to like the man. It felt impossible. Yet so much in her life lately had felt impossible—like the possibility of her impending death, like letting go of Lucas—that maybe she just needed to try harder.

Waving good-bye to her mom, Kylie headed back to the office to face the Brightens. And she had another case of stomach flutters. And for good reason, too. One's very first conversation with your recently discovered grandparents shouldn't be about pregnancy. Even when the conversation was about *not* being pregnant.

Stopping at the office door, mentally exhausted, she thought about how her day started on a downward spiral ever since Miranda had turned Nikki into a kangaroo with pimples.

This was definitely going down as one of her most bizarre days.

Squaring her shoulders, determined to get through this meeting with Daniel's adoptive parents, hopefully without having the sword appear again, Kylie decided that after this visit, she was going to go to her cabin and either cry or eat a lot of chocolate.

Maybe both.

She recalled her dad's promise that the Brightens would love her, and while she trusted her dad with all her heart, she couldn't help but worry. Then again, maybe they were going to be so thrilled to have a granddaughter that they wouldn't even care if they thought she was sleeping around and possibly pregnant.

Right before she reached for the knob, Kylie experienced a bit of déjà vu. She'd been right here before—walking into the office thinking she was to meet the Brightens. Of course, that turned out to be her real grandfather and aunt. But the point was, she recalled with clarity the fear and anxiety she'd felt then.

A crazy sense of accomplishment tugged at her heart. While she'd just admitted to being worried and either wanting chocolate or a good cry, what she felt now was so much more manageable.

No matter what happened in there, Kylie would be able to deal with it. She could almost hear Nana, her mother's mother, whispering from the outskirts of heaven, *My little Kylie is growing up.*

Suddenly feeling a bit more confident, and deciding that maybe all she'd need this afternoon was some good chocolate, Kylie walked into the office.

Holiday came rushing up to her. "Burnett has the Brightens in the conference room sipping tea. He took the sword to my house and locked it in a closet so . . . maybe that won't happen again. I explained the whole pregnancy situation to the Brightens, too." Holiday bit down her lip in concern. "Oh, Kylie, I'm so sorry. All this is my fault. I got you into this jam."

"It's fine," Kylie said.

Holiday gave her a quick soothing hug. "Are you really okay?"

Kylie inhaled. "A little nervous, but yeah, I'm okay."

"Do you want me to come in with you?"

Kylie considered it, and then said, "No, I . . . I think I can handle it."

Holiday sighed. "You are growing up."

Kylie stared at the fae. "I could swear I just heard my grandmother say that."

"She did," Holiday said. "She was just here."

Kylie grinned. "Really?"

Holiday nodded. "She pops in at the oddest times."

Kylie felt her Nana's love stir inside her. "Tell her I love her," Kylie said, and went to meet the people who had raised her father and probably contributed to the great man, and ghost, that he turned out to be.

• • •

When Kylie walked in, Burnett was already standing up, ready to excuse himself. "I'll let you three visit."

As he walked past, he rested his hand on her shoulder and gave her a squeeze. It was a cold touch, but came with warmth and a feeling of *go get 'em, girl.* She was hit again with how lucky she was to have the people at Shadow Falls in her life.

The moment Burnett left, and she felt both Mr. and Mrs. Brighten's gazes on her, the flutters in her stomach returned full force.

She gave herself a second just to study them. Mr. Brighten was balding, with brownish gray eyes, and he had a kind face. Mrs. Brighten had a head of thick gray hair and what looked like hazel eyes. She had a gentle, kind look about her. A little plump and with a likable face. Like someone you would pick out of a crowd to play the part of loving grandmother.

"Hi." Kylie forced a smile, but she didn't force it too hard. She took one step into the room and decided to clear the air first. "I just want to reconfirm that you know that I'm not pregnant."

Chapter Twenty-five

"Your principal explained that." Mrs. Brighten continued to stare.

"I also want to say that . . . that I know you might think my mom and stepdad are nuts after witnessing the whole parking lot scene, but . . ." She remembered to breathe. "But . . . well, sometimes they are a little nuts, but for the most part, they're really good people." Emotion tightened her throat and she swallowed. "They both love me."

Mr. and Mrs. Brighten nodded again. A strange kind of awkwardness filled the room. One Kylie hoped to send packing. She really wanted this to go well. And not just for her dad, she realized, but for her.

"I'm sorry we're staring," Mr. Brighten finally said. "It's just . . . you look so much like your father. It's amazing."

Kylie smiled again, this one completely genuine. She moved in and sat down across from them at the table. "I know."

"You've seen pictures?" Mrs. Brighten asked.

Yeah, his real father and aunt brought them to me when they were pretending to be you. Yeah, she had to lie. "My mom had a few photos of him." Then Kylie remembered her mom had kept the obituary clipping that had Daniel's image.

Almost a frown appeared on Mrs. Brighten's expression. "I do not understand why she wouldn't have contacted us about you. We could have . . . we would have loved to have seen you grow up." She paused. "It would have helped . . . helped with our own loss of your father."

Kylie remembered her mom saying that the Brightens would hate her for this. "She knows it was a mistake," Kylie said, recalling her mom saying almost as much. "But in her defense, she was young, pregnant, and scared. My stepdad, he was someone who knew her and loved her. He agreed to marry her, but he wanted . . . he wanted to raise me as his own." She paused. "He was wrong, too, but they were both just trying to do the best they could."

Mrs. Brighten nodded. "I imagine that was a hard place to be."

Kylie's knot of worry lessened. "I hope you'll forgive her. Because . . . she's been a pretty amazing mom."

"I'd like to chat with her."

Kylie tensed. "I'm sure that's possible. If you don't mind, I'll check with her . . . and get back to you on that." Kylie sent up a prayer that her mom would be agreeable. But oh, lordy, that was going to be a hard conversation.

Tears filled Mrs. Brighten's eyes. "I brought some more photos with me, if you'd like to see them."

"I would love to," Kylie said. "Thank you."

Mrs. Brighten pulled a small photo album from a large beige purse. As Kylie flipped through the pages, she recognized some of the same images she had. Her real grandfather had snuck into the Brightens' house and had copies made to bring to her so they would appear like the real Brightens. But there were many images that Kylie hadn't seen. And seeing images of her father, she felt emotion swell inside her.

"If you would like you can keep it," Mrs. Brighten said. "I made it up for you."

Kylie smiled. "Thank you so much! I will cherish this, I promise."

Mr. Brighten sat up. "You even act like your father. He was so . . . polite."

"Yes," Mrs. Brighten said. "He was such a good boy. Always kind-hearted. A gentle spirit. A little shy sometimes, but—"

"I can be shy, too," Kylie said. "I hate it when I'm called on to stand up and talk or give a report in school." *Or everyone is looking at my weird pattern. Or thinking I'm pregnant.*

Mrs. Brighten smiled. "He really didn't like school very well. He always said he felt as if he didn't fit in anywhere."

"Oh boy, do I know how that feels," Kylie said.

"Not that he got into trouble. Well, there was that one time in his last year of high school. There was a kid at school, Timmy. He was slow, and while walking home from school, Daniel came upon a group of older boys picking on him—really mistreating him. There were maybe six of them, and Daniel lost it. We still don't know how he did it, but he gave all of them bloody noses and black eyes. And there wasn't a scratch on our boy."

Kylie listened to the story with a hungry heart—a daughter eager to know about a father she knew so little about.

"The school suspended him," Mrs. Brighten continued, "but when Timmy's parents found out, they went to the local news channel and they interviewed Timmy about what happened, and the news channel honored Daniel as a hero. And the boys got in trouble. The school was forced to drop Daniel's suspension. Of course, Daniel was embarrassed about the attention. The news channel gave him a trophy, and the next day, he went over to Timmy's house and gave him the trophy. He said that Timmy was the real hero having to deal with those bullies all his life."

Pride for her dad swelled in Kylie's chest. He'd been a protector just like her, and like her, he didn't want the credit. She wished again that she hadn't lost the man whom she'd taken after. Sure, she still had a part of him in spirit form, but she could have used so much more.

"But you know after he graduated from high school, he just sort of found himself. As a matter of fact, one day he came home from a trip and he told me he was finally figuring out who he was."

Kylie remembered her dad telling her about meeting an old man who'd told him he wasn't human. She wondered if that was the same trip.

"I told him," Mrs. Brighten continued, "that I already knew who he was. He was a kind and gentle soul." She stared at Kylie. "I see the same in you. As if . . . as if you had some magic spirit that very few people have." She reached across the table and rested her hand on Kylie's.

The aged hand reminded Kylie of how her great-aunt had touched her when playing the part of Mrs. Brighten. There was no extra warmth from the real Mrs. Brighten's touch as had come from her great-aunt's. Yet it didn't make the real Mrs. Brighten's touch any less special. And just like that, Kylie knew how easy it was going to be to love these people, and how lucky her father had been to be raised by them.

It was almost five that afternoon before Burnett and Holiday, holding hands like two lovebirds, walked Kylie to her cabin. Della waited inside to take over shadowing duties.

"You sure you'll be all right?" Holiday asked.

"Yeah." And amazingly, Kylie sort of believed it. Yes, she was still craving some chocolate to counteract the freaking crazy day, and yes, her heart would forever be broken over Lucas, but she was going to be okay.

Thinking of her other roommate, Kylie asked, "Did you talk with Miranda about the Nikki episode?"

"Yes," Holiday said, her eyes frowning. "Although I haven't come up with her other punishment yet."

Kylie couldn't help but put in her two cents. "I'm not saying Miranda didn't do wrong, but Nikki was being overly obvious about her crush with Perry. I even warned her about it. But she didn't listen."

"I know," Holiday said. "Nikki was wrong, but Miranda can't go around turning people into kangaroos."

"Really? You seemed to enjoy hearing about it when she did that to me," Burnett said sarcastically.

Holiday hiccuped. "That was funny." She sent him a devilish grin.

Kylie watched them leave before stepping inside. She found Della sitting at the kitchen table, sipping on a glass of blood, with schoolbooks in front of her. The little vamp took her homework seriously.

Della looked up. "I agree with Holiday. It was funny when Miranda turned Burnett into a kangaroo."

Kylie slumped down into a chair. "Where's Miranda?"

Della rolled her eyes. "She and Perry went off to have make-up 'almost sex'—her words, not mine. Personally I didn't need to know that. Although I have to admit I wonder exactly what 'almost sex' is." She frowned. "Then again, it probably involves Perry sucking her earlobes and I'm really not willing to hear about that. Again."

Kylie chuckled. "When you think about it, all things sexual are sort of . . . I mean, even French kissing . . . having someone's tongue in your mouth. It's gross."

"Unless you're doing it." Della's words came out dreamlike. Kylie felt certain her friend was thinking about Steve. "And then it's not gross. It's almost magic."

Kylie remembered French-kissing Lucas and even doing more the night they'd been coming back from the graveyard. It *had* been magical. But all that magic was over now. No more Lucas. "Yeah, it's not so gross then, is it." Popping up, she went and looked inside the tiny pantry. "Do we have anything chocolate in this kitchen? Anything?"

"I think there's some chocolate syrup in the fridge. But we don't have any milk. Not that it was me who drank it. That would be the witch." Della glanced back at Kylie.

Kylie reached into the refrigerator and found the chocolate syrup. Oh, hell, beggars couldn't be choosy. She squeezed a line of chocolate all the way up her index finger and popped the digit into her mouth.

"So the meeting with the Brightens didn't go well?" Della asked.

"No, it went fine," Kylie mumbled around her chocolate-covered finger. When the sweetness disappeared, she pulled her finger out and aimed the top of the bottle down and gave the digit another squirt of sweetness.

"Then why are you sucking chocolate syrup off your finger like it's whiskey? Wait! I know why, I heard about the fiasco with your dad and mom—the whole pregnancy thing. Hilarious." Della dropped her elbows on the table and laughed.

"Not hilarious." Kylie frowned. "How did you hear about it?"

Della shrugged, looking a little guilty for bringing it up. "Someone heard it go down. Everybody was talking about it. Sorry." She made an apology face.

Kylie moaned. "Will I ever stop being the source of gossip around here?" She held her head back and squeezed a good squirt of chocolate straight into her mouth.

"Now that's gross!" Della chuckled.

Kylie brought the bottle down and licked her lips. "I didn't touch my lips to the bottle. I just poured it into my mouth."

"And on your chin."

Frowning, Kylie wiped her chin with the back of her hand. "Sorry, I'm feeling desperate." She snagged a bowl and spoon and went back to the table and emptied a half a cup of the sweet feel-good stuff into her bowl.

"Damn," Della said. "You are feeling desperate."

Kylie scooped a spoonful of chocolate into her mouth, licked the spoon clean and said, "Monique crawled into the stall with me."

"Who? What stall?"

"Monique. Lucas's Monique. She climbed into the bathroom stall with me in the restaurant bathroom."

"Oh, shit! Did you two like duke it out or something?"

"No." Kylie licked the spoon. "I just peed all over myself." She took another spoonful of chocolate into her mouth.

Della sighed. "Are you okay?"

"I will be after I finish off this bottle," Kylie said.

Della half grinned. "If I was a real friend, I'd stop you from drinking it."

Kylie shook her head. "If you were a real friend, you'd help me finish it."

"Shit. Why not?" She pushed over her glass of blood. "Give me a couple of shots."

Kylie arched an eyebrow. "For real?"

"Yeah." Della pushed her schoolbooks to the side. "Screw homework, let's get drunk off chocolate. I could use a pick-me-up, too."

Kylie saw pain reflect in her friend's gaze. She gave an extra-hard squeeze of chocolate into the vamp's glass. "What really happened while you were away, Della?"

Chapter Twenty-six

The vamp stared down at her glass of blood laced with chocolate. She swirled the glass and seemed to watch the two ingredients blend together. "I skipped out on Steve the first night and went to see Lee."

That didn't surprised Kylie, she knew Della was still hung up on Lee, but it didn't explain how she ended up getting hickeys from Steve. Unless it wasn't Steve who gave her the hickey, but Kylie didn't think she'd lie about that. And something told Kylie this wasn't all about Lee. It was about a shape-shifter with a cute butt.

"And?" Kylie asked, dipping her spoon back into her own chocolate.

"And he went out on a date with his new fiancée." She brought the glass to her lips and sipped. "Hey, this shit is really good."

"Yeah." Kylie waited for Della to continue. She didn't have to wait too long.

"He took her to a Chinese restaurant. I followed them." Tears filled Della's eyes.

Feeling her friend's pain, Kylie set her hand on Della's. Della pulled it away.

"Then they spotted me and I realized I looked like an idiot. I was all kinds of embarrassed." She took another sip of her chocolate blood and looked up. "Then like some damn knight in shining armor Steve showed up. He'd followed me. He saved my ass from looking like a total fool. Pretended we were on a date. He kissed me in front of them. Like we were this hot couple."

Kylie took another spoonful of chocolate into her mouth. "And the kiss was pretty good so you guys made out later?"

"No. I mean yes."

Kylie pointed her spoon at Della. "Which is it?"

"Yes it was good, but it didn't happen until the next day." Della leaned in and frowned.

"The mission went bad. I was stabbed," Della confessed.

Kylie's mouth dropped open. "But Burnett said—"

"I made Steve promise not to tell him. It wasn't life threatening." She moaned. "The bad thing is that Steve saved my ass. Not just at the restaurant in front of Lee, but again with the rogues and then when we ran into some nasty weres. I was in pretty bad shape, couldn't fight. I hated it." She paused. "He checked us into a hotel and was taking care of me. I don't know how it happened, one minute he was doctoring me and the next we were playing doctor."

"Oh my!" Kylie said. "So you actually—"

"No, we didn't. Came close. Thankfully blue balls don't really kill a guy."

"Blue balls?" Kylie asked.

Della rolled her eyes. "You don't know what blue balls are?"

"No. Should I?"

Della grinned. "At least you should know if a guy ever tells you he can die from it, he's lying. And believe me, some guys will actually say that to guilt a girl into doing the bumping dance. I had one try it on me once, before Lee. I told him I'd go to his funeral, and never dated him again."

"But what is it, really?" Kylie made a face. "Or is it too gross? It must be gross because they never mentioned it in any of the pamphlets my mom gave me."

Della chuckled again. "It's when a guy gets really turned on and is ready to do the deed and then the deed gets canceled."

Kylie leaned in. "Do their balls really turn blue?"

Della burst out laughing. "I don't know, I've never gotten down there and checked."

Kylie blushed, but then she didn't really care in front of Della, so she just laughed. "So you think Steve had blue balls?"

Della rolled her eyes. "He looked pretty uncomfortable. I shouldn't have let it get that far. I was just . . . mixed up in the head."

"Or maybe you really like Steve." Kylie pointed her spoon at Della. "I'm not saying you should have had sex, but the guy's crazy about you and you obviously like him, too. So why are you treating him like a disease now?"

Della took a big swig of her chocolate blood. "Because . . . when I realized what was happening, all I could think about was that in a year or so I'll be standing in another restaurant watching Steve with his fiancée. I can't do that again." Tears filled her eyes.

"But you don't know that will happen."

"I don't know it won't happen, either." Della reached for the bottle of syrup and added another squirt to her glass. "So now I've spilled my guts. How do things stand with Lucas?"

Kylie stirred her chocolate in her bowl. "It's over."

Della's eyes widened. "Why? Did Monique say they'd fooled around? We should get Miranda to give him a case of mange on his balls!"

"No, Monique sort of said they didn't."

Della picked up her glass. "Then why's it over?"

Kylie clanked her spoon against her bowl. *Because if it isn't he'll lose everything.*

Della studied her. "But it he didn't cheat—"

Anger stirred in Kylie's chest. "Even if he didn't do anything, it still feels like he did. I mean, he was getting engaged, behind my back." She shook her head. "First Trey. Then my stepdad cheats on my mom. Then Derek and now Lucas. Why do guys do this?"

Della kind of shrugged. "At least Lucas didn't have sex."

It still feels like a betrayal. A big one. "What's downright infuriating is that I still love him." Love him so much that she couldn't stand by and watch him lose everything because of her. "But I'm still so mad at him I could . . ."

"Give him a set of blue balls?" Della chuckled.

"No, punch him!"

"Then maybe you should." Della looked down at her glass.

"Should what?" Kylie asked.

"Punch him. Then maybe you wouldn't be so mad and you could move on."

Kylie shook her head. "I wish it was that simple."

"Maybe it is. You won't know until you try. Just go up to him all casual like and then go all crazy on his ass. Seriously, then maybe you could put it behind you and forget it."

"Like you're trying to do with Steve?" Kylie pointed the spoon at her again.

"Hey, I'm like a good parent. I don't want you to do as I do, but do as I say!" She chuckled.

Kylie shook her head.

"And besides, now it's . . ." She shut her mouth, unsure if she wanted to talk about this.

"It's what?" Della asked.

She might as well spill it. "It's not just about what he did." If it was, Kylie suspected she'd be halfway to forgivness. "He gave up everything when he refused to sign that engagement paper. He's not going to get on the Council, his own pack is pissed at him. Monique's dad is threatening to have him killed. Sooner or later he's going to hate me for this."

"I think you're overthinking it."

Kylie ran her spoon around the bowl for the last bit of chocolate. "And I think we gotta change the subject," she said.

Della relented and picked up her glass. They didn't speak for a few minutes, then finally she spoke up. "Before I went to Lee's place that night, I went and played peeping tom at my house."

"How were things?" Kylie asked, sensing it didn't go well.

"Good. So good it made me mad. They were playing board games like this happy little family. Dad told jokes and they were all laughing. I don't think they even miss me." She stared at the table for a few minutes.

"They miss you, Della. They're just trying to get by."

Della nodded. "Have you ever considered just telling your mom and stepdad? I came so close to just walking in there and laying it out on the table. Look, Dad, I'm not being difficult or lazy. I'm not on drugs. I'm just a vampire." She shook her head.

Kylie bit down on her lip, unsure what to say, so she didn't say anything.

"I guess I'm scared they'll think the truth is worse than what they already believe."

Kylie wished she could tell Della it wasn't so, but she wasn't sure. "I thought about telling my mom, too. I just don't know if she would handle it."

Della nodded. "So we just hide from the people we love. Sad, isn't it?"

"Yeah." Kylie ran her spoon around her bowl. "At least you don't hide from the supernatural world."

"You don't hide either," Della said.

"Yeah, I do. I'm basically hiding from the FRU. I mean everyone here has seen my pattern, so it's a little late to worry about that, but I know the majority of people here think any day now my brain tumor is going to become apparent."

Della offered her a sad look. "They are actually betting on it."

"Just great." Kylie paused. "When Monique came in the bathroom, I tried to change my pattern. I just wasn't fast enough. She even said something about me having a brain tumor. And I'm like, 'I'm sure that's what it is.'" Kylie dropped her spoon in her bowl and listened to it clatter. "Most of the supernatural world doesn't even know my kind exists." Even Hayden hides what he is, Kylie thought.

"Then maybe it's time you change that." Della sat back in her chair.

"Change what?" Kylie asked.

"Come out of the closet. You know, like . . . 'I'm gay and here to stay.' You'd need a different slogan, but maybe, 'I'm a lizard and if you don't like it, I'll eat out your gizzard.'" Della chuckled. "Okay, it needs some work, but you get what I mean."

"I'm serious," Kylie said.

"I know, and so am I. Besides the silly slogan, I mean. You can't do it with the humans, but you should be able to do it with supernaturals."

Kylie ran her finger around the rim of the bowl to collect the last remnants of chocolate and considered what Della said.

She's right, the voice in her head said. The same voice from earlier. The one that popped up inside her head at the oddest times.

"Who the hell are you?" Kylie muttered.

Della scooted back in her chair. "Okay, I'm rethinking the brain tumor now."

"Not you."

"Oh, shit." Della's eyes grew big. "Do we have a ghost here?"

"No, not a ghost," Kylie muttered. "Just a voice."

Della tilted her head to the side. "I didn't hear anything."

"In here." Kylie pointed to her head.

"Have you ever heard of schizophrenia?" Della asked in a sarcastic voice—which meant she was teasing, but Kylie didn't think it was too funny.

"I'm not crazy," Kylie said.

Della grinned. "If you were, I'd still like you. If for no other reason than for teaching me how good blood and chocolate are together." She drained her cup.

Kylie stared at her empty bowl while her brain raced on how she could come out of the closet. She had made it her quest to save other chameleon teens from living a life of seclusion, but maybe before she could do that, she needed to make sure it was safe for them to come out. Maybe Della and that annoying voice were right. If she could force the supernatural world to accept her—for what she really was—then other chameleons might follow her out in the open.

Sort of like Rosa Parks on the bus in the fifties. Someone, some chameleon, needed to stand up so they could be counted as part of the supernatural world. They should be proud of who they were, and not have to hide their true selves.

Instantly, her chest swelled with emotion that was both warm and affirming. This was her quest. Her new quest or maybe just part of her old one. And it felt like the right thing.

Yup, all she had to do was figure out how to come out of the closet.

That night, head buried in her pillow, the tingly feeling of another presence stirred her awake. It wasn't a cold presence, which meant whoever was here wasn't dead. Opening her eyes, the sweet floral scent tickled her senses. She spotted the red rose on her bedside table.

Only one person left her roses.

Lucas? Her heart whispered his name and went straight to hurting. Last night, she'd lain in bed and accepted what had to be. Letting him go. As much as it hurt, she couldn't let him destroy his life because of her.

She inhaled and listened. Was he still here? Or had he come and gone? She noticed her white curtain fluttering as a soft night breeze floated inside. If he'd left, he'd have shut the window.

She closed her eyes again, wondering if she pretended not to wake up he would just leave.

"I know you're awake," his deep voice spoke into the still darkness.

"And I know you shouldn't be here." She swallowed and fought the swell of emotion climbing up her throat. She rolled over and pulled her pajama-covered knees to her chest. It took another couple of seconds to gather her courage for her to look for him—knowing that seeing him would hurt.

She was right. His hair looked windblown as if he'd gone for a run. His eyes looked hurt. Raw pain rained down on her. Her chest ached with loneliness.

"I couldn't sleep," he said. Silence filled the room. He moved closer. His knees touched the bed. He sat down. The mattress dipped with his weight. Her heart raced, remembering the times she had curled up with him here on this bed. She'd even slept beside him here and he'd held her, made her feel safe, protected. Loved.

"It can't be over, Kylie. You are the only thing that matters to me."

She shook her head. "Not true." Just like her, he had others in his life. He had things that were important to him. He had quests. "Your pack is important. It has been all along. Your grandmother. And you can say you don't like your dad, but you put up with him, so he has to matter to you. And then there's your sister." *And you'll lose them all if you choose me.*

"Fine, I care about them—everyone but my father. Right now I don't care if he rots in hell. I'm tired of him manipulating my life—but the others, yes, I'll admit it, I care. But they aren't you," he said, and growled.

"Monique's father is considering putting a hit out on you!" she blurted out.

"That rich pompous ass is always running off his mouth. He's nothing but hot air. He knows what my dad would do to him if he hurt me." Lucas stopped talking and just looked at her. "But this proves it. You care about me. If you didn't, you wouldn't care if he planned to kill me. You may still be angry, and I deserve that, but you love me and that's why it can't be over."

She shook her head. "Love isn't enough!" Tears clouded her vision. That was what she'd finally realized last night. "Can't you see, Lucas? We're Romeo and Juliet; we're the Hatfields and McCoys. We are every bad love story that ever existed. We are people who only hurt ourselves and others by selfishly letting our emotions guide us instead of logic."

"That's stupid," he growled, and tried to reach for her.

"No!" She scooted away from his touch. "Do you want to know what's stupid? I keep seeing you kissing Monique in my head. I keep hearing you vowing your soul to her, and I get so hurt and so angry that I want to scream. But at the same time, I completely understand why you did it. And if I were in your shoes, I might have done the same things. I have my own quests, the ghosts, figuring out how to help other chameleons, and I'm going to complete those quests no matter what."

She swallowed and offered the last piece of truth, the last piece of reasoning that they couldn't be together. "I'm going to do it even if it hurts you. That's how I know, Lucas. That's how I know that this isn't right. When doing the right thing for yourself can hurt someone you love this much, it can't be right! We *aren't* right. So please, let's not hurt each other any more than we already have. Just leave."

She had never seen anyone look so hurt. It took everything she had not to call him back as he climbed out her window.

Chapter Twenty-seven

The next day during science class, Kylie sat at her desk barely listening to Hayden Yates talk about Newton's laws of motion and $E=MC^2$. Not that she didn't respect science, but how could any of that explain a sword that could move on its own? And didn't Hayden say that both Einstein and Newton were supernaturals? Did that mean they didn't have magical swords following them around?

Not that she was completely consumed with worry over the sword right now. Her morning had been bat-shit crazy. Starting with a ten-minute conversation with her mom that entailed both of them apologizing. Mom for overreacting to the news of the pregnancy tests and making a scene, and Kylie for not informing her she'd used the card for the items. It hadn't been a bad call, but it hadn't been a good one, especially when her mom launched into a conversation about how John was possibly her soul mate.

Somehow she'd managed to tuck her mom worries away. Her Lucas issues weren't so easy to tuck away. Between hurting for him, she'd also fretted over finding a method of coming out of the closet.

She'd even skipped Campmate hour and breakfast to try to formulate a plan. And she came up . . . empty.

Of course, she wasn't at her all-time best. After Lucas had left, the spirit, as if jealous that Kylie wasn't fixating on her, had decided to pop in every hour last night. She hadn't brought her severed head and sword, for which Kylie was forever grateful. But on her last visit the spirit brought something even more upsetting. Grief. She sobbed in her hands and muttered something about her son being killed.

Having lost too many in her own life, Kylie hurt for the spirit and told her so, but the spirit was too upset to even respond.

Kylie wondered if the ghost meant her son was killed in the present time, or if she was revisiting something in her past. Time just didn't compute with spirits, which could be confusing as hell to the living who were trying to help them.

Then again, nothing seemed to compute much with this spirit. She wouldn't answer any of Kylie's direct questions. As in: *Who is it exactly that you want me to kill?* Or, *Why me? Why did you choose me to do your killing?*

When Holiday had stopped by the cabin last night, she'd reminded Kylie that a spirit usually had a connection with the person they were visiting.

"Find that connection and you might start to understand what she really wants," Holiday had advised.

Easier said than done.

So far, the spirit hadn't said one thing that led Kylie to believe she had known her, or that they knew anyone in common.

She'd first run into the spirit on her way to see Lucas's engagement ceremony. Kylie considered that maybe she had been killed in those woods and Kylie had just stumbled by. She even found herself hoping that was the case. Call her a prude, but she didn't want to be connected with someone who chopped heads off people and carried them around like trophies. And if Kylie had known someone like that, wouldn't this person stand out in Kylie's memory bank?

Sure, Kylie was almost certain the ghost had brought the head around just to get attention, but something a little less dramatic would have worked just fine. Holiday also said to consider everything the spirit did or brought with her to be a clue. Like the sword that kind of looked like the one that appeared at the falls.

Was the head a hint or a sign? Then again, weren't clues supposed to be subtle? There was absolutely nothing subtle about a severed head. That last thought led Kylie back to believing it was just a ploy to get attention—mostly because the ploy was working. Here Kylie was worried about the ghost and not her quest.

Not that she didn't need to figure out both; she did. But her quest seemed to take priority right now. Or it would if the ghost would stop pulling her thoughts away.

Hayden stood by the board and pointed to the homework assignment. She started to jot it down when something landed in her lap with a thump. A pretty heavy thump.

Startled, her butt came off the desk chair a good half inch. Only her dislike of being singled out in the class had her swallowing the yelp that rose in throat and planting her butt back down.

Considering there was a desktop covering her lap, the whole "thing falling in her lap" didn't make sense.

Then again it didn't have to make sense, because nothing else in her freaking life did!

Kylie hesitantly reached under her desk to feel the cold metal object. Just as she suspected, it had a long vertical shape with a handle. The sword was back.

Kylie heard a clearing of a throat a couple of seats away. She glanced over at Derek, who was on shadowing duty, and he mouthed the words: *You okay?*

Obviously Derek had sensed her emotional dilemma, but hadn't seen the sword, or he would have at least glanced down at the dang thing. She nodded.

After only a minute, Hayden dismissed class. Kylie pretended to be reading her notes and didn't move. Burnett didn't want anyone to know about the sword, and suddenly brandishing a weapon in the middle of science class that looked like something straight out of a video game would likely draw some attention.

"Kylie, you coming?" Derek asked from the door.

"Uh, no, I need to discuss something with Mr. Yates. I'll be out shortly." She glanced at Hayden, who studied her with concern.

"Just wait outside," a worried-looking Hayden told Derek.

When Kylie glanced up at Derek, she saw Lucas standing right outside the door. His blue gaze met hers, but dang it, she had too much on her plate, not to mention a sword in her lap, to start fixating on losing him, on how much it hurt. Yet, when she saw the concern in his eyes, the complete affection with which he looked at her, her heart did another nosedive anyway. Begrudgingly, she couldn't deny that there was a part of her that wanted to hang on to him, to grasp on to what they felt. But that would be foolish, wouldn't it?

"Shut the door," Hayden told them, and walked over to her desk.

Shut the door. Hayden's words echoed in her head. She had to shut the door to her feelings about Lucas. But how?

"Is something wrong?" Hayden asked.

My whole freaking life. Kylie met the teacher's eyes, pushing away her ache over Lucas. "Yeah, there's a sword in my lap."

"*The* sword?" he asked.

She made a face. "Well, I haven't looked at it, but I'm assuming I've only got one sword that just magically appears and breaks all the rules and theories you just covered in class."

Hayden grinned and tilted his head down to see the sword. When he rose up, he said, "Yeah, those theories aren't worth a crap sometimes when magic is involved."

"Same sword, I assume?" Kylie asked.

He nodded.

"Great." Then she realized something he'd just said. "You think it's magic doing this, like Wiccan magic?"

"Or something equally baffling," he said.

"So you really don't think it's some chameleon powers?"

He twisted his mouth. "Chameleon powers are in part Wiccan powers."

"Yeah," Kylie said, and her mind went back to her latest quest. "Which completely confuses me as to why it's bad to be us."

He looked puzzled. "It's not bad to be us," he said, and then, "Let me get my hoodie and I'll wrap it up and we'll take it to the office."

He went and snatched his sweatshirt from the cabinet behind his desk, then came back with it stretched open. "Do you want to bring it up?"

No. She didn't like touching the thing, didn't like it sitting on her lap, but she did it anyway.

She reached down and carefully grasped the handle and brought it up and out. Before she had it all the way up, it started glowing again. She dropped the weapon in the hoodie then looked up. "If it's not bad to be us, then why do you hide your pattern? You even wear a hoodie so no one will see it. And why do the elders think they have to hide all the kids?"

"I hide the pattern because people wouldn't understand, because in the past that led to us being persecuted, but not because it's bad to be a chameleon."

"But wouldn't it be better if you didn't have to hide it? If we could just wear it proudly like the others do?"

He stared at the sword as if half listening to what she said. "Someday that will happen."

"No it won't," Kylie insisted. "Not if everyone keeps hiding."

He gazed up at her. "You don't understand how bad things were for our parents."

"You're right, I don't understand. And maybe that's why I see things clearer. Change needs to happen. But somebody has to make it happen. It's not going to happen on its own, or by accident."

"Okay, it sounds as if you've actually given this a lot of thought. How would we change it?" he asked.

"I haven't figured it out yet, but I will." She stood up.

He sighed as if he didn't like what she said. "When you do figure out something, you run it by me first. I know you wouldn't want to put anyone in jeopardy."

"I just want to help. And I'll run it by you if I can." She cut her gaze to the sword.

"What's that mean . . . 'if I can'? Why couldn't you run it by me?" he asked.

She looked at him. "I'm just being careful not to make promises that I don't know if I can keep."

He frowned. "Don't do anything stupid, Kylie."

"Now that I can promise," she said. "I'll avoid stupid at all costs."

He didn't appear content with her answer, but he looked back at the sword. "Your grandfather called me at lunch and wanted to know for sure if the sword had any markings." Hayden rolled the weapon over. "I don't see a thing on it."

"Me either," Kylie said.

"Does it hurt you to hold it?" he asked, and looked up at her.

"Hurt? No. Freak me out? Yes. Why?"

"Would you hold it for me again? For a few seconds, and let's see if anything appears. We know it starts to glow; maybe something else will appear on it."

Kylie frowned. "Fine, but if it or I go bananas and kill you or something, it's not my fault. I mean the last time Holiday had me try something, Burnett nearly ended up sterile."

Hayden frowned. "Maybe we should wait and try it when we get to the office and Burnett and Holiday are around."

"Good idea," Kylie said.

"Are you sure this is a good idea?" Kylie asked. "What if it's like the paperweight incident?" She glanced from Hayden to Burnett, who'd gotten ball-busted by the paperweight.

Not surprising, the vamp was the one who looked the most concerned, but he was also the one to speak up. "You've held it before and the only thing it did was glow."

"But I never held it for more than a few seconds."

"If you really don't want to do it, then don't," Holiday said, and Derek, standing beside her, nodded. Burnett, remembering Derek's computer skills, had asked him to be here so he might research any information on the sword.

Kylie looked at Holiday. "I just don't want it to go crazy and start killing people."

"Why do you think it would do that?" Holiday asked.

"I . . . I don't know, maybe because of the ghost's sword," Kylie said. "And the fact that she carries around a head with the sword."

"Do you really think the ghost and this sword are connected?" Holiday asked. "Because I still can't see how a ghost could have sent the sword here."

"I don't know what to think," Kylie said. "But I think the two swords look alike."

"But it's a very common-looking sword—for what it is," Burnett said.

"And I don't think you'd hurt anyone," Derek said. "You're a protector; if the sword is reacting to you, then I think it's connecting to that part of you. I don't think it's evil."

"I agree," said Hayden.

"Okay, it's your lives on the line." Kylie reached for the weapon.

"But just in case," Holiday said, stopping Kylie. "Let's all be prepared to duck and run if need be."

Kylie frowned.

Holiday shrugged. "Just in case."

Kylie reached for the sword. Burnett pushed Holiday behind him and then everyone took another step back.

Chapter Twenty-eight

The moment her palm wrapped around the grip of the blade it started to glow again. Warmth from the weapon soaked into her hand and started climbing up her arm.

"You okay?" Holiday asked as if sensing Kylie's unease.

Kylie fought the urge to drop the weapon and took a breath. Instead, she gripped the handle tighter, trying not to let the weight of it make the sword wobble. It wasn't so heavy, probably only weighed three pounds, yet it felt awkward. She felt awkward holding it.

"Yeah, I'm okay," she said. "It's just warm."

"Don't let it burn you," Holiday said.

"It's not hot. Just warm," Kylie said. The sword continued to grow brighter, not so bright it hurt to look at. It was like filtered light. She took her second breath since holding the weapon and suddenly she wasn't afraid anymore. It was . . . not even the least bit frightening. It felt . . . like picking up something familiar. A worry stone, or a picture frame she'd held and stared at for a long time. And yet she'd never touched this sword until a few days ago. How could it feel so comfortable in her hand?

As if her sense of calm spread, Burnett and Hayden took a step closer. Derek followed them and then Holiday.

"I don't see any new markings on it," Hayden said.

"Me neither," Burnett said.

Kylie looked at the sword and realized it didn't even feel cumbersome anymore. The awkwardness had vanished. Her grip on the sword felt solid, the object in her hand became almost a part of her. She turned her wrist and saw an inscription on the knob at the top of the handle.

"Here. There's an inscription." Kylie nodded, then pointed with her left hand.

All four of them moved closer.

"It's in Latin," Holiday said. "It says *holy warrior*."

"You know, I can check the Internet and see what I can find, but . . ." Derek looked at her as if with an apology, as if he knew what he was about to say was going to upset her. "But there is someone here who knows a lot about swords."

Burnett nodded. "I just now remembered that." The vamp looked at Kylie with the same apologetic look as Derek.

Oh, shit! She knew without them saying who it was.

Burnett pulled out his phone. "I'm calling Lucas."

Kylie shook her head. "How? What does a werewolf know about swords?"

Burnett arched a brow. "His ancestry goes back to the Scandinavians."

History wasn't her forte. "And what does that mean?"

"Fighting with swords had been in his family a thousand years. He was trained when he was a kid."

A moan slipped out of her mouth. She'd hoped to keep as much distance as she could from Lucas.

"Fine, call him. Show him the sword. But can I go now?" Kylie started to set the sword down.

Burnett frowned. "Actually, I'd like him to see it glowing."

"Lucas," Burnett said into his phone. "Can you come to the office? I have something I want you to see." Burnett looked at Kylie. "Yes."

Pause. "Yes. No, she's fine." Pause. "You'll see when you get here." Pause. "Great." Burnett hung up.

"He's actually just at the dining hall," Burnett said.

Kylie knew then that he'd probably followed them to the office and was waiting to see if something was wrong. The fact that he cared did another number on her heartstrings. She closed her eyes for just a second and prepared herself for seeing him.

The sound of rushed footsteps on the office's porch filled the silence. The office's front door banged open.

A knock sounded on Holiday's door. "Come in," Burnett and Holiday said at once.

Lucas rushed in, his gaze shooting to her. His eyes, filled with worry, met hers with a touch of panic. She felt that look of concern brush against her nerve endings. Nerve endings that felt raw, exposed. Real physical pain stirred in her chest.

"What's . . . wrong?" His gaze shifted to the glowing sword, which she now held by her side, and his breath caught. "Damn!"

"Do you know anything about this type of sword?" Burnett asked.

Lucas moved in. He reached for her wrist, gently, but his touch shot tiny pinpoints of pain inside her. Her focus shifted off the sword and on his touch.

He raised her hand and the sword. She heard him breathing, soft easy breaths that somehow seemed emotional. She sensed his mind wasn't only on the sword either. She bit her lip to keep the sigh from leaving her lips.

"And?" Burnett asked.

Lucas inhaled. "It's from the twelfth century." He turned her hand a bit to get a good look at both sides. "More than likely a crusader sword."

"I pretty much knew that," Burnett said. "Any knowledge of why it would be glowing?"

Lucas looked up at her. "It has to be Kylie."

His thumb brushed over the bottom of her wrist. His touch was sweet and bitter at the same time. She wanted to cry. She swallowed again, praying to keep the tears at bay. But damn it! Even angry at him, even feeling certain their relationship was doomed, she loved him so damn much. The desire to lean against him, to beg him to hold her, was strong, but she forced herself not to give in.

"Yeah, we know that, too," Burnett said. "But why?"

Lucas's gaze continued to caress her. "That I don't know. I mean, I could guess."

"Then guess," Burnett said, lacking patience.

Lucas glanced at Burnett. "She's a holy warrior."

"No, I'm just a protector." Kylie pushed her Lucas issues aside to focus on the issue of the sword again. "I'm not a warrior. I don't even like war."

"But that is exactly what the sword says," Burnett said. "Holy warrior."

Lucas looked back at her. "Where?" He glanced down at the sword again.

Kylie turned her wrist and showed him the inscription.

"Holy shit. You really are a holy warrior." He looked awed. Impressed.

There was a time she'd been thrilled to see that look in his eyes for her. But not right now. And oh yeah, she wasn't so impressed either. She didn't want to think of herself as Joan of Arc, or any kind of warrior. "You can't believe everything you read," she said.

Lucas looked puzzled by her reaction. "It's almost the same thing as a protector, but to me, it's even more amazing. There are legends written on it. I don't remember them all, but my grandmother has a book on them."

"But you've never actually met a holy warrior, right?" Kylie asked.

"You," he said again with a sense of pride.

"Before me!" she snapped.

"No," Lucas admitted.

Kylie turned to the others in the room. "Have any of you met a holy warrior?"

They all shook their heads no.

"Then there's my proof," she said adamantly. "They are just legends. They really don't exist." Face it, she didn't want to think of herself as a warrior. She was still trying to come to grips with being a protector.

Holiday moved in and rested a hand on Kylie's arm. "We didn't know chameleons existed until a few weeks ago."

"She's right," Derek said to Kylie.

Well, hell, there went that argument, Kylie thought, and tried not to panic.

Lucas, who still held her wrist, gave her hand a slight squeeze. "It's not . . . a bad thing. Being a protector is practically the same thing. You have to fight to protect someone."

She looked down at the glowing sword and realized that Lucas's touch was warmer than the sword.

"Okay, so we're guessing she's a holy warrior, but what does this really mean?" Burnett asked. "Why has the sword just now appeared? Is it a rite-of-passage thing? Just timing? Or . . . is it something else?" The way he said *something else* made it sound bad.

And Kylie could guess what it was, too. And she didn't like it. Nope, not even a little bit.

Lucas glanced at her with sympathy. "I think she's being presented a weapon for a purpose. Yes, it could just be that she hasn't been ready to receive it yet. But I think it's more that . . ." A look of protectiveness crossed his face. She knew they were all thinking the same thing.

"More what?" Burnett and Holiday asked at the same time.

"It could be she's going to need it. The sword appears when it's time to prepare for battle."

"This is exactly what the elders said," Hayden spoke out. "If she's given a sword, it's because she'd going to need it."

"Is there a way we can find out for sure?" Burnett asked.

Lucas shook his head. "I wouldn't know. But . . ." He inhaled and met Kylie's gaze. "Do you know how to use one of these?"

"Why would I know how to use this? I don't even know how to use a potato peeler. And that's why this whole thing doesn't make sense. I am *not* a warrior."

"I've seen you fight," Derek said. "You're pretty amazing."

"He's right," Lucas said. "You've got a holy warrior's heart, too." He looked back at Burnett. "But she needs to learn to use a sword."

And obviously she wasn't going to have a say in the matter. She frowned.

"Can you teach her?" Burnett asked.

Lucas's gaze met hers again.

No, Kylie thought, and she finally pulled her hand away from his. This was not a good idea.

"If she'll let me," Lucas said.

"Kylie?" Burnett asked.

Did she have a choice? Could she say hell no and the sword would disappear?

She didn't think so. She couldn't run from this.

She knew that. Knew it with certainty—if for no other reason than how the sword felt in her hand—as if it belonged there.

She nodded, knowing it was the right thing to do, but hating it all the same.

"Good," Burnett said. "First I want you to get me those books of legends from your grandmother and then your job is to teach Kylie how to use that sword."

Lucas turned and looked at Kylie. "I look forward to it."

And I don't, she thought, but kept those words to herself.

Ten minutes later, Kylie walked back to her cabin with Derek, her official shadow until Della returned from her meeting with her vampire sisters. Lucas was gathering supplies, and lessons would start tomorrow.

"I know you're not happy about this," Derek said.

"You're my shadow, I'm not upset."

"Not about that. I mean the lessons with Lucas."

Kylie sighed. "I don't see where I have a choice."

"You could have insisted Burnett find you another teacher."

"I didn't think about that." *But why hadn't I? Am I wanting to be with him?*

Derek glanced at her. "It's probably best this way, though."

"Why?" Kylie asked, sensing there was something he wasn't saying.

He smiled, but it came with a small touch of sadness. "You love him. I felt it so strongly in there. I also felt your anger."

"I have a right to be angry," she muttered, even when she knew her anger wasn't the biggest issue. Not that it was exactly a small issue either.

"Yes, you do," Derek said, and he stopped walking and just looked at her. "But what you were feeling was bigger than that."

She thought he meant her knowing that Lucas would eventually resent her, but then Derek continued.

He made a sheepish face. "I felt it. The same anguish you used to feel when we first met. When you were hurt over that ol' boyfriend of yours. Then it was the pain you feel toward your stepdad—you know, for cheating on your mom. Then there was the feeling of being betrayed by me."

She wanted to deny it, but couldn't. "So I guess this just means all guys are pieces of shit!" Her heart knotted and she swallowed to keep the tears from rising to her eyes.

He sighed and reached out and touched her shoulder as if wanting to console her. "What Lucas did was wrong, Kylie. Hell, what we all did was wrong. And I'm not saying Lucas doesn't deserve your anger, but he doesn't deserve to pay for everyone else's mistakes."

In spite of her efforts tears blurred her eyes. Damn Derek for being right! Her anger at being betrayed by others was all wrapped up in her anger at Lucas.

Derek's warm touch soothed her emotions, but it didn't fix things. Because this wasn't fixable. "Even if I could get over being mad, our relationship wouldn't work."

"Why not?" he asked.

She shook her head. "I already told you. He'll lose everything. His family. His pack. And even more importantly, his dreams. I refuse to be the reason he loses all that." She took off walking again. Fast. Wishing she could run, run away from everything she felt. From everything she'd lost.

He caught up with her, and she slowed down as they cut to the path back to her cabin. The sun seemed to come at a different angle than a few weeks before. There was a fall feel in the air and it seemed to say that life was changing.

Change was hard.

He cleared his throat and spoke into the fragile silence. "Then you just find a way around that."

She looked at him, unsure exactly what he meant. "Around what?"

"Around him losing everything."

"I don't think that's possible," she said.

"Anything is possible. You're Kylie Galen." He offered her a sincere smile.

She shook her head. "You know, people give me way more credit than I deserve."

He grinned. "You just don't see yourself like we do."

She let go of a frustrated puff of air and the earlier issues rose in her chest. "I'm not cut out to be a warrior, Derek."

"You are going to do fine," he said. "Besides, remember what you told me about accepting my gifts when we first got here?"

"It was probably bad advice," she said.

"No it wasn't. You told me I needed to embrace the gifts. You were right. I can't imagine not using my powers now. They are a part of me. And this whole sword thing and being a warrior is part of who you are."

She shook her head. "I have so much on my plate, I don't need something else."

"What's on your plate?" he asked.

"My resident ghost. I need to get her crossed over before she makes me crazy. And my quests," she said.

"But don't you think the whole sword thing is part of your quests? I'd think it glowing when you touch it is a sign that it has to do with you."

"Well, it's not the part of my quest I would choose to work on right now," she snapped.

After a second, he asked, "Can I help you in any way?"

She actually considered it. "I don't think so."

"Tell me about your ghost," he said.

She told him about the spirit. About the head and the sword.

"Shit, that would be freaky," Derek said. "They have to be connected somehow. She's got a sword and then a sword shows up." He paused. "I know that Lucas is going to bring those books from his grandmother's but I'm still going to do some research on the Internet. Maybe I'll find something."

"Thanks," she said, and then glanced at him. "For everything, too."

"Everything?" he asked.

"I don't deserve your friendship."

"Oh yes you do." They walked a few minutes in silence. The sound of their footfalls on the rocky path joined in the melody of nature. A few bird calls, insects buzzing.

"You want to know something?" he said.

"What?" she asked.

"You did the right thing . . . with us. I needed you to tell me that. As crazy as it sounds, I actually feel better."

"Are you just trying to make sure I don't feel guilty?" she asked.

"No. I'm serious. This is right."

She looked at him and sensed he was being completely honest. "We'll be okay, won't we?" she asked.

"Yeah, I think we will. But I'm also serious about being your friend."

"Me too," she said.

They walked a little way in silence again.

"What are your other quests?" he asked.

She didn't want to explain everything about coming out of the closet to Derek, so she explained the other half. "I want to help the other chameleon teens. The elders keep them secluded from everything. It's no way to grow up."

"Like that girl Jenny?" he asked. "She seemed . . . pretty normal."

"Yeah, like her, and she's normal, she's just . . . very secluded from the world." She told him about them not having cell phones or friends outside the compound.

"That's sad. Jenny seemed . . . nice."

"Yeah, she is," Kylie said, and remembered seeing Jenny clinging to Derek's back as he ran around in circles trying to buck her off. Kylie almost smiled.

"I know what you're thinking about," he said.

"It was funny," she admitted.

"It was not. I could have hurt her."

"You wouldn't have," Kylie said.

"Not on purpose, but she lunged at me from nowhere. I had no idea it was a hot chick latched on to me."

"So." Kylie pointed a finger at him. "You thought she was hot. I knew you did. I saw the way you two looked at each other there."

He shrugged. "I didn't look at her any way."

"Yes, you did. You were checking her out. And she was checking you out."

He arched a brow. "Was she really?"

Kylie laughed. "Yes, she was."

"Then I'll have to look her up, I seem to have a thing for chameleon chicks."

"Good luck with that," Kylie said. "I hear her kind can be difficult."

"That's true," he said, and chuckled. They walked a few feet in silence.

"How bad is it really for them, for the teen chameleons?" Derek asked.

"They basically aren't allowed to go in public until they can change their patterns. And that doesn't happen until like their late teens or twenties."

"You can change yours."

"Yeah, I'm different for some reason." She frowned. "It seems to be the story of my life."

"That does suck for them," Derek said. "Why don't you see about bringing them here? I'll bet Holiday would allow it."

"Believe it or not, I've given it some thought, but it's not going to be that easy." First Kylie had to figure out how to get the chameleons to come out of the closet.

"Well, if I can help, you know I will."

"I'll remember that."

When they got to the cabin Della was already there. So was Miranda. They sat at the kitchen table, sodas in their hands and troubled expressions on their faces.

"Good, you're here," Miranda said as if they'd been waiting for her to hold some important roundtable, Diet Coke discussion. Then both her roommates looked at Derek as if it was a party and he wasn't invited.

Derek looked at Kylie and half chuckled. "The last time I saw that look from girls, there was a handwritten note on my neighbor's tree house that read 'No boys allowed.' I'll see you. And if I get anything from my computer research, I'll let you know."

Kylie watched him leave. Then she turned to Miranda and Della and tossed out her own roundtable, Diet Coke issue to discuss. "Why couldn't my heart have picked him? Life would have been so much easier."

"Because hearts are ornery, sneaky little bastards, designed to cause misery. They want what they want, and they don't give a damn about what would make life easier or harder for the heart's owner," Della snapped. "It sucks big toads!" she screeched, and hit the table so hard, Kylie wouldn't be surprised if it had cracked. "I say we get drunk on chocolate again. Do you think you could score another bottle of chocolate syrup from Holiday?"

Kylie looked at Miranda with the unspoken question: *What the hell is going on?*

Miranda shrugged and obviously read Kylie's silent inquiry, because she answered it. "Steve's been calling her about twice an hour and she won't even answer the phone."

Chapter Twenty-nine

The next day after school, Kylie still sported a chocolate hangover. Yes, they did exist. She was living, breathing, nauseous proof. Holiday, claiming they all three deserved to drown their sorrows in cocoa, had not only come through with the chocolate syrup, she'd had Burnett buy them a gallon of chocolate ice cream and a pack of Oreos.

Of course, more than half the Oreos were gone by the time Burnett and Holiday dropped them off, and Holiday still had crumbs on her chin. "I'm eating for two," she said, excusing herself.

Della had stuck with just her Bloody Chocolate Marys, but Kylie and Miranda had gorged on everything. Kylie wouldn't be surprised if she never touched the stuff again. She couldn't deny that the chocolate had managed to temporarily soothe all their issues. Soothe, not solve.

Della had bitched about Steve not accepting it was over. Miranda had whimpered about having to apologize to Nikki. Kylie had almost gone into a serious whine about how all guys were no-good cheats. But no sooner than the words were about to leave her lips did she recall what Derek had said about her dumping all her past anger on Lucas. Again seeing truth to the statement, she bypassed that rant and talked about being pissed she was a holy warrior.

Of course, after bringing up the warrior issue she had to go into the whole thing of what happened with the sword, making them vow not to repeat it. Miranda, of course, thought the whole holy warrior thing was cool, and Della was jealous. Kylie was still pissed and downed another bowl of ice cream to help deal with it all. Ahh, but before the night was over, they were laughing themselves silly over all things stupid. Among the topics they discussed were sex, boys, and what was more appealing on those boys, briefs or boxers.

Boxers won.

"Okay, so maybe chocolate and blood don't go so well together," Della said, looking pretty gloomy this afternoon as well. It was Kylie who should be in the worst mood. She was about to meet Lucas to have her first sword fighting lesson. By the lake, too.

Why had he chosen that spot to practice?

Oh, damn, she knew why—because that was sort of their make-out spot. But what she didn't know was if he thought there was a chance in hell that they'd be making out today. If he did, he had another think coming. She'd come here to fight, not French-kiss!

She spotted Lucas waiting, leaning casually against a tree. She hadn't seen him since yesterday in the office, but for some reason it felt like a long time ago. He had missed school. When Ms. Cane asked about his absence, Fredericka popped up and said he'd had to go pick up something from his grandmother. Kylie figured it was the books Burnett had wanted.

Moving closer, her gaze continued to shift toward him. He stood there appearing as natural and rugged as the woods behind him. For some reason, he came off more were than human, and she surmised it was getting close to the full moon. About two weeks before a full moon she started noticing he would appear more masculine. The closer she got to where Lucas stood, the more she realized just how hard this was going to be.

His jet black hair needed a trim and flipped up in places. Those tiny almost-curls stirred in the breeze and made her want to run her fingers through them. He wore jeans that were just tight enough to showcase a lower body of a man, not a boy. The aqua blue T-shirt fit snug across his wide shoulders and defined the shape of his chest beneath the thin cotton. The hem of his short sleeves landed perfectly to draw attention to the muscles in his arms. And the color of his shirt just made his blue eyes look a tad untamable. He looked like he'd just walked off some magazine ad selling some super-masculine product.

He pushed off the tree and started walking toward her and Della, but she felt him moving right at her as if she and she alone was his destination. Not that he hurried; his gait was slow, but confident. Her stomach fluttered and she could feel her hands start to sweat.

Della leaned her head down and whispered, "You do know a were can smell your pheromones, don't you?"

Friggin' great, she thought, but then realized that while she couldn't control being attracted to him, it didn't mean she had to act on those feelings.

"If it makes you feel any better, you're not the only one polluting the air right now."

Kylie hadn't purposely dressed to draw his attention. Had she?

The pink scooped-neck tee didn't give more than a hint of cleavage. Sure it fit snug enough, but most of her clothes did since she'd grown a cup size. The color was feminine, but could she help it that she liked pink? Her shorts were cutoff jeans, nothing too short, her shoes just plain white tennis shoes worn over pink socks that matched her shirt. And the only makeup she wore was mascara and lip gloss.

Lucas stopped in front of her. Crazy, how he smelled like the outdoors; fresh, earthy with a hint of mint.

"I'm here." She tried to appear unaffected by his presence.

"Good," he said, and there was a softness to his tone.

Their gazes met and held a second. Her heart picked up speed.

Della waved her hand at Kylie as if to say she was feeling like a third wheel. "Did you want me to stay?"

Kylie's yes and Lucas's no chimed out at the same time.

"Sorry," Lucas said, not sounding so sorry as he looked at Della.

"But I need Kylie's full attention to teach her, and you would just distract her."

"Right," Della said in a tone of complete disbelief.

Lucas frowned at the vamp.

"Okay," Della said. "I'll just mosey along." She focused on Kylie. "Call me when you're ready to go and I'll come back when you're finished."

"I'll walk her to the cabin," Lucas said.

"I'll call you when I'm done," Kylie said.

Della took off, leaving them alone. Kylie looked at the water for a second and tried to find the strength to get through the next hour.

Neither of them spoke for several minutes. She continued to stare at the water and she could feel him staring at her. The butterflies playing bumper cars in her stomach revved their engines and went into high gear. Taking a deep breath, telling herself she was being silly, she faced him. "Where do we start?"

"Let me get the supplies out." He went back to the tree where a big cloth bag rested beside the trunk. He pulled out a towel from the bag and then shook it out on the ground. Reaching into the bag again, he pulled out a sword. She recognized it immediately as the one stalking her. Something close to a shiver spiraled up her spine. But not fear, something else. Like some crazy form of recognition.

Lucas rested it on the towel. Just the way he carried the weapon spoke of respect, reverence. She hadn't even realized he knew how to use a sword. Perhaps the topic of fighting and such just didn't come up in their conversations.

Kylie moved closer and watched as he pulled out a second sword, a little different, but similar. The size and shape seemed almost the same and it had the same look of antiquity.

Did another one just magically appear? "Where did that one come from?" she asked.

He glanced up. "This one's mine. When I got the books for Burnett I also brought my sword."

"Where did you get a sword?" Kylie asked.

"It's a family heirloom. It's been in my family for a long, long time. My grandfather actually gave it to me before he died."

She noticed again that the swords sort of looked the same. "Were they crusaders or holy warriors?'

He grinned up at her—one of his sexy bad-boy smiles. And damn if her toes didn't curl inside her tennis shoes at that smile. She remembered feeling that smile against her lips. Tasting it. Loving it.

"Actually, they were Vikings. I'm told that they were the Robin Hoods of their kind, not the murdering pirates, but I wouldn't swear on it."

She brushed her sweaty palms on her back pockets. "Has Burnett had a chance to look at the books yet? Did he learn anything useful?"

He reached back in the bag and pulled out two wooden swords. "I saw him right after lunch and he said he was still making his way through them."

"Have you read the books?" Kylie asked.

"Yeah. When my grandfather was giving me lessons, I devoured them. I used to pretend to be a holy warrior." His smile brightened. "Saving damsels in distress."

She could see him playing that role. She remembered when they were kids and he'd caught the rock that the bullies had thrown at her. At six, she'd considered him a hero.

At sixteen, she considered him a heartbreaker.

"Okay," he said. "Here's my plan. First I'm going to teach you how to hold the sword, and then to do some very simple defensive moves. Then we'll actually spar for a while."

He picked up her sword and moved behind her. She immediately swung around.

"Turn around, I want to guide you on how to hold it."

"Why can't you just show me?"

He frowned. “This is how my grandfather taught me. Please, turn around.”

She frowned right back at him, but she swung around. Then she held her breath and waited for his touch. Waited to feel his body against hers.

Waited for the pain that came with touching him—emotional pain—that was both sweet and bitter.

She felt his chest, warm and solid, come against her shoulder blades. His right hand reached down and pressed two fingers down by her elbow. Then he slowly glided his hand down to her wrist. The feel of his touch was both wanted and unwanted. She swallowed and it sounded almost too loud.

“Take the sword.” His voice, deep and hoarse, whispered in her ear.

She hadn’t realized until then that she’d closed her eyes.

Popping them open, she saw he’d reached around her and held the sword in his left hand. Reaching for the sword, she wrapped her palm around the handle.

“Now, move your wrist just a little to the . . .” He paused at the same time the sword started to glow.

His intake of air said he was again awed by the sword’s action. Kylie was too centered on the feel of him pressed against her to care about the sword.

“This way,” he said, and shifted her wrist to the right ever so slightly. His head turned also and she felt his cheek on the back of her head.

She thought she heard him inhale, but she couldn’t swear on it.

“Do you feel how the sword is level in your hand?”

She nodded, not trusting her voice. His scent surrounded her. The strongest waves of pain stopped, but she still felt a dull ache. She also felt . . . the wonder of his touch. She felt his skin wherever he pressed against her.

“You’re doing good. This is the way you need to hold it.”

They stood like that for several long seconds. His firm form pressed again her, his arm encircling her, the sword in her hand.

For a second she thought she heard his hum, the powerful hypnotizing sound meant to weaken women. "Now what?" she bit out, fighting the feeling of being lured, of being seduced.

He inhaled sharply and stepped back. "Now I get my sword and show you some moves." His voice sounded extra low.

He shifted quickly to reach for his sword. He moved to stand right beside her. His dark blue gaze turned and he looked at her. She saw the heat in his eyes, she saw the desire. "I'm sorry. I didn't mean for that to happen."

She looked away quickly and while part of her wanted to call him on it, she simply stood there and waited for him to show her the next move. And hoped it only involved sword fighting and not seduction.

Chapter Thirty

She spent the next thirty minutes following his moves. Over and over. Swiping the sword this way, then that. He barked out commands. Not really in a rude way, but as if this was the way he'd been taught. She couldn't help but imagine a younger Lucas taking stern directions from his grandfather.

"Not like that," he said. "Keep the sword pointing out to where your opponent will be. And don't look down. Now look where you're holding your weight. Put your weight into your moves."

Over and over again, they did it.

It was actually grueling. The sun felt hot on her skin, the air thick. Her leg muscles from all the partial squats and forward thrusts burned. She didn't complain. Not once. She'd take this to him touching her.

"That's good," he said, doing the same moves beside her. "You're doing it."

Oh my. You are a natural.

Out in the open, she actually heard the voice before she felt the spirit's cold. The spirit stood to Kylie's left, holding her own sword, following Lucas's direction to a tee.

"What are you doing?" Lucas asked. "Shift your body weight back and then forward."

Kylie ignored Lucas, but continued to move—her focus now on the spirit's weapon and not following his directions.

Comparing the swords, she realized the spirit's sword wasn't really like the one glowing in Kylie's hands. The ghost's blade was more slender and tapered. And the hilt, as Lucas called the handle, was longer.

What kind of sword do you have? Kylie asked the spirit, thinking maybe if she could get her to open up, she might give Kylie something to help send her away.

A bastard sword. I stole it from a bastard. She laughed, but she didn't miss a step in her moves. Her form looked practiced.

Whoever she was, her skills with the sword matched, if not surpassed, Lucas's.

I'm serious. Kylie missed a step.

"You okay?" Lucas asked and she felt him studying her.

"Yeah," Kylie answered, but continued to focus on the spirit. She needed to get this figured out. The sooner the ghost was gone, the sooner she could work on her other quests.

Who is it you want me to kill? she asked, and kept moving, but obviously not well enough because Lucas had stopped moving and was now just staring at her.

"Do you want to take a break?" he asked.

Who is it? Kylie demanded, and stopped moving.

The spirit stopped her motions and looked at Lucas. *Listen to this guy. He's a good teacher. With a little practice you'll be ready. You'll kill my enemy and then I'll leave you be and take my place in hell.*

Hell? Kylie's breath hitched. She hadn't ever dealt with a spirit heading to hell. She couldn't help but hope the ghost was wrong. But knowing what she knew, all the people the spirit had claimed to have killed, she might be hell bound.

The spirit faded.

Kylie let out a frustrated puff of air and then wiped the sweat from her brow with the back of her left hand. Again she got the distinct feeling that this spirit was somehow connected to her receiving the sword. But what could that mean? Was Kylie actually supposed to do the ghost's bidding, and kill someone for her?

The thought of taking a life sent a shiver down Kylie's spine. Just another reason she questioned her ability to be some holy warrior.

"You need some water?" Lucas asked.

She looked at him. His skin, already golden from the sun, glistened with heat. The front of his T-shirt clung to his upper torso, showing off his chest even more. Sweat always did look good on him.

She glanced down at the sword. "Is there such a thing as a bastard sword?" she asked, focusing on the ghost and not wanting to think about how good he looked.

"Yeah, why?" He moved to his bag and pulled out two bottles of water. He handed her one. His hand brushed against hers. She pulled her hand back, and he must have noticed her suddenness because he frowned.

"Nothing," she said, knowing he wouldn't want to know. He didn't like ghosts. *But he went into the cemetery for me, to help me. Even when at the time I was a vampire.*

She put the sword down and watched it lose the golden hue.

"That's so strange," he said.

"Yeah." The bottle he'd handed her chilled the inside of her palm. She unscrewed the top and took a long sip.

They drank without talking, her mind on the ghost one second and on how good Lucas looked the next.

"You ready to spar?" he asked.

She looked at his sword and the one resting on the towel. Real weapons that could kill. A slip of a wrist and someone could be seriously injured. "I don't think so."

"Not with these. You're not ready for that." He pointed back to the towel and the wooden swords. "With those."

She wanted to say no, but then realized the sooner she learned to fight, the sooner she wouldn't have to meet Lucas and be reminded of all she'd lost. Screwing the top on the water, she dropped it beside her sword and then picked up one of the wooden weapons. "Let's go at it."

Twenty minutes later, they were finally doing just that. Going at it. Kylie finally started to understand how to do this. Using the moves he'd taught her earlier, she was able to block most of his offenses. Most of them, but not all.

Three times he found his way around her sword and touched her chest with the wooden edge. "Two points for the teacher," he'd said each time. Then they'd go back swinging, swiping, moving back, forth, and sometimes in circles. The sound of their wooden blades clashing rang in her ears. Sweat poured down her brow again, but she ignored it, determined to earn a few points of her own.

Watching him, studying him, she started noticing his patterns of movement. Using what she learned against him, she waited for her opportunity and then took it. She tapped his chest with her own wooden blade. Breathing heavy, she felt the sweat rolling down between her breasts. "Two points for the student," she said, reveling in the moment of success. As crazy as it was, she enjoyed this.

He stopped and lowered his sword. His blue gaze froze on her. He drew in a deep breath. "You have no idea how much I've missed seeing that smile."

Sobering, realizing what she'd offered him, she tapped her wooden blade to his. "We came here to fight."

He held up his sword and then went back to sparring.

"I miss you," he said, right after he stopped her blade.

She pulled back and swung her sword extra hard to the left. His wooden blade blocked it. She pulled back and then went back for more.

"You are my soul mate," he said, blocking her at every turn.

Emotion filled her chest. Some from the memory of hearing him say those words to Monique, but mostly from knowing all he had to lose. She swung harder, and her sword hit his with a cracking thud. The impact sent his sword flying out of his hand, and hers broke in half.

"You should do what your father wants. Go to Monique, agree to marry her. Get on the Council like you planned."

"I'm not agreeing to marry Monique!" he said in a stern voice. "I should have never agreed to it!"

"I think we're done," she said, her heart racing and a world of hurt sitting on her chest.

A soulful expression filled his gaze. "With sparring today, we're done. But not with each other." He went and picked up his sword and then moved back to pack their things, while she stood there, trying to get her breathing under control. He found the other half of her sword and picked it up.

She couldn't help but wonder if these weren't the same swords he and his grandfather used. And if so they probably meant something to him. Guilt filled her chest. "I didn't mean to break it."

"I know. It's okay. It happens a lot." He paused and from the look he sent her he was about to say something she didn't want to hear.

Kylie's phone rang. She pulled it out of her pocket.

Lucas frowned. "If it's Della tell her I said I'd walk you to your cabin."

"It's my mom," Kylie said as she stepped a few feet away. She pulled the phone to her ear, a bit concerned that her mom was calling during work hours.

"Hey, Mom?" Kylie said, and she could still hear her heart thumping in her ears from the exertion of the sparring match. Or because of what Lucas had said.

"Hey? That's what you're going to say to me!" her mom bit out.

"What should I say to you?" Kylie asked.

"How dare you do this to me, Kylie Galen." Her mom's tone sent her back to the time that she and her mom couldn't see eye to eye on anything—back to the days when Kylie called her the Ice Princess. She took a deep breath and told herself not to panic, but wasn't this just what she worried about? That with John in the picture the fragile relationship they had would be put in jeopardy?

"Mom, what did I do?" Kylie moved a couple more feet away, not wanting Lucas to hear her fight with her mom.

"You know what you did; don't play innocent with me."

"I'm not playing," Kylie said, growing a little more concerned, and when she looked up she saw Lucas studying her with empathy.

"You met with Mr. and Mrs. Brighten, didn't you?" Her mom spoke so loud, it hurt her ears and she was certain Lucas could hear.

Kylie moved a few more feet away. She'd planned to tell her mom as soon she got back to the States, but after the pregnancy fiasco it just hadn't seemed like a good time. And yesterday morning with all the apologies and John praise, it didn't feel right. Besides, it might just be something they needed to talk about in person.

"Yes, and I was going to tell you."

"Was? *Was* going to tell me? Don't you think this is something you should have told me before you did it!"

"I did tell you. I mean, I told you I wanted to do it. We talked about it months ago, remember?"

"You should have discussed this with me first."

And you should have discussed it with me years ago. Kylie found some emotional reprieve in her own anger, but she knew better than to let it out right now. Her mom was never reasonable when this upset and adding fuel to her mom's emotional fire wasn't smart.

"Did they call you? Were they upset?" Kylie had thought the Brightens had agreed to wait and meet with her mom later. Why had they gone ahead and called? But even annoyed that they had called, she couldn't imagine the Brightens being rude with her mom.

"Yes, they called me! And do you have any idea how awkward that conversation was?"

"I'm sorry. But you were in England," Kylie added.

"How long has this been scheduled, young lady?"

"They've been out of the country and I don't even think they got my message until they got back. They called and wanted to come by immediately."

"You should have run this by me first, Miss Galen."

Oh, hell, whenever her mom referred to her as Miss Galen, Kylie knew her goose was cooked. And like so many times in the past, she didn't think her goose deserved to be cooked.

"I should have been prepared to speak to them. Instead, I get this phone call out of the blue."

"I'm sorry," Kylie said.

"John was with me when the call came in. Do you have any idea how awkward *that* was."

Tears filled Kylie's eyes and she couldn't hold back her anger anymore. "That's why you're upset, because of John?"

"I haven't told him that Tom wasn't your father. It was completely embarrassing."

"You're embarrassed about me?" Kylie asked, and shook her head.

"Don't turn this around," her mom said.

"Turn it around?" She shook her head. "I'm sorry, Mom, but you are so wrong here."

"I was not embarrassed about you. I'm . . . I'm embarrassed that I got pregnant by someone I barely knew."

Kylie swiped at her tears. "You said you loved him."

Her mom gasped. "Of course I did, but . . ."

"But what?" Kylie asked. "But you were afraid that your precious John would see your omission of the truth as a lie?"

"Kylie, don't be—"

"And that wouldn't be good, would it?" she continued. "Wait, you don't have to answer that, because I can tell you how it feels. How it feels when someone you thought you knew keeps something from you, something that might have mattered! I can't believe you're mad at me for not telling you I contacted the Brightens when you friggin' didn't tell me about my own father, or about my grandparents, all these years!"

Her mom's intake of air said a lot. "I . . . I thought I explained that?"

"Yeah, you explained that you were so in love with my father, and now you claim you hardly knew him."

"I . . . I don't think this is something we should discuss over the phone."

"Really? That's sort of how I felt about telling you about the Brightens." Another few tears rolled down her cheeks.

She hung up so angry she almost wanted to throw the phone down. She didn't, but she did turn it off just in case her mom tried to call back.

"I'm sorry." Lucas's words came behind her.

She wiped her tears away again and turned around. She hadn't known he was so close and unintentionally ran right into him. Her face landed on his oh-so-perfect chest. His arms, warm and gentle, came around and held there for two or maybe three seconds before she pulled away. Just long enough to remember how good it was to lean on him—to recall how good it had been to be able to count on him. Just long enough for her to come to her senses and remember she shouldn't be leaning on or counting on him anymore.

The following Friday, almost midnight, Kylie lay in bed staring at the ceiling, playing mind games with her issues. Round and round they go, which one to fret over, nobody knows.

Her mom, whom Kylie was talking to but was still mad at, and her seemingly impossible quest to save the teen chameleons.

Her completely impossible ghost and the impossible and infuriating Lucas.

And an unbearable longing to talk to her dad again, who she hadn't felt or heard from since right before the Brightens' visit.

And last, but for sure not least, an impossible rogue, whose threat still rang in Kylie's ears. *You will come to me, Kylie Galen, come to me willing to die, to suffer at my hands for my pleasure, because the price will be too great! Your weakness will take you down.*

Right now, Kylie's weakness seemed to be her inability to figure anything out. Everything in her life felt as if it were in limbo.

The only issue Kylie felt productive in this last week was her skill at using the sword. At times she wondered if her good feeling about that wasn't just because of Lucas. Being with him for an hour or two a day.

Oh, she hadn't succumbed to any of his advances. Subtle things, like walking so close that his shoulder brushed up against hers, his tactic of showing her a move by standing behind her and guiding her through a certain stance or motion. And then there were his not-so-subtle advances. They would be sparring with the wood swords and he'd just pop out with something like "I still love you" or "Do you know how beautiful you are?" or "Do you remember the night we were coming back from the graveyard and we almost made love?"

She'd broken three more wooden swords when he said those things, too. One would think he would learn to keep his mouth shut. But nope. Lucas had even laughed the second time she'd done it. He didn't seem to care that his comments ended up with him having to replace another sword. And she knew that for a fact when the very next day he said something else that ended with her breaking the third sword. Not that she was doing it on purpose; it was just so dang hard not to let her emotion come out in her blows.

Today when they had been leaving, she'd called what they were doing "fencing" and Lucas had corrected her. He told her that she wasn't learning to fence. That entailed a completely different set of skills. She was learning to fight. He didn't say it, but she read his thoughts. She was training to kill.

But who?

And how? Oh, she knew it would happen with a sword, she just didn't know how she would be able to do it. To really take a life.

Letting go of a deep breath, she rolled over, gave her pillow a thump of her fist, and recalled Collin Warren when she'd tossed him across the room. Her intent hadn't been to kill but to protect. She hadn't killed him, but she could have.

And maybe that was how "this," whatever "this" was, would go down. Maybe if her protective mode was in gear, she'd be able to do it and not think. But when she thought about it afterward, would she be able to live with it?

Perhaps if it was to save someone she loved.

Or to kill someone you loathe.

The cold washed over her. Kylie sat up and the ghost sat at the end of her bed holding her sword. Kylie had seen her every day while practicing with Lucas. She would show up and complete the exercises with them, but no matter how hard Kylie had tried, she hadn't spoken once.

"Who do I loathe that much?" she asked.

You know, the ghost said.

"Tell me, damn it! I'm tired of your games!"

Della, looking half asleep, burst into Kylie's room. "Are you okay?"

"Yes!" Kylie told her. "Go away!" When she didn't do it immediately, Kylie said, "It's a ghost issue."

Della shot out. But when Kylie looked around the ghost was gone. "Who do I loathe that much?" she repeated her question. The ghost didn't return, but suddenly Kylie knew. She knew with clarity.

Mario.

She was supposed to kill Mario.

Deep down she'd known this was going to happen. Known that they would face each other again. What she didn't know was how in the hell she was going to win against him. He'd had years to build his powers. How could she match that?

Then another question filled her head. Did this mean that Mario was who the ghost wanted her to kill? How was she connected to Mario?

Chapter Thirty-one

Saturday morning, standing in the dining hall, Kylie waited for her mom to show up to parents' day. She hadn't said anything about John coming, but Kylie didn't know if that meant he wasn't, or if she didn't feel the need to ask Kylie if it would be okay. She really prayed he was a no-show. Already feeling as if her relationship was on shaky ground with her mom, she didn't need John around.

On the other hand, Kylie's stepdad had to leave town on a business trip and wasn't going to make it—which was fine with Kylie. Without him, the combustion level would at least be lessened a degree. She hadn't stopped loving Tom Galen, but right now the father figure Kylie ached to see was her real father. Ever since the Brightens' visit, Kylie had been longing to spend some time with Daniel. Almost every night before bed she'd pull out the photo album the Brightens had left her, and nearly every night, she'd end up crying. Feeling as if life had cheated her.

Cheated him, too.

Kylie watched a few parents stroll through the door. Miranda's parents walked in and found her waiting, prim and proper-like, at a table. Seeing Miranda like that felt wrong, like wearing your shoes on the wrong foot.

Miranda's mom sucked all the confidence and personality out of the witch. That was just so wrong.

Derek's mom moved in with exuberance, as if eager to see her son. That's the way parents should be, Kylie thought. The woman's gaze shifted around the room, obviously looking for Derek. When her gaze found Kylie's she grinned and waved and started moving toward her. Thankfully, Derek called to her from the other side of the room and spared Kylie the awkward conversation. What did you tell the mother of the boy whose heart you'd just broken?

Helen's parents walked in with worry on their faces, even though they'd just dropped their daughter off a few days earlier.

Jonathon hadn't stopped smiling since Helen had returned. Kylie had sat with them at almost every lunch break, letting Della and Miranda sit with their own kind. Yesterday during lunch, Kylie had studied all the different species tables and wondered if there would ever be a chameleon table at Shadow Falls.

Next, Della's parents and sister walked in. Her father looked as he always did, pissed off and unhappy to be here. Della's dad had even told her once that the only reason he came was because her mother made him. Part of Kylie would have loved to knock some sense into that man. How could he not know how much those words hurt his daughter?

Across the room, Della frowned at her family walking through the door. Kylie's heart went out to Della. If possible, her home life was even worse than Kylie's.

"You okay?" Holiday moved to stand beside her.

"Yeah. Just wondering why families have to be so screwed up. Why can't people just love each other?"

Holiday brushed her shoulder against Kylie's, offering a bit of emotional calm. "They do love each other. Family drama is a trade-off for having family. What you see in this room right now is probably the worst it's going to be."

"What do you mean?" Kylie asked.

"The hardest time in any relationship is change. And nothing brings more change in a family dynamic than when a teen is becoming their own person. That's true for humans as well as supernaturals."

Holiday must have seen Kylie glance from Miranda to Della, because she said, "In a few years, Miranda will no longer care if her mother approves of her choices. And her mom will gradually accept that Miranda is her own person. Della will grow up and do great things, because Della won't accept any less from herself. Her father will have to admit that while he didn't understand the changes in his daughter's life, she grew up to be a success."

"And you don't think that these hard feelings will hurt the relationship?"

Holiday sighed. "Oh, there'll be scars and some mending to do, and yes, there are some cases that don't end well." She paused. "But for the most part, the problems you see here are things that families can and probably will recover from."

"That's hopeful," Kylie said.

"Did you return the Brightens' call?" Holiday asked.

Kylie had gotten the message yesterday that they'd called. "Yes, I spoke with them. They wanted to come to parents' day and meet my mom."

Holiday tensed. "You didn't tell me they were coming."

"They're not. I didn't think my mom was ready to meet with them. After the argument we had about me seeing them, we've barely spoken about them. She apologized, but now we're both pretending it didn't happen. I'm kind of scared to bring it up."

"It will work out. Your mom doesn't come across as the unreasonable type."

"Obviously you don't know her very well." While Kylie said it half jokingly, the other half had merit.

Kylie looked at Holiday and remembered her visit with the ghost. "I had a visitor last night."

"Did she talk to you this time?" Holiday asked, knowing exactly who Kylie meant.

"A little." She bit her lip. "I think it's all connected. The sword, the ghost, and Mario."

Holiday's brow tightened. "Why do you think that?"

Kylie leaned in. "Something she said, and . . . just a gut feeling."

"Miss Brandon?" someone called from across the room.

Holiday pressed a hand to Kylie's arm and frowned. "We'll talk later."

Kylie nodded, and as the camp leader walked away, she saw Lucas walk in. He moved to sit down with a group of weres. One of the weres said something and then they all shot up from the table and left Lucas by himself.

It was starting, she realized. They were pushing him out. Pain for him cut deep.

"Sad, isn't it?" a voice said behind her. "And it's your fault." Kylie recognized Clara's voice. Kylie turned to face Lucas's sister, but she shot away. Breath held, she looked back at Lucas. She longed to go to him, to soothe him, but that would only make it worse.

Five minutes later, Lucas's grandmother came walking painfully slowly into the dining room. Kylie glanced around the crowd. Lucas still sat alone at a table in the back. The elderly woman's gaze roamed the room and found Kylie.

When she started shuffling toward Kylie, her heart stopped. *Oh, shit!* She had no desire to hear Lucas's grandmother scold her for ruining her grandson's goals and quests.

Kylie went to dart out the side door when she heard her mom. Turning she saw . . . her mom with John. *Oh, crap, he came.* Nevertheless, she'd take John over Lucas's grandmother hands down—especially since her mom wasn't playing feely-touchy with John's butt.

Kylie took off toward her guests with fake eagerness, praying that would deter the elderly woman from approaching.

After a quick hug with her mom, and ignoring John, Kylie led them to an empty table as far away from Lucas as she could find. Her heart didn't find a normal rhythm until she saw Lucas's grandmother head to his table.

"Thank God," she muttered, and motioned for them to sit.

"Thank God, what?" her mom asked, still standing.

Kylie opened her mouth, praying something intelligent, albeit a lie, would fall out. Lately, Kylie's prayers had been going unanswered and this was no exception. Her lips opened, but nothing, not a thing, came out. Even worse, her brain had shut down.

"Thank God, what?" her mom asked again.

"That the pain in my stomach went away." Kylie pressed a hand on top of her belly.

"You've got stomach pains?" Alarm laced her mom's voice.

"It's nothing."

"You don't know it's nothing," her mom insisted.

"I do." Kylie's voice rang high pitched, fearing her mom would drag her to the emergency room. Heck, she might accuse her of being pregnant again.

"How do you know it's nothing?" her mom asked.

"Because it's just . . . gas. I had a little gas."

Her mom, blushing, glanced at John. Kylie could feel her own face heating up like a Betty Crocker oven. Of all the things she could have come up with, why gas?

Her mom leaned in a little. "Do you need to go to the restroom?"

"No. It went away."

Her mom leaned in. "You sure?"

"Positive." Kylie dropped in a chair and prayed this wasn't a premonition of how this meeting would go.

Forty-five minutes later, Kylie, John, and her mom still sat at the table chatting. Well, Kylie did very little chatting, while her mom and John never stopped. They talked about her mom's new job that she'd be taking in two weeks and they talked about England.

"Oh, I brought you something." Her mom pulled a bag from her purse. "I know how you like T-shirts," she said.

Kylie couldn't help but think, *My mom went to England and all I got was a T-shirt,* but she smiled and pulled it out of the bag and then chuckled when she read the script across the front: *My mom went to England and all I got was this T-shirt.*

"Perfect," Kylie said, and loved that it was pink.

"I also got you this." Her mom pulled out a small white box.

The charm bracelet caught the light and sparkled, almost magically, when Kylie opened the box. Her heart skipped a beat when she saw the charms. A sword that looked very much like a crusader sword, a cross that looked too damn close to the one on the sword, and a Joan of Arc emblem.

"I bought it at one of the castles and it didn't have a wide selection of charms, but . . . for some odd reason I felt compelled to pick those out. I hope you don't think they're stupid."

Define "some" reason, Kylie wanted to ask, but she didn't. "No. I like them. Thank you." A certain familiar chill fell on her like a light rain.

Daniel was there? Had her dad led her mom to buy these charms? She glanced around hoping to see him, but he didn't materialize.

Soon, Kylie. Soon. The words echoed in her head, fear filled her heart.

I miss you, Kylie said in her mind. *I don't know if I'm ready to die, but I do miss you.*

Footsteps echoed in the room, and Kylie noticed the other parents leaving.

Her mom looked around. "These visits fly by. I should run to the girls' room before we leave." Her mom popped up and hurried off.

Kylie was about to stand to follow her mom when John rested his hand on hers. The feel of his palm sent a shiver down her spine. It wasn't cold or hot. Just emotionally wrong. She pulled her hand away.

"I was hoping to get a chance to speak to you," he said.

And I was hoping you wouldn't. She glanced toward the restroom. "I think I'll—"

"Is there a reason you don't like me, Kylie?"

She looked at him. Decisions, decisions. Was she going to be diplomatic, or honest?

Who was it that said honesty was the best policy? She couldn't remember, but she decided they were brilliant.

Chapter Thirty-two

"Let's see," Kylie said, not skipping a beat. "Let's begin with the fact that you started a fight in front of my whole school with my stepdad."

John squared his shoulders, almost defensively. "He's the one who hit me."

"After you insulted me and charged at him. And you also stuck your tongue down my mama's throat in front of all the students and their parents. Would you like me to continue? I think I could come up with more really quick."

Anger filled his eyes, but he seemed to rein it in. "You don't hold back, do you?"

She sent him her swallowed-a-mosquito smile. "That *was* holding back."

"You are such a joy to speak with," he said. "However, the problem is that your mom really likes me and I her. I don't think I'm going out on a limb to say that it would be helpful if we could get along."

Kylie leaned in. "I don't think I'm going out on a limb to say that you haven't known my mom long enough to be saying this to me."

Kylie could swear his eyes brightened. A nonhuman kind of bright. She tightened her brows to check his pattern.

What was this man?

His human pattern appeared clearly. Not that he couldn't still be a chameleon, but . . .

Anger filled his gray eyes. "This could end up *hurting* your mom." His words came out so cold, so . . . threatening that Kylie's protective instinct buzzed.

"What do you mean?" She curled her hands into fists.

He glanced away as if to calm himself. When he looked back his eyes were normal. "Just that problems between us would hurt your mom."

She stared him right in the eyes. And God help her, but she sensed he was lying, that his words *had* been a threat. She tried to calm the buzzing in her veins down, but it continued. Over John's shoulder she saw her mom step out of the restroom.

She leaned across the table and whispered to John, "If anyone dares hurt my mom, they will die regretting it."

Right then, Kylie knew two things: she did have the ability to become a holy warrior. Because if John laid one finger on her mom, she could, and would, kill him with no regrets. And secondly, she simply couldn't die, not right now. Not if it meant leaving her mom with this asshole.

"Is everything okay?" Her mom stepped up to the table, obviously picking up on the tension.

Kylie waited to see how John decided to play this.

"It's fine," John said. "We were just talking." He stood up. "I guess it's time to go." They started walking, but the fear for her mom built higher with each step. Kylie couldn't let her mom leave with this man—not without a warning.

She reached for her mom's arm. "There's someone I want you to meet."

John turned.

"Can you give us a minute?" Kylie sent John a look that dared him to intervene.

He hesitated but then said, "I'll wait by the car."

Kylie watched him walk out, wishing he'd keep walking right out of her mother's life.

Her mom looked around. "Who do you want me to meet?"

"Mom, I know you're not going to like what I have to say, but John scares me. I'm worried about your safety."

"Scares you?" her mom asked. "I don't understand. What has he done?"

"I don't trust him. He gives me the creeps. And I'm a good judge of character."

Hurt flashed in her mom's eyes. "So am I, young lady. Sorry you don't like him, but I do."

The hurt in her mom's eyes vibrated in Kylie's chest. "I just want you to be careful and not let this thing move too fast."

Her mom scowled. "This is because you want me and your dad to get back together."

"First," Kylie said, now feeling annoyed, "Tom's my stepdad. Second, yes, I did want you to get back together, but this isn't about that."

"It has to be, young lady, because John is the sweetest man I know." She leaned in and kissed Kylie's cheek. "Now, please accept the fact that your stepdad and I are not getting back together." She left. Kylie stayed, fearing what she might say to John if she had to face him again at the car.

"Are you okay?" The masculine voice came near her ear.

Kylie's first thought was that it was Derek. He always knew when she was in emotional trauma. But she quickly recognized the deep, sexy voice. The voice of the person whom for the last week she'd tried to beat to smithereens with a wooden sword.

She turned around. "Yes." Then her pent-up anger crowded her chest and she knew what would help. "Do you want to go practice?"

"Now?" Lucas asked.

"I need to burn off some aggression."

"On me?" He half smiled.

"Not . . . Do you want to practice or not?" she snapped, in no mood for humor. Face it, someone had sent her a sword to learn to fight—and if they expected her to fight, then they obviously meant for her to stay alive. And she planned to stay alive to protect her mom from creeps like John.

Yup, staying alive sounded like a good idea.

"Sure." His blue eyes filled with concern. "Let me tell Burnett." His gaze didn't move from her face. "What happened?"

"I don't want to talk," she said. "I want to fight."

Thirty minutes later, Kylie had already broken one sword without Lucas having said anything about loving her, how beautiful she was, or about them making out in the grass.

He made her go through some stretching exercises, insisting he could see the tension rolling off of her. It wasn't rolling off of her, it was rolling around inside of her. Fear for her mom's safety chopped away at her sanity, fear for Lucas and what would happen to him if the pack completely turned against him ate at her peace of mind.

"You still don't want to talk?" he asked as their swords banged against each other.

Yes, but I just don't know what to say. "No," she lied, changing her stance and managing to get her sword past his, and then tapped the tip against his chest.

"You are getting good." He stared down at the sword pointing at his heart.

She pulled back to let him get his footing. In a few seconds, they were back to sparring when she felt the cold wash over her.

Too good. The student is besting the teacher. You need a new teacher.

Kylie glanced at the ghost standing there with her sword. *Who else can teach me?*

Me, of course. But no pansy stuff fighting with wooden swords. You must learn to fight with a real weapon.

Kylie's heart raced, remembering her main fear. *Am I going to die?*

The ghost sighed. *That is up to you.*

How sad was it that she preferred to take the word of a murdering spirit than that of her father? But the fact remained that she wanted to live.

"You ready?" Lucas asked.

Kylie faced him. "One second." She looked back to the spirit. *Do you know my father?*

Her question left her lips at the same time the spirit vanished.

Facing Lucas again, Kylie held up her sword and the sparring resumed.

"Do I need to teach him a lesson?" Lucas asked as his sword clashed again hers.

"Who?" she asked.

"Your mom's boyfriend." Lucas blocked her sword.

"No, I need to stop him," she said. If she didn't die first.

Then she felt a fire burn in her belly. She wasn't going to die. She was going to fight and win. And Lucas had to do the same, she realized.

"You're getting gutsy," Lucas said, but suddenly she lost her focus and his sword got around her and tapped her shoulder.

Kylie looked at the sword's point. "That wasn't a death blow. You can't count that as a win."

"No, but you'd be bleeding so badly that you wouldn't last much longer."

"Fine. Count it." She stepped back and prepared to start again.

This time she was more careful, blocking him blow for blow. Sweat poured down her brow. Her muscles ached, her heart ached. She opened her mouth to say something about his new moves. But something completely different came out.

"You should have told me about Monique," she said, not realizing what she meant to say. The sound of wood being slammed together filled the air like thunder. "If I had known . . ." What would she have done? Was there any chance in hell that she would have said it was okay? Probably not, but perhaps she wouldn't have felt so betrayed. Maybe she wouldn't have lumped him together with all the other betrayals of her past.

"You wouldn't have accepted it," he finished for her. It was the truth. He started those fancy foot moves around her again. "And you would have been right not to accept it. It was a bad judgment call on my part."

"Bad for us, yes. But maybe it was the right call for you," she said. "You have too much to lose, Lucas."

"I have you to lose!" Their swords slammed together; the loud noise crackled in the air.

They backed away from each other. "I told you that we're over. Find Monique, tell her you'll marry her."

"I am not marrying her. I never planned to."

"Then go back to your original plan, say you'll do it, get on the Council, and then back out."

"No. It was a bad plan then and it would be a bad plan now."

She breathed in and caught the air in her lungs. "Everyone blames me for ruining your dreams," she said. *And someday you will, too—if I live.* And that was what hurt the most right now. Not dying. But the fact that forgiving him seemed easy compared to accepting that he would one day resent her. Resent the choice he'd made.

He lifted his sword to start sparring again. She went along with it because just looking at him hurt too much.

He started talking as he moved. "Anyone who blames you is a fool. I was the one who chose not to sign the betrothal agreement. Not you." The swords hit again.

"Your sister believes it. Even your grandmother believes it. I saw it in her eyes today when she started to come over to talk to me."

"My sister is stupid. I love my grandmother," he said, and the sound of his sword slicing through air sent a chill down Kylie's back.

"But that doesn't make her right. She follows a lot of the beliefs of the elders."

"Your pack is turning away from you. I saw that." Her throat tightened again. "You can't lose them, Lucas. You've told me a thousand times how important they are to you."

"But you are more important to me," he said. "I can't lose you."

"You've already lost me!" she seethed, and blocked his sword again. She couldn't let him do this. She couldn't let him sacrifice everything he had wanted. She couldn't watch him grow to hate her someday.

He pulled back. She expected him to come to the left, but he came to the right, and she failed to block him. He placed his sword right over her heart.

This one was a death blow.

"No." He purposely tapped his sword to her chest. "Your heart belongs to me. Don't ever forget that."

She stumbled back, anger vibrating through her. Anger, not so much at him, but at knowing how much he could lose. She slung the sword down and turned around and stared at the water, her throat knotting, her vision becoming blurry.

He came up behind her—not touching her, as if he knew she wouldn't allow it.

Instead, he stood so close his words brushed against her cheek and sent shivers of regret down her spine. "I became blinded by what I thought I needed to do. I was wrong. I was stupid. But not for one minute did I ever stop loving you. And that's why I deserve to be forgiven."

Just like that, she felt the tight emotion in her chest lessen. He was forgiven. But as she'd known for a while, forgiving him wasn't the biggest issue. A tear slipped from her lashes. She moved a few feet away.

"I'm finished," she said. "I want to go back to the cabin."

"Okay," he said, but he sounded rejected and she felt the same emotion echoing inside her chest.

When he went to pick up the swords, she turned to watch him.

He looked up. She saw so much in his eyes—hurt, regret, a longing for her to say she forgave him.

But if she gave him that, he would only work harder to convince her to come back to him. And how could she when she knew that someday he would resent her for it?

After a few seconds, he said, "I think you're ready to start practicing with the real swords."

She considered how many times her sword had touched his body accidentally, but then she remembered what the ghost had said. Dying was her choice. And she chose to live.

She needed to be ready—ready to fight for her life.

"Okay," she said, and tried not to let the fear into her voice.

Are you ready?

Kylie had just fallen asleep that night, after fretting for a good hour, when the voice and chill woke her up.

"Ready for what?" she asked, not opening her eyes.

For practice. I told you. You need a better teacher.

"He's a great teacher," she said, defending Lucas before she even realized it.

He's great to look at. And I'll admit he has some skills, but you need more. So wake up.

Kylie pried open one eye and saw the spirit, her face inches away. "You do know that the living need eight hours of sleep?"

That's the rule for humans. Supernaturals can survive on much less. Now get up and let's get started.

"I don't have my sword."

Ahh, but if you get up, you'd see it's already here.

Kylie remembered Holiday saying it wasn't possible. "A ghost can't move objects."

I didn't say I moved it. I said it was here.

"So who's moving it?" Kylie asked.

Don't pretend that you don't know. The same ones who delivered the sword to you. The death angels.

Kylie's breath caught. "So they want me to kill Mario?"

Well, I haven't spoken to them directly. She leaned in. *Frankly, they make me very nervous, but as for killing Mario, it would appear that way, now, wouldn't it?*

"And you?" Kylie asked. "What do you want? The same thing?"

You know, I've tried to figure that out myself. But every time I get close to the answer, it's as if it moves farther way. Why is that? She sounded genuinely puzzled and vulnerable.

Kylie recalled the ghost grieving over her son. Maybe she wasn't all bad.

Kylie sat up and saw the clock. "It's two in the morning. You really want me to get up?"

I don't think you can fight reclined in your bed. I'd have you gutted before you ever raised your sword.

Okay, the spirit was bad after all. However, her words had Kylie crawling out from under the covers. She spotted the sword at the end of her bed. And she also spotted Socks, his little feline face barely sticking out of the dust ruffle.

"Okay . . . where do we begin?" Kylie picked up her sword.

Put on a white gown. Or something white, the spirit said.

Kylie looked down at her black nightshirt. "Why?"

Don't you want to die in white?

Kylie's heart stopped.

The spirit laughed. *You are so easy to tease. Put on white because how else will you know if you're cut and bleeding?*

Kylie put the sword back down. "I'm not sure I want to play."

The spirit laughed again. *Don't fret. I'm just going to mark up your gown. I can't actually cut you. Though the latter is a much better teaching tool.*

Kylie relented and grabbed a white shirt and pair of boxers. They went into the living room. Kylie's sword glowed a bright yellow.

They had just started to spar when Della shot out of her bedroom, eyes aglow, and looked at Kylie holding up the sword.

"I'm just going to practice a bit," Kylie said.

"In the middle of the freaking night? With a freaking glowing sword?"

Kylie nodded. "You drink blood, I play with glowing swords."

Della wrapped her arms around herself as if cold. "You've got company, don't you?"

Unable to lie, Kylie nodded.

"Oh, hell!" The vamp went back into her room, slamming the door behind her.

That girl had some serious issues.

Kylie frowned. "Not as many as other people I know," Kylie said to herself. "Now, let's do this and get it over with."

The next fifteen minutes were the hardest Kylie had ever fought. She used every technique she'd learned from Lucas, but this woman didn't abide by the normal techniques. She fought dirty. And was proud of it.

Every time the spirit's sword came in contact with Kylie's body, a red mark would appear on her white shirt or boxers. Every time Kylie's sword made contact with the spirit's body, she would show an open wound and blood. Of course, the ghost only had one little scratch on her upper left arm. Not a lot of damage considering Kylie's clothes were covered in red marks.

It only made Kylie feel more vulnerable and less capable of facing a real battle. A battle that Kylie sensed was her destiny. A battle with Mario. A battle she very well might lose.

After a few minutes, the spirit started spouting orders, much like Lucas did. Move this way, hold her sword this way. Move quicker. Never lose sight of her sword.

Kylie finally got the hang of it and actually blocked some of the spirit's blows. But all that stopped when the front door to her cabin cracked open and then was knocked off its hinges.

The wood panel landed with a big *clunk* on the floor.

Before Kylie got a good look at the cabin's intruder, Della's door hit the floor with the same sharp noise.

The vampire rushed out, her eyes glowing bright green and her fangs fully extended.

Chapter Thirty-three

The intense cold faded with the spirit. Kylie stood, feet apart, body tense, her sword poised to fight. She looked from Della, all fangs and fury, to the front entrance.

Confusion had Kylie holding her stance. Burnett stood atop the downed door, his eyes brighter than Della's. Behind him was an army of Shadow Falls campers: Lucas, Derek, Chris, and Jonathon. All of them stood mesmerized by the glowing weapon.

"Holy shit." The words came from Chris and Jonathon. While Jonathon had seen the sword, he hadn't seen it glowing.

"You don't repeat what you've seen here!" Burnett snapped.

Kylie lowered her sword and breathed, hoping air would lessen her adrenaline.

What the hell was happening now?

She met Burnett's gaze. "What's wrong?"

He looked around. "Who's here?"

"Just the spirit," she said.

Chris and Jonathon stepped back.

Derek, accustomed to the whole ghost issue, stayed where he was. So did Lucas. She noticed the were's bright orange eyes, as if he was prepared to fight. His gaze stayed trained on her.

Burnett's posture lost some of its fierceness. But not nearly enough to put Kylie at ease.

Another set of footsteps sounded from the porch. Hayden entered, giving the door a quick glance.

"What's going on?" Kylie asked.

"Can I second that question?" Della bit out, and brushed a curtain of straight black hair from her face. Her eyes no longer glowed, but their green hue remained, made even more noticeable by the solid black nightshirt that hung just above her knees.

"Someone jumped the fence. Broke into the camp." Burnett took another step inside.

"Who?" Miranda walked out of her bedroom, holding on to her teddy bear, wearing Smurf pajamas, and yawning.

Kylie's grasp on the sword tightened as only one person came to mind. Was she ready to stand up to Mario?

Probably not, the answer came back. But nothing would stop her from trying. Not when so many people she loved were standing around as possible victims for the rogue.

Burnett said, "I heard the alarm. Then I heard you fighting and assumed you were being attacked."

"Told you practicing in the middle of the night wasn't good," Della muttered.

"Where's Perry?" Miranda asked as if she suspected he would be involved in this.

"Circling the property to see if he sees anyone." Burnett turned to Hayden and nodded as if giving him a silent order. The chameleon moved back out on the porch. At first Kylie was confused, then she understood. Burnett had instructed Hayden to turn invisible to see if he heard any other chameleons. She considered checking herself, but with everyone's eyes on her, she didn't want to freak everyone out.

In a few minutes, Hayden reappeared behind the others. "It seems clear," he said.

But Kylie knew that if an invisible intruder remained completely still, he might not be detected.

Burnett shifted his gaze to Della. "Stay and guard Kylie. We'll go look around."

"If you don't mind, I'd like to stay here as well," Lucas spoke up.

His words caused an emotional flinch in Kylie's gut. Letting go was hard. Letting go, with him always around, felt impossible.

Burnett nodded. Then footsteps thundered down the porch steps as everyone left.

Kylie looked from Lucas to Della, and then Miranda.

The witch still clung to her teddy bear. "Who do they think is here?" Miranda asked.

No one answered. Then Miranda's gaze shot to Kylie. "Oh, him."

Della sighed. "Looks like it's gonna be a long, bat-shit crazy night."

Lucas planted himself in the living room chair. Kylie, trying to ignore him, placed her sword down on the coffee table. She watched it lose its glow and then she glanced at Miranda. "Do you feel anything?"

The witch closed her eyes. After a long second, she opened them and looked at Kylie. "Yeah."

Kylie's heart tightened. Oh, shit. Was Mario here? She almost reached for her sword.

"But it's not evil this time." Miranda glanced at the weapon on the coffee table. "Maybe that's what I'm feeling."

"You didn't feel it the other night, did you?"

"No. But it has an aura, so it makes sense I might feel it."

Kylie let out a deep breath. She hoped Miranda was right—that whoever was here wasn't evil.

The sudden sound of footsteps on the front porch had everyone on alert again. Lucas shot up from the chair. Della shot across the room. Kylie however, moved fastest and was closer to the door. If it was Mario, no way in hell was he going to hurt them before getting through her.

Steve walked inside. His gaze shot past Kylie, to Della.

Della frowned. "What are you doing here?"

"Making sure you're okay."

Della frowned. "I don't need you to protect me."

He stomped out at the same time Kylie heard a roar. Not a human roar. She'd bet anything that the shape-shifter had just turned himself into a big pissed-off feline. Kylie considered going after him to help soothe his ego, but since she'd nearly become supper for one angry lion when she first got here at Shadow Falls, she decided to let Steve handle his own ego.

Miranda made a disapproving noise. "That's no way to treat the guy who gave you a hickey."

Della growled. "What? You saw how quickly he left. If he'd really been concerned, he'd have stayed."

Kylie rolled her eyes at Della's logic.

Lucas raised his brows—probably at the hickey comment. Then his gaze shifted to Kylie with a look of protection. But in less than a second, something softer flashed in his eyes, something tender. *Love you,* those blue eyes seemed to say.

The lion somewhere out front roared again and then a huge prehistoric bird came down with a loud thud in the open threshold.

Miranda squealed, lost her teddy, and went to hug the bird.

Kylie plopped down on the arm of the sofa. The vamp had hit the nail on the head when she said it was going to be a very long and batshit crazy night.

"What's the tape for?" Kylie asked Lucas the next day as he unloaded his bag again and prepared for practice. Kylie had slept in and missed classes, and Lucas had called a little after eleven and asked if she wanted to cancel practice since they'd been up most of the night. She'd wanted to say hell yes, but heeding her heart, as well as the ghost's warning that she needed to learn to fight, she agreed to practice.

"For protection. We wrap the ends of the blade." He looked up the line of trees as if he'd heard something. Or someone.

Kylie's thoughts went from fighting with real swords to Lucas's cautious surveillance. "Who's out there?"

"Chris and Will," he answered.

Since the intruder hadn't been found last night, and they hadn't gotten another security alarm saying anyone had left, the entire camp was on Red Alert. For now she didn't just have one shadow, she had three.

Lovely.

Just lovely.

As she watched Lucas pull out the swords, a breath of cold moved across the back of her neck. Make that four shadows.

He's such a pansy. Tell him not to the tape the blades. You need to learn to fight for real! Time is running out.

Looking over her shoulder, Kylie saw the spirit had donned her blood-soaked gown again.

What happened to you? Who killed you? Kylie asked.

The spirit looked down at her gown and frowned. *I'm not important. You are.*

Suddenly feeling desperate for answers, Kylie continued, *How do you know me? How are we connected? I need answers.*

You need to learn to fight. Or you will be as dead as I am.

The warning sent dread stabbing at Kylie's heart. She watched Lucas crouch down and start to wrap the end of the blades. "Do we really need the tape?"

He looked up, surprise in his eyes. "Are you serious?"

She nodded. "You need to teach me how to fight for real."

He stood up, concern in his face. "Why? What is it that you know?"

"Just a feeling," she lied.

"I don't like that feeling," he said.

"Join the crowd." She blinked. "Just teach me to fight, Lucas."

Appearing resigned, he picked up the two swords. Her weapon

started glowing the instant she wrapped her hand around it. Perhaps it was her imagination, but it seemed to be glowing brighter. What did that mean? Did the sword, like the ghost, know the time for battle drew near?

Lucas stood beside her and commenced doing warm-up stances. She immediately followed suit.

Kylie's phone, tucked in her pocket, beeped with an incoming text. She waited for the next break before she pulled it out. It was from Derek.

Call me.

Was he back to trying to convince her to rekindle their relationship? She recalled seeing him frown last night when Lucas had insisted on staying at the cabin to protect her.

"Who is it?" Lucas asked.

She hesitated, then just spit it out. "Derek."

He frowned but remained silent. They went back to the basic form exercises.

"When are we going to spar?" she asked as she copied his moves.

"When are you going to tell that fairy that it's really over between you two?"

"I already did," she answered before she realized the wisdom against it.

He stopped moving. His sword, pointing upward, came down in a whoosh. He faced her. "You did?"

It was too late to take it back. "Yes."

He smiled. "Thank you."

She frowned. "I didn't do it for you. I did it for him."

His smile remained strong and one eyebrow arched up. "But I'm the reason you did it."

It wasn't a question, but she could deny it. Then too much time had passed for her to do it. It would've sounded false. It would've been false.

An even bigger smile appeared in his eyes. A smile of confidence. Of hope.

"I love you," he said, his voice almost musical with happiness.

She shot him a scowl. "Isn't saying that a bit dangerous considering these aren't wooden swords and the ends aren't even taped?"

He laughed. A real laugh, and the sound of it washed over her like a soft summer rain on an extra-hot day. Then flashing in her mind was the look on his face when the weres had left him alone on parents' day. Then she recalled that Will and Chris were out there, probably listening to every word they said. Will was supposed to be a friend, but would he, too, turn his back on Lucas?

She cut her eyes to the woods and whispered, "We're not alone, remember?"

"I don't care who hears it. I love you!" His voice rose louder this time.

She frowned. "Nothing's changed."

"Everything has changed," he said.

No it hadn't. He might think he could walk away from everything that had mattered to him, but she wasn't about to let him do that. She loved him too much.

"Are we going to practice? If not, I'm leaving."

"Then let's practice," he said.

They continued with the exercises for another ten minutes. Finally, he faced her. "We'll start, but remember, this isn't wood. We start slow."

He wasn't joking about slow. They moved at a snail's pace and continued for the next fifteen minutes. "Who were you fighting with last night?" His question broke the long tense silence as they finally started picking up speed.

"The ghost."

"Is she good?" he asked.

The fact that he asked about a ghost surprised her.

"She claims she's better than you."

"I knew I didn't like her," he said, and half smiled. After a pause, he asked, "Who is this ghost?" His gaze stayed on the swords.

"I don't know," she answered truthfully. And just like that, Kylie sensed it was imperative that she find out.

Kylie didn't remember to call Derek. She and Lucas had a good practice. They didn't really let loose and spar like they would have with wooden swords, but almost.

When she checked her phone at almost midnight that night and found another text from Derek, she felt guilty. *Call me now!*

She'd seen him at dinner—that had been after his text—and he hadn't said anything. He hadn't even sat with her; instead he'd grabbed his dinner and left.

Still a bit worried, but not knowing if he'd still be awake, she texted him back. *What's up?*

She waited up for a good forty-five minutes to see if he would text her back. Nothing.

Frustrated, she flopped back on her pillow. The ghostly chill waved through the room for about the third time since she'd come to bed, but the spirit didn't stay.

Kylie's conversation with Holiday this afternoon added merit to her feelings. If she could just figure out the spirit's identity, it might help to answer a lot of questions.

While the spirit hadn't confirmed it, Kylie was almost certain the ghost was connected to Mario.

"Who are you?" Kylie asked the wisp of cold moving like a quick shadow in the room. "Tell me. Or at least show me something."

No answer came. Accepting that no spirit spoke before they were ready, Kylie rolled over and tried to sleep. Tried to think about something other than the ghost.

Anything other than killing someone.

Anything other than dying.

Anything other than Lucas and the hope she'd seen in his eyes.

Sleep had just about lured her in when she heard a slight noise. Footsteps on the wood floor. She opened her eyes and reached under her pillow for the sword.

Under her pillow? She didn't sleep with the sword.

Instinctively, she knew they were coming after her.

Who was coming for her?

Something wasn't right. Yet Kylie pulled out the weapon and lunged out of bed. Her feet landed on carpet. She looked down at the Oriental rug. Plush. Expensive.

Where was she?

Or a better question was: Who was she?

Heart pounding at the sound of the approaching footsteps, she looked around the room. A bedroom. Not Kylie's bedroom.

Heavy, expensive-looking wood furniture glistened from the little moonlight filtering through a large bay window that looked out at palm trees.

The taste of fear and fury lingered on her tongue. She raised her sword. Only to realize it wasn't the sword that had been delivered to her, but the sword of . . .

Everything made sense now. She was the spirit and she was in a vision. She spotted a heavy framed mirror over a dresser. For a flicker of a second, she stared at the image. Her dark hair hung loose, uncombed.

But causing Kylie's first stirring of panic was the gown. The one the spirit had obviously been wearing when she'd been murdered.

And Kylie was going to live it. Her first impulse was to scream out "Hell, no." Her second was to be aware, to find the answers she needed.

The thundering of footsteps drew closer, thudding as if climbing old wooden steps. Instinctually, Kylie knew that the spirit had expected her attackers. She had known that the night would bring her death. She'd chosen to wear white, yet had questioned if the sign of purity would do her any good.

Now as she waited for the end to draw near, a surge of regret, remorse for the life she had lived, crossed her mind. But deep down she accepted it was too late. Too late to change how she'd lived. But she could and would change how she died.

Who are you? The question whispered through Kylie's mind. She prayed the answer would make itself clear so she could leave this vision before she had to live this woman's death.

The spirit looked to the window almost as if considering escape. *Get out,* Kylie told her. *You don't have to die.*

Even before the thought was complete, Kylie knew the actions of the spirit on this eve of her death had already been written. Kylie had not been brought inside the body, or the memory, to change what was. She'd been brought here to live it.

To learn the truth.

What truth? Why hadn't the spirit left? Kylie sensed that leaving had been an option. The spirit had chosen to die. For what cause?

"Mama." The young boy ran through the door.

"He found us." His eyes rounded with fear and tears. "He found us. Now what do we do?"

She grabbed the boy by his shoulders. The spirit wanted to embrace him, to bury her face in his hair so she could die with the smell of her only son still filling her senses. But time had run out. She pushed him into the closet. "Use the trapdoor like I showed you. Run and don't look back." She shut the closet door at the same time the bedroom door crashed open.

Chapter Thirty-four

The woman, with Kylie living inside her, turned to fight. Not because she thought she could win, but for the little time her son would need to escape. She knew she would die, but it was for her son.

They moved in. There were three of them. They wore black, no masks, and she recognized them.

Knew them well.

Had eaten at their tables.

Laughed at their jokes.

She also recognized the look in their eyes, the drive to complete a job. Killing her was their duty.

She raised her sword and fought. Fought for her son. For a few seconds, she actually bested them, blocked their attempts to draw blood. No one could say she had gone down easy.

The first piercing pain went into her ribs. Kylie screamed for it to stop. She tried to tell herself it wasn't real, that it wasn't her, but it felt real. She felt the pain the spirit had felt those last horrific moments of her life.

Felt their weapons slashing into her skin, hitting bone.

Her body grew limp, the pain too much. She dropped to her knees and fell forward to the floor. Her own blood oozed out. The thick flow of fluid warmed the sudden chill. She didn't fight it. She willed the blood to flow faster. The faster it flowed, the less she hurt.

The coppery scent of blood filled her senses. The stickiness of it seeped beneath her cheek pressed to the cold floor. The last thing she saw was the closet door ajar and her young son watching in horror as she took her last breath.

He hadn't run. Fury filled her soul.

Would he know? Would he know that the reason she died had been to keep him safe—to protect him from the kind of life she and his father had lived?

The second before death took her, she vowed revenge. Not revenge on the ones who killed her—they were nothing more than pawns doing the devil's work. She knew, for she had been one of them. The revenge she sought was for the one who'd sent them, the devil himself. As well as the one who had allowed it, the devil's son.

"Don't get too close. She might cut your head off with that thing." Miranda's shrill voice registered in Kylie's mind, but it was in the distance.

"She won't kill me," Della responded.

"I don't mean she'd want to." Miranda's voice came again. "But hell, you saw how she was dancing around with that sword."

Her consciousness fought against the void of blackness. She wanted to fall back into the void. It held no memories. It offered escape from what she'd just experienced. The damn voice, the one she couldn't really identify spoke again. *You need to remember.*

Taking a breath, she opened her eyes.

Della's black, slightly slanted eyes came into focus. "She's back," she said in a singsong voice, sounding like a horror film.

Kylie tried to push up but felt too weak.

Della helped her sit up. Kylie looked around. She was in her cabin's kitchen. Still clutched in her hand was the sword. The vision must have provoked her to pick it up. Remembering parts of the vision, she dropped the sword and ran her hand over her stomach to check for wounds.

None. Only the memory of pain remained. It was over. Everything but the crying. Tears welled in her eyes. How could life be so brutal? So evil?

"You're not going to kill us, are you?" Miranda asked. Kylie shook her head. As painful as it was to remember details, she needed to remember—she needed answers.

A flash of the little boy in the closet filled her mind, something familiar tickled her memory. Yes, *he* was familiar. Even more, bits and pieces of the story played déjà vu with her mind. Someone had told this story. Who? All of a sudden she knew.

She stood up. Her knees buckled. Della caught her.

"We've got to go," Kylie said.

"It's kind of hard to go when you can't stand up," Della said.

"I can." Kylie forced herself to stand on her own accord and pushed Della's hand away.

"Okay, you're standing," Della bit out. "Step two is being able to walk."

Kylie took a few steps and glared back at the vamp.

"Step three is making sense. And it doesn't make sense for me to walk out of this cabin before I know where we're going."

Kylie inhaled. "To Derek's. I need Derek."

"Derek?" Miranda said. "And here I thought she'd given up on him and was almost back with Lucas."

Kylie shot the little witch a pleading look to give it a break. "I'm serious."

"Can I get my bra on first?" Della asked.

"You don't need one." Miranda snickered.

Della shot her a scowl. "You are the witchiest bitch I know."

Kylie, too emotionally distraught to deal with their bickering, started for the door. She had to know.

Della must have decided Miranda was right about not needing boob support, because she followed Kylie out the door. Pajamas and all.

"You know Burnett will have my head for letting you do this without calling him."

Kylie started running, her need for answers giving her will. She felt the wind in her hair and the tears run wet down her cheeks.

In less than two minutes, Kylie came to a stop beside Derek's cabin.

"Okay, wise one, are you going to knock on the door?" Della looked at her, and her smartass expression vanished into one of concern once she saw Kylie's tears.

"I'm sorry," she said. "It must have been bad."

Kylie nodded. "I'll try the window." She ran to the side of the cabin. The windows were a lot taller than she was. Jumping up, she latched her fingers onto the top of the window ledge and pulled herself up to peer inside.

And what she saw had her . . . had her . . . confused.

Befuddled.

Shocked.

She blinked—as if it would change what she was looking at.

But two or three flutters of her lashes later, she could still make out not one, but two people in Derek's bed. One was Derek. She could clearly make out his masculine form. But the other was . . . Kylie couldn't see her face.

But it was definitely a *her*. She had long black hair and a very feminine-shaped pajama-covered butt protruding from the blanket. And Kylie just happened to recognize those PJ bottoms as Derek's.

The girl shifted. Kylie held her breath, hoping she'd roll over so she could see who was warming up the other side of Derek's bed.

Kylie took a second to ask herself if she was jealous. Somewhere deep down, very deep, there was a touch of green emotion. But with it came a sense of rightness. Derek needed to move on.

But did he have to do it so dang fast?

The girl rolled over.

Kylie saw her face and . . . "Crap!" Her fingers accidentally let go of the windowsill and she fell, landing with a thump on her butt.

How? How could this be?

Chapter Thirty-five

"What is it?" Della asked, looming behind her.

"Nothing," Kylie lied, still on the ground where she had fallen.

"Try again," Della said, obviously having heard her heart's untruth.

"Let it go. And please . . . give me some privacy to talk to . . . him."

"I'm shadowing you," she said and watched Kylie stand up.

"I know," Kylie answered. "But I'm begging you. Please. I need some privacy."

"To do what? Go jump his bones?" Kylie didn't even reply to that. Della swung around and stomped off.

Kylie pulled back up on the windowsill, hung on with one hand, and knocked with the other. Both parties in bed bolted up.

Derek's sleep-filled gaze shot toward the window. Kylie wasn't sure what Jenny—as in Hayden's sister, Jenny—did. She'd vanished.

Brushing a hand over his face, Derek came to the window. Kylie dropped down as he lifted the window up. He reached out and offered her a frown and a hand to pull her up.

"It's about damn time," he muttered as he hoisted her up. "What the hell took you so long?"

Feet on the bedroom floor, Kylie frowned. "You saw me at dinner and didn't say anything."

"What could I say in a room filled with vampires?"

Hell, he was right. "What's going on?" She looked around. "And Jenny, you can make yourself visible. I already saw you."

Jenny appeared and her cheeks turned red. "This isn't what it seems. We weren't . . ." She pointed to the floor where a blanket and pillow were thrown.

"You were supposed to sleep on the floor," Jenny snapped at Derek.

"I couldn't sleep, so I just . . ." He glared at Jenny. "I didn't touch you."

Kylie shook her head. "I don't care about that."

"I do," Jenny said, and glared at Derek.

"I didn't touch you!" he repeated.

Kylie moaned. "Jenny? What are you doing *here*?" Right then Kylie remembered the alarm. "That was you that jumped the fence."

Jenny frowned. "I didn't know the place was wired. Even the compound doesn't have an alarm."

But the chameleons weren't waiting on a psycho rogue to attack. Kylie shook her head, reminding herself to focus on one issue at a time. And this was a big issue, too. "Shit!" she muttered. "Does Hayden know you're here?"

Both Derek and Jenny shook their heads.

Kylie looked at Jenny. "You ran away, didn't you?"

Jenny nodded and gripped her hands together. "Please don't . . . don't be mad."

Derek looked at Jenny with empathy and then stared at Kylie as if frustrated. "Why are you upset? You said you wanted to help her."

Kylie frowned. "I do, but . . . running away isn't the answer."

"Please," Derek muttered. "For someone who ran away a couple of weeks ago, I don't think you have a lot of room to judge."

"I didn't run away. I told everyone I was leaving. And I'm not judging." Frustrated and yet a bit amused at Derek's defense of Jenny, Kylie inhaled and looked from Jenny to Derek. "If a chameleon runs away before they're mature they are excommunicated from their family."

Derek cut his eyes to Jenny, up and then down. "She looks pretty mature to me."

Kylie rolled her eyes. "I'm not talking about her body. I'm talking about her being able to change her pattern." Moving her gaze to Jenny, Kylie realized something. "But you're able to go invisible. I thought that didn't happen until later?"

"It doesn't normally. I've been working really hard on my own for the last couple of years so I could leave early. But I still can't control my pattern." A sadness entered the girl's eyes.

"Are you really ready to completely walk away from your family?"

Jenny dropped on the bed and bunched a handful of Derek's loose-fitting pajamas in her hands. "It hurts like hell, but that family is trying to force me to marry someone I don't love. And he doesn't love me, either. I don't want to live like that."

Kylie's mind raced. She had told Holiday that what the chameleon elders were doing was almost as bad as the weres. Now she realized how right she was. The elders were doing to Jenny what Lucas's father was doing to Lucas.

Did that mean Lucas was right to stand up to his pack, and to his dad? Everything felt so mixed up. Realizing Derek and Jenny stared at her, she decided now wasn't the time to think about Lucas. One problem at a time.

Problem one, her grandfather and the entire chameleon community were going to blame this on Kylie because she was the reason Hayden was here. How in the hell was she going to fix that? She looked at Jenny again. "Okay, so now explain to me why you haven't gotten with Hayden?"

"Because," Jenny said. "Every time I talked to him about me leaving, he'd tell me it was wrong. To stick it out until I matured. But everyone knew that the day I matured, I was out of there, so the elders were trying to find another way to stop me. They were going to force me to marry Brandon next week." Her expression grew solemn. "Besides, I didn't come here because of Hayden. I came here because of you. I thought you'd understand. I guess I was wrong."

Guilt filled Kylie's chest. "You're not wrong, I just . . . I don't know how to make this right." Kylie looked around. "How did you end up with Derek?"

"You always had people around you. I saw Derek and I figured if you trusted him, then I could, too."

Kylie sighed. "Are you really ready to lose the right to see your family?" Was Lucas?

Tears filled the girl's eyes and Kylie felt the same emotion stir inside her.

"No," Jenny said, "but I wasn't ready to marry Brandon, either."

"I know," Kylie said. "We just have to figure out how to deal with this." The same went with Lucas. But God help her, she didn't have a clue how to do either.

She glanced at Derek and remembered why she'd come here to begin with. "We have a lot of stuff to deal with," she muttered.

"What stuff?" Derek asked.

Kylie hadn't realized she'd spoken aloud. Then parts of the vision played in Kylie's head like a horror movie. "Do you remember when you told me about Roberto, Mario's grandson? You said he witnessed his mother's murder?"

"Yes."

"Do you remember how she was murdered?"

He ran a hand through his dark hair. "I think one article said she was stabbed."

Kylie frowned. "I was afraid of that."

"Why?" Derek asked.

"She's my ghost."

Derek looked concerned. "Roberto's mom is your ghost?"

"Please tell me she's not here right now." Jenny pulled her knees up to her chest and hugged them.

"It's okay." Derek moved closer to the girl. He rested a palm on her shoulder to ease her fear.

"Stop it!" Jenny slapped his hand. "I don't like you touching me. You . . . make me feel things I don't . . . feel."

Derek frowned. "I was trying to make you feel better."

"Maybe I don't want to feel better!" she snapped, and they stared at each other.

For some reason their bickering reminded Kylie of Burnett and Holiday, or better yet, Kylie and Derek in the beginning, and she knew why. Sexual tension. If Kylie was a vampire she'd bet she could smell the pheromones.

Derek looked at Kylie. "Do you see what I've put up with the last twenty-four hours?"

The only thing keeping Kylie from smiling were the remnants of the vision and the realization that she didn't have a clue how to deal with Jenny. If she went to Holiday, she wasn't sure the camp leader would or even could allow her to stay. But how long could they keep her hidden?

All of a sudden, Derek's window shot up and Della lunged inside. "Okay, here's the thing. I just got a call from Burnett. He was doing walk-bys of our cabins and realized we're gone. He's on his way here. You've got one second to hide Girl Wonder over there, or he's gonna know she's here."

Jenny vanished. Della, seeing the vanishing act for the first time, looked stunned. Burnett came bolting through the opened window. "What the hell is happening now?"

"I had a vision." Kylie offered part of the truth. "I wanted to ask Derek about it."

"And you couldn't have called me first?"

"You know how I am after a vision, I was crazy, all I could think about was finding out the truth."

"What truth?"

"I know who the ghost is now. She is . . . was connected to Mario. She was his daughter-in-law, Roberto's mother. Mario had her killed." Kylie's heart ached, remembering the last few minutes of the woman's life. Remembering how Roberto had witnessed the terrible death.

Burnett sighed. "And the sword? Is it from her, too?"

"No, she says it's from . . . the death angels."

A long pause filled the room as if everyone had to take a few seconds to believe it. "Do you know why they sent it?" Burnett finally asked.

Kylie frowned. She suspected it was because she was going to have to face Mario. And deep down she figured that Burnett suspected it as well. But nobody wanted to say it. "No, not really." It wasn't even a lie. There was a difference in knowing something and suspecting it.

"Come on, let's go talk to Holiday about this vision," Burnett said.

Kylie left Derek's cabin to deal with one issue, knowing that sooner or later, she would have to deal with the one she was leaving here. Jenny.

How long could they hide a runaway chameleon? Hopefully long enough for Kylie to come up with a plan.

Both Burnett and Holiday walked Kylie back to her cabin after their powwow. She'd managed to get through the talk without lying by keeping the topic on the vision. Kylie hadn't told them anything about Jenny or about her father repeating his message concerning them being together soon. To be honest, she tried not to think about her dad's message. Hadn't Holiday said that a person who started preparing oneself for death cheated themselves out of what little life they had left? And . . . somewhere deep in her gut, she held on to the fact that her dad could be confused. That his definition of soon could be in about eighty or ninety years.

The first thing Kylie did after Burnett and Holiday walked away was grab her phone.

Derek answered on the first ring. "You survived?"

"Barely," Kylie said.

"How did you lie to Burnett?"

"By avoiding the truth."

He sighed. "Speaking of the truth. I reread the articles about Roberto's mom. The cause of death had been listed as multiple stab wounds. Oh, and her name was listed as Lucinda Esparza."

"Thanks." Kylie repeated the name in her head.

"So what's the plan with *my* problem?" he asked.

So he considered Jenny his problem, did he? "I don't know, but would you mind continuing to hide her until I brainstorm a plan? Since you don't have a vampire rooming with you or Burnett doing walk-bys. She has less chance of being detected with you."

"I planned on her staying here," Derek said, sounding almost insistent. It was then Kylie knew for sure. Her old flame had managed to fall out of love with her and was on his way to falling for Jenny. Kylie felt their connection, just like she'd felt the thing between Burnett and Holiday, Perry and Miranda, and Jonathon and Helen.

She could almost hear Derek and Jenny telling their kids how they'd first met. "Your mom just jumped out of nowhere expecting me to give her a piggyback ride!"

Jenny was lucky. And Derek deserved to be happy.

And so do I. And her happiness was tied to Lucas. It was as if something switched in her head and she realized how wrong she'd been. She shouldn't have been trying to push him away. She should have been pushing him to find a way to make it right. "Hey . . . uh, I just realized I need to do something. Can we talk tomorrow?"

"Do what?" Derek asked, obviously reading something from her.

Convince someone I'm worth fighting for. "Bye." She hung up, and then went to dial Lucas's number. An instant before she hit the last number, she changed her mind. There was another way. A better way.

• • •

It took ten minutes to fall asleep, and another few to get in control and dreamscape her way to Lucas's cabin and into his bedroom. He looked adorable asleep in his bed. The sheet came low on his waist and she couldn't help but wonder if he had anything on at all. She really doubted it.

Mentally dressing him in a pair of long boxers, she slipped into his mind and into his dreams.

"Lucas," she whispered his name. While she could have taken him anywhere, she hadn't. They remained in his bedroom. She eyed his bare chest again and wondered why she hadn't dreamed him in a shirt. Probably because she liked seeing his bare chest.

Then she looked at his bed and her mind went to joining him there. That's when she decided she needed to get them away from here.

Lucas sat up. "Hey." His voice came out deep and sleepy.

"Come on, let's go," she said.

"Go where?" he asked.

"Somewhere to talk," she answered.

He patted the bed and looked at her through his dark lashes with a sexy grin. Had he read her earlier thoughts? she wondered.

"We could talk here," he said in a husky voice.

She rolled her eyes. "Nice try."

He laughed. Then he pulled up the sheet and glanced beneath it. "At least they don't have smiley faces on them," he said, referring to the time she'd dressed him in another dreamscape.

She concentrated and moved the dream to behind the office where they often went to talk.

He looked around, and then back at her. The night was dark; only a few stars brightened the sky. "I think I liked the lake dream better," he said, talking about the dreamscape they'd shared of them skinny-dipping.

Reaching out, he caught her shoulders and pulled her against him. His chest was so warm. So inviting. She would have loved to stay there. To explore all the things she wanted to explore between them. *But not yet.*

"Behave," she said, and pulled loose.

His smiled faded. "Is something wrong?"

"No. Well, yes, it's wrong. Everything's wrong." She inhaled. "You have to get on that Council, Lucas."

"I'm not marrying Monique," he growled.

"Not by marrying Monique. You have to find another way."

"I need my father to vouch for me, Kylie. He's not going to do that now."

She gritted her teeth. "Talk to him. You said he's protective of you. He obviously cares. Maybe if you—"

"You don't know him," he said.

Fury rose in her chest. "Then find another way. Find someone else to vouch for you. Or talk to the Council yourself. You've told me all the young people want change. Make the elders see this. They were young once. Can't you make them remember what it was like? I mean . . . who was it that said if the door is locked, find a window. If the window's locked, well . . . break it. If it won't break then find a freaking sledgehammer and make a new one."

He shook his head. "You don't how they are."

"Yes, I do! The elders of the chameleons are just like your elders. They want to arrange marriages and tell all the young chameleons what to do. I don't know how I'm going to change things, but I'll be damned if I'm not going to try."

"It's not the same," he said, as if taking offense to her accusation.

"Maybe it's not exactly the same. But you're still giving up."

"I'm not giving up on us," he said. "That's what matters."

She shook her head. "But you are giving up on us. If you don't get on the Council, Lucas, there is no us."

"You don't mean that!" he said, his anger thickening in his voice.

"Don't think I want it," she said. "But I know if you lose who you are and all you ever wanted, you will resent me for it. Maybe not now, but someday you will. And I can't go into this knowing that you'll hate me someday. I can't."

In a flash, Kylie ended the dreamscape and shot up in her bed. Then she cried herself asleep. But right before she did, she heard her father one more time.

Soon. Soon we will be together.

She couldn't help but wonder if, when she was dead, would she still ache for Lucas?

The next morning, Kylie, running on only an hour of sleep, stood with the crowd waiting for Chris to do his dog and pony show and get Campmate hour under way. Perry, her official morning shadow, stood beside her, with Miranda leaning against him. Della had a vampire meeting and was going to miss out.

Lucas wasn't here. But she'd gotten a text from him that read: *I think I found a window.* Hope gave her energy. Energy to reminisce over how good Lucas had looked in the bed last night and how tempted she'd been to curl up with him and let things just happen. Pushing the sexy were from her mind, she searched for something else to think about—like figuring out how to proceed with Lucinda, who was standing in the crowd as if she belonged but wasn't speaking to Kylie. Was Kylie's fighting Mario honestly what the spirit needed Kylie to do to pass over? Pass over to hell?

It was one thing to encourage the souls destined for the pearly gates to leave their lonely existence on earth and move on. But how could she encourage someone to head off to hell?

Kylie shivered at the thought.

"You're quiet," Miranda said. "Everything okay?"

Kylie nodded and spotted Derek moving into the crowd. Her thoughts shot to Jenny and how she was going to deal with that. Her gut told her the right thing to do was to confront Hayden.

She knew Jenny was frightened he would insist she return home, but Kylie wasn't so sure Hayden would do that.

The chatter in the circle of students quieted. Kylie looked up. Chris moved into the front of the crowd, drawing Kylie's attention from her own woes. "Today we have . . ." He looked down into his hat and then glanced up. Up right at Kylie.

Oh, hell, Kylie thought, who was it this time?

"Kylie Galen." Chris smiled. "The girl who happens to be the person who has brought us more blood than any camper in the past." He hesitated. "You, my friend, get the pleasure of . . ." He paused for dramatic effect. "Of Steve's company."

Kylie saw Steve, the shape-shifter with the cute ass, the one who'd given Della a hickey, start strolling over. Not for one minute did Kylie assume Steve had an interest in her. She knew he was merely looking for some romantic advice.

Advice Kylie didn't have. What the hell could she tell him? Her normal reply to someone trying to gain someone's attention was to be patient. But Della was the most adamant and stubborn person Kylie knew and it would take the patience of a saint to wear the vampire down.

"Be patient? That's all you've got for me?" Steve complained ten minutes later.

Kylie glanced up at Perry, circling them as they sat behind the office, and then frowned at Steve. "I don't know why everyone thinks I'm the love guru."

"Come on, give me something that would help me. You know her better than anyone."

Kylie dropped down beside the tree. "What can I tell you? Della's difficult." So difficult that if Della found out that Kylie had offered Steve advice, the vamp would revoke Kylie's best friend card.

"You think I don't know that?"

Kylie looked up into his desperate eyes. "She was hurt really badly by someone."

"I know that, too." He crossed his arms over his wide chest. "She deserves so much better than him."

"Oh, hell," Kylie said, and decided to throw caution to the wind. "Okay, here's all I can tell you. Della loves a good fight."

"I don't want to fight," Steve said. "What I want is . . ." He blushed as if thinking about what he really wanted.

But damn it, Kylie liked Steve.

"Look, I don't mean to fight with her. Fight *for* her. When she tells you that you can't sit with her at lunch, sit down anyway. When she tells you to leave, don't. She's gonna get pissy. That's Della, but I think it'll win you brownie points."

The shape-shifter paused as if contemplating. "Damn. You're right. When we were on the mission, she tried to push me away, but I didn't let her. I couldn't because Burnett warned me if anything happened to her, he'd have my head on a platter. And that's when we . . . Hey! I know what I have to do."

"What?" Kylie asked, afraid of what she'd set in motion.

"Just wait and see." A smile spread his lips. Sparkles started popping off around him. He changed into a bird, not one as big or magnificent as the one who guarded her from above, but still impressive. Flapping his wings twice, he flew off, squawking at Perry as he did.

Perry came in for a quick landing. "You are good at this," he said, still in bird form. "She'll be putty in his hands. Of course, she'll have already ripped your heart out for betraying her."

"Don't talk to me when you're not a human!" She dropped her forehead on her knees.

Crap! Perry was right. Della was going to kill her. But since destiny may already have Kylie earmarked to die, she wasn't sure it really mattered.

Chapter Thirty-six

"You waiting for a call?" Kylie asked Hayden Yates when she walked into his classroom ten minutes later and he was holding his cell.

"Hoping." He frowned and looked around as if making sure they were alone. "It's Jenny. She's left home. God only knows where she is."

Kylie bit down on her lip. "If you found her, what would you do?"

"What do you mean?" Suspicion made his eyes tighten.

"Would you take her back to her parents? If she's run away, it's probably because she's like you when you were young, and she can't handle that lifestyle anymore."

His suspicion faded. "She doesn't know how hard it is to be completely alone."

"She wouldn't be alone," Kylie said. "She'd have you."

He frowned. "I know nothing about dealing with a teen."

Kylie rolled her eyes. "You're a teacher. You deal with us daily."

"I teach, I don't parent. There's a difference. But discussing this is silly." He ran his fingers through his hair. "She's young, she's naïve."

"She's not that naïve." Kylie remembered Jenny standing up to Derek and how she helped them escape. "What if I knew where she was?"

Hayden glared at Kylie. "Christ! The alarm?"

Kylie nodded. Hayden frowned. "Do Burnett and Holiday know?"

"Not yet."

He blew air through his teeth. "If the elders find out she's here, they'll expect Burnett and Holiday to bring her back."

"I know," Kylie said. "That's the problem."

Hayden locked both of his hands behind his head. "And Holiday and Burnett will have to do it. They can't legally keep her without some serious consequences."

Kylie sighed. "That's the other part of the problem."

He pressed a hand on his desk. "This is so screwed up."

Kylie's mind raced. "I want to talk to Holiday and Burnett about it, but if this whole Mario thing calmed down, I think I'd have a better chance of convincing them."

He shot up. "Where is she right now?"

"She's staying at Derek's."

He looked puzzled. "Derek?" Hayden's expression went from teacher to big brother and Kylie got the feeling Derek could be up against some issues.

"It's better than my place because Burnett is watching me like a hawk. When Jenny jumped the gate, she couldn't get close to me because I had shadows. Jenny and Derek met the night I escaped and she thought she could trust him. And she's right. Derek's the nicest guy I know. He would never . . . you know."

"He better not . . . you know!" Hayden bit out.

"I think it would be safer to move her to your place. Not because of Derek. But . . ."

He exhaled. "It would be safer if she went back and—"

"No!" Kylie said. "Just give me some time. I think I can solve this."

"How? She's not mature yet."

Kylie pointed to her pattern. "I'm not completely mature and I'm doing just fine."

"You can really say that with a straight face?" he asked. "You have a murdering rogue after you. The FRU is chomping at the bit to get their hands on you to test you. In my book that's not doing okay."

"Just give me a few days. Please."

"You can't fix this, Kylie," Hayden said.

Hayden's earlier words echoed in her head. *The FRU is chomping at the bit to get their hands on you to test you.*

For the first time, Kylie saw this for what it was. A window! "I can try to fix it," Kylie said. Maybe die trying, Kylie thought, but maybe not. Besides, staying alive might not be in her cards anyway.

She popped off Hayden's desk and started walking backward to the door. "I gotta go. I'll tell Derek to bring Jenny to your place after classes today."

During lunch, Kylie waited to see if Lucas showed up. She sat beside an angry Della, who scowled at her the whole time because she'd heard Kylie had gone off with Steve. Across from her sat a suspicious Miranda, who'd been pre-warned by her shape-shifter and Kylie's shadow that she was acting strange.

Perry was wrong. She wasn't acting strange, she was acting scared. Yet even scared, she knew it was the right thing. Her gut told her.

Her mind shot away from her fears when Lucas walked into the room. He wore a navy T-shirt and his older jeans, the ones that were faded in all the places the material caressed his body. His hair looked windblown as if he'd been out on a run. In less than a week, they'd see a full moon. No doubt he ran to burn off some of the anxiousness.

He looked around the room.

She met his dark blue gaze head-on.

He started toward her, without even going to get a food tray. When he sat down, his shoulder brushed against hers. She dropped her fork and glanced at him. "Would you be up to skipping class for practice?"

His brows tightened. "What's up?"

Was she that readable? "I've already cleared it with Holiday." And the camp leader had asked the same question. *What's up, Kylie?*

She gave Lucas the same answer she'd given Holiday. "I feel like practicing." Face it, she couldn't tell the truth. Not here. But she planned on telling him when they were alone.

"How's your window?" she asked.

"Still jammed. But I'm working on it."

The optimism in his voice had her smiling. He grabbed the roll off her plate.

When she looked at him oddly, he said, "I'll need some kind of nutrition to take you on. You seem extra feisty today."

"You're right. You'd better eat the rest of my salad, too," she teased.

He leaned his head down and whispered, "I love you."

Love you, too, Kylie thought, but couldn't bring herself to say it yet. She wanted to save it until all their windows were open and life offered them promise. And more than anything, she wanted that promise.

As they walked to Lucas's cabin to collect the swords, Kylie tried to figure out how to tell him about what she was doing. Instinctively, she knew he would fight her on it. And today of all days, she didn't want to fight.

"So this window you mentioned, you got a plan to get it open?" she asked.

He nodded. "It was what you said about the elders being young at one time. I remembered not too long ago my grandmother asking about one of the elders on the Council. She said he and her twin sister had fancied each other when they were young, but that she'd already been promised to someone else. I hadn't even known my grandmother was a twin. When I asked about her sister, she said she'd died. But I got a feeling there was more to the story. I went to see her this morning."

"And?" Kylie asked.

"She confessed that her twin killed herself the day before she was supposed to marry the other guy."

"So you're going to go and talk to this elder?"

"It's not that easy. He wouldn't agree to see me. But he might agree to see my grandma and she could perhaps talk him into seeing me."

"Did your grandma agree to do it?" Kylie asked.

"No," he said, frustration sounding in his voice. "She's stubborn. I'm supposed to go meet her for tea in a couple of hours." He sighed. "Tea always softens her a little. I think I'll be able to convince her."

"I think you will, too."

They arrived by the lake, and Kylie still couldn't find a way to tell Lucas her plans. So she just let it slide for now. They warmed up for a good twenty minutes, practicing the same moves he'd taught her. Kylie didn't need to watch him to keep up. But she watched him all the same. She loved how his body moved, with strength, with control, and the way his muscles rippled under his jeans and cotton T-shirt. Cotton had never looked so good.

He stopped the warm-up exercises and faced her. "You ready?"

She nodded. They held up their swords against each other. He pulled back and moved in, his blade swiping in the air a good six inches from her. She followed his lead, and after five minutes, she felt like they were really fighting for the first time.

The sense of danger didn't hold her back, it actually enthralled her. Who knew deep down she was such a thrill seeker?

She felt the sweat pour from her brow. And in the quick glances she caught of him, she saw the sheen on his skin and the damp shirt clinging to his chest. Wet cotton looked even better than dry.

"You're amazing when you fight," he said, sounding winded.

She looked up and lost her focus, never realizing how deadly that little mistake could be until she felt her blade make contact.

Chapter Thirty-seven

Kylie's breath trapped in her lungs. She dropped the sword. Lucas's sword slipped from his hand and landed beside hers. He stepped back. His shirt hung open, ripped by her blade.

"Oh my God! Are you—"

"It's okay. Just a scratch." He pressed his palm on his upper abs.

"Let me see." She moved to him.

"I'm fine." He took another step back. "It's my fault. I made you lose your concentration."

"Let me see!" she demanded again.

"It's really a scratch," he said.

She took the last few steps separating them and reached for his shirt. Her heart clutched, fearing what she'd see. Tears filled her eyes and air slipped from her lungs when she saw the red mark running over his belly button.

"A scratch, see?" His voice came out deep.

He was right. It wasn't much more than a scratch, but it still looked painful. She pressed two fingers to his bare flat stomach. Inhaling, she concentrated on healing. Her hands grew warm, and slowly she moved her touch across the wound.

She heard him groan, or was it a growl? She met his eyes. "Am I hurting you?" Then she recognized the heat in his eyes.

"No," he said, the hypnotic hum vibrating from him signaling that his body sought a potential mate.

Feeling brave, she brushed her hand up and over his abdomen. The soft, warm ripples of muscle and skin felt wonderful against her palm. She wanted more. More of him. More touching. She wanted to be touched.

As if reading her mind, his hands were on her waist, pulling her against him. His lips found hers and the kiss was smoldering. Deep and demanding from the moment his mouth met hers. She wasn't sure how they ended up on the ground, but suddenly they were there. The soft grass tickled her neck, but she mostly felt Lucas. Felt his hand brushing under her shirt. His sweet, soft touch on her breasts. Felt his weight half on her, his leg positioned between hers.

Everywhere a part of him touched her, she burned and ached for more. His hum filled her ears like music and she was lost. Lost in the moment, in the desire. Lost with yearning.

She wasn't afraid. She wanted this, wanted Lucas. She slipped her hand inside the back of his shirt.

She heard him make another sound, a mixture of both pain and marvel. And then his weight and all the wonder were gone. Opening her eyes, she saw Lucas standing over her, his eyes ablaze and looking almost wild. His hands were locked behind his neck and he breathed in and out as if he needed more oxygen.

"We can't . . . I'm not prepared . . . I don't have . . ."

Doing her own share of trying to breathe, it took her a second to understand what he was attempting to say. He didn't have condoms. Even if he did, this shouldn't happen as an accident.

"We need . . . Not like this," he said.

"I know." She sat up and the cumbersome feeling crowded her chest and she felt her cheeks heat up.

Standing up, she swallowed the tightness down her throat. "I'm sorry, I shouldn't have . . ." She looked away, not sure how to put it.

He closed the distance between them and gently turned her face to his. "You didn't do anything wrong. We didn't do anything wrong. We just need to plan it."

She nodded. Her phone chimed with an incoming call. She hadn't reached for it when Lucas's started to ring.

She inhaled and pretty much knew what this meant. The FRU were here. Early. She pulled her phone out and saw the call was from Burnett and knew she was correct.

"It's Burnett," she said. "I'm sure it's Holiday calling you, too." She reached for the swords. "Don't answer it. We just need to get to the office."

He studied her. And she felt guilt swirl in her chest. She should have told him. Now it felt as if she'd kept it from him.

"Why shouldn't I answer it?" He opened the bags and pulled out the cloths to wrap the swords in.

"I was going to tell you, but . . ." *I knew you would fight me on it.*

"What's going on, Kylie?" he asked as he put the swords in the bag and then picked it up.

"It's my window," she said.

"What's your window?"

"The reason Burnett and Holiday are calling. It's the FRU, they're here for me."

"Why the hell are they here for you?" he asked.

She swallowed and started walking. He grabbed her by the elbow, questions in his eyes.

"I agreed to be tested."

He shook his head, his eyes went from blue to burnt orange instantly. "No!"

"I have to, Lucas. It's my quest. Just like your quest is to change things with your kind. I have to do this."

"No, you don't!" He moved in front of her and stopped her from taking another step. "Are you forgetting that I saw part of the vision of what they did to your grandmother?"

"That was over forty years ago. Things are different." That's what she'd been telling herself, that's what she had to believe. She moved around and continued forward.

"No!" He grabbed her arm.

She looked at him, pleading for understanding. "I have to do it, Lucas. And you have to let me."

"Burnett and Holiday won't allow this," he seethed.

"Burnett doesn't believe they would hurt me," she insisted, feeling a cool breeze brush her skin. And she knew she wasn't alone. Her father was here. She prayed he approved of what she was doing.

"He believes there could be risks to doing it, he told me that himself. He told me he hid your grandmother's body because of it."

"There's risk in everything, Lucas." She touched his stomach. "In learning how to fight. In not learning how to fight. I'm doing the right thing. I know it."

"We didn't contact her," the male voice came from Holiday's office. "She contacted us."

Kylie and Lucas walked inside the office. Lucas remained furious. She could tell from his posture, his silence, but he didn't try to stop her. She knew he sensed how serious she was.

"Kylie wouldn't have done that. She wouldn't even know how to get in touch with you," Holiday demanded.

Kylie stopped at Holiday's door. "I called my mom and got his number. Told her I needed to talk with him about something I was doing for Holiday." Kylie met the camp leader's worried eyes. Burnett stood beside her, his eyes showing signs of anger. She just hoped it wasn't targeted toward her.

Holiday shook her head. "I refuse to let this happen."

Kylie moved all the way inside, followed by Lucas. She looked at Burnett, hoping she would find an ally in him. "From the very beginning, Burnett said that they wouldn't intentionally harm me."

Holiday stood up. "He also admitted there could be risks, which was why he . . . agreed that you didn't need to do it."

"She's right," Burnett said. "I don't want to chance—"

"The risks are practically nonexistent," the gray-haired FRU agent spoke up. "It's what we've been telling you from the beginning. But you refused to listen."

Kylie ignored the agent and spoke to Holiday. "It's my quest. You yourself said that it was a good quest."

"But I didn't mean you should put your life in jeopardy."

"It's not in jeopardy," the FRU agent said again.

"Then why couldn't a regular doctor perform the tests?" Holiday asked, her tone sounding like an angry parent. No doubt she was going to make a good one.

"I already told you when we spoke months ago. It's nothing more than a brain scan and some blood tests. And the reason they can't be done in a regular hospital is because these tests aren't for humans."

"But they could do a brain scans and blood tests in a regular hospital," she accused.

"It's different," the man answered. "The scan is set to look for things a regular brain scan doesn't search for. The same for the blood test. A regular lab can't do this."

"And how many of these tests have been done?" Holiday asked.

"Thousands," he said. "It's been used by the FRU for several years."

"For what?"

He frowned. "Research."

"On who? What kind of research?"

"Mostly to study criminal cases. But—"

"You use it on criminals and you think it's fine to use on a teenager?" she demanded.

"It's safe."

"You're going to tell me that there haven't been any negative side effects?"

"None to speak of."

"So there have been some that you won't speak of!" Holiday snapped.

"I have to do it, Holiday. It's the right thing. I know it. Please, don't try to stop me, because I won't let you."

Kylie saw tears appear in Holiday's eyes, and it was killing Kylie that she was causing her friend pain, but everything inside her said it was the right thing.

She looked at the agent. "Did you bring the papers I asked for?"

"What papers?" Burnett asked.

"A written document from the FRU containing their promise that if they prove that I'm found to be a special race that they will acknowledge that we exist to the supernatural world."

"But then what?" Hayden appeared, standing in the corner. "Are you going to insist everyone that comes forward go for these tests?"

The FRU agent looked puzzled at Hayden's appearance, but he didn't miss a beat. "We will need to confirm it with at least one other of your kind. But once we have Kylie and this other person on record, all we'd require is a blood test to be registered."

Hayden looked at Kylie and she knew what he was thinking. "You don't have to do it," she said. Putting her life on the line was one thing, asking someone else to do it was another.

"Yes, I do. You were right. It's time things change." Hayden's gaze went back to the agent. "You have your second person."

The agent, right along with Lucas, tightened his brows and stared in awe at Hayden's pattern.

"I still don't like it. What if they don't keep their word?" Lucas asked.

Kylie glanced to Lucas and then Burnett and pleaded for him to speak up. He'd never lost his loyalty to the FRU and she trusted his opinion more than he would ever know.

"They wouldn't do that," Burnett said.

• • •

The room was cold and reminded Kylie too much of the vision she'd had with her grandmother. But she held tight to the knowledge that Lucas, Burnett, and Holiday all waited outside. First, they had her dress in a hospital gown. Beautiful.

The nurse came over. "I'm going to give you a couple of shots to numb you. It's sort of the same thing a dentist uses when he's working on a tooth. We need to get blood from your radial artery for this test, so it's slightly more uncomfortable than just drawing blood. But these injections should help."

The nurse was right, it was more uncomfortable. Kylie didn't know if the prior injections helped, but it still hurt like the devil. She closed her eyes and squinted tight, waiting for them to be done.

In a few minutes, it was over. Before Kylie was led to the other room for the brain scan, they let Lucas, Holiday, and Burnett come in. She knew they'd done Hayden's brain scan first.

"Is Hayden okay?" It was the first thing she wanted to know when they walked in.

"Just saw him," Burnett said. "He's fine, said it was a piece of cake."

Kylie nodded. Holiday still didn't look happy.

"You can still call it off."

"Holiday," Kylie said. "I'm doing this."

The fae exhaled as if exasperated and pressed a hand on her stomach. "I hope my kid isn't half as stubborn as you."

Kylie glanced at Burnett and grinned. "With the daddy being who he is, I'd say you don't have a chance in hell of the child being anything *but* stubborn."

"Hey, I'm not that bad." He smiled, but she could tell it was forced. He was trying to lighten the mood, but the concern shined in his eyes as well.

In a few seconds, Burnett and Holiday left. Lucas stayed behind and moved to stand beside the bed. He picked up her hand with the Band-Aid and brushed his thumb over the bandage. She could tell he was thinking about her healing him.

"When all this is over with, we need to talk. I don't like the fact that you didn't tell me what you were planning to do, or that the other teacher was chameleon. And I know, I didn't deserve for you to tell me about it then. But you were right when you told me that day that we didn't need any secrets. I don't want any more between us."

She swallowed. "Me either."

Suddenly, Kylie remembered something. "You were supposed to meet your grandmother for tea."

He shook his head. "This is more important."

"No it's not, Lucas. You have to get on that Council."

He frowned. "I haven't given up. I just postponed talking to her." He exhaled. "But I don't care what you say. If I make the Council or not. I'm not losing you."

"Okay." A nurse walked in. "We're going to take her now."

Lucas frowned but let go of her hand.

Kylie refused to be wheeled into the lab where the scan would take place. She wasn't sick. But she did make sure her gown was tied before giving everyone a peek at her pink bikini underwear.

Holiday squeezed her hand before she walked into the lab. Burnett gripped her shoulder. Lucas, looking half-pissed and half–very concerned, stayed back. The nurse walked ahead of her into the room, Kylie turned to follow her and was tugged back.

Lucas's mouth pressed against hers briefly. The words *I love you* sat on the tip of her tongue, but she didn't say them. She didn't want him to think the fear of what was about to happen was the only reason she said them. And then there was that little doubt that if he knew he had her now, he might not work as hard to get on that Council.

The door swished shut behind her. A chill ran up her spine, but not from a spirit; the room was simply that cold. Kylie glanced around, noting the lack of color in the room. Not a speck of color. Everything was white or off white.

"Okay," the nurse said. "Have you ever had an MRI?"

Kylie nodded. "When I was having night terrors."

"Well, this is very much like that. The machine is a little loud and you might feel crowded, but you'll need to remain completely still. It will take about ten minutes to complete the test. You don't have claustrophobia, do you?"

"Not really," Kylie said, but then remembered being caught in the small grave with the three dead girls. Then again, it was more the dead girls than the small space that freaked her out.

"Good," the nurse said. "Here's some earplugs. Now climb up here and we'll get this done."

Kylie put in the earplugs and swallowed a sudden feeling of anxiety. In the back of her mind, she heard her father's words. *But soon. Soon we will discover this together.*

Her heart raced to the tune of fear, but she climbed onto the table and laid down, trying to fight the chill, and yet wishing she could feel another cold. That of her father. A little word from him that she wasn't about to die would be good.

The machine pulled her inside. Her nose was less than an inch from the top and the sides of the machine actually touched her forearms. *A machine, not a coffin,* she told herself. But that's where her mind took her—being in a closed coffin.

The noise started. Even with earplugs, the sound grew so loud she could hardly hear herself think. She closed her eyes. Tried not to listen. Tried not to think. She wasn't sure how long she was in there when she felt a light tickle in her head. That tickle grew until it was a pain. A sharp pain.

She opened her mouth to scream, tried to move but couldn't. Suddenly she felt like a light exploded in her head and all she could see was darkness.

Soon, baby, soon we'll be together.

Chapter Thirty-eight

Someone was holding her hand. In the distance angry voices rumbled. One she recognized. Burnett. Kylie opened her eyes, unsure of where she was. The moment she saw the white ceiling, she remembered the pure white room. The big white machine.

The pain.

She didn't hurt now.

"Thank God." Kylie turned toward Holiday's voice. Ah. Holiday was the hand holder. Worry pinching her brow, she pushed some button on a remote control and called for the nurse. "She's awake."

"What happened?" Kylie asked.

"You passed out." Holiday had tears in her eyes. "Scared the shit out of us! Are you okay?"

"I can feel my fingers and toes," Kylie said.

The door burst open and Burnett, a very angry-looking Burnett, came storming into the room. Right behind him was a man wearing a white coat. And following the doctor was the agent who'd picked her up. Following him was Lucas—a very worried-looking Lucas. And last was Hayden Yates—looking equally concerned.

"I told you she was going to be okay." The doctor looked at Kylie and then Holiday. "Is she talking?"

"Yes," Holiday said.

"Is she moving?" he asked Holiday.

"Yes, and I can hear you, too," Kylie said.

He frowned at Kylie. "Of course you can."

"Wait," Kylie said. "Did they finish the test?"

The doctor nodded. "It was wrapping up when you started experiencing pain."

"Do we know anything yet?" she asked the other agent.

"We need others to read it," he said, "but it appears you have the markings of all the supernaturals, just as Mr. Yates does."

Kylie sat up a little. "Does that qualify as a new species?"

"I'm under the impression that it would, but again, others have to review it."

Kylie bit down on her lip. "How much of this did you already know from the tests in the past?"

The room went silent. Kylie saw Burnett's shoulders tighten.

The agent paused. "The results we had pointed to the same thing, but ninety percent of the evidence was destroyed by the doctors and administrators running the study to hide their wrongdoings. What evidence we did have, we didn't know if it was valid."

"If you even suspected what was done, why haven't you tried to make it right before now?" Hayden asked.

"We tried," the agent said. "Maybe not hard enough, but in our defense, the one thing your species is best at is hiding. We searched for family members of those few that we maintained files on. They and their families had disappeared. At one point we considered putting out notices asking people to come in, but no matter how we tried to approach it, it sounded like a witch hunt. And considering what had already happened, it just didn't feel like the right thing."

"And how soon will this information be released to the supernatural world?" Kylie asked.

"Probably no later than a few weeks. We'll also be announcing the internal investigation on the FRU and our wrongdoings in the past. Anyone affected by the studies, or their family members, will receive financial compensation if they come forward."

Kylie thought of her grandmother. "Money won't bring back lives."

"No," the agent said. "But it's the human way of showing the organization's wrongdoing. And since we live in a human world, it's the best we can do."

"Why?" Kylie asked.

"Why what?" The agent looked confused.

"You don't just admit wrongdoings and offer compensation for no reason. Someone is threatening to expose you. Who is it?"

The agent's expression went cold. "What's important is that it's being done."

Kylie got the feeling they didn't know the person forcing their hand. But she had a feeling she did know. A few minutes later, the doctor and the agent walked out.

Kylie looked at Burnett. "You wouldn't know anything about this, would you?"

He shook his head. "Not a thing." It was a lie, she could see it. He'd been trying to make the FRU do right by her the whole time. She knew she loved this man.

Kylie glanced at Hayden and smiled. Hayden returned the gesture. They had done it. Well, with the help of Burnett. She knew it wasn't completely over, they still had to convince the elders to trust that things would be different, and they still had to come clean about Jenny, but at least now chameleons wouldn't have to hide.

The next morning Lucas dropped by at five A.M. Kylie was still asleep when he jumped through her window. He'd rescheduled his meeting with his grandmother for this morning and just wanted to check on her before he left. As he started out, she pulled him in for a kiss.

When the kiss ended, he was humming. "You trying to convince me to stay?" he asked, his eyes bright with need and passion.

"No," she said, and laughed. "Go. We can do this later."

"Promise?" he asked.

"Promise," she told him, and she meant it. She didn't tell him all bets were off, that she'd take him any way he came. On the Council, or off. If he didn't make it and grew to resent her later, she'd just face it then. But she loved him too much to turn away from him now.

As Kylie pulled her clothes from her closet, Della invited herself into Kylie's bedroom.

"That was a quicky," Della said, referring to Lucas's short visit.

"He just came by to tell me he's meeting his grandma."

"I know, I heard," she smarted off.

Kylie frowned. "You could cover your ears and not listen in, you know."

"And you could stop buddying up with Steve!" she hissed.

Kylie just shook her head. "Look, I need to get dressed. I'm going with Hayden to confront Burnett and Holiday about Jenny."

"Burnett's gonna be pissed," Della said.

"I know," Kylie said. "But when he's done being pissed he's usually reasonable."

"Yeah," Della said. "But it's always that pissed part that scares the shit out of me."

Kylie laughed. Della eyed her. "Why would you talk to Steve behind my back?"

Frowning, Kylie answered, "What was I supposed to do? He paid blood for the hour."

"Tell him no. Believe it or not, that's usually enough to send him packing."

Maybe not anymore, Kylie thought.

"What did he want anyway?" Della dropped on Kylie's twin bed.

Kylie rolled her eyes. "You know what he wanted. Advice on how to deal with you."

"So what did you tell him? And remember I can tell if you lie."

Kylie picked up her brush and started putting up her hair. "I told him to be patient. To fight for you, because you were worth it."

"Stupid advice," Della said.

Kylie put her brush down. "Not stupid. True. You are worth it." Moving to the bed, she hugged the vamp.

"What's with all the hugging stuff lately?" Della whined.

"I love you," Kylie said, and grinned.

"You told me that already. So seriously, what's up?"

She couldn't lie to Della, so Kylie vagued up the truth. "You tell people you love them so if anything happens, they'll know how you felt." Now if she could just find the courage to go and tell Lucas.

Della looked suspicious. "What do you think is going to happen?"

"I hope nothing," Kylie said, thinking she'd lived through the FRU testing, which hadn't turned out to be nearly as scary as she'd thought, but she still had to face Mario, and that might not be quite so easy.

"What do you mean?" Della asked.

A light knock sounded on the door of the cabin and saved Kylie from having to explain. "Hayden's here. Gotta go."

As Kylie walked out she heard Della's parting remark. "Perry's right. You've got secrets. You can't hide them from us!"

Yes, she could, Kylie thought.

Soon we'll be together. Her father's words whispered through her head. She bit down on her lip.

If you don't mind, Daddy, I'd like to hang around about a hundred years first.

Hayden and Kylie walked into the office. Burnett met them at the door. Holiday was standing behind her desk looking worried.

"What's wrong?" they asked in unison.

"Nothing, really," Kylie said.

"We need to talk," Hayden said.

Burnett motioned for them to sit with a concerned look. As soon as Kylie and Hayden sat down, Burnett spoke. "Are the elders having a problem with you two being tested?"

"It's not that," Hayden said. "Supposedly they have contacted all the elders of the other compounds and the consensus is that it is a good thing. Of course there is still a lot of suspicion of the FRU. Something like this doesn't change overnight. There will be a lot of fences to mend. Trust to build." He glanced at Kylie. "I personally think a few of the elders are just ashamed that it took a sixteen-year-old girl to force us to face our fears."

"I didn't go in alone," Kylie said, giving Hayden his credit.

"No, but I wouldn't have gone if you hadn't set it up." Hayden glanced back at Burnett and Holiday. "But this isn't why we are here."

"Why is it I don't think I'm going to like this?" Burnett sat down on the edge of Holiday's desk.

"Don't start projecting." Holiday touched his leg.

"First, I want to say I take full responsibility for this," Hayden said.

"No," Kylie said. "If you are going to blame someone, blame me."

"I'm still not liking it," Burnett snapped. "But I'd like to find out what it is I'm not liking, so I can do what Holiday says and stop projecting!"

"Remember when I told you that one of the other chameleons helped Derek and me escape?"

"Yes," Burnett said, and Holiday nodded.

"That girl was Hayden's sister."

"And?" Burnett said.

"She ran away."

"And?" Burnett snapped, motioning for Kylie to move faster.

"She ran here," Kylie said.

"Here?" Burnett asked. "She's here now?"

Both Kylie and Hayden nodded.

"How could she be . . ." He scowled. "The night the alarm went off?"

Both Kylie and Hayden nodded one more time.

Kylie saw one of the crystals in the room flicker. For some crazy reason, she sensed Jenny had walked past.

Kylie met Burnett's eyes. "Please don't get too mad and start yelling. Not for my or Hayden's sake, but for Jenny's. You make her nervous."

"She's been here all along, and now is when you decided to tell me? You let me search this whole damn camp for almost twenty-four hours and you knew the whole time who it was?" He stood up from the desk and started walking back and forth.

Holiday stood up, and as he moved past her, she placed a calming hand on his arm and brought the vampire to a halt.

"We didn't know right away. She was hiding, she . . ." Kylie didn't see any reason to throw Derek to the wolves. "I didn't find out about her until a day later and Hayden didn't know until I told him."

"Is she still here?" Burnett barked out the question.

"Yes," Kylie said. "And she'd like to stay here. To finish school."

"Will her parents sign for her?" Holiday asked.

Hayden's jaw tightened. "I don't know how they are going to feel when they learn she's here. With the news of the FRU, they may allow it. If they don't, I'll be taking legal action to get custody of her."

"Is she here now? In this room?" Holiday asked.

Kylie nodded. "Jenny."

Jenny appeared, standing against the wall farthest away from Burnett. Kylie didn't know if it was just Burnett's warm and fuzzy appearance right now, or if it was because Jenny knew he was part of the FRU that had sheer panic in the girl's gaze.

Burnett must have recognized the look, because immediately his posture softened. He offered her a nod.

"Hello, Jenny," he said. "Welcome to Shadow Falls."

Kylie saw Holiday beam with pride at her soon-to-be husband's transformation. No doubt Holiday was schooling him on softening his approach. And it was working.

Kylie just hoped that this meant Jenny's chances of staying on at Shadow Falls were good.

Holiday and Hayden were going to have a conference call with Kylie's grandfather to talk about the possibility of Jenny staying on. Until then, Jenny was going to hang out with Holiday, with plans to introduce Jenny to everyone at lunch.

Kylie suggested she introduce Jenny to some of her own friends first. Maybe Jenny wouldn't feel as if everyone at Shadow Falls were rude gaping individuals.

Kylie made some phone calls and asked everyone to meet her in the office at 10:45. She didn't tell anyone what it was about, but she had good faith they would all show up.

As Kylie left the office, Della met her outside and they went to wait for Campmate hour. Miranda came running up with Perry. "So what's the meeting all about?"

"You'll find out," Kylie said, not wanting to explain with so many ears around. Since Della already knew about Jenny, or as Della had dubbed her, Girl Wonder, she'd told Della the truth.

"I know," Della said, teasing Miranda.

Kylie frowned at Della.

"Why did you tell her and not me?" Miranda asked.

"I promise you'll understand later."

Miranda frowned. "You aren't leaving again, are you? Because you pinky promised me you wouldn't." Tears actually appeared in the witch's eyes.

"I'm not leaving," Kylie assured her. Not by her own accord, Kylie thought, and then thought again about the sword and what it all meant.

"You're gonna come clean and tell us that you and Hayden are lovers," Perry said.

Kylie scowled at him.

"Hey, I'm just guessing. I mean there's something going on between you two."

Lucas showed up right then and growled at the shape-shifter for the comment. Then Lucas leaned down and kissed her.

"What happened with your grandma?" she asked in a low whisper.

"Window's open." He kissed her again. "She's going to talk to him about meeting me. He could tell her hell no, but it's a start."

"It's a great start." Kylie let out a squeal and for just a few minutes, she felt certain everything in her crazy life was going to work out.

Then Chris, announcer of the grand event, pulled his hat from behind his back and his gaze started moving around the crowd and stopped on Kylie. She wanted to scream, enough was enough. But then his gaze shifted a little to her right.

Was he looking at her? Or was he looking at . . .

"Okay," Chris said. "One of our own vampires brings in a little blood. About time."

Oh, hell, Kylie thought, and got a feeling she knew who'd paid blood for Della. And she wasn't sure this was a good thing.

"Della, our friend, you get the pleasure of spending an hour with Steve, the amazing shape-shifter."

Della's mouth dropped open. She looked around, eyes bright with fury for the culprit.

Steve strutted out of the crowd, and went to confront the pissed-off vamp with a confident gait.

Kylie knew she'd told him to fight for Della, but she hadn't meant for him to do it in front of everyone. Della, not liking being shown up, was likely to fight back.

"You ready?" Steve asked.

Della scowled. "I'm not going to spend an hour with you."

Steve just stood there. "I paid good blood for you."

"Then you really screwed up."

"Nope." Steve looked back at Chris and then the forty or so other students enjoying the show. "What are the rules, Chris? Hasn't everyone pretty much agreed to honor the blood drive?"

Chris looked shocked that Steve dared to argue with Della. But he shook his head. "Yup, that's pretty much it."

Steve turned back to Della. "You ready?"

Della tilted her chin and glared daggers at the boy.

Perry leaned over and whispered to Kylie, "If she kills him, it's your fault."

Chapter Thirty-nine

Oh, hell, Kylie thought, and prepared herself to intervene.

"I'm not going!" Della snipped, and put her hands on her hips.

"We'll see about that." Steve shrugged and looked as if he was going to walk away, but then he swung around and grabbed Della by her lower legs and tossed her over his shoulder and started walking.

Everyone started hooting and hollering with laughter.

Kylie didn't laugh. She saw a very pissed-off vampire brace her hands on Steve's butt and look up. Her eyes were green with fury, but there was something else there, too. Something that told Kylie that Steve's ass wasn't about to get chewed up.

With every fraction of a second that passed, Kylie felt more confident that Della wasn't going to go ape-shit on Steve, she was actually going to go with him.

Damn, Kylie thought. Maybe she really was good at the whole matchmaking thing.

"Can I vanish?" Jenny asked Kylie as they stood in the door of the lunch room with Holiday.

"I wouldn't recommend it," Kylie said. "Just smile. Believe it or not, you sort of get used to it."

The meeting with Jenny and Kylie's friends had gone off without a hitch. Everyone genuinely seemed to like her. Derek, of course, showed the most interest.

Lucas had come up behind her and said, "Another secret."

Kylie offered a quick "Sorry," and nothing else. She had the feeling keeping him at bay until he met with the Council was going to be tough. For both of them. But she was determined.

"Don't they know it's rude to stare?" Jenny asked.

"Yeah, but they just can't seem to help themselves," Kylie said.

Hayden stood up from his seat and moved to Jenny's side.

He wasn't smiling and she saw the big brother protective attitude in the way he looked at all the students. "Eat your lunch and stop gawking," he ordered.

Holiday spoke up next. "Mr. Yates is right. This is no way to welcome a new student."

Kylie and Jenny both looked at Holiday with questions in their eyes, and Holiday smiled and nodded. Then she turned back to the crowd. "Everyone, I'd like for you to meet Jenny Yates. She's Hayden's little sister. So mistreat her and you might be getting extra homework assignments."

"Is she the same as Kylie?" someone asked.

Hayden took a step forward. "And the same as me."

Everyone's eyes tightened and gasps filled the dining hall. Kylie went to sit with Hayden and Jenny at what she realized was the chameleon table. A feeling of rightness filled Kylie's chest. This was part of her quest and she'd accomplished it.

Of course, all Kylie's friends quickly joined them. Lucas included. And that was just fine—because while it was nice to have someone like you around, a person's pattern shouldn't dictate who you welcomed into your life, or at your lunch table.

• • •

Later that evening, they went down to the lake to swim because with fall upon them, the water would be too cold soon. Kylie had almost declined but when she saw Della wanted to go, she gave in. She put on her bathing suit and slipped a black coverall dress over it. As everyone swam, Kylie moved to sit on the pier and call her mom.

She hadn't shaken the feeling that John was up to no good. The conversation was short. Her mom and John were out to eat at one of the nicest restaurants in Houston.

Hanging up, Kylie stood there and tried to soak up the sunset. Just when the sun slipped away, nightfall came and turned the sky an array of colors. The birds flew from one tree to another, feasting on insects. Kylie was about to rejoin the others by the water's edge when the spirit's cold washed down on her. Kylie looked around and the spirit sat on the edge of the pier as if in a stupor, looking lost, looking so damn sad.

"I know who you are, Lucinda," Kylie said. "You were Mario's daughter-in-law."

I know. I've figured that part out. But things came to me one piece at a time, like putting a jigsaw puzzle together. I could almost see what my whole life was like, but when those last dozen pieces fell into place, I saw the whole picture. Her voice sounded tight, ready to break. *I didn't like it.*

After a long pause, she looked at Kylie. *I lived a terrible life. Did terrible things. Hurt so many people. And my own son paid the price. I should have lived to be a good example for him.*

Kylie looked up at the beaconing sky. The hues of gold and oranges had faded and it was now ten different shades of pink. She noted the birds were now flocking around the pier. Could they, like her, see the dead?

Looking back at the sadness in the spirit's eyes, Kylie said, "He's in heaven."

The spirit shook her head. *I don't think so. I'm sure his grandfather taught him all his evil ways. He was so young and impressionable. Then his own grandfather killed him.*

The mood surrounding the spirit—devastation, doom—pressed on Kylie's heart. "You were an example for him. He died saving someone else, just the way you did to save him. You taught him that. And that's what saved his soul."

The ghost's eyes grew wet with emotion. *Are you sure? How do you know this?*

Kylie hesitated, worried the spirit might blame her. "He died saving me."

The spirit sat as if lost in thought for a second. *Then that's why they sent me here?*

"Who sent you here?" Kylie asked, pretty sure she knew, but she wanted to hear it.

The death angels.

"Is that whose voice I hear every now and then?"

That would be them.

"But why do I hear them more than . . . Holiday and other ghost whisperers?"

They watch over protectors closer. They have to because you can only fight to protect others.

"Do they want me to kill Mario, or is that just you?" Kylie hoped she was wrong about her assumptions.

At first I thought it was just me, but then I realized it was their plan, too.

Kylie's heart clutched.

He has to be stopped. You are the chosen one. No one else has been able to stop him.

"But if I can't protect myself, then . . . who will I be protecting when I fight him?"

I cannot see that future.

"But what if I can't do it? I'm not that good with a sword."

Then you die trying. Sometimes that's all we can do.

Kylie knew the spirit referred to herself, too. She'd died trying to save her son. Yet as much as she felt for the ghost, fear bit down on Kylie.

"I'm not ready to die."

Then you have to practice. That's another reason I'm here. To help teach you to fight—because if you fail, bad things will happen to so many people. People you care about. People who trust you to protect them.

She felt the sting in her blood at being a protector. "Then I'll have to win," Kylie said. Because damn it, she wouldn't let Mario hurt anyone else that she loved.

"What?"

Kylie looked over her shoulder at the sound of Lucas's voice. His lack of a shirt had her staring. His hair was still wet. A few droplets of water still clung to his chest. He'd been in the water just a few minutes ago. He must have slipped his jeans over his swim trunks. She could see the edge of suit sticking out over the waist of his jeans.

Her gaze moved across that spot on his belly button where she'd run her hands to heal him, and then just to touch him.

"You okay?" he asked.

She nodded, but it was a lie. Her heart was caught on the possibility of dying, of others suffering because she couldn't rise to the challenge. And just like that, seeing him made her realize how much she wanted to live.

She looked back at the water and heard his almost-silent steps on the pier as he moved closer.

"You got company?" he asked, now standing beside her.

She looked around. "No, she's gone now."

His phone rang and he grabbed it out of his pocket as if he'd been waiting for a call. He frowned at the little screen, and then turned it off.

"Is something wrong?" Kylie asked.

"No, it's just Will."

"He still calls you?"

Lucas nodded. "He's not persuaded by the old rules."

"He's a good friend," she said.

"Yeah." Lucas slipped it back into his pocket. "I was hoping it might be my grandmother."

She saw the concern in his eyes. "About meeting with the elder?"

"That and she told me she wasn't feeling well this morning. I called a bit ago and she didn't answer. She probably went out to play bingo. She's like this bingo fanatic. Bingo and gardening, that's her life."

"You really love her, don't you?" Kylie asked, hearing the devotion in his voice when he talked about her.

He inhaled the way a guy does when he's worried something he's about to say is going to make him sound weak. "She was there for me when my parents decided I was too much trouble. She was the best thing that ever happened to me, but I didn't know it then. I felt abandoned by them. I made her life hell for a while. Then when my parents split up and my dad came to get me, my grandmother threw all kinds of hell to keep me. I wouldn't be who I am today if she hadn't done what she did."

"You are lucky to have her." Kylie felt a little guilty for disliking the woman and for avoiding her last Sunday.

"Yeah, I am," he said. They grew quiet. "I've been practicing what I'm going to say."

She looked at him. "Say to who?"

"The elder I'm hoping to get the meeting with."

She smiled. "That's good."

"I'm going to be accepted. Because if that's what it takes to get you back, then that's what I'm going to do."

She swallowed. "No, you do it because that's your quest."

"That, too," he said. He reached out and brushed a strand of hair from her cheek. "But lately, I think you're my quest."

He moved in and slipped his hands around her waist.

She put her hand on his chest, felt his were heat, felt the thumping of his heart.

He leaned down and kissed her. She knew she shouldn't let it happen, but she wanted it, needed it. His taste and the wet slip of his tongue moving across her lips was heaven, but the kind of heaven one found in life and not in death.

And she wanted to choose life. Hoped it would be so.

She heard the humming coming from him instantly, and it would be so easy to let it lure her in.

He ended the kiss, smiled down at her, and exhaled. "I'd better go before I can't leave."

She watched him go and then looked up at the dark pink sky, and hoped with everything she had that she wasn't taken from this world until she had experienced life. And she truly hoped that Lucas was part of that life.

That night, after listening to Della and Miranda bicker for the last two hours, Kylie darted out of the bathroom, wearing a towel, and headed to her bedroom. She barely got two steps when Della shot in front of her.

"No. Solve it yourself!" Kylie snapped, certain that was what Della wanted. "I'm tired of being the referee!"

Della paused, smiled in an evil little way, and then said, "Never mind."

Skirting around Della, Kylie shut her bedroom door with just a touch of attitude. She tossed her towel on her dresser and turned to the bed where she'd left her PJs. Only it wasn't just her PJs on the bed anymore.

Lucas, eyes wide, sat on the foot of her bed, about four feet from where she stood completely naked.

She squealed.

He laughed.

She dashed for the towel.

Once she had it around her, she glared from a still grinning Lucas to the door. "I'm killing Della!"

He laughed again. "I'm afraid I might have to protect her for this one."

"I tried to tell you," Della called out, laughing, and Miranda laughed with her.

Kylie's fury faded to embarrassment, then when she saw the sexy way Lucas looked at her, her emotions changed into something else.

He stood up and started walking toward her. "You are so damn beautiful."

She tightened her hold on the towel.

He stopped about a foot from her. "I just came to tell you that I got a call from my grandmother. The elder has agreed to meet with me."

Kylie smiled. "That's great."

His gaze traveled up and down her towel-clad body. "I don't suppose I could get another peek of what's under that piece of cotton, could I?"

She cut her eyes at him.

"I don't want to be too presumptuous, but you do know that sooner or later I'm probably going to get to see it all anyway."

"I know," she said, and she was actually looking forward to it. Just not with her two roommates listening in.

His smile widened. "Okay, so just a kiss good-bye."

She nodded. He moved in. In less than two minutes he'd left. The kiss was hot, wet, and toe curling. He'd run his hand inside her towel and touched her bare back.

Fifteen minutes later, she was still only wearing the towel, staring up at the ceiling in a happy haze, when her phone rang.

She snatched it up, thinking it would be Lucas. "I don't know why you left in such a hurry," she teased. But she had known, he'd wanted her.

"Uh, I didn't leave. This is Sara?"

"Oh. I thought you were . . ."

"You thought I was who? Or should I say which one."

Kylie blushed and decided to just come clean. "I thought you were Lucas."

There was silence for a second and then Sara asked, "Can I ask you something?"

What was it with Sara wanting her to lose her virginity? "Sure, ask away." At least this time, Kylie could tell her that it would probably be happening soon.

"Do you consider you and Trey completely done with? Like . . . last year's news? Or is there a chance you two might—"

"It's so over." Kylie gripped the phone tighter. "Look, if he's trying to get you to talk to me, it's not going to work."

"No. It's not . . . that. It's . . . Where do you stand on friends dating another friend's old boyfriend?"

Kylie stared at the ceiling and tried to wrap her head around this. "Wow. Uh. Well, I would tell this friend to be careful because Trey has a few flaws."

Sara sighed. "I know, but . . . he's sort of been there for me during the whole cancer thing, and you know . . . some people deserve a second chance. I got one. Maybe Trey deserves one."

Kylie heard something in Sara's voice she liked. She heard the old Sara. Kylie smiled. "You're right. Everybody deserves a second chance. And when I think about it, until he got all sex crazed, he was a pretty good guy."

"So you really wouldn't object?" Sara asked, sounding unsure.

"No, I give you my blessing. I'll sing at your wedding."

"Please." Sara chuckled. "I'm probably one of the few people who knows you can't sing worth a damn. Remember in the sixth grade when our moms made us try out for the play? And you had to sing. You got out a couple of words and then you puked on the stage."

They both laughed. And Kylie accepted that while she and Sara would probably never be as close as they once were, Sara was a part of her life that Kylie would forever cherish.

When the laughter stopped, Sara cleared her throat. "So, when are you going to come clean about healing me?"

Kylie tried to think how to say it. "You know what, Sara? If you want to believe I healed you, then believe it. But I wouldn't tell a lot of people. They'll think you're crazy."

Thursday night Kylie practiced with Lucinda. The last three days had passed without major chaos. Steve and Della were actually speaking. Kylie couldn't swear on it, but she'd bet the vamp and Steve were seeing each other on the side.

Jenny was adapting, though she still had issues with everyone staring. While Hayden didn't like it, she and Derek were hanging out a lot. Derek had even come to see Kylie and basically told her he had feelings for the chameleon.

At first, Kylie thought he was there to make sure Kylie didn't want a second chance with him before he moved on, but then she realized what he'd really come for. He wanted relationship advice. She gave it to him, too. "Just be yourself, Derek. You're a hell of a catch and she's gonna love you."

Holiday had gone to the doctor and found out she was farther along than she'd thought. For that reason, she decided to move the wedding up to this weekend. It wasn't going to be a big event. Just Holiday's immediate family, the students, and a few of Burnett's FRU coworkers.

Della, Kylie, and Miranda all helped Holiday pick out her wedding dress from the Internet. They had laughed, stayed up way too late talking, munching on junk food, and trying to come up with names for Holiday's baby. She really didn't want to name it Burnett Bankhead James Jr., and nobody could blame her.

Kylie and Lucas met every morning before he took off to spend his time with the elder. The man had not only listened to Lucas, but had agreed to help him polish his case to the Council that he was supposed to present next week. So far, the old man kept Lucas busy every day debating and listening to all of Lucas's arguments and helping him with his points he needed to make. Which was great, but other than those short practices, she hadn't seen Lucas and she missed him something terribly.

What made it worse was that he hadn't touched or kissed her since the night he'd seen her naked. She knew why. The closer it came to the full moon, the less willpower he had. She noticed the change in him, too, body and mind. His body had grown buffer, the muscles in his arms more pronounced. She sensed his lack of patience. Not that he once got abrupt with her; she just sensed it, how he held himself, how he walked and talked.

Their sparring matches had grown more intense. Not that those scared her anymore. Her nightly practices with the spirit prepared her. The red marks where the spirit's sword touched her gown had lessened tremendously. The open wounds the spirit wore from Kylie's sword had increased.

"I think I'm done," Kylie said, looking away from the wound she'd just caused Lucinda.

You're getting better.

"I'd practice more if I didn't have to see you bleed."

It needs to feel real, Lucinda said.

"It already does," Kylie answered. She watched Lucinda check her wounds. "Do you think I have what it takes to fight Mario, to win?"

With the death angels' help, maybe. Without them, you don't stand a chance.

"Gosh, you know how to boost someone's confidence," she said.

I've only seen one person able to take him. His own son.

Kylie remembered the story Derek had told about him disappearing. "Whatever happened to him?"

I don't know. I hope he's rotting in hell. But chances are he is still alive. Her gaze met Kylie's. *It's always the good that die young.*

"Then maybe I should run out and do something bad," Kylie said, half teasing.

You couldn't. Good is bred into you. Sort of the way my husband's evilness was bred into him. Only because of you was my son saved.

"No, it's because of him that I was saved."

You see, that's part of your goodness. You won't even take credit.

Kylie pushed that thought away. "Was he behind your murder? Your husband?"

No, but he allowed it. And he allowed his father to take our son. To raise him to be evil. Crazy thing was, my husband hated his father, but envied everything he had. She looked over her shoulder as if she heard something or someone. Then she disappeared.

Kylie went to her room and grabbed her nightshirt, then headed for the shower. Sweat ran from the back of her neck down her back. Even with the spirit's cold, she always worked up a sweat.

Turing the water on to lukewarm, she dropped her clothes on the floor and stepped into the shower. Closing her eyes, the warm rush of water hit her skin and she waited for it to soothe the muscles she'd overworked during practice.

The sudden change of temperature had her eyes popping open. Her breath hitched. She stared at the shower wall. The cold sent goose bumps racing across her naked body. A thick steam billowed up around her.

She wasn't alone. Someone was in the shower with her. And it was a different cold. One she hadn't felt before.

Can't avoid me this time, can you? The voice, a voice she didn't recognize, came behind her.

Chapter Forty

Kylie turned, hiding what she could of her most embarrassing parts with her hands. The steam was so thick she could barely make out the figure. But a vague outline of a body stood behind the curtain of vapor.

All the scary tunes of horror movies with deadly shower scenes played in her head, but more than afraid, she was furious. Didn't ghosts have any sense of privacy?

"I'm in the shower!" Kylie demanded. "Couldn't this wait?"

No, it can not, the voice said. *He is about to find me and it is going to hurt him so badly. He does not need to be alone.*

The properness of the voice tickled some memory. Kylie knew this person, but from where?

No longer caring about her nudity, Kylie waved a hand through the air, the steam smearing like condensation on a mirror. When she saw who stood in the shower with her, her heart clutched. Not from fear, but from grief. And not for the woman who stood before her, but for her grandson—Lucas.

He's on his way to check on me now. Hurry. He can't be alone.

Kylie jumped out of the shower and ran to get dressed. As she fought to put clothes on her shower-wet body, her heart ached for Lucas, of how he would feel finding his grandmother's body. "Where do you live? Wait? Doesn't Burnett know?"

The vampire? Is this the person you imply?

"Yes," Kylie said, wishing that it didn't take so damn long to speak in a proper tone.

She nodded. *Yes, he's been there.*

"Della!" Kylie called out the girl's name.

There's a letter in my desk drawer that he needs to read. Make sure he gets it.

Della came running into the room in a flash. "What?"

He was right, you know.

"Who was right?" Kylie asked the spirit, ignoring the panicking vampire standing in her Mickey Mouse pajamas.

You are part of his quest, and he yours. I see things clearer up here. You see, you have been a part of each other's quests since you met all those years ago. You are the reason he will complete his life's mission and he will be there to save you when you need help to complete yours. But go now. Go help him.

"Is this a vision?" Della asked, staring at Kylie with uncertainty.

"Let's go!" Kylie shot out of the cabin. She was almost to Holiday's before she realized she was flying and that she must have turned herself into a vampire.

"I hope we're going to a pajama party," Della said in her sassy voice.

"Gotta get Burnett," Kylie answered as a few hot tears trickled down her cheek.

They landed with a thud on Holiday's porch and hadn't taken one step when Burnett yanked open the door while still zipping up his jeans. "What's wrong?" he asked.

"Do you know where Lucas's grandmother lives?"

He looked confused, his eyes still dazed with sleep. "Yes. Lucas called about ten minutes ago, he was going to check on her."

"We need to get there."

"Why?" Burnett asked.

"She's dead," Kylie blurted out as more tears filled her eyes. "He doesn't need to be the one to find her."

"Oh, hell!" Burnett rushed back to the bedroom with his phone. He looked at Kylie. "He's not answering."

"You stay here," he said to Della, and then he and Kylie took off. Her feet only hit the ground three times before she was in full flight beside Burnett.

In less than ten minutes Burnett finally started his descent. They stopped at a large one-story white brick house. It spoke of money and a love of gardening. The yard looked like something from a magazine.

Not that Kylie spent much time appreciating the landscape. Her feet had barely hit the manicured lawn and she was listening for life inside the house.

She heard deep intakes of air that expressed grief and sadness. "He's already here," she said to Burnett. "I'm going inside."

Burnett stepped in front of her. "No. I'll go in."

"No!" Kylie demanded, and started forward, her heart aching for Lucas.

"Kylie!" Burnett caught her arm. "When a were is distraught, especially this close to a full moon, he sometimes lashes out with anger. He can't control it. Especially with a vampire."

She brushed a few tears from her eyes. "You don't get it. He loves me. He won't hurt me. He would never hurt me."

Burnett hesitated.

"It's just like you and Holiday," Kylie said.

He exhaled and stepped back from the door. She moved into the house. It smelled like the lemon Pledge that Nana used to use. Everything in the house, from the antiques to the fancy oil paintings, spoke of wealth.

"Lucas," she called his name.

He didn't answer. She moved down the hallway where she heard the sounds of anguish.

Lucas sat on the edge of the bed. His grandmother's lifeless body was centered on the mattress.

"Lucas," she said again, and walked in.

He swung around. His eyes were the deepest, darkest shade of orange she'd ever seen.

"Leave!" he growled.

"No," she said. "You need me now." His grandmother had said so.

He bolted across the room and backed her against the wall. There was nothing but wild pain in his eyes. He growled, and for the first time she saw his canine teeth extended.

"It's me, Lucas," she said, feeling his fingers dig into her forearms.

She felt the instant he came to his senses. He dropped his hands from her arms, shifted away from her, and pressed his head against the wall.

She went to him, wrapped her arms around his waist, pressed her face between his shoulder blades, and held him.

"She's gone," he said, his voice hoarse with grief.

"I know." She hugged him tighter.

He turned around and pulled her to him. They stood there for the longest time, just holding on to each other.

"I'm so sorry," Kylie whispered, and she felt his pain, remembered with clarity how she'd felt when they told her Nana had died.

He released her, and then met her eyes. His gaze was still bright, but the wildness was gone. The dampness on his cheeks wasn't a sign of weakness, but a sign of devotion, of the love he felt for the only real mother he'd known and then lost.

"I knew she didn't have long, but I wasn't ready yet. I thought I had another year, maybe two."

Kylie reached for his hand. "I'm so sorry. I know how it feels."

He exhaled and looked back at the bed and her body. She heard his breath come short. She pulled him out of the room.

When she stopped, he met her gaze. "How did . . . how did you know?"

"She came to see me. Told me you might need me."

His eyes filled with more tears. "Even in death, she was watching out for me."

He fell back against the wall and let out another low growl. "I'm going to miss her so damn much. She was my grandmother and my mother rolled into one. She was the only one who cared about me when I was a kid."

Kylie moved to him. He folded his arms around her and held her. She finally pulled back and looked at him. "She said there was a letter for you in her desk drawer."

"I'll look." He ran a palm over her cheek. "I left a message on my uncle's phone. He and the other family members might be here any minute. I need you to go."

"I want to be here," she said. "I want to be here for you, Lucas."

"I know, and if it were my choice you could stay. But the were custom to prepare one for death is closed only to blood relatives." He reached down and kissed her. "And even if it weren't the custom, you are a vampire right now. I can't chance you being hurt. Please understand," he said. "Because if anyone lays a finger on you, I'll kill them."

She nodded. She didn't like it, but she understood. "Will you be okay?"

"Thanks to you," he said.

"I didn't do anything." She pressed a hand to his chest, knowing his heart was breaking.

"You came." He stopped as if remembering something. "God, I'm sorry. Did I hurt you when you first came in?"

"No," she said.

He pushed the sleeves of her T-shirt up and no doubt saw bruises on her arms. "Damn it! I did." He closed his eyes in more pain.

"It's nothing but a couple of bruises." She reached up on her tiptoes and kissed him gently, hoping to ease his pain. "I'm fine, Lucas. Look at me."

He opened his eyes. She smiled. "I'm fine."

He let go of a shuddering breath, then tilted his head up and sniffed the air. "Is that Burnett outside?"

She nodded.

He frowned. "He shouldn't have let you come in. He knows it's dangerous."

"He tried to stop me. I insisted. I knew you wouldn't hurt me."

"But I did," he fumed, and glanced down at her arms.

"This is nothing. It will be gone tomorrow."

He looked deep into her eyes. "I love you, Kylie Galen. Hurting you is the last thing I want to do."

She smiled. "I love you, too."

The shadow of pain in his eyes changed for one second. He leaned down and pressed his forehead to hers. "Did I hear that correctly?"

She looked up. "Yes, you did. And you also need to know that while I want you to get on that Council really badly, it's not going to change anything between us."

"I wasn't going to let it." He kissed her again and then set her back down. "I wish I didn't have to send you off."

"I know," she said.

He walked her to the door, his hand holding hers, and she could tell he really didn't want to let her go.

As soon as they opened door, Burnett met them.

"I'm sorry for your loss," Burnett said.

"Thank you." The way Lucas spoke, the manner in which he held himself in front of Burnett, was him hiding his pain. And yet he'd let her see it. He hadn't hidden from her. He trusted her that much. For some crazy reason that endeared him to her all the more. Tears tightened her throat again. He needed her just as she needed him. Which meant she couldn't die.

Lucas looked at Kylie. "Tomorrow is the full moon, then there are ceremonies. I probably won't see you for several days."

She nodded, again not liking it. She wanted to be with him in his time of grief. But she accepted that this was something she couldn't change.

Burnett looked over his shoulder and then back at Lucas.

"Someone's coming."

"Go," Lucas said.

"Is it just Lucas, or something more?" Holiday asked the next morning.

Kylie looked out at the falls. She had gone into Holiday's office at first light and asked if they could come here. Burnett as usual waited outside.

"I just needed this," Kylie said. She'd woken up this morning worried about Lucas and worried about . . . what the ghost had said. That if she fought and lost, people she loved would suffer.

She needed to feel the warm energy from the falls telling her it was going to be okay. She didn't want to die, she wanted to be there for Lucas through all of life's ups and down. But she especially didn't want to die knowing she'd let the people she loved down.

Holiday looked at her. "What's wrong, Kylie?"

Kylie forced a smile and fought the tears from rising in her throat. She felt it here. The peace, the acceptance that all would be well. She just didn't know if she'd be alive to see it herself.

"Haven't you ever just needed to come here?"

"Normally there's something picking at my sanity. So what's bothering you?"

"It's everything," Kylie said. "I'm worried about Lucas. He was so upset, Holiday. He cried. And I don't think he can do that in front of his father or his family. He needs me, but I can't be there because of some stupid were rule! And I'm worried about my mom, I still don't trust John." *I'm worried about leaving everyone I love and if they will be okay.*

The ambience of the falls seemed to enter her chest and calm her. That along with Holiday's touch on her forearm.

"It'll be okay." Holiday hiccuped. "And if you want, I'll have Burnett do another check on John."

Kylie inhaled. "No. You're right. It's going to be okay." She had to believe it. She had to.

"Have you told your mom how you feel about him?" Holiday asked.

"Yes, and she thinks I'm just upset because she won't go back to my stepdad." Kylie dipped her toes in the cool water. "I actually called her before I came to see you. Woke her up and everything. She's staying at his beach house—using up her vacation days before she quits her job to go work for him. It's as if he's sucking her in. She's practically living with him; now she's going to be working for him."

Holiday gave Kylie's arm another squeeze. "As much as we wish we can make our parents behave, they are as bad as we were when we were in our terrible twos sometimes. My mom actually dated a stripper after the divorce."

Kylie looked at Holiday and chuckled. "Okay . . . enough about bad stuff. What do you want me to wear to the wedding?"

Holiday got that giddy look in her eyes. It happened every time someone mentioned the wedding. "You can wear shorts for all I care. You're my maid of honor. You should wear what you want."

"I have a paisley dress in pastel colors that I think would work."

"It sounds perfect," Holiday said. "Oh, did I tell you I invited Blake to the wedding?"

"You mean, Blake, the ex-fiancé?"

"That would he him," Holiday said.

Kylie made a face. "Does Burnett know?" She envisioned Burnett ripping off some of Blake's limbs for showing up.

She grinned. "It was his idea. He said he wanted the man to see it so he'd realize I was off the market."

Kylie grinned. "That sounds like Burnett."

"Of course, Blake declined. I think Burnett scares him a bit."

"That goes to show you, you only fall for smart men," Kylie said, and giggled.

They lay back and stared at the roof of the cave. "I know you're young, but Burnett and I were thinking, we'd like to make you the godmother of the baby. I mean, it is because of you that we got together."

Kylie grinned. "I would be honored."

After a few minutes of silence Holiday spoke again. "I got the college forms you asked for. Burnett or I can help you guys fill them out whenever."

After another moment of peaceful silence, Holiday sighed. "Can you see it?"

"See what?" Kylie said.

"I just got this glimpse into the future. You finishing college in about five years and coming back to Shadow Falls to work here."

"You'd hire me?" Kylie asked.

"In a snap," Holiday said.

Kylie grinned. "Since you have it all figured out, what am I going to take in college? What kind of work am I going to be doing here?"

"Psychology, of course. You'll make a great counselor."

Kylie grinned. "You know, that's exactly what I was thinking about." Kylie paused. "When you look in the future, can you see if Miranda and Della and I will get into the same college?"

"If you guys want that, it'll happen. Heck, maybe we'll hire all three of you. Miranda would make an excellent teacher. With her own disabilities, she'll know how to work with other students with problems. And Della, heck, she'll be working with Burnett on security."

"I like your idea of the future." Kylie paused, then asked, "Will Lucas be here?"

"You bet." She sighed. "He'd be working with Burnett at the FRU and here part time."

"I love him," Kylie said.

"I know."

"Wow, none of this 'you're too young to be in love' talk?"

Holiday sighed. "You are young, but damn it, you have an old soul, and sometimes that just makes you wise before your years."

Holiday reached over and patted Kylie's hand. "It's really going to be okay."

Yeah, Kylie thought. She really liked Holiday's glimpse into the future. All she had to do was stay alive.

Chapter Forty-one

That night Kylie sat in her bed watching the clock and twisting the charm bracelet her mom had given her around her wrist. Almost midnight. Lucas would be shifting soon. She'd spoken with him today twice. He'd called the last time just to hear her say it again. She knew what he was talking about, so she obliged him.

I love you.

He hadn't said he'd come by tonight, but she still hoped.

Kylie's gaze shifted to the bright light on the other side of the room. The sword hadn't stopped glowing all day and she wasn't even touching it. It was as if it was trying to tell her something. Obviously, Kylie didn't speak swordese.

Not that she hadn't tried. After dinner, she'd actually sat down and had a conversation with the thing. Asked if there was something she needed to know. Told it her concerns about staying alive.

It didn't talk back. Not that she expected it to, but seriously, she wouldn't have been too shocked if it had. Face it, crazy shit happened at Shadow Falls.

Seeing it was almost twelve, Kylie got up. Della walked out of her bedroom the moment Kylie stepped out of hers.

"Where are you going?" Della asked.

"I just want to sit on the porch. Alone."

"You're hoping he'll come, aren't you?"

Kylie nodded.

"Fine," Della said. "But if tomorrow you have doggy breath . . ."

Kylie giggled and went outside. She gazed at the moon and wondered if shifting would help Lucas deal with his grief. She hoped so.

The memory of him as a wolf when he'd stopped Fredericka from charging her still teased her memory, and she ached to see him in that form again. There were so many things she wanted to know about him. What he looked like when he first woke up in the morning. What side of the bed did he normally sleep on? Did he snore?

Pulling out her phone, she checked her e-mail to see if maybe he'd sent her something earlier. She had only one, from Derek. He had forwarded her all the links he'd found in connection to Lucinda Esparza. Since the spirit hadn't actually passed, Kylie suspected she wouldn't leave until after the confrontation with Mario. Or maybe she just wasn't eager to head off to hell.

The thought sent a shiver down Kylie's spine. She went to cut off her phone, but she accidentally hit one of the links. She read it, not really learning anything new. Then she read the last one on the list, an old newspaper clipping announcing the wedding of John Anthony Esparza and Lucinda Edwards.

Kylie pulled up the link. She saw a picture of Lucinda in her wedding gown. She was pretty, young, and innocent all dressed in white. The next picture was the couple cutting the cake.

Kylie looked at the picture. Her heart stopped. Completely stopped. She blinked, praying her eyes were playing tricks on her, but no, it was him.

No wonder she didn't like him. John, her mom's John, was John Anthony, Mario's son.

Thrown instantly into protective mode, her blood buzzed, as adrenaline spread from limb to limb. The sword appeared beside Kylie—glowing, beckoning her to action. With clarity, Kylie remembered Mario's threat. *You will come to me, Kylie Galen, come to me willing to die, to suffer at my hands for my pleasure, because the price will be too great! Your weakness will take you down.*

He'd had this plan all along.

Kylie considered calling for Della, or going after Burnett, but something inside her knew this was her fight.

Hers to win.

Or hers to lose.

She didn't have an exact address for John's beach house, but her mom had said it was on the same street as one of the old plantation homes they had visited a while back. The sword flickered and Kylie sensed it might know exactly where they were going.

Picking up the weapon, Kylie could swear she heard something stir in the woods. She looked back, didn't see anything, then willed herself invisible and took off.

She flew over the gate knowing the alarm would go off, but never looked back. Burnett would be livid. Yet everything in her said this was right. Living or dying wasn't even important. Saving her mom was.

Right then she knew exactly what Mario had meant by her weakness. Love.

Weakness or not, it was the only thing worth dying for.

She followed the coast past Galveston, to the next little island. The moon hung in the dark sky, round and bright. The sound of ocean moved with the wind and carried Kylie closer. She found the street where John's beach house should be, and as she moved lower to the ground the sword grew brighter. When she came up to a large yellow house on stilts with an eight-foot-high block gate around the property, she instinctively knew she'd found it. She noted the house backed up the beach, but they only had a small gate opening up to the sand and ocean. Who bought a house on the beach and then closed it off? Someone afraid of intruders.

The sword seemed to pull her even closer to the property. Hell, maybe she and the sword did speak the same language after all.

Kylie almost landed inside the block fence, but she realized John might have an alarm system that rivaled the one at Shadow Falls.

Heart racing, blood fizzing in her veins, she told herself to slow down and think before taking some action that could get her, or her mom, killed.

Remaining in one spot, she checked out her surroundings. Vegetation was sparse compared to Houston and the hill country area. Palm trees and some large oleander bushes with salmon-colored flowers lined the block fence. She heard voices in the distance. She darted to the black shadow lining the gate, away from the moon's glow, and followed the tall block gate around the property, closer to the voices. Instantly, the sword's light faded as if to keep her from being seen. But her hand holding the sword still felt the weapon's power, its energy.

Around a slight bend, she spotted a side driveway and an iron gate. She moved in quietly until she got to another large oleander bush. Peering through the limbs and leaves she saw two men behind the thick gate sharing a conversation. Guards.

What kind?

She needed to know what she dealt with. Tightening her eyes, she focused on their foreheads—chameleons. But their patterns were murky, almost black.

Evil.

Her breath caught for one second, knowing and accepting just what she was up against.

The humming sound of a motor caught her attention. The silver Cadillac they stood beside had the engine running. Another motorized sound filled the moonlit night. The gate clinked and started to open. She watched from the shadows as one of the guards got into the white car.

This was her chance. Maybe her only chance. She had to get inside that gate. She had to save her mother.

The thought hit her that she might be too late. She pushed it away, unable to accept it.

Willing herself invisible, aware that she dealt with other chameleons, she listened to hear if anyone else was in the invisible realm. The sounds made by another invisible always seemed almost closer. Louder.

Only silence echoed in this unique world, but like her, they might be standing silent.

Listening.

Aware her footsteps might be heard, she waited for the gate's motor to grow a bit louder, offering the tiniest advantage. When the gate opened a few more inches she could slip inside.

Breath held, trying to make herself as light on her feet as possible, she moved in. She got just inside the gate when she heard another sound—a footstep. She wasn't the only one invisible.

Another guard appeared a few feet from the other. He cut his eyes around.

"Do we have company?" the first guard standing by the gate asked.

"Maybe? Get the damn gate shut off so I can know for sure."

Knowing now, before he faded again, was her only chance, she took off at a dead run. Crouching behind a prickly bush, realizing her odds of being seen in the visible realm might be less than being heard in the invisible sphere, she willed herself to appear.

The buzz in her protective mode still ran high and she found herself needing more oxygen. Still gripping the sword, she closed her eyes one second, and that's when she heard it—a deep angry growl.

Shit. They had guard dogs.

Opening her eyes, she stared at a snout with snarling teeth exposed and glowing yellow eyes. The black spiked collar told Kylie she was right, it was a guard dog, but the wild look in his eyes told her the animal was at least part wolf.

Kylie swallowed her fear and smelled the animal's breath. It jerked its snout up, showing more teeth. His growl became lower, more intense. The tags hanging from its collar clinked and seemed too loud.

Looking the animal right in the eyes, she tightened her hold on the sword. *Don't make me kill you. My fight is not with you. I even kind of love wolves.*

Instantly the animal backed up. His yellow eyes never blinked. He crouched down on his haunches, his gaze shifting away from her eyes. Kylie remembered the wolf she'd run across at Shadow Falls and how it had shown submissiveness.

She didn't understand it, but she'd take whatever advantage she had right now. Because face it, she had a feeling she was going to need it.

She glanced back where the men stood by the gate. Only one remained. The other had gone back into the invisible realm. He could be anywhere.

Willing herself invisible again, she listened. Heard the footsteps moving in front of the bush. They slowed down. Her heart pounded so loud, she was certain he could hear it.

The dog/wolf turned and bolted out of the bush.

"Damn it, you mongrel," the guard's voice rang out. "I thought I had something."

Through the leaves, Kylie saw the man appear. He stomped over to the animal and kicked his back leg. Hard. The dog yelped, and Kylie's blood raged for the defenseless animal. When the man drew his leg back again, Kylie reached down and picked up a stone and tossed it to the bushes to her right.

The man swerved around and went to look in the bush beside her. The closer he came the harder it was to breathe.

"Got anything?" the man from the gate yelled out.

"I don't think so," he muttered, and started toward the gate. "Just that damn ugly-ass dog."

That ugly-ass dog just saved my butt, Kylie thought, her heart still bouncing off her breastbone with the need to protect.

When the man remained visible and started chatting with the other guard, she knew this was her opportunity to move away, maybe find a place to actually get inside.

Becoming invisible again, she quietly moved around the house looking for an entrance. The wolf/dog came limping toward her, confirming her suspicion that it could see her.

Willing herself visible, she reached down and touched the dog's back leg. She felt her hand grow warm. *Get me inside the house, friend,* she told the animal with her mind, unsure if it would work, or if she was simply hoping. Then again, Derek could communicate with animals. Maybe she'd changed herself into fae.

The canine turned and started moving beneath the stilts holding up the beach house. She started to continue on her own way, but the dog stopped and looked back at her almost as if to say, *This way.*

Chancing it, she followed the dog. After moving in and around multiple beams, she questioned her decision, but then the dog stopped at what appeared to be a ramp that led up to a doggy door. Still invisible, she tried to move in rhythm with her canine friend. Not an easy feat carrying a sword.

She accidentally hit the sword on the edge of the door. If anyone lurked inside this dimension, they would have heard her.

Inside, she stopped and listened. Not a sound echoed in the darkness. She saw a couple of sleeping bags and empty dog bowls. *Bet they don't feed you regularly, either, do they, buddy?* But if they were fed here, that meant there had to be a door into the house. Whether it would be locked was another matter.

Scanning the dark room, she saw the door. She petted the animal again. *Thank you.* She stood up and reached for the doorknob. It turned in her hand. An almost silent twist of the wrist. She inhaled, feeling successful so far. But she didn't kid herself, the hardest part was finding her mom and getting them out of here.

Getting them out alive.

The sword seemed to vibrate in her hand, as if reminding her that escaping tonight wasn't that simple. Tonight she would use the weapon, only this time it wouldn't be practice. It would for be real.

At first she thought everyone in the house was asleep. She moved her way through a big kitchen, then she came into a large living room with a big rock fireplace. This room seemed to be the center of the house. A door led off from both sides. She spotted a light at the end of one hallway. She heard voices. Moving with baby steps down the hall, she listened to see if she could hear her mom.

One voice was clear: John. A second voice spoke and chills ran down her spine. She swallowed the taste of fear down her throat: Mario.

No female voices entered the conversation. Debating what to do, she decided to search for her mom. At this time of night, her mom would be asleep. She turned down the other hall, where it looked like bedrooms would be.

The first room appeared to be a guest room. With hopes her mom might be sleeping there, she opened the door. The room stood eerily silent and empty.

She saw a room at the end of the hall and figured it was the master bedroom. Right then, she somehow knew that's where her mom slept.

She'd been sleeping with John.

Sleeping with the enemy.

But Kylie was here to fix that. She held tight to her sword as she quietly turned the knob.

In the bed was a familiar shape. A nightlight cast a glow onto her mom. Kylie recalled all the nights as a kid that she'd walked into her mom's bedroom with nightmares, or a stuffy nose. Not once had her mom gotten angry. She might not have been the biggest on offering affection, but she had always been there. The anger Kylie felt over the whole Brighten situation suddenly seemed irrelevant.

Moving in, she got to the side of the bed. "Mom?" she whispered.

Her mom didn't budge, and for one second Kylie panicked, then she saw her side shift with an intake of air.

Looking at the dresser, she saw a wineglass. The nightlight shined on the glass and showed tiny flecks of something filming the bottom. Picking it up, she held it to the spray of light, and sure enough, it appeared something other than wine had been in her mom's drink—like crushed pills. John had drugged her mom?

Putting the glass down, feeling another surge of protectiveness moving through her veins, she gripped the sword and leaned down. "Mom," Kylie said.

Her mom stirred a bit, but barely.

Reaching for her shoulder, she gave her a slight shake. "Mom, I need you to wake up."

Her mom's eyes popped open. "Kylie? What are you . . . ?" She looked around as if she couldn't concentrate. Was it because she was she still asleep or the drugs? "Where's . . ."

"John?" Kylie finished for her mom.

Taking a deep breath, Kylie realized she hadn't taken the time to figure out exactly what she was going to tell her mom. With no time to come up with something clever, she knew it would have to be the truth.

Was it time to spill everything? Could her mom handle the truth? Or maybe just part of it?

"John?" her mom called out.

Kylie pushed two fingers over her lips, praying she hadn't been loud enough for him to hear. "No, you can't . . ."

"My God, what is that?" Her mom lurched back, looking at the sword, which was now gleaming, it was so bright. Her mom made a face. "This is a dream, right?"

"Mom." Kylie tried to speak calmly. "John is not what you think. He's not a good guy and we need to leave."

Her mom looked away from the sword back to Kylie. "You need to stop thinking that. I know it hurts that your dad and I—"

"Mom, I really need you to be quiet and just do what I say, okay?"

Her mom's brow wrinkled and Kylie felt certain she was partially drugged. "How did you get in here?" Her mom gave her head a little shake as if trying to wake herself up. Then she glanced at the sword again. "It has to be a dream."

"Come on." Kylie pulled her mom up.

Her mom rose to her feet, but then fell back to the bed. Kylie pulled her up again and this time noticed she wore a sexy nightgown. But she didn't have time to worry about that. She had to get her out of here.

She took her hand and started walking her to the door. Right before they got there, it swung open.

John stood staring at Kylie. Then, as if out of an evil dream, Mario appeared beside him.

Kylie pushed her mom behind her and held out her sword. "Get out of our way."

Mario's answer was a devilish smile that spoke of evilness. "I told you that you would come to me."

"Who are you?" her mom asked, and tried to move in front of Kylie.

Kylie caught her mom by the arm and held her back.

"And look what you brought." Mario motioned to her sword. "A toy for us to play with."

Chapter Forty-two

Kylie wasn't sure what to do next. But she went with the first thing she thought of. Tightening her hold on her mom, she willed herself and her mom invisible. Her mom screamed, obviously from not being able to see herself or Kylie.

Unable to give in to her mom's panic, Kylie didn't hesitate and bolted for the door, dodging the two men. Unfortunately, her mom was yanked from Kylie's hands. Swinging around, Kylie couldn't see her, but she heard her mom gasping for air and she knew Mario had gone invisible and now had her.

"Let her go!" Kylie seethed, and willed herself visible.

Mario appeared seconds later with her mom. His hand gripped her mother's throat so tight her face looked blue.

Kylie brought up the sword.

Call him a coward! The spirit's voice rang in Kylie's ears at the same time the cold shot down her spine.

Insist he fight you like a man.

"Don't be a coward. Stand up and fight me like a man!" Kylie bit out and prayed it worked.

Mario, his hand still around her mom's throat, stared at Kylie, his eyes growing tight. "Fine." He threw her mom at John.

Her mom fell at John's feet gasping for air. He picked her up, none too gently. Everything in Kylie wanted to attack. To forget the sword and use her bare hands to rip these two men apart. The only thing that stopped her was the spirit standing there repeating the same words over and over again.

The power you have is in the sword. The power is in the sword.

The moment her mom got air into her lungs, she yanked free of John and charged at Mario. Her mom might not be supernatural, but a mother's love was pretty damn powerful.

Just not as powerful as the magic of these two. John snagged her back by her hair. "Stop fighting, you fool!"

Her mom's eyes went wide and she cut them toward John. In her expression, Kylie knew she saw John for who he really was for the first time: someone evil, someone who had used her.

Kylie's heart ached for her mom and she prayed that this wouldn't be her last moments of life. For no one should die thinking only of their mistakes. Consumed with regrets.

Mario waved a hand through the air and a sword appeared. "I will kill you slowly, and your mother will get to watch. How much fun will that be?"

"No!" Kylie's mom screamed.

John pulled her mom's arms behind her back and held them there, making her struggles useless.

"Not here," John said. "I paid over fifty thousand for this rug."

Her mom screamed again and John yanked her against him. "Shut up or she will die sooner."

Mario looked at his son. "The blood would add to its worth!"

Her mom looked at Kylie, tears spilling from her eyes. The spirit stared at John. *You will rot in hell for all you've done.*

Kylie could only pray the spirit was right and his trip to hell would come soon.

"But then again, a little more room to play would be appreciated." Mario moved to stand in front of John and put the tip of his sword to her mom's chest, looking at Kylie. "We will walk out of here. If you choose to not follow, or try anything foolish, I'll kill her. And with pleasure."

Kylie's mom let out a horrible sound, a cry of pure terror. When she glanced up, Kylie read the plea for forgiveness in her mother's eyes. She thought they were doomed, and Kylie wasn't so sure she was wrong.

"I'll follow you," she said.

And she did. She followed him down the hall and into the living room.

Mario waved a hand and the furniture moved back, giving them the entire room to fight. Kylie had no idea where Mario got his powers, but she could guess it was from evil.

"Give me a second, I want to enjoy the show." John, dragging her mother with him, opened a drawer and pulled out a roll of duct tape and wrapped it around her wrists. Then he did the same with her ankles. Roughly, he pushed her down against the wall as she fought him and begged him to stop. His laugh rang out cruelly. He ripped off another piece of tape and put it over her mouth.

Kylie watched in horror and fury, barely able to stop herself from leaping on the sorry excuse of a man and ripping out his black heart.

Not now. Not yet. Patience, patience, the spirit whispered in Kylie's ear. *There is a plan and you must follow it if you are to cheat death.*

Kylie didn't understand what the spirit meant, but she had no time to contemplate. The scream of the spirit warned her just in time of Mario's charge. She brought her sword down against his. The clatter sounded in her ears, but she barely heard it over the sound of the blood humming through her body.

He came at her again, and Kylie responded blow for blow. Their swords clanked, clattered. Lucas would have been proud. But as good as she was at blocking his blows, she never got the chance to go on the offensive, she was too busy defending herself.

While she never stopped to look, she could imagine her mother watching in horror. And while she tried not to listen, she heard the desperate screams, muffled by the tape.

Help us. Kylie cried out the words in her heart, cried out to the death angels, to God, to anyone who might listen. In the distance, the howl of the half wolf/half dog broke through the air, as if he prayed for her as well.

Don't lose sight of his sword. Watch him, he will move low this time. The spirit's orders came quick and fast. Kylie tried to listen, tried to forget that this was life or death. She took orders and listened to the sound of metal against metal.

For one brief second, Kylie caught sight of Mario's face. He grinned as if he were simply toying with her. How long could she do this? How could she win?

Don't stop believing in your gifts! the spirit called out.

Then Kylie saw John appear behind his father with his own sword. Two against one? The memories of the Lucinda's vision filled her head. Yet only the slightest bit of fear entered Kylie's heart. No time to be afraid.

Like Lucinda on the night she'd lost her life, Kylie didn't think of death, she simply fought. Fought with everything she had with a prayer on her lips.

She watched in revulsion as John swung his arm back and thrust the sword into his own father's back. The end of his sword plunged through the man's chest. His shirt front darkened with blood around the extended blade. Mario's eyes turned bright green just before the life went out of them. A black wisp of fog-like smoke billowed out of the man's mouth.

Kylie knew it was the man's soul—stained and evil from all his sins. Then the ugliest sound Kylie had ever heard bled into the air—like rats screeching and cockroaches feeding. Several shadowy beings, hell's minions, swept through the room and took Mario's black soul with them.

John yanked the sword out, blood squirting from the hole in Mario's chest. With the sword no longer holding up his body, he crumbled to the floor.

Death wasn't pretty.

• • •

Kylie stared at the body, her own sword held motionless before her. Why had John done this? Had she been wrong about him?

When she glanced at the man's face, the cold smile he wore told her she'd been wrong about nothing.

How fitting, the spirit said. *You killed the man who killed your son. But not for our son.* She moved closer to him, looking him in the eyes. Then her gaze shifted to Kylie. *Don't trust him.*

"Why did you do that?" she asked John, keeping her sword poised to fight.

"I've been waiting for him to die so I could take his place. This was just the opportunity I sought."

Kylie felt the despicableness in his gray eyes. "Now what?" she asked.

"It's obvious, isn't it?" He smiled. "You have choices. Accept that you and your mother belong to me. You do what I say, your mother lives. You don't, and she dies." He cast a glance at her mom, who stared up at him with hatred.

"I think we'd both rather die," Kylie said, "but I don't plan on doing that right now."

"You think you can best me? You are nothing but a child with powers you can't even control."

He came at her with fierce swiftness. His sword moving in and out. She could barely keep up.

Go left. Now right. The spirit yelled instructions.

Kylie fought to defend herself. Her sword came down, but his came faster. She felt the razor-sharp edge slice into her left forearm. The sting and the blood followed.

She didn't slow down. She couldn't. To slow down, to take her eyes off his sword for one second, would mean death.

For her.

For her mom.

Then she felt the cold, a familiar cold of her father. He was here. But was it to help her, or take her with him?

A loud crash sounded somewhere nearby. She forced herself not to think or to focus on anything but the fight.

Then a low ugly growl vibrated in the room. She saw the wolf leap up from across the room. His mouth opened, his teeth exposed, as if ready to tear into flesh. Her friend had come to fight with her.

Recognition hit in a flash.

This was not the half-wolf outside.

The wolf flying in the air toward John was Lucas.

John swung his sword toward the new threat, ready to pierce Lucas's chest.

Using every ounce of strength she had, feeling her blood hot with the need to protect, she brought her sword down on his, knocking it from the man's hands. John roared with fury, dodged Lucas, and reached again for his sword.

Before he got to it, Kylie got to him. She buried her sword into his side. She pulled the weapon out and started to go at him again.

He collapsed.

His body shook.

He gasped for air.

Blood dripped from the tip of Kylie's sword.

Kylie looked at Lucas, his eyes ablaze, his teeth still barred.

Then, just as before, the hideous sounds filled the room as the devil sent his own to collect the dirty soul that seeped from John's mouth.

Dropping her sword, Kylie felt soiled for taking a life. Then she swung around to her mom, who still lay staring at the scene. The realization came quickly. She hadn't taken a life, she had saved one.

Dropping down on her knees, she struggled to get the tape off her mom's mouth.

Lucas, in all his wolf beauty, moved toward her. Her mom squirmed as if in fear of the wolf. Lucas brushed against Kylie's side, met her gaze briefly, then turned and left. Kylie remembered again what his grandmother had said. *You are part of his quest, and he yours.*

"Mom," Kylie said. "It's going to be okay." She finished pulling the tape from her mom's mouth.

Her mom's scream bounced off the walls.

"It's okay," Kylie said again. "It's okay. Now, be still so I can get the tape off of you."

As soon as Kylie took the tape off her mom's wrists, she grabbed Kylie and held her. Held her hard and long. "This is the worst dream I've ever had."

Kylie pulled back and debated what to say, but then just nodded and ripped the tape from her mom's ankles. Her mom curled up in a ball, rocking back and forth, as if just waiting to wake up.

Kylie looked back at the two bodies. She needed to call the police, didn't she? She glanced back at her mom and wondered how it would play out with her spouting out things about dreams and wolves.

Then Kylie remembered, she might have come here alone, but she had friends. She grabbed her phone and started punching in Burnett's number. Right before her finger hit the call button, another noise filled the room. A soft comforting sound. The sound of trickling water. The sound of the falls. The warm feeling, the sense of rightness, of justice, filled Kylie's chest.

The moment of peacefulness was shattered when her mom screamed again, her eyes focused on something behind Kylie.

"He . . . What? How?" Her mom started scooting back.

Kylie swung around, grabbing her sword as she did, and praying it was her mom's panic talking.

She was wrong.

Chapter Forty-three

Standing before Kylie, fully manifested, was her father. Not just fully manifested but brighter than ever before. The sound of the falls grew louder. The hum of peaceful water.

"Daddy?" she whispered.

Hey, baby girl.

"Hey," she said.

He looked over her shoulder and frowned. *Your mom's passed out.*

Kylie glanced back. "She's had a hard night."

So have you. He motioned to the blood on her shirt.

"Just a flesh wound," she said, or was it more? She glanced down wondering if she'd only imagined it was small and now her father was here to take her with him.

Blood had soaked through her shirt, not a lot of blood, but enough that the peaceful feeling lessened and fear took its place. Oddly, it was not fear for herself, but fear that her death meant she'd let others down. Or had her victory over John and Mario resolved that? And it was simply her time to go?

Glancing up, she stared at her father, her vision slightly blurred with tears. "Am I going to die? Are others going to suffer because—"

No, Kylie. He rushed to her. His hands holding her shoulders. His cold a comfort she welcomed. *You have so much life to live, child. I'm not here to take you. I'm here to help you explain this to your mother.*

She blinked. "Did the death angels give you more time on earth?"

Only a little more, but what they offered me was better. I have a place with them now.

It took Kylie a second to understand. "You're going to be a death angel?"

I will be after I help you this last time. But the beauty of it is that from now on, I will always be watching out for you. The wisdom you hear in your heart will be from me, daughter.

Tears filled her eyes again. She realized something he said about helping her explain this to her mom. Kylie had been so intent on saving her mother, she hadn't even considered how she was going to explain it. "How am I ever going to get Mom to accept this?"

That is what I am here for. We will do it together.

Then Kylie recalled. "She could see you . . . before she passed out."

Yes. She had always felt my presence, but I was granted enough energy so she may see me. He looked around, frowning at the dead bodies. *But for now, call Burnett.*

Kylie picked up the phone and redialed Burnett's number.

"She is almost awake." Kylie's father appeared. Kylie, sitting in a chair beside the bed in the extra bedroom in John's house, looked up at her daddy.

Her mom had been out for almost four hours now.

Burnett and Holiday had shown up minutes after she'd called them. And he'd immediately called a crew to clean up the mess. The FRU were going to make it look like a code red, which was a car accident. How they would make being stabbed with swords appear to be a car accident, she didn't know.

She didn't want to know.

After a good long cry on Holiday's shoulder, Kylie explained what went down. She'd also told them about Daniel. Holiday was in awe that Kylie would have a personal connection with a death angel. Kylie had almost told her that she would have preferred to have had her dad with her in life, but this wasn't about choices and she reminded herself that she had much to be grateful for.

When she explained that Daniel was here to help her explain things to her mom, Burnett expressed concern that Kylie's mom couldn't handle the truth. Kylie was worried about the same thing. Yet when he suggested they bring Derek in to erase her mother's memory, Daniel had appeared and disagreed.

She needs to know the truth, Daniel had insisted. He hadn't given explanation; he didn't have to. Kylie had to trust her dad, even when her heart feared how her mom would take the news.

It was Holiday who pointed out that Kylie's mom wasn't just a normal human. Being a descendent of a Native American tribe had made her intuitive of supernatural powers.

So, with the help of Daniel, a future death angel, Kylie was about to tell her mother everything. And she wasn't looking forward to it.

Her mother opened her eyes. She focused on Kylie and then the words spilled from her mom's lips. "I had the worst dream." She sat up and looked around.

Kylie looked around as well, not knowing if Daniel was still visible. He wasn't. She supposed he'd show up when she needed him. But she felt pretty needy right now. Looking back at her mom, Kylie knew the moment when her mom realized they were at John's house. Her breath came short. "What are you doing here?"

Kylie took her mother's hand. "You were in trouble."

Her mom blinked, shook her head, and fell back against the pillows. "I'm still dreaming."

"No, Mom. It wasn't a dream."

"Yes, it was. It was awful, Kylie. At least parts of it were. You were fighting and—"

"It was awful. But it wasn't a dream." Kylie knew only one way to prove it. She pulled the collar of her shirt down and showed her mom the cut. It probably could have used some stitches, but Kylie had been too busy to worry about that. Of course, Holiday had seen the blood on Kylie's shirt and hadn't been happy until she searched the house for something to clean the wound.

Her mom's eyes got big as quarters.

"Are you . . . okay?"

Okay was such a vague term, Kylie realized. It didn't come close to expressing what Kylie felt. But at the same time, words failed her.

She'd seen her mom nearly choked to death. Kylie had been forced to fight for their life with a glowing sword. She had watched her abductor kill his father. She'd been stabbed with a sword. Then she'd had to kill a man.

"Yeah," Kylie nodded. "I'm okay." She inhaled and tried to remember how she planned to tell her mom the truth.

"Of course you're okay," her mom blurted out. "It's just a dream."

Kylie gave her mom's hand another squeeze. Daniel had said he was going to try to go into her mom's dreams and help make all this easier. Had he been successful?

"Mom, do you remember telling me that you thought there was something magical about Daniel?"

Her mom nodded. "Yes, but—"

"Well, you were right. He was magical. And that made me magical."

Her mom gripped the bed sheets as something occurred to her. "I dreamed about him, too. Oh, goodness. This isn't making sense." She dropped back and covered her eyes with her hands.

"It will, but you're going to have to listen to me, Mom." Or maybe it wouldn't make sense. Hadn't it taken Kylie weeks to accept all this?

She paused. The expression *to make sense* was another vague term.

"Do you remember the stalker I thought I had? You know, when you sent me to see that shrink."

Her mom nodded, but weakly, almost as if she was about to pass out again. Then Kylie realized why that might be.

"Breathe, Mom."

Her mom took a big, deep swallow of air and Kylie continued. "Remember I told you he was dressed in army clothes?"

Her mom nodded again. "I realize now that probably freaked you out because . . . well, my dad died in the army? Isn't that part of what upset you?"

"He said you would tell me all this. What's happening, Kylie?"

"Just what Dad told you," Kylie said calmly. "I know it sounds crazy and I know what you've . . . what we've been through here is hard, but you have to try to believe."

Her mom's eyes, focused over Kylie's shoulder, suddenly went large. The cold hit at that exact moment when her mom gasped and Kylie knew Daniel had appeared. And if her mom's expression was any indication, she could see him, too.

"Breathe, Mom." Kylie got tears in her eyes at the look of loss that passed on her mother's face as she gazed at the man she loved so much so long ago.

"The dream I had . . . you . . ." Her mom's voice wavered.

I told you that you would see me. Daniel moved closer to the edge of the bed. *Now, I want you to listen to our daughter. She's going to explain things to you better than I did. I have to go now, but remember what I said. You will find love again. Don't fight it.*

Daniel leaned down and kissed her mom softly on her lips. *You were the love of my life,* he said.

Tears filled her mom's eyes again as Daniel pulled away. He glanced at Kylie and then placed a soft kiss on her cheek.

Daniel looked back at her mom and motioned to Kylie. *We did good, didn't we?*

Her mom nodded.

Her dad glanced back at Kylie. *I'll always be here when you need me.* He faded and Kylie wiped her own tears from her cheeks.

Her mom looked at Kylie. "I had a dream, he told me that he'd been watching over us the whole time."

Kylie nodded. "He has been, Mom. I only started seeing him recently, but he knew things about my life."

Kylie crawled in bed with her mom and hugged her and they cried. Cried for someone who had died years ago, but who they would forever miss. After a few good tears had passed, Kylie told her mom about Shadow Falls being for magical teens, and about Mario and Roberto, and how John was actually Mario's son. In a gentle tone, she told her mom that they were magical, but Mario and John were actually the bad kind of magic.

Her mom gasped. "I just remembered. John killed someone, some man? Where are the cops?"

"That was Mario. And, well, Burnett took care of that."

Her mom gripped Kylie's hand. "Burnett from . . . your school?"

Kylie nodded and noticed her mom had stopped breathing again. "Breathe, Mom."

She gasped and then asked, "Is he, this Burnett, magical, too?"

"Yeah." Kylie decided to wait and explain the whole different species thing to her mom later. Vampires, werewolves, and such might freak her out. It certainly had Kylie, at least until she became best friends with one and fell in love with another.

Her mom closed her eyes as if trying to forget something, or maybe trying to remember. "Then there was a wolf and then you killed . . . John. Oh, God, baby, you had to kill him. What are the police going to say?" She sat up some. "We'll tell them I did it. Do you hear me, I did it, not you."

Kylie's heart clutched at her mom's willingness to confess to murder for her. How, Kylie wondered, had she ever doubted her mom's love? "There's not going to be any police. Burnett works for an organization like the FBI. He's taking care of it for us. That means we can't ever talk about this to anyone."

Her mom nodded and then she leaned in. "But, Kylie, how is

Burnett going to explain the bodies? People will know I was dating John."

"Burnett is taking care of that, too."

She sank back into the pillows. "It's going to take a long time to believe this."

"I know," Kylie said. "It did me, too."

The following Monday morning, Labor Day, Kylie went down early and started breakfast for her and her mom. Kylie had stayed with her, and she had to remind her to breathe a lot. They slept in the same bed at night. Talked sometimes until after midnight.

Her mom asked a lot of questions. Some required difficult answers. Yup, she went into the whole species issue. Vampire and werewolf being the most difficult because of instinctual fear due to all the folklore surrounding them. Kylie told her mom she was a chameleon, and decided to wait until later to explain that meant she actually had a little of all of the species in her.

Over the weekend, Kylie had also spoken to Della and Miranda. Della was furious Kylie had disappeared on her watch again.

"It's beginning to look bad on my record," Della said.

Kylie promised to talk to Burnett and take all the blame.

Miranda reminded Kylie of her pinky promise to never leave, and Kylie assured her that she was coming back. And today was the day. It also just so happened to be Burnett and Holiday's wedding.

She and her mom were going early to help set things up.

Lucas had called Kylie three times. He had been staying at his uncle's since the full moon. Supposedly, a funeral was a several-day ordeal for weres. And today, before the wedding, he had his meeting with the Council as scheduled. She'd offered to go with him, but he assured her that he needed to do this alone. Kylie prayed they accepted him.

Not that it would change anything between them. As his grandmother had said, they were part of each other's quests—quests that had been ongoing since they met all those years ago. Some things were just meant to be.

Kylie hoped it was true what Daniel had said about her mom finding another love. Sadly, Kylie got the feeling it wouldn't be her stepdad. She'd actually spoken with Tom Galen this morning. They'd spent a good twenty minutes making plans for their next summer trip. Before they hung up, she told him she loved him, and she meant it. Even knowing she'd have Daniel close as her guardian death angel, her stepdad had his place in her heart and always would. She knew Daniel wouldn't want it any other way.

Kylie went to the refrigerator to pull out the eggs. The steam rose from the carton in an odd way.

Guess what?

Kylie recognized the spirit's voice.

"What?"

They aren't sending me to hell.

Kylie looked back at the spirit sitting on her mom's countertop and smiled. She wore a nice gown with no slashes, no blood, and she'd left the sword behind, too. "You're going to heaven?"

No, well, not yet. They're giving me a second chance. You know, to do some work for them to make up for all my wrongdoings. Then, if I earn the right, I'll get to go there. I'll be with my boy. She beamed.

Kylie smiled at her. "I like second chances." She paused.

Do you know why they are giving me this second chance?

"Why?" Kylie asked.

Because I loved my son.

Kylie smiled and remembered Mario had called it a weakness, and yet it was that very thing that took him down.

"It's a powerful emotion," Kylie said. And she thought of all the love she had in her life. Her family. Her friends. Lucas.

I have to go now, the spirit said, her image fading.

"It was nice knowing you," Kylie said.

You, too. The voice faded with the last of the cold. Kylie turned back to her breakfast-making when her mom walked into the kitchen.

"Who were you talking to just now?"

Kylie debated telling the truth and decided to hold off. "Phone's been ringing all morning."

"Who called?" she asked as she went for a cup of coffee.

"Dad, Lucas, and Sara," Kylie said.

Her mom's eyes widened. "Your dad?"

"Tom," Kylie clarified.

Her mom nodded. "I guess . . . your dad wouldn't use a phone to contact you."

Kylie grinned. "I don't think so."

Her mom poured her coffee and added a teaspoon of creamer into the cup.

"Is this Lucas guy . . . is he . . . important to you?"

Kylie nodded. "Very much so. I love him."

Her mom's eyes grew wide. "Are you two . . . you know?"

Her mom still couldn't say sex. "Not yet," Kylie said. "But it's going to happen soon."

Her mom nodded. "You should probably see a doctor about getting . . ."

"On the pill," Kylie finished for her.

Her mom nodded.

"I will," Kylie said.

Her mom inhaled as if the conversation had been painful, then she asked, "Is Sara coming by before you head back?"

"No, she's in New Orleans at a family reunion. That's what she called to tell me. That and to tell me her aunts were smothering her with their boobs."

Her mom giggled and then her expression went flat. She just stood there, staring at her coffee, stirring it around and around. The spoon clinking against the side of the cup seemed to be the only noise in the room. She finally looked up, concern tightening her brows. "When I took Sara to see you, she told me you healed her. You didn't really . . . did you?"

Okay, Kylie couldn't keep everything from her mom. "Yeah." Kylie got busy making the French toast and pretended it wasn't a big deal.

"Is there anything else you can do?" her mom asked, caught her breath, and waited.

"Why don't I just tell you a little bit at a time?" Kylie said.

Her mom released a deep breath that sounded like relief. "Good idea."

Chapter Forty-four

Kylie had been holding her phone on the ride to Shadow Falls waiting for Lucas's text or call. Had he made the Council? Had he not? If he hadn't was he already beginning to resent her? Oh, she knew he'd said he wouldn't, but she knew how important this was to him, too.

It was around three that afternoon when they parked in front of the Shadow Falls Academy sign. Holiday and Burnett met Kylie and her mom at the gate. Hugs were given; even her mom was open to them. Yet as she started into the gate, her mom slowed down.

"Something wrong?" Burnett asked.

"Just a little nervous," her mom answered. "I mean, I'm just not sure I'm ready to meet any vampires or werewolves."

Burnett glanced at Kylie over her mom's shoulder and Kylie offered him a shrug that said she hadn't informed her mom about who was what. He looked back at her mom and smiled. "Don't worry, they're not nearly as intimidating as you'd think."

"Were any of them at the parents' day meetings?" she asked, sounding hesitant.

"A few," Burnett said.

Kylie rolled her eyes and knew her mom was going to give him hell when she learned what he was.

"So what should we start doing?" her mom asked, looking at Holiday as if wanting to forget the whole supernatural issue. "I mean we're here to help pull off this wedding."

Holiday walked them to where they were going to have the ceremony. Several of the students were already helping to set up chairs.

The first chance Kylie got out of earshot from her mom, she asked Holiday, "Have you heard anything from Lucas yet?"

"No, he called earlier and said the meeting with the Council had been delayed a bit, he'll be here in about an hour. But he can't be late," she said. "He's one of Burnett's groomsmen." For the first time, Holiday's eyes pinched with worry. She reached over her shoulder and twisted her hair. Then she hiccuped.

Holiday glanced over to Kylie's mom. "How is she really doing?"

Kylie spotted her mom chatting with Chris, clueless that she was talking to a vampire. "Better than I thought," she said. "Of course, when she finds out that she's already had conversations with two vampires, she's gonna flip."

Holiday grinned and then grew serious. "How are you doing?"

"Better than I thought, too." Kylie smiled. "But I'll be better when I see Lucas."

"I'll feel better, too," Holiday said.

"Where's Della and Miranda?" Kylie asked, expecting to see them by now.

"They drove into town to pick up the cake and some flowers for the reception. If they get into an argument and drop the cake or something, I'm going to cry. I swear, I've never seen two girls love to fight as much as they do."

Kylie grinned. "Yeah, but they love each other. But enough about everyone else, shouldn't you be soaking in a tub, relaxing for the big event?"

Holiday smiled. "Believe it or not, this whole thing with your mom has been a blessing. I've been more worried about you two than the stressing about the wedding."

The next hour flew by as Kylie and her mom finished helping put out chairs and assisted decorating the dining hall for the reception. Kylie had broken down and texted Lucas, but he hadn't answered. Nor had Kylie seen Della and Miranda, and she was having withdrawals.

Suddenly Kylie heard a couple of squeals. Familiar squeals. Della and Miranda squeals.

Kylie wrapped her arms around her two best friends and it turned into a group hug. "Have I told you how much I love y'all?" she said.

"Yeah," Della said. "And the only reason I'm letting you get mushy now is because I heard you kicked ass the other night."

Kylie pulled back and smiled. "I did kick ass!"

Kylie, Della, Miranda, and her mom had gone back to get dressed at Kylie's cabin. Kylie had enjoyed sharing Della and Miranda with her mom. Or she would have if she weren't still worrying about Lucas. Where was he? Fear that he hadn't made it and hadn't wanted to face her filled her heart. Kylie left the bathroom, where they were all putting on their makeup, to check her phone.

"You know a watched phone never rings," Della told her, having followed Kylie out.

Kylie looked up. "I'm just—"

"Worried. I know. But my gut says he's fine."

Kylie looked up at her vamp friend. "Since when are you the positive one?"

"Since I was forced to room with a damn optimist." She grinned.

Kylie laughed and hugged her. A few minutes later, her and her mom and her two best friends started walking to the front. They had told Holiday they'd arrive thirty minutes early to help out with seating. Kylie had almost texted Holiday and asked if she'd heard from Lucas, but decided not to worry Holiday any more on her wedding day.

The four of them had just turned the last bend when Kylie saw him.

He walked toward them slowly. His blue eyes, dark and hungry, were fixed on her. Obviously dressed for the wedding, he wore a navy suit coat, navy slacks, and a solid white shirt. There wasn't one spot on him that wasn't completely gorgeous.

Kylie hadn't realized she'd stopped walking until her mom leaned down and whispered, "Breathe, Kylie." There was a teasing tone in her voice. "That's your Lucas, isn't it?" she asked.

I sure as hell hope he's mine. Lucas stopped in front of her. "Mom, you remember Lucas, don't you?" Kylie asked, but she couldn't take her eyes off him.

"Why don't we let these two have a few minutes?" Miranda said.

Kylie's mom looked as if she was nervous. "Sure, as long as . . . there's not any vampires or werewolves around."

Della coughed to cover up her laugh.

"Don't worry," Lucas said, "I'll protect her."

And he would, Kylie thought. He had protected her. He'd save her life.

"Oh, I was worried about me," her mom said. "Kylie's friends with them. And I'm sure that eventually I'll get used to them, but the thought of it still creeps me out."

"I understand," Lucas said, and cut his eyes to Kylie.

As her mom and Della and Miranda walked away, Kylie heard her mom say, "Do they only come out at night?"

Kylie rolled her eyes at Lucas and leaned in. "I'm not sure what she thinks they look like."

"Don't worry," he said. "She'll get used to us. Her daughter did."

Kylie grinned. "Why didn't you answer any of my texts? I've been worried sick."

"I had to cut it off and when I got out it was late and . . . I wanted to tell you in person."

"You got on the Council?"

His blue eyes brightened with a smile. "I did." He looked over his shoulder, as if making sure her mom wasn't looking. Then he pulled her against him and kissed her. A soft kiss.

"I got you something," he whispered, his lips breathing words against hers.

He reached into his coat pocket and pulled out a ring. A gold ring with a large diamond. A beautiful, teardrop-shaped diamond that looked like an engagement ring. Kylie's breath caught.

"It was my grandmother's ring. In her letter she wrote you should have it. And before you start panicking, let me say that I know maybe we're too young to call it an engagement. That's why I got you this, too." He pulled out a gold chain. "I want you to wear it around your neck. Call it a promise—a promise that when you do slip a ring on that finger . . ." He ran his hand down to her left hand. "That it'll be my ring."

Emotion rose in her throat. "You don't have to give me anything for me to give you that promise."

"Perhaps," he said as he slipped the ring onto the chain and then reached around her and clasped it around her neck. "But this is just a little reminder for all the Dereks in the world that you're taken."

She lifted on her tiptoes and kissed him again. This time, he pulled her into the line of trees and deepened the kiss. A kiss filled with promises. Promises of more kisses . . . of just more. She slipped her hand inside his coat and circled his warm waist. His hum vibrated through her body and she ached to give herself over to the lure of that sound. She came close to pulling his shirttail out and touching his naked back.

He pulled back, a little breathless. "I'd better get you to the wedding. Or we won't make it."

"If I wasn't the maid of honor, I might take you up on that." She arched a teasing brow.

He grinned. "Next week, I'm making a trip to Dallas to start to sort out my grandmother's estate. Do you think . . . maybe you could come with me? We could stay in a nice hotel."

Kylie's heart raced, knowing what he was asking, and she didn't hesitate. "That sounds perfect."

As they walked up, Burnett came moving toward them. He looked concerned. "The Brightens are here," he said.

"For the wedding?" Kylie asked.

"No, they didn't know about the wedding, they just stopped by in hopes of seeing you." He frowned. "And just to make things difficult, your grandfather and aunt are also here. I could just send them all away, or I could ask them to the wedding. It's your call."

Kylie looked over at her mom talking to the other wedding guests mingling by the chairs.

"No, I think it's time."

Thirty minutes later, Kylie stood up at the front waiting for Holiday to walk down the aisle. Lucas stood across the row watching her, caressing her with his gaze. She knew he was thinking about next week. God help her, but it was going to be hard to think about anything else.

Beside Lucas, Burnett fidgeted. She had never seen Burnett like this. He looked like a kid who needed to go to the bathroom.

When Kylie confronted him earlier about appearing nervous, he'd told her, "Hell, yeah, I'm scared shitless that she'll realize she can do better than me."

The music started. Kylie looked back at the crowd. Her mom sat by the Brightens. She had been nervous about meeting them, but Kylie assured her that they would like her. On the opposite side of her mom sat Kylie's grandfather and her great-aunt Francyne. Kylie had introduced her mom to them, too. And a few minutes later, Kylie introduced the Brightens to Malcolm Summers and her great-aunt.

Because she couldn't tell them these were Daniel's real father and aunt, she introduced them as friends of the family. It was awkward for just a second, but then her grandfather shook Mr. Brighten's hand, then embraced Mrs. Brighten and told them sincerely what a pleasure it was to meet them. Kylie could tell her real grandfather was grateful to the Brightens for the love they'd had for his son.

Everyone from that row looked at Kylie and smiled. Oddly enough, they looked like one big happy family. And they were her family. Kylie had never been so proud. And deep inside she heard her father's voice say, *Perfect.*

In the row behind them, Kylie saw Miranda sitting beside Perry. Kylie would bet her best bra that those two were already planning their own wedding. And beside Miranda was Della, who stared at the row of chairs to her left. Stared at Steve. Would Della ever accept him? Yup, *for a few days* Della *had cratered slightly where Steve was concerned, but she was back to pushing him away again.*

Hayden, sitting next to Jenny, smiled at Kylie. To Jenny's right was Derek. Kylie didn't miss that his shoulder pressed against hers. Those two had something special and they deserved it.

Kylie's gaze shifted to the very back row to Fredericka, who sat with the new teacher. Kylie hadn't heard anything from Holiday about Fredericka's asking about seeing him. But Kylie got the feeling that something had happened and it had been in Fredericka's favor.

Inhaling, Kylie felt love in the air. All of a sudden, Holiday started moving down the path between the chairs. The "Wedding March" started to play. Burnett stared at Holiday, mesmerized. Kylie didn't blame him. Holiday, in all her fae glory, was beautiful. Her green eyes sparkled. Her skin practically glowed.

For some reason, Kylie recalled the day her stepdad moved out, how she'd thought it was the suckiest day of her life, and how she'd felt everything in her world was changing, and nothing would ever be the same again.

And she'd been right about one thing. Everything had changed.

Everything.

Some of it had been hard to deal with, but most of it . . . Wow.

She reached up and touched the ring hanging around her neck and looked across to Lucas, who was smiling at her. He mouthed the words, "I love you."

Kylie whispered those words back and she couldn't help but think that today might just be the best day of her life.

Stay tuned for an all-new series about Shadow Falls' favorite vampire, Della Tsang!

Available 2014

Visit www.cchunterbooks.com for the latest news.

Welcome to Camp Shadow Falls.
Once you visit,
you'll never be the same.

Awake at Dawn
c. c. hunter

c. c. hunter
Taken
at
Dusk

Whispers at
Moonrise
c.c. hunter

NEW YORK TIMES BESTSELLING SERIES
Chosen
at Nightfall
c.c. hunter

St. Martin's Griffin